Hope

H. K. Jensen

* * * * Lariat Cross * * * *

H. Kelvin Jensen

PublishAmerica
Baltimore

© 2007 by H. Kelvin Jensen.
All rights reserved. No part of this book may be reproduced, stored in a retrieval system or transmitted in any form or by any means without the prior written permission of the publishers, except by a reviewer who may quote brief passages in a review to be printed in a newspaper, magazine or journal.

First printing

All characters appearing in this work are fictitious. Any resemblance to real persons, living or dead, is purely coincidental.

At the specific preference of the author, PublishAmerica allowed this work to remain exactly as the author intended, verbatim, without editorial input.

ISBN: 1-4241-6935-6
PUBLISHED BY PUBLISHAMERICA, LLLP
www.publishamerica.com
Baltimore

Printed in the United States of America

i

* * * Chapter 1 * * *

A scorching sun lay heavy across the southern plains, creating a heat-crazed environment of living hell. A killer to anything that lived; plant, animal, or man it mattered not. They all fell victim to the life-sucking heat.

In barren prairies like this, life if any was drawn to the water holes. With plenty of luck a seep might be found, sometimes a pot hole, and seldom a natural spring. Above all this, the water discovered in such places was seldom fit to drink.

Alkali, arsenic saturated soil, and rotting animal carcasses were responsible for many of the sources of water being posted with a wooden cross. Though faint the sun-dimmed letters quickly became, the meaning was more than clear. A dire warning to the unwary—a skull and cross-bones perhaps; oft-times just two words—Poison Water!

All was quiet on the vastness of the Texas prairie; the terrible heat was responsible for this. A vulture hovered high overhead, a tumbleweed bounced hither and yon, being harassed by a prairie thermal. The vulture would not move on. It was watching with interest a man on a horse nearing an old prairie waterhole.

Bone-tired and ready to drop, the buckskin dun horse staggered up to the waterhole and thrust a dust-caked nose into the slimy residue of a once respectable pool of water. The rider, who had been slumped low in the saddle, stumbled as he slid to the ground and hung on to the saddle horn to keep from falling. He was in bad shape, the same as his horse. His whiskered face was burnt a scarlet red, his lanky body sucked dry of any existing moisture. His mind was wandering like a demented soul; he struggled to retain his sanity.

It felt good to be standing on the ground, eased his mind some too. He cursed when he saw what the horse was attempting to drink.

"Reckon I'm sure a sorry hombre," he mumbled, as he loosened the cinch of the old Texas saddle. "I'm plumb ashamed to let ya drink this…terrible lookin' stuff." He knew that his horse was in bad shape as well, having been without water for far too long.

"Reckon its drink this devil's brew or the both of us will be goners for sure—keel over dead in our tracks." He checked his canteen and found little there, enough to rinse out his mouth some, and that was about it. Hard times were upon Matt Brannon and his beloved horse Buck. The young cowboy, known as Brannon, knew this and cursed his luck. What little luck he had was mostly the bad kind it seemed.

It was not only the lack of water on this sun-baked prairie, but the blasted bounty hunter who had been dogging his trail for days on end. He scanned his back-trail, to the far horizon he looked, and cursed once more. Here on the sun-baked Texas prairie the horizon was dancing with mirage after crazy mirage appearing as if a whole damned posse was hot on his trail. Brannon knew different, was wise to the crazy patterns that beckoned from the distant sky. A lone rider was closing in on the waterhole, not a posse as the mirage suggested. He could have ambushed the self-made lawman several times as of late, shot him down like a dog, but that was not Brannon's way. The paper on Matt Brannon read:

Wanted Dead or Alive
—$500. Reward—

Brannon figured he had been pushed far enough, he would make a stand right here and now. He'd sure had enough of being stuck between a rock and a hard place. If what the poster said was true, why prolong the agony? It was time to settle this thing for good. He knew the bounty hunter was a man out of Abilene by the name of Jones. Jones had a reputation of bringing in his man…dangling across the saddle of the unfortunate's horse. Brannon knew he would be shot on sight, never given any thought of taking him back alive.

He turned and looked across the southern plains, scanning the horizon for any signs of life. Maybe it was his sun-burned eyes but the crazy mirages were more abundant now, suggesting all sorts of weird things in that direction. More prominent than the rest was an object, a dark object that appeared to be on the move, coming towards the waterhole as well. Brannon hunkered down in the shade offered by his trembling dun horse, pulled off his Stetson and relaxed for a spell. The slight decline in temperature made by the shade, sure felt good. His mind began to wander, perhaps nature's way of helping the mind forget the deadly plight that his body was in.

High in the sky, nothing more than a mere black dot, that vulture continued to soar a lazy circle, watching with keen interest the man and the horse! The cowboy known as Brannon relaxed, his mind was on the move, back to where this confounded mess all began.

An hours ride from the ranch where Brannon and five other cowboys rode for the brand, was a crossing of trails near a good spring of water. A lone building stood at the crossing, a trading post sporting a back-room saloon, dance hall, and the girls to go with it. It was known as Tumbleweed. Come payday all six of them shaved, cleaned up in the water trough, and rode into Tumbleweed for a night on the town. It would be a chance to unwind, let their hair down, and have a good time.

They stayed mostly together, some had a go at the poker tables, others never strayed far from the old plank bar, and Brannon and his pard, Joe Hawk—a half-blood Comanche Indian, were entertaining two dancehall girls at a back wall table. Brannon and Hawk were keeping the girls supplied with drinks, enjoying the sound of their chatter, and just having a good time being in the presence of the happy girls. Other than having seen the rancher's wife, none of the six had laid eyes on a woman for six months. Reckon it is going on a year for me, Brannon reminisced. Rudely, a husky barkeep walked up to their table and demanded the girls leave. Said it was high time they shared themselves with the rest of the crowd. Brannon fired right-up, and in no uncertain terms suggested the barkeep leave them be, and to mind his own damned business. Besides, their money was just as good as any mans.

Brannon had a temper, and when something like this happened he was hard put to control it. The barkeep grabbed the girl who was sitting beside him and drug her from her chair, gripping her arm until she squealed with pain. Then all hell broke loose in the old frontier saloon. With a roar Brannon was out of his chair, and swung a rock-hard fist at the barkeep's jaw. The girl managed to break free from his grip as the cowboy's fist found its mark. As if pole-axed, the barkeep was down, wondering what State of the Union he had wound up in.

Several rowdies arrived at the table ready to take on the cowboy, when Joe Hawk entered the fray. Nothing Hawk liked better than a good fight, and he was more than willing and able. At this time a sound brought the whole house to attention. It was the wild rebel yell of the fighting southern cowboys.

Six cowboys who rode for the same brand were now banded together, fighting as brothers, up against a houseful of hide hunters, whiskey runners and border riff-raff. The cowboys were holding their own, doing a good job of it too, when a shot was fired, then another. Two of the cowboys went down, one of them Joe Hawk who died with a long knife still clutched in his hand. Spotting the two gunmen, Brannon downed them both, and they were down for good. No more hell-raising would these two be involved in.

A silence filled the old smoke-filled saloon. A silence broken by Brannon who announced the fight was over, his hand hovering near his still smoking six-gun. "Make way," Brannon roared. "Leave us be—we're a takin' Injun Joe back to the ranch, bury him thar on the prairie." A way was cleared for them to leave. Six cowboys had come to party and have a good time, six of them left. Four of them walking, one being helped along by his pard, and Indian Joe's body carried out in the arms of Matt Brannon.

Indian Joe was buried on a knoll overlooking the prairie, after which the remaining cowboys went about their daily chores with heads hanging low. Brannon was out riding the range the day the Marshall came to the ranch with a warrant for his arrest. Said he was being charged with the murder of the two men back in Tumbleweed. He told the boss to send him in, else a posse would come and get him. The posse came and Brannon wasn't there, had rode away a week ago. The posse scoured the country side, they found tracks and sign, but never spotted the big cowboy. Brannon smiled through cracked lips as he remembered leading them in circles out on the prairie, always working farther away from Tumbleweed. The posse eventually dwindled in numbers until such a day as Brannon no longer had to keep looking over his shoulder.

It was some time later while still in hiding and suffering from lack of supplies, an Indian lad found him, Indian Joe's nephew in fact. He told Brannon that Jones the bounty hunter was on his trail. The boy left him a hefty bag of jerked meat and disappeared as quietly as he had arrived. Brannon knew he was in bad trouble, a man and his horse with little water and trouble closing in on him. The bounty hunter was gaining ground fast; Brannon could make out the man's face, and see there was a pack horse in tow. Looked like canteens in the packs...water canteens! Brannon settled his long gun across the saddle, and waited.

About a hundred yards out, Jones pulled in his outfit and shouted, "That you Brannon? Throw down your gun and come out where I can see you...won't be any trouble if you do." Jones continued, "I'm a takin' you back to Tumbleweed to hang for murdering them two hide skinners."

Though the cowboy could barely speak, his throat and tongue swollen from a long stretch without water, he mouthed the words. "The hell you say!" and fired a shot that kicked up a cloud of dust in front of Jones' horse. His lips moved again, no sound came from his mouth. "Reckon it was self defence, the son-of-a-gun was shooting at us—killed Injun Joe—my ol' pard. Would a shot us all, you hear!"

The bounty hunter's horse was under stress from the intense heat of the day, and the miles it had covered. Brannon's shot had caused an eruption to occur right under its nose. This was more than the animal could handle and with a squeal and a wicked leap, Jones was unseated and tumbled under the horse's flying hooves. The heat-crazed horse continued to buck and stomp and squeal. When it had recovered from the fright and frustration it had endured, Jones' lifeless body was not a pretty sight.

Brannon watched in amazement and, though too weak to walk much, hobbled the fifty-yards to the wreck using his rifle as a crutch. Finding several over-sized water bags on the pack horse, he managed to uncork one and have a life saving drink. After a few hearty swigs, Brannon knew he must slow down. To satisfy the intense urge to drink the bag dry would be fatal. Chances are he might founder himself, die right there at the waterhole.

After a couple more cautious drinks, he could feel the effects of the water coursing through his heat-ravaged body, it sure felt good too. Dragging the water bag in one hand, the other holding his rifle and an old blue-enamel bean pot found in the pack, he returned to the waterhole and his long-suffering dun horse. Using the same method he had used on himself, just a few swallows at a time; Buck drank from the bean pot and soon felt much better.

Later, after a feed of oats, thanks to the bounty hunter's supplies, the horse lay down on the barren prairie and proceeded to roll from one side of his back to the other. Then stood upright again and vigorously shook his large frame. Though strange it seems, this is a toilette common to various members of the animal kingdom, including the horse.

The cowboy was feeling much better now, munching on jerky and still drinking small sips of water. It sure seemed good to see Buck recovering from the ordeal they both had endured; he was thankful, plumb thankful they both were alive.

Sitting Indian style in the shade offered by Buck's lanky frame, he just couldn't keep his eyes open. His heat-tortured body was fighting to come back from what it had endured, sleep was what it needed, a good sound sleep. The cowboy's chin settled on his chest and his awareness slipped away. The buckskin dun knew his cowboy pard was sleeping, he sensed it was something his friend was in need of, he knew the cowboy had suffered from thirst the same as he. Buck dozed himself some, yet would not move from the cowboy's side. Except from the snoring of the horse's friend, all was quiet on the lonely prairie.

An hour passed before the cowboy stirred. He was no longer sitting as before, his body had slumped over to the ground. Awareness was returning, awareness that prompted caution, a survival instinct that he must not ignore. Slowly his hand moved down his body making sure his six-gun was still in place, it was there as it should be. He removed the leather whang that kept it in place, and struggled to sit up once again. His mind was still cloudy, having a dickens of a time getting rid of the cobwebs. He sensed a presence close by, a human presence. This must have been what woke him, he reckoned, an ingrained sense of survival.

A voice spoke out of the void. "No need to pull that hog-leg o' yourn son—I'm a peaceful sort—too old for any gun fightin'.

"I'm a hand on a ranch 'bout twenty miles south-east o' here. The Medicine Pipe, and she's a good un too. I bin a checkin' this far end of the range for Medicine Pipe cows, condition of waterholes and such."

Unable to do much talking yet, Brannon's eyes were starting to function as they should. In the background stood a ranch wagon pulled by a team of mules, and the old timer who had greeted him was standing close by. He was an older cowboy wearing a full moustache; his hair was long and in dire need of a good trimming. Sick as he was Brannon smiled, reckoned the old timer had shied away from the shearing shed for at least a year, possibly two or three. He was a pleasant fellow, showing concern for his fellow cowboy. "Most folks know me as Amarillo; reckon that's a good enough name for now. "What's yours?" inquired the old timer.

The big cowboy hadn't attempted to speak any words yet, but reckoned this was as good a time as any to give it a try. "B-bb-rrr—," And it was an effort to do this, and a failure. His throat and voice box were still badly swollen from the ordeal his body had suffered.

"Reckon you come mighty close to cashin' in your chips," Amarillo said. He could tell what the young cowboy had been through. He had been there himself a time or two, and it was a terror all right. "Appears this dog-goned sun and heat has about done you in, young fella.

"Reckon I got here in the nick of time, another hour and you would be food for that vulture that's a hangin' 'round these parts. It's that big bird up yonder," the old cowboy gestured high in the sky, "who has saved your bacon son. I spotted it a hangin' around here, and reckoned some critter, or the like…was in bad trouble.

"Tell you what I'm gonna do is load you in this here wagon and get you back to the ranch. Old Hugh's wife is as good a doctor as you'll find in these parts." "I've got room for your gear and what not, and whatever that dead one over there's got scattered around."

Amarillo went to work, and he was no slouch either. He talked while he worked, not expecting Brannon to answer. He located the bounty hunter's six-guns and rifle, along with his hat, boots and belt, which he brought back to the wagon. "Reckon I can use this stuff, these here boots just might fit me. Sure a sick-lookin' mess back there, nuthin' much left to bury. The vultures and coyotes will clean it up—save me digging a hole."

After watering the stock, he tied Buck and the packhorse at the rear of the wagon, and they were ready to roll. He would have nothing to do with the killer horse, and in his own way had figured out what had happened here. He knew the cowboy would tell him later, no need for that now. But for now, to an old plainsman like Amarillo, the drama that took place here was like reading a page from a book of life on the prairie. Jones' horse was set free to follow if it wished, or run with the wild ones that inhabited this lonesome prairie. "It's the critter's decision," Amarillo said. "No reason we should bring a man-killin' critter like that along."

Brannon was sitting on the seat beside Amarillo, a blanket around his shoulders. "I've seen some survivors of this country." A wide grin spread across Amarillo's face. That the old teamster was prone to a bit of jest now and then, there could be little doubt. "And you're the sorriest lookin' one of the whole bunch." exclaimed the old cowboy.

The wagon was on the move, Amarillo was smiling as he looked up in the sky. The vulture was still there, had been all the time. It was hovering much closer to the ground now, showing more than a little interest in the ground litter strewn around the old water hole. His smile was turning into a full-fledged chuckle, and Brannon heard him say, "Sure beats a diggin' a hole in the ground."

Amarillo drove about ten-miles before nightfall. Spotting a small draw in the prairie, he pulled in and set up camp. In no time at all a sage brush fire was blazing, a coffee pot bubbling a merry tune, and bacon and warmed-up beans sizzling in a skillet.

Brannon was sure sick, he still couldn't speak and intense chills were racking his body. Sitting close to the blazing fire, with two blankets around him now, Brannon knew that he had indeed been mighty close to cashin' in his chips. He was able to drink his coffee, cup after cup he drank, and reckoned he sure felt better for the doing. With a smug look on his face—reckoned that coffee would be all the medicine he would ever need in this life.

Late the next day they rolled into the ranch yards of the Medicine Pipe ranch. Brannon was on the mend; his voice was back, but still weak as a newborn calf. There to meet them were the owners, old Hugh Arnett and his good wife. After listening to Amarillo's story, the good lady hustled Brannon into the house to be looked after properly. She insisted that Brannon take a bath, and then tucked him into bed with clean sheets and a night gown that he had to wear. "I'll be back soon," she said, "with some good hot soup, and a beef sandwich."

"It is nourishment you need—food and drink—to get you back on your feet." Unknown to Brannon, she left with his filthy clothing in hand, to be given a good scrubbing. "You must stay in this bed!" she counselled. "You must get lots of rest—it is good food and rest that will return you to your health."

He soon discovered that Old Hugh's wife loved to talk, a real chatter box. Seemed like the chance for him to talk was a rarity, somehow he managed a respectful "Yes ma-am…No ma-am." She was like a mother hen, tucking the cowboys under her wing like a brood of chicks. Brannon loved her for it, treated her as he would have his mother if he had known her.

A few days were all that it took for Brannon and Buck to recover from their ordeal on the prairie. Old Hugh gave him a full time job riding the range, and within a month's time advanced him to foreman of Medicine Pipe, with the authority to hire and fire as need be. The cowboys must all answer to Brannon, carry out his orders and ride for the brand.

Amarillo was Brannon's favourite; after all he had saved his big boss's life. So Brannon let him pick his own jobs. The old timer was a loner and preferred to work alone. He was happiest when checking water holes, salt licks, cattle that were tick infested, and keeping track of the general location of old Hugh's longhorns. The old timer would load his wagon with water and supplies, a bedroll, a rifle, and oats for the mules. He would then hitch his mules to the rig and take off across the prairie.

He would leave on Monday morning and return in five or six days, never longer. One day Amarillo never came home, he was a day overdue and everybody was in a tizzy, including old Hugh and Matt Brannon. The hands that were at the home ranch were paired up in twos and scattered throughout the range. Though there were others out there who hadn't reported in from assignments of their own, top priority at Medicine Pipe was to find Amarillo, all else would have to wait.

It was breaking daylight when the search began with all heading for their assigned sections of this big sprawling prairie. Brannon had left several hours earlier, riding a big, strong bay horse. Buck was trotting along side. He would alternate riding the two, giving the other a much needed rest. He planned on covering plenty of ground, keeping track of the search parties as best he could.

After the excitement of the cowboys riding out on the search for Amarillo, the preparations and all; Old Hugh and his wife sat in their rockers on the covered porch of the Medicine Pipe ranch house. They were saddened by the disappearance of Amarillo, and prayed that he might be found safe and sound. He was not only one of their working cowboys; he was their good friend as well, as were all the nine-man crew. They fretted some about the big foreman they knew as Brannon, riding out alone and all, yet they trusted him, and felt more secure for his being here.

Several days passed with no sign of the missing teamster. Some of the groups returned to the ranch for water and fresh mounts, all had reported a shortage of longhorns. There were small bunches scattered here and there, but nothing of the great herd that once roamed the Medicine Pipe range.

Brannon kept on the move, he rode as a loner, making like a wolf on the hunt. Reckoned he could cover more ground this way. Like the others he was finding that the longhorns had been moved off of Medicine Pipe. His heart was saddened; a picture was unravelling that told of a well-organized group, cattle rustlers robbing old Hugh Arnett of a lifetime of sweat, blood and tears. And he was fuming mad, damned mad in fact. He blamed himself; after all he was the foremen of the crew. He now knew he should have spent more time on the range, kept closer track of the line-riders and what they were doing. But dog-gone it all, he had trusted them, never realized they were working hand-in-hand with a bunch of rustlers.

In a far corner of the range, roughly five-miles south of the waterhole incident, Brannon rode upon a scene of much activity, sign of a large herd of longhorns being gathered and driven away from Medicine Pipe. The sign was like an open book, thousands of cloven-hooves chewing up the virgin grass of the prairie. Showing up at random across this large bedding ground were the tracks of a wagon pulled by a team of mules, overlapping those of the rustled herd.

He now knew Amarillo had been here. "Sure hope the old mule-skinner hasn't got in more trouble than he can handle!" "I reckon he's still alive though—I can feel it in my bones!" Buck's ears perked up, he listened with interest to the sound of Brannon's voice, hadn't heard him speak for several days. To hear the big cowboy talk as they travelled gave the big dun horse confidence. He then knew his cowboy friend was his old friendly self again.

Brannon followed the wagon tracks, which were following the herd of cattle. As he rode, he was struggling to unravel this mystery. By the sign, most of old Hugh's longhorns had been gathered here by the rustlers. That old Amarillo was on to them, and following them, was evident by the wagon sign in the dust left by the departing herd. He was sure proud of the old timer, and prayed in his heart his old friend hadn't been killed. Not only had Amarillo saved Brannon's life at the waterhole, he was now determined to save old Hugh's longhorns from the rustlers.

Brannon's mind was in turmoil as he rode, he had to find his friend. He was sure Amarillo had got himself in trouble, might be holed-up somewhere in the scorching sun all bloodied and shot up. Just a laying there all helpless and sick, watching a circling vulture waiting for him to die!

The vulture is the death bird of the southern plains. Excitement surged through the cowboy's body, excitement and hope. "Vulture!" he whooped, couldn't help it he reckoned. "Why didn't I think of it sooner?" The buckskin dun was startled by the whoop, buck-jumped a hop or two then turned his head to see what was wrong with his friend.

Brannon was cursing himself for not thinking of this sooner. It was the answer he had been searching for in his mind, a living clue to the finding of old Amarillo. "Reckon I'm sure a dummy, Buck," he was talking to his horse again. "Reckon we've got to watch the sky—one o' them big birds will show us where old Amarillo is holed up!"

Several hours later, all sweat-caked and covered with dust, the over powering heat was getting to Brannon. Though he was tipping his canteen on a regular basis, his body was slipping into the old pattern of before. "Must be my body's still a sufferin'; from…from the waterhole affair," he muttered.

Fortified with plenty of water to drink, it was late afternoon when Brannon hit pay dirt. The mirages were back again, creating all sorts of fantasy images—including several wagons pulled by mules—always heading in his direction, but he knew he was nearing the end of his search for Amarillo when he spotted a vulture that was soaring in a lazy circle high above the mirages. He continued on and spotted the wagon, tipped on its side, a wreck if he ever saw one. That fool vulture was hovering above the wreck, descending quite rapidly. Pulling his six-gun, Brannon fired at the vulture, and then fired again. In a dramatic show of raw energy, the big bird put on the brakes and went flapping back into the sky. A feather, then there two, floated to the ground carried by a prairie thermal.

Although it was too hot to sweat, a tear or two showed on Brannon's cheek when he spotted Amarillo. The old teamster was still alive—just barely. He had been shot, had lost a lot of blood, and was trapped under the wagon with a broken leg. He was game though, had his six-gun in hand, and wasn't about to die without a fight. When he sensed it was Brannon standing there, and not one of the rustlers, he relaxed some and his gun slipped into the tinder-dry grass below him. A slight smile was on his whiskered face. "Reckoned you would find me," he mumbled. "'bout the only one with any know how." Brannon scrambled down beside his friend, pressing a canteen to his trembling lips. Memories flooded back as he watched the old-timer struggle to drink. "A feeble smile returned to his face. "I pulled you out of a tight spot one time pardner, remember? Reckon it's now your turn to do the same for me!"

On their arrival back at Medicine Pipe old Hugh was overjoyed to see them. The old rancher had faith and was a praying man, which is how he knew that Brannon would find Amarillo and bring him back. Tears began to flow down his good wife's cheeks when she heard the news. This was a trying experience for both of them, a bombshell in fact. They too had been informed of the missing herd, and the unfaithful line riders who were nowhere to be found. They thanked Brannon and Amarillo, bowed their heads and went inside the ranch house to offer a silent prayer. The good lady of the ranch returned in a few minutes and escorted Amarillo into her kitchen. He was in dire need of some cattle country doctoring, and a good dose of her loving care. Brannon went to the bunkhouse and collapsed on his bed. He was bone-tired and sure needed sleep, sleep he had been deprived of for so long a time.

Though refreshed from a good nights sleep, Brannon was fuming mad over the recent chain of events at Medicine Pipe. He would hunt down the turncoat cowboys and read'em from the good book. Reckoned he would ride out to the Adobe Flats line camp, the gathering place for the roundup that was due to start in ten days time. Unknown to Brannon, the roundup had been taking place much earlier than expected. He had been unaware of this since he had been tied up in his search for old Amarillo.

With two canteens full of water, his saddle bags stuffed with food and a coffee pot, he left before dawn for Adobe Flats. Arriving there late in the afternoon, he could sense things were not as they should be. There were three men stationed there, two men were shoeing horses, the third, just a boy, greeted Brannon with tears in his eyes, said he would like to talk with the big cowboy in private. Brannon gigged the buckskin with his spurs, leaned over and spoke to the boy, "Follow me son to the water trough over yonder—we can talk thar without them jaspers a listenin'." "Stay on the far side of my buckskin, never know what them two might be up to!" He dismounted, loosened the cinch and turned to the boy. "What's on your mind son? Don't worry none'bout them two over yonder, tell me what you got to say."

The story the boy revealed was a shock to Brannon, the worst being that three men had rode for Medicine Pipe, said they were going to kill everyone there and steal the old couple's life savings. He knew the boy was telling the truth, the tears in his eyes were proof enough of that. The boy spoke again and gestured toward the two men. "Them two, Mr. Brannon...are in on it too...bin a rustling Medicine Pipe longhorns for a long time."

"Stay here son," Brannon cautioned. "I'm a goin' to read'em from the good book!"

He freed the Peacemaker, shrugged his shoulders and turned to go. From behind came the voice of the boy, "Luck, Mr. Brannon, best of luck." Matt Brannon walked towards the outlaws he was a raging inferno ready to erupt. "Draw them six-guns of yourn," he roared. "Time you cattle rustlin' devils were taught the ways of the west." The two had been ready, drew their weapons, and were surprisingly fast. Brannon had them beat, their shots went wild as he watched them fall in the leavings of the horse corrals at Adobe Flats.

Turning back towards the boy, he found him on the ground, a bullet hole in his chest. One of the outlaw's flying bullets had struck the boy down. He knelt by the boy and heard him say, "They made me join'em, Matt...I overheard their talk, they just wouldn't let me be." "I was scared, didn't know what to do." "Should a told you sooner...tried to Matt. Never had the nerve, I reckon. I'm sure sorry Matt—!" With the dying boy's words ringing in his ears, the cowboy picked up the sign of the remaining rustlers and headed back to Medicine Pipe.

The big cowboy rode hard and fast, the buckskin dun enjoying the run, no need for spurs, the big horse sensed the urgency. They arrived at the ranch in a cloud of dust. Brannon stepped to the ground and hurried to the house. The door was open and things were sure messed up. He discovered old Hugh and his wife, both dead, the two of them had been shot, and old Hugh hadn't died easy by the looks of things. The house had been ransacked, it appeared the bunch were after the Arnett's life savings for sure. The ransackers had made a clean sweep of everything they owned—cattle, gold and even their lives. Glancing toward the bedroom where Amarillo had been convalescing, he spotted the old timers body in the hallway, his shooting iron still in his hand. Amarillo had been killed as he attempted to defend the Medicine Pipe Ranch.

Uttering a savage curse, the big cowboy left the terrible scene and picked up their sign. He must find them if it was the last thing he ever accomplished on this earth!

* * * Chapter 2 * * *

Far out on the sun-baked plains a summer storm was erupting in fury. Billowing up from the heat-hazed horizon were huge, threatening clouds slashing out lightning accompanied by the ominous explosion of thunder. Having out-paced the storm, a trail-worn cowboy, riding a line-back dun, entered the main drag of Fort Worth, Texas. They appeared the worse for wear, the rider and the horse, dust-caked and soggy with sweat from the miles they had covered but they held their heads high, alert to whatever fate might have in store.

Fort Worth, a burgeoning hub of commerce north of the Brazos was stirring, preparing for the lucrative night that lay ahead. A rowdy din could be heard along the rut-scarred trail where the cowboy rode, boisterous laughter and shouts of those who were there to party and have a good time.

Reining up to a hitch-rail, Matt Brannon stepped down from the saddle, loosened the cinch and looked around in awe. "Don't ya get all spooked up now, Buck? All these people take a gettin' used to…for both of us I reckon." With an affectionate hand, the cowboy caressed the big stallion, talking to him as if he were human. "I'll be back soon," he said, "and find ya some oats and a stable…reckon we'll stay the night."

His had been a long ride up from the Brazos country. He was hungry and dry, bone dry. It was a steak he was wanting, one with all the trimmings, and coffee, a pot of it would sure be welcome. Adding to the confusion of this wide-open town were gunshots, the high-pitched squeals of ladies of the night and, above all else, the melancholy strains of a fiddle.

With rifle in hand, Brannon stepped up onto the fresh-hewn boardwalk. His Mexican spurs were jingling, singing a merry tune as he sauntered a few doors down to a saloon that advertised 'Eats'. With his free hand, Brannon shoved the bat wings aside and stepped into the haze of the smoke-filled room. He moved quietly to the side and stopped, keen eyes sweeping the crowded room, his right hand hovering near the Colt Peacemaker hanging on his hip. All seemed as it should he reckoned, no trouble he could sense as he strode to a wall-side table. The big cowboy known as Brannon seated himself, back to the wall, facing the crowd and the street-side door. A bar maid hustled right over and with a come hither smile and a toss of her unruly curls, asked. "What'll it be stranger, a bottle of our best, and a pair of glasses, just for you and me?"

With a harsh look that withered the girl of the night, Brannon shook his head and replied, "It is food I want, Missy. A steak that's not bawlin' and coffee…a pot of it will do." Tossing a coin on the table, he leaned back in the chair and appeared to relax some, yet his inner self was a raging inferno waiting to erupt.

The Medicine Pipe cowboys, he mused, the ones who had turned on old Hugh, even killed the rancher and his wife, were here in Fort Worth. Their tracks were simple to follow then, were lost in the confusion of the countless users of this up-and-coming cross roads of the west.

His had been a long, tedious ride up from the Brazos country and from the Medicine Pipe ranch where he had been employed as foreman. Brannon had only been on the payroll a couple of months. He remembered, riding herd on old Hugh's longhorns, and the nine unruly cowboys who should have been riding for the brand. It was roundup time on the range before he found out the extent of the rustling.

Under Brannon's orders the Medicine Pipe cowboys had scoured the plains and rough country beyond looking for old Hugh's longhorns. A Brannon discovered the truth, he was plumb disgusted with himself, should have figured it out much sooner, he reckoned. The rustlers were living and working on Medicine Pipe, eating the old couple's grub and taking their wages. At the same time they had been rustling the Arnett's herd. They took a few cattle at a time, so that no one would notice. He knew a lifetime of work, sweat and tears had been decimated with no trace, there were only a few cattle left, only the stragglers.

Five of the nine man crew were involved, the other four were too old for the rigorous life of a rider, instead were kept around the home place doing the chores and odd jobs. The young lad who had been shot at Adobe Flats was a messenger boy for old Hugh. The other four were traitors of the worst kind. When the youngster had alerted Brannon to the extent of the rustler's murderous plans, Brannon had returned to the ranch to try and save old Hugh and his wife from the scheming devils. He had wanted to alert the old rancher, let him know what was going on and receive fresh orders, but he never made it in time. The big cowboy had been shaken at what he discovered, the tragic demise of two old friends.

Hugh Arnett and his wife had been kind and good to him. A bit timid perhaps, but both honest and God-fearing residents of this harsh land. They took care of any, and all who passed by Medicine Pipe. Fed them and took care of their needs, ever willing to furnish a grubstake; even gave them a job riding for the brand. The Arnett's, never able to have children of their own, had a way of sharing the love that was so much a part of their simple lives with others.

After finding his slain friends back at the Medicine Pipe, Brannon had uttered a terrible oath, left the ranch house and rode back to the Adobe Flats roundup camp. Here he picked up the rustlers tracks and took off across the prairie, hot on their heels. Brannon was frightening to see that day at Adobe Flats. With the memory of his dead friend's words still fresh in his mind, the big cowboy picked up the sign of the killers and tracked them all the way to Fort Worth. It was here that Brannon was set to avenge old Hugh and his good wife, who both lay dead at their Medicine Pipe ranch.

The saloon was crowded with the trade of the night, every table taken, people of all sorts milling in and out of the swinging doors. The bar maid arrived with a sizzling t-bone steak which he dug right into savouring every bite. Been a long spell since his feet had been under a table, he reckoned. The tables were shoved close, the diners rubbing elbows with those of the table beside them.

Four cowboys were seated at a table beside Brannon, three not much more than boys, the other an older pleasant looking type. He was sporting a full moustache, which along with his thinning hair, were showing streaks of grey. Through the din of the crowded room Matt Brannon was able to listen to their talk. The old one was telling his cowboys how it was, and to Brannon it was plumb interesting.

Tom Lynch was the old cowboy's name, a former Confederate soldier and Indian fighter who had drifted into the cattle business. Under his supervision, a herd of longhorns had been gathered for a trail drive into the northern territories, Montana was the destination. Lynch and his crew of youngsters had ridden far and wide buying and gathering a herd. There were plenty of cattle on the Texas plains, countless thousands of them, most running wild and free as the buffalo. Regardless of this, Tom Lynch chose to buy from settlers, small ranches and big ones too. He paid in gold, which was welcomed in this part of the country where cash money was a scarce commodity. It gave them an opportunity to pay their bills, and possibly have a little left over to jingle in their pockets. In his quiet way, Tom Lynch was helping to restore a shattered economy that ensued from the long years of Indian turmoil and the Civil War of the States.

Here on the Texas plains, Lynch paid four-dollars a head at the owner's gate. In the northern territories where they were heading the longhorns would fetch twenty dollars a head. Some of the herd would be used as brood cows, the remainder to be fattened on the nutrient-rich grasses then sold as beef.

Lynch planned to follow the Western Trail north, it began along the Rio Grande River, crossed the Chisholm west of Fort Worth, then on to Dodge City, Kansas. The rivers would be a challenge for this kind of venture, one most cowboys were plumb scared of. "Always the damn rivers," one of them lamented. He couldn't swim a stroke, as was the case with most of the crew, but cross them they must. Lynch knew these Texas boys and knew that the river crossings would be a frightening experience for them. In fact plumb traumatic for those born on the arid plains, where the dew of the night was a rarity, a reason for them to marvel and rejoice. To soak in a creek or a puddle was carried out with much concern for their well being in this arid land.

Matt Brannon smiled as he listened to the old soldier down play the dangers, as well as building up the excitement and romance of a cattle drive, the likes of which none had experienced in their short lives.

Lynch told of the Red River. Yes, it was feared the most, he told them. Sometimes it was an easy crossing, more often than not a raging hell. The Red would be the first, then on to the South and North Canadian, the Cimarron, and the Arkansas just to reach Dodge City, Kansas. Pointing into the northwest, they must conquer the South and North Platte rivers to reach Fort Laramie in Wyoming Territory. Onward into the northwest were his plans, the next river the Powder, then on to the Yellowstone in Montana Territory, their final destination. It would be here in the vicinity of Miles Town that the herd would be sold, then scattered far and wide on this great northern prairie.

Brannon was all ears by now. He was excited and wanted nothing more than to be a part of Lynch's outfit. Confound it all, he mused, if this Medicine Pipe chore was wrapped up, old Hugh and his wife avenged, then he would be free to hire on with Tom Lynch. He knew he had to ride away from the land of his birth, make a new start. There were too many memories here, too many heartaches and sorrows.

It was then that a strange thing happened, a pulling at his inner self, an urgency that he couldn't explain. He now knew that he must be a part of this exciting new adventure into the northern territories, he must be a part of pushing a herd of longhorns up the trail. His thoughts were piling up, plumb out of control urging him on. It was a reality he must face. Before he could leave Texas he had a chore to finish. He must find the four remaining killers and settle this confounded mess once and for all. He would never be able to rest or look himself in a mirror if he failed.

Brannon turned his chair to face the old cattleman. "Good evening amigo...couldn't help overhearin' yer talk, was a wonderin' if ya could use another rider? Matt Brannon is what they call me. I have a chore to do here in Fort Worth, and then a cowboy and a buckskin hoss will be ready for a long drive."

Tom Lynch listened to what the big cowboy had to say, looked him in the eye and liked what he saw. "Why, it's a good evening to you cowboy," he replied. "I'm sure a needin' another wrangler or two." With a friendly smile the old cattleman continued to talk, "Could sure use you if you're willin'. What's this unfinished business you're a speakin' of? Anything I can do to help out?"

Brannon was hesitant at first, then, with a sigh related the Medicine Pipe affair, the murder of the ranching couple, and his sworn vendetta against the remaining outlaws. Chick, a young rider at Lynch's table then spoke out. "Sounds like two hombres who were across the road in the Dusty Spur, braggin' about a streak o' luck that happened their way. Those boys were drinking heavy...and flashin' a wad o' cash and gold around."

Brannon's relaxed manner changed. His eyes were terrible to see. With a curse he shoved back the table. "Might as well get this over with right now," he told his new boss. "Thanks Chick, fer tellin' me this."

Lynch reared right up and spoke his mind. "Now hold your hosses, Matt Brannon...me and the boys are comin' along...we'll back you if the play gets outta hand!"

His Mexican spurs were jingling a merry tune as the big cowboy shoved through the crowd and left the saloon. Lynch and his boys had to hurry to keep up. Crossing the hoof pocked roadway, Brannon entered the two-bit dive and paused to let his eyes adjust to the dimness of the saloon.

It took only a moment for the big cowboy to spot the pair of wayward cowboys then came a chilling shock to those that were there. Rising above the din and confusion of the sordid house of ill repute, a wild shout rang out across the room. A cold chill rippled up the spine of many, the unexpected cry was reminiscent of the high-spirited rebel fighters who fought for the south in the not so distant Civil War, and they knew it well. A hush spread across the room, all eyes on Brannon...Lynch and his boys standing along side.

The big cowboy's rage was terrible to see. He called them right to their face so everyone would know what kind of vile scum they were. "Turn around and draw...ya cowardly killers!" he roared. "Let's see how ya like facin' someone who aint old and unarmed! Ya murderin' skunks tortured and killed yer boss, old Hugh Arnett, then gunned down his wife...shot her in cold blood!"

Astonished gasps disturbed the hush that had settled over the room, followed by silence. Two outlaws were standing at the bar, nursing whiskeys, shaggy heads hanging low. With a sneer on his face, a third one stood up from a table where he had been entertaining a bar maid and a bottle of booze, then joined the others at the bar. Here they stood facing the bar, hands hovering near their six guns. The stage was now set, the curtain ready to be drawn.

A slight nod from the leader was the cue. In unison, all three swung to face Matt Brannon; their six guns spewing hot lead. They were slow, much too slow, their bullets slashed into the tobacco stained floor as their lifeless bodies wilted away like scarecrows in a Texas norther.

The cowboy was still standing, a terrible sight to see. In the blink of an eye a roll of death brought fear to those who witnessed it. Three shots so close together that most assumed it had only been one. The trio died in the Dusty Spur, their trigger fingers loosened in death, their guns dropping into the sawdust on the bar room floor.

Brannon's .44-40 was still smoking as he ejected three spent cartridges. The bar room bunch were stricken with awe and fear. Never had they witnessed a real live gunfight before this night, and forget it they never could. Brannon would now be famous, known to one and all as the Brazos gunfighter, a reputation that he sure did not need.

For those who were wise to the ways of gun fighting, the intricacy of sight and sound, the feat was spoken of and marvelled at for years to come.

The foreman of Medicine Pipe had garnered a just revenge; an eye for an eye had been achieved. Old Hugh and his good wife had been avenged, his good friends who had taken him in, offered him kindness when the chips were low.

23

A tremor coursed through his body, his countenance softened. He turned to Tom Lynch and asked, "Ya still want me after all this? My duties with Medicine Pipe are now over." Still absorbing what he had just witnessed, Lynch took his time in answering the cowboy's question. "You're on my payroll Matt Brannon...I wouldn't have it any other way." A slight smile appeared on the cowboy's face, ever so slight. "I'll ride fer the brand Tom Lynch," he replied. "To hell and gone if ya say the word."

* * *

It was a beautiful night in northern Wyoming; the herd was bedded down with the night crew out in the dark singing them to sleep. The flicker of a campfire reflected off the weathered canvas of a travel-worn chuck wagon, two large coffee pots sat bubbling among the glowing embers. Relaxing around the buck-brush fire, Lynch's weary cowboys were nursing a last cup of the day before retiring to their blankets. The boys had been through a tough time of it, they were bone-tired, edgy and spent. It was the heat that made them so miserable. "The damned heat," one of them moaned. "I can take the dust, but this gad-durned heat is just too much!"

Not only was it in the high 90's here along the Montana border country, the heat produced by the bodies of 2500-head of moving longhorns increased it considerably. It was nearing the end of August, in the year 1877. The four-month long drive from Fort Worth to Miles Town was nearly over. The drive up through Wyoming territory was through a desolate wilderness, hot and extremely dusty. The long days and shorter nights were filled with the usual hazards of the times, but Tom Lynch and his fourteen cowboys had been up to the task.

The drive was now in the Powder River country, an arid wind-blown region where the grass was short and dry. With barely enough water in the Little Powder, Lynch was pushing them north in easy stages. The old cattleman sauntered up to the fire, poured himself a cup of coffee and sat down with his cowboys. These young cowhands respected old Tom, would drive the longhorns to hell and gone if he asked them to.

"I'm concerned about this stream we're a followin'," he said. "Reckon they call it the Little Powder...sure hope the water holds out until we reach the big river. Takes a heap of water to satisfy 2500 head, what do ya think Matt?"

The big cowboy who was sitting on the far side of the fire looked up with a grin on his whiskered face. "We'll make it Tom. I figure if we're lucky, we're about four-days south of the Powder, most likely ten days south of the Yellowstone. We'll make it, don't ya worry none, you hear?"

Suddenly, and with no apparent reason, old Tom began to fidget he arose from where he sat and began pacing around the fire ring. It appeared as if the old timer was upset about something, he kept peering off into the darkness.

Brannon noticed it right off; he got up and approached his boss. "What's wrong Tom? Ya feelin' all right, reckon yer' actin' kind o' strange."

Lynch never answered his foreman's question. Not right away anyhow, he appeared as if he was deep in thought, concentrating on something out there on the prairie. Brannon sure didn't know what was wrong with him unless it was something to do with the longhorns.

This had been a day when they had pushed the herd to the limit; it was almost brutal in fact. There had been no water since early that morning. Knowing the Little Powder was somewhere ahead of them, Brannon and the cowboys had been ruthless in keeping the longhorns on the move.

Sundown was closing in on the barren prairie before the staggering herd reached the Little Powder River. The scent of water in their dust caked nostrils created bedlam within the herd. In a crazy unyielding fashion, the cows scattered up and down the modest stream, desperate to get a drink.

There was no way the hard driving crew could swing the herd into a circling pattern, and bunch them together for the usual bedding ground procedure, they were strung out for a half mile. After slaking a raging thirst, the longhorns dropped in there tracks and could not be moved. Twilight had turned to the dark of night and Brannon decided all they could do was leave them alone. As weary as the herd was, the big foreman figured the longhorns would not move until morning.

He did, however, double the night crew just in case of trouble. The cowboys followed Brannon back to old Ike's chuck wagon to eat a welcome meal; this was the first food since morning for most of them.

Suddenly, Lynch stopped his pacing. "Listen!" he spoke loudly, his voice demanding attention, "You jaspers over yonder shut up and listen!" A hush was evident from the eating cowboys; they could hear nothing but the crackling of old Ike's sagebrush fire. But wait, something far off in the darkness, a droning sound was becoming stronger slowly increasing as the minutes passed.

The mysterious drone turned into a rumble, a scary rumble. Above all this a whoop and a holler from a fast riding cowboy charging into camp from his night hawk duties with the herd. "Brannon!" he shouted, "and Mr. Lynch, we've got a stampede on our hands. It's buffalo that are comin'."

The night hawk cowboy vaulted from his saddle and ran up to the fire. Brannon and Tom Lynch were standing beside him waiting for the boy to catch his breath. "Well, speak up boy," Brannon roared. "What's goin' on out there?"

"We got a bunch of buffalo mixin' in with the herd! All night these critters bin a stragglin' in on the drag bunch up river a ways, a few at a time. The critters are sure enough buffalo boss, they fill up on water then are a beddin' down with the herd—seem to be in worse shape than our longhorns, been a runnin' like crazy."

The night hawk, Chick, accepted the last cup of coffee that was in the pot and continued, "There's more a driftin' in all the time, must be a hundred at least, no end to'em. Reckon there are thousands still a comin'. Boss, what would ya have us do?"

Brannon knew they must act quickly to save the herd. It sounded as if a full out migration of buffalo was taking place, thousands of them by the sounds of it, and the Lynch herd was trapped right in the centre of the action.

"Mount up boys!" Brannon roared. "Reckon we got us a stampede on our hands, a stampede of the wild ones a huntin' new graze and water. Follow me ya hear."

The cowboys followed Brannon with old Tom in the lead. They rode hell bent for leather up river to the bedding ground of the straggler bunch. Orders were issued as they rode. Brannon sent two cowboys up river with Chick, and left six at the place where the stampede was mixing with the longhorns. "Cut out about fifty head or so of longhorns. Fire yer six guns to push them up river—longhorns and buffalo together. Do yer best boys, the rest of us will start the main herd movin' down river, get'em separated as best we can."

Brannon and the remaining cowboys cut in on the terrified longhorns and started moving them north. It was bedlam with cattle bellowing in terror, horses squealing in fright, and the ominous roar of stampeding buffalo. Lost in the intense noise were the shrill yells of the cowboys and the bark of their six guns firing into the air.

Somehow the plan worked, the tail end of the Lynch herd took off up river which caused many of the buffalo to follow, leaving a gap in the middle for the stampeding buffalo to flow through.

Old Tom and his bronc were at the top of a rise in the rolling prairie, worried sick over the safety of the cowboys and his longhorns down below. He had been ordered to stay there by his foreman and knew it was in his best interest to obey Brannon's orders. He listened to the intense sounds of the passing buffalo as they crossed the small stream and continued on into the eastern prairie.

He heaved a big sigh of relief and felt certain that the herd had been saved. Lynch was thankful that his big foreman, Matt Brannon, had been at the helm. He didn't know what he would have done without Matt. Confusion and chaos remained for the rest of the night. The cowboys were scattered hither and yon, some gave up trying to wrangle the longhorns in the dark, others stayed with small bunches and kept working until first light.

It was nearing dawn when Brannon returned to camp. Old Ike had hot food and coffee waiting for the cowboys who had rode in, after eating they had collapsed on their bedrolls and were instantly asleep. All the cowboys were accounted for except Chick and his boys who had driven the drag bunch up river.

After drinking nearly a whole pot of coffee, Brannon saddled a fresh bronc and headed out to find Chick and his five riders.

He met up with Chick who was coming back to see what the others had accomplished. Matt and Chick returned to the straggler bunch. "How many longhorns ya got here?" Brannon asked, glancing at Chick who was practically riding asleep in the saddle.

"Reckon it's been a long hard night," the boy replied, looking kind of sheepish, as he rubbed his bloodshot eyes. "I tried to count'em, near as I can tell there's about ninety head of longhorns. Reckon we got twice as many of them ornery buffalo mixed in."

"Don't worry none'bout them buffalo," Brannon replied. "Let's circle around and head'em back down river, buffalo and all...catch'em up to the big herd. Reckon these here longhorns are already homesick fer the herd, the buffalo will do their own thing—work out toward the edge of the cattle, then drift away after their own kind." All went as planned, and on the way back to the main herd, they encountered many dead longhorns and buffalo that had been trampled by the stampeding head strong bison of the plains.

The majority of Lynch's trail herd had been saved, were headed down river, on their way to Miles Town and the end of a long hard journey.

After a stop over of a day to give everyone, including the longhorns, a much needed rest, the herd was moving deep into Indian country, the home of the Sioux, Crow and Cheyenne. The further north they travelled, the more sign was spotted. Sightings were becoming more prevalent with no incidents to speak of. There was nothing ahead but Indians, the US Cavalry, and the growing cow town of Miles Town, Montana Territory. The Yellowstone River in the background would be the finale of the long drive.

Daylight the next morning found Brannon preparing the outfit to 'move'em out'. He was riding his favourite horse, Buck the line-back dun he had raised from a colt. As was the way of the trail, his worldly possessions were tied on the saddle, tucked in saddlebags and stuffed in his pockets. The sun bronzed trail boss was eager to get the herd moving while it was still cool. He peered long into the confusion of the rousing longhorns, ears straining to catch old Tom's signal to start the herd moving. Brannon insisted that Lynch start the herd on the move each morning. It was a token of respect to the old cattleman, one that Lynch appreciated and enjoyed. The sharp bark of a six-gun signalled the start, accompanied by the shouts and whoops of the cowboys, sure enough trail music to Tom Lynch's ears. "Move'em out! Let's head'em north boys, head'em north to Montana!"

Slowly but surely, the trail crew pushed the herd north along the Little Powder. Two days it took to cover thirty miles, and here old Tom called a halt. The cattle needed a rest, and so did the cowboys. Brannon was saddling a night horse for his turn at riding nighthawk when old Tom sauntered up and started to visit. Pausing to light his pipe, fragrant smoke curling around his whiskered jowls, he drawled, "Matt, I need you to go scoutin' in the mornin', why don't you put that hoss back in the remuda and get yourself some sleep? I don't mean to interfere none, but come first light could you go out ahead o' the herd a checkin' on Indian sign. Find out if there's enough grazin' for the herd, and see if you can locate that tradin' post. Them hide hunters we met'bout a week back, says there's a tradin' post where this here Little Powder meets up with the big river."

Showing the old cattleman the respect that he deserved, Brannon relaxed and listened to what he had to say. "Reckon I can do that," he answered. "I suppose you're right...I could sure use some shuteye."

With an ember from the fire, Lynch fired up his pipe once more, then continued his talk, "As scarce as the grass is around these parts, the hosses will be needin' some oats to get us to the Yellowstone and another problem," he grinned. "Old Ike's plumb put out…his coffee's'bout gone. This is the worst bunch of ha-wgs I ever laid eyes on fer drinkin' coffee. These Texas boys will have old Ike's scalp if we happen to run out."

Matt Brannon was smiling at his boss. "I'll leave at first light Tom. We sure don't need our camp cook losin' any more hair…not much there to start with."

"And Matt, I don't mean to appear bossy, but keep a sharp lookout fer Injuns…you hear?" insisted Lynch.

Tom Lynch was worried about Indians, he always had been. It was just a year ago, June of 1876, that Custer and his 7th Cavalry had gone down to defeat at the Little Bighorn River. The site wasn't far from here, roughly a hundred miles as the crow flies. This was Indian country and the old cattleman knew it.

Lynch had grown fond of Brannon, depended on him to handle the herd and trusted him to the limit. He knew the big cowboy was plumb salty when riled, and rode for the brand. Before leaving Fort Worth he gave Matt Brannon the position of trail boss, he hadn't regretted it for a minute.

* * *

A star lit sky was softening over the Wyoming plains. The Lynch trail camp was stirring, young punchers gathered around the glow of the buck brush fire, a pleasant aroma of frying bacon, coffee and fresh-baked sourdough biscuits drifting in the night-cooled air.

Old Ike was dishing out grub to the hungry cowboys, some had eaten and were saddling their day broncs. Matt Brannon, who was heading down the trail for a scout along the Little Powder, already had his dun horse saddled and waiting. The big cowboy shoved a saddle carbine into the steer-hide scabbard, rolled a blanket, coffee pot and a bait of grub in his slicker, then secured all this behind the saddle. He was now ready to ride down this lonely tributary of the Powder River.

Out beyond camp a night bird uttered a timid refrain. Nearby a sage grouse cackled a startled alarm, exploding from out of a nearby clump of sage as Brannon stepped in the saddle and swung aboard the hurricane deck. This was all the buckskin needed. He humped up right now and began to buck and squeal. Brannon was grinning as he stayed in the saddle, attempting to keep Buck away from old Ike's fire. The cowboys were whooping in unison, urging their big boss to stay aboard. It was diversions like this that made the harsh life of a cowboy bearable. Camaraderie, friendship, and even pride were thick and strong. It is the cowboy way.

The big cowboy known as Brannon survived the violent outburst. He was still grinning and knew Buck's show of spirit wasn't all that serious. It was the buckskin's way of telling Brannon that it was five-o'clock in the morning, that he didn't care for the noisy sage hen, and that he was sure enough ready to go. The cowboy calmed him down, talking to the horse as if he could understand. "Why, ya son-of-a-gun, it's been a coon's age since ya tried to buck me off." "Thought ya had me didn't ya?"

With the stampede over, he gave the horse his head and let him go. A good run would take the ginger out of him.

Late that afternoon he rode up a high grass-covered bluff to see the country ahead. Using old Tom's field glasses he could make out the main valley of the Powder off in the distance, and the winding course of the smaller stream leading up to its namesake. He reckoned another ten miles to the trading post.

"We'll camp down yonder by those rocks, Buck," he told his horse. "There appears to be a trickle of spring water…and this here bunch grass will make a fine supper fer ya."

* * * Chapter 3 * * *

Somehow, and it baffled Matt Brannon to know why, it seemed right to be riding down this river valley, almost as if he was heading for home. It was as if some unknown force was beckoning him to come to this trading post. A strange sense of urgency he could feel, as if a new chapter in his life was set to unfold.

He had came from the south, riding down the Little Powder, the coolness of the wooded valley a welcome reprieve from the sun which was now high in the sky. Located in a stand of cottonwood on the far side of a bunch grass clearing sat the trading post he had been searching for.

The modest outpost consisted of several log buildings, a lean-to barn, a horse corral and a stack of hay. There were several horses in the corral, chickens scratching in the dusty yard, and a lazy curl of wood smoke was lifting upward from the chimney of the store itself.

The big cowboy and his dun horse were nearing the buildings and the strangeness of it all, an essence of the unknown, bode heavy upon his mind. An inner feeling it was, one that was deep inside and hard for him to understand. Brannon shook himself, rubbed his eyes, and wondered if it was the heat that was causing him to be this way. "Must be the heat," he muttered. "That's it! The damned heat has sure enough addled my brain."

Moving away from the loafing corral bunch a striking pinto mare came to the edge of the corral. Her inquisitive nose was showing above the top rail, she nickered a greeting to the dun horse and his rider. Brannon could see she was well put together. He knew good horseflesh when he saw it. A glance was all that was needed to convince him he was looking at one of the best of the breed.

The big dun stallion returned the friendly greeting, his entire body shaking in a 'howdy' of his own. "Easy does it," Brannon said with a grin. "Ya sure got yerself an eye for the ladies…ya rascal. She's a sure enough beauty, I reckon."

Continuing on, he reined the dun up to the hitch rail, was preparing to step down when an old frontiersman walked out of the store. Must be the trader himself, Brannon thought. 'Riley's Trading Post', the sign above the door read in large printed letters. Shoving the Stetson back from his sun-bronzed brow, the cowboy drawled, "Howdy amigo."

Relaxing in the saddle some, the big Texan continued his talk, "Heard there was a tradin' post in these parts, decided to drop by...be needin' supplies fer a trail herd headin' this way. Reckon it should arrive here in'bout two days time, if all goes well."

"Well crawl down off that horse and come on in," the trader said. "My Lynn's got us some coffee a brewin'."

With a wink and a smile he spoke again, "I'll bet she can find us some of her doughnuts too. Why stranger, you've never et real doughnuts till you sample some of Lynn's!"

"Reckon I will," the cowboy was quick to reply. "Most folks know me as Brannon, Matt Brannon. And I thank you Mr. Riley. I reckon ya are Riley, the owner of this here tradin' post?"

"Aye lad, my name is Ben Riley. My daughter and I run the place together. Lynn is her name...we bin here going on four years now." replied the trader.

Brannon stepped down from the saddle, loosened the cinch, and with his Stetson in hand, pounded a cloud of dust from his travel-worn clothes. With Riley in the lead, he followed him into the coolness of the store. All was quiet except for the jingling of the cowboy's spurs.

There was no mistaking the strangeness that had invaded his soul, he was almost light-headed. Far up the Little Powder he had first noticed it, a faint whispering on the prairie wind, pleasant in a way, yet so intense. Almost as if someone was urging him onward, begging him to come on home.

It had been a long time since he had been exposed to this sort of thing. The trading post was small, yet stacked to the rafters with the necessities of the frontier. Most noticeable was the scent that filled the room—an essence of birch-tanned pelts, saddle leather, and kerosene too. Gun oil and plug tobacco, and above all this, was a more pleasant reminder of roast beef, baked-bread hot out of the oven, fresh brewed coffee, and something else. A faint hint of an enticing perfume!

With a flick of a smile, the cowboy reckoned he just might enjoy this assignment after all. The trader escorted the cowboy to the far end of the store where they sat down at a modest well-scrubbed table. Ben Riley and Tom Lynch's trail boss were no sooner seated when a curtain parted from a back-room kitchen and out walked the trader's daughter, a pot of coffee in one hand, a heaping plate of doughnuts in the other. Glancing up at the approaching girl, Brannon's heart skipped a beat; a silent gasp escaped his sun-chapped lips. He was plumb thunderstruck and speechless, never in his life had a young woman affected him this way nor had he seen one so beautiful.

"Lynn," spoke up the trader, "this here hombre is Matt Brannon, dropped by to arrange for some supplies."

With his Stetson in hand, Brannon arose from his chair and somehow managed to speak. "Sure good to meet ya Lynn Riley...I reckon it's sure my pleasure to do so." The girl flashed him a smile, a contagious happy smile that unsettled the cowboy even more.

"Sure good to meet you too Matt," she answered with a toss of her long auburn hair. Standing there, hat in hand and at a loss for words, it was then the cowboy reckoned it was she who had drawn him to this place, it had to be. He knew from the moment she entered the room that she must be the one.

Brannon somehow was able to return to his chair. For the first time in his life he was mindful of his shabby looking appearance. His trail-worn clothes, the trail dust embedded in himself and his beard, he hadn't shaved since leaving Fort Worth.

Lynn Riley was excited to have company and she sat down at the table with the cowboy and her Dad. Pouring her own coffee, she picked up a doughnut and looked directly at the big Texan, her deep brown eyes twinkling as they delved into his very soul. The girl appeared relaxed, so right for the time and the place. Yet, her eyes never left those of the cowboy. One look into her eyes is all it took and Matt Brannon found himself smitten by this vibrant, exciting girl. She had him licked, had beaten him to the draw. It had taken only short minutes for the trader's daughter to subdue Matt Brannon, the wild Brazos gunfighter.

Brannon was still squirming in his chair some, but managed to explain his reason for being here. He told of the advancing herd of Texas longhorn cattle and most of all inquired about the presence of Indians in these parts.

It was the doughnuts that were his saviour, helping him to settle down, helping him to accept the fact that he had fallen head-over-heels for this girl and that it was she whom he must have. He ate many of them, one after the other he consumed the girl's tasty treats. They were food from the God's as far as Matt Brannon was concerned.

Old Ben was aware of his daughter's treatment of the cowboy, and suppressing a grin, told the big Texan there were sufficient supplies here at the Post to take care of his needs. Filling his cup for the third time, maybe it was the fourth time; he settled back in his chair and began to talk.

"Since the big fight over yonder at the Greasy Grass…'bout a year ago it was…after them Sioux and Cheyenne massacred Custer's outfit to the last man, well the Injuns scattered you see. 15,000 of them were camped at the Little Big Horn, countin' about 4,000 fighting warriors. They broke up into bunches, small clans…scattered all over the country." Pausing to light his pipe, tobacco smoke thick around his greying locks, Riley continued his story. "Sittin' Bull took a bunch o' Hunkpapa Sioux up to the Cypress Hills in Canada, others drifted into the Dakotas. There is still quite a few in this here Powder River country, south and west o' here.

"There's a few in these parts that stop by now and then to trade. Mostly peaceful though—can be a downright quarrelsome bunch at times." The old trader added. "There's a cavalry outfit camped at the mouth o' the Tongue River over Miles Town way, been a pilin' up all kinds o' supplies and what not. Talk is they're aimin' to build a fort. Keogh some calls it."

After the trader's lengthy oration the cowboy was settling down some. With traces of sugar showing on his three-month growth of whiskers, Brannon finished another doughnut and asked, "How far to Miles Town?"

"Why, it's not that far from here," Lynn told him. "About a three day journey by team and wagon, much faster if I'm riding Star."

"It's sure a hot, dusty son-of-a-gun,'bout a 100-miles to the fork of the Yellowstone and the Tongue," her father added.

Brannon shoved back his chair and prepared to leave. "I sure do thank ya for your hospitality, best doughnuts I ever had the pleasure of eatin'. Reckon I could use a sack o' that Arbuckle's over yonder; old Ike will have my scalp fer sure if I forget to bring it. It's sure been swell a meetin' ya like this, Miss Riley. Reckon it's a day I'll never forget!"

Tom Lynch's trail boss left the trading post, secured the sack of coffee behind the saddle, and was ready to step into the saddle when old Ben approached the hitching rail. He was grinning when he spoke, "Wait up a minute Matt. Here is a bait o' oats for your hoss…do him good'fore you head back south."

The dun was greedily crunching the unexpected treat and the cowboy was still fussing with his outfit when out of nowhere Lynn was standing beside him offering him a bulging canvas bag. "I have something for you," she said with a smile, "I fixed you some sandwiches."

"Why, thank ya Ma'am," Brannon said, and accepted that which she offered. "Ya didn't need to do this for me."

"And there's doughnuts as well," she said with a smile, once again giving him a going over with her piercing eyes. "I am happy to give you this food Matt Brannon, but please do not call me Ma'am! My name is Lynn Riley!"

"Sure hope ya accept my apologies Lynn Riley! I'm sure sorry...I do enjoy yer doughnuts though, the tastiest I ever'et." exclaimed the cowboy.

Swinging into the saddle, Brannon looked down at the trader's daughter. "The herd will pass by here in a few days," he told her. "Reckon I'll be seein' ya then."

Outwardly, Lynn Riley appeared at ease, yet her inner self was in turmoil the same as Brannon's. "Don't you go a worrying none," she smiled as she spoke. "I'll be here...you hurry back, you hear?"

Reining the dun horse high on his back legs, his big Stetson waving at arms length, the cowboy called back, "This cowpuncher will be back for sure...bye Lynn Riley." With his spurs urging the stallion across the bunch grass prairie, Matt Brannon vanished in the brush along the Little Powder. The trader's daughter was certain she heard a shout off in the distance, one that sent shivers racing up her spine. It was the wild rebel yell of a Texas cowboy.

* * *

The sun was hours above the horizon of the next day before Matt Brannon met the herd in the vicinity of the big bluff, the same place where he camped on his ride down river. Riding point of the herd, Tom Lynch spotted him right off and spurred ahead to meet him. After a hearty handshake, the two riders of the range rode side-by-side, the cowboy and his boss Tom Lynch, listening to his trail boss telling it like it was.

It wasn't long before old Tom reined in his bronc, an accusing look was spreading across his face when he asked, "Dog-gone it all...you a holdin' out on me? I swear I can smell fresh doughnuts!" Brannon was laughing when he opened a saddlebag. He was pleased to share Lynn Riley's doughnuts with his good friend.

* * *

Lynn Riley was fidgety and downright restless. Ever since she watched the cowboy vanish in the brush along the Little Powder, she had been this

35

way. The tall, handsome cowboy was all she could think of, she just knew that her life would never again be the same. Every now and then, more often than she realized, Lynn left the store and peered off into the distance.

Old Ben was settled in the shade of the porch awning, in the comfort of a well-used rocking chair. "The herd's a getting' closer," he drawled. "Every now and then I kin hear'em. See the dust cloud a boilin' from above that willow thicket yonder? I figure they'll make the Powder here'fore long…most likely cross over and bed'em on the big sage flat. Make a good place fer a night camp."

Lynn was trembling and confused. She went back in the trading post reluctant to let old Ben see her this way. "What is wrong with me?" she wondered. What she was sure of though, was that ever since Matt Brannon rode into her life, life as she knew it would never again be the same. She smiled some as she remembered how she had never let up on the cowboy. She had brazenly, perhaps, met the big Texan as a woman, a very desirable woman.

Lynn knew that her lack of propriety had unsettled the cowboy. That he had been ill-at-ease she now regretted. From the first time she saw him sitting by old Ben she became aware of it. "Wonder if this is love at first sight?" she murmured.

A frown came to her pretty face as she remembered the traders from Belle Fourche. It was the young one that troubled her, she couldn't even pronounce his name it was French she had assumed. He was the one who proposed to her, and his visits were coming more often it seemed. Deep in her heart she knew that she never loved him, she never could.

It was just the loneliness here on the frontier. She needed someone to associate with, someone to love. "I have so much love to give," she mused, "and it is locked up inside me going to waste." Lynn Riley was frightened of her future she had been for a long time. She was sure she couldn't hold out against the advances of the big, burly trader much longer.

Her emotions were raw and on edge as she thought of it. She compared the Frenchman with the cowboy there was no contest in her mind. She had made her decision in mere moments, a few short minutes after Brannon walked into her trading post. She was certain her father would be upset, old Ben had visions of turning the business over to his daughter and the French trader. His wishes were to retire and go back to Missouri.

The lonely girl longed for her mother who had died so long ago. If only her mother could be here, to talk to, to confide in, and share her thoughts and desires with. Glancing into the cracked mirror that hung on a nail behind the pine-slab counter of her store, she spoke as if her mother was standing beside her. "I just know I have…I have fallen in love with a tall, handsome cowboy!"

Love, the thought of really being in love unnerved Lynn. She paced the floor of her little store. Matt would be returning soon. In preparation she took the time to brush her long auburn tresses and to dab on another touch of her treasured perfume. As she settled down another thought entered her mind…she would bake a batch of doughnuts. She had to calm herself, keep herself busy. Besides Matt might like some more, he had assured her they were sure enough good.

The scorching heat along the Little Powder was hovering above 100 degrees in the shade. Ben Riley and his daughter could hear the rumble of the advancing herd, all 2500 of them by the sounds of it. A huge dust cloud hovered above the longhorns, and they could hear the shrill high-pitched yells of the cowboys. Never had they seen or heard the likes before. The herd passed on the far side of the Little Powder, a few hundred yards east of Riley's Post. Protected from the searing heat of an unforgiving sun, Lynn and her Dad sat under the porch awning watching an unfolding drama.

The first to be seen were the point riders, there were two. Lynn just knew that one of them was Matt Brannon. She could detect a large Stetson waving through the dust, she was then sure. Following close behind plodded a pair of large rangy steers, a glint of sun bouncing off the massive horns showing through the dust. Their mission in life was to lead the rest, creating a bond that influenced the herd to follow. As the herd and dust flowed by, Lynn could detect the flank riders doing their job, and doing it well. Next were the cowboys on swing, hurrahing and swinging their lariats high in the air. Hidden from view by the river brush and the namesake of the Powder River, namely dust, were the vigilant drag riders. Their job was to protect the rear of the herd and urge on the stragglers, a job none of them wanted, yet it had to be done.

More times than once the trader's daughter heard a chilling sound, a sound that sent shivers rippling down her spine. It was a wild, rebel yell originating from Tom Lynch's cowboys. "The herd sure hasn't slowed down any," commented old Ben, "the cowboys must be a pushin' 'em across the river all right.

* * *

A demanding, searing thirst now satisfied, the longhorns scrambled up the far bank of the Powder River. The Lynch trail herd was tired and ready to stop for the night. Matt Brannon knew his profession well. Push them hard after the mid-day break come evening it was a simple chore to swing the leaders into a circling pattern, which would stop their advance. This night the bedding grounds would be on an extensive flood plain overgrown with sage brush.

Tom Lynch and his big trail boss were really fussy with the herd, watching over the longhorns like a pair of hawks. In a sense this was a trial run. Though a few herds had ventured north before them, this one was the first into this northern portion of the Great Plains of America. The enticement that lured them here was grass, an abundance of nutritious grass untouched by the hooves of beef cattle. The northern plains offered an exciting new market for Texas beef. Vast fortunes could be made. They were fussy all right, and with good reason to be so.

Under the capable hands of old Ike, night camp was set up and supper cooked for the hungry crew. The nighthawk boys were assigned their respective shifts, Brannon and his boss then rode across the Powder River to Riley's Post.

A scorching Montana sun had settled into the vastness of the west. The intense heat of the day softened, a soothing coolness crept along the breaks of the Powder River. The kerosene lanterns were lit at Riley's Post. Relaxing outdoors on the raised pine-slab porch, Lynn and her Dad were enjoying the coolness of the night. Old Ben was sitting in a time-worn rocking-chair; his daughter was resting on a cushion placed up top on an empty nail keg. Lynn had made the cushion special for the nail keg, and though not exposed to the talents of a seamstress, was proud of her handiwork just the same.

Lynn's heart gave a flutter as she sensed the approaching horses and the easy banter of the riders. She just knew one of them would be Matt Brannon. "Ho, the Post," Lynch called out, as they neared the hitch rail. "Askin' permission to ride in?"

Rising from his comfortable roost in the shadows, the trader answered, "The store is still open strangers, tie up your broncs and come on in. Is that you Matt? I reckoned that was your dun hoss."

Stepping down from their saddles, the two riders moved into the lantern-lit doorway. Lynn came from the shadows and stood by old Ben. She appeared a bit shy, yet was smiling when she spoke, "Hello, Matt...I'm so glad you've come back." "Sure is good to see you again!"

Although it was too dark to notice, the cowboy's sun-bronzed face showed a touch of red at the girl's warm greeting. He removed his hat, and with a smile as wide as a crescent moon, the trail boss replied, "Howdy, Lynn Riley...sure is good to see ya too! Lynn and Ben Riley, this is my boss, Tom Lynch."

With a twinkle in his eyes old Tom removed his hat. "It's sure my pleasure, Lynn and Ben Riley." Then looking at the girl he said, "This trail boss of mine has been tellin' me all about you...even shared your doughnuts with me." Turning toward the open door, Lynch suddenly stopped. "Is that doughnuts I can smell? Tarnation...it is doughnuts!"

Chuckling, Ben answered the cattleman, "It sure is Tom. My Lynn's been a fryin' up a storm all day. She just knew this trail boss o' yourn would be a hankerin' for some more."

It was now Lynn's turn to blush. "Come on Matt, walk with me for awhile," she asked, gently tugging the cowboy's arm. A harvest moon, seductive in a brilliant hue, was showing above the distant breaks. Lynn hooked her arm through the cowboy's and drew him toward the corral.

The moon rose higher in the sky, the landscape grew brighter. The pinto mare sensed their presence, she neighed a greeting and trotted towards the girl and the cowboy. "Isn't she a beauty? Her name is Evening Star," exclaimed Lynn, as her face beamed with pride.

Thrusting an inquisitive nose through the cottonwood rail, Star eagerly awaited the girl's gentle touch and cooing flattery. Hoisting a dusty boot on the bottom rail, the cowboy answered her question. "Star's a mighty fine hoss, Lynn. The best looking pinto I've ever laid eyes on. We'll have to go for a ride sometime?"

"Why Matt Brannon, that would be wonderful," she replied with a happy giggle. "I won't let you forget you offered, you hear?"

Continuing their walk, Lynn led the cowboy towards the river. He was settling down some, feeling much more comfortable around this lovely lady. He had even bathed in the river over near camp, had put on a clean shirt and shaved off his beard.

Presently, he stopped walking so he could look at her lovely face in the moonlight. He turned her towards him and spoke, "I'm not much fer fancy talk Lynn. But I reckon there's something we've got to find out...right here and now. You see Lynn—the herd's moving on. In the morning, at the crack o' dawn we move'em out. We are going North to the Yellowstone and beyond."

"Reckon it is a hundred miles from here, maybe more. Could be I'll never see ya again, never again be able to look into yer pretty eyes, listen to yer wonderful laughter, or eat yer delicious doughnuts." His voice became unsteady, his talk was faltering, yet he was determined to finish what was bothering him so.

Interrupting, the girl gently chided, "Tell me Matt. Please tell me what you want to say."

Words were difficult to find for the cowboy, yet, he was determined to lay the cards on the table. He must find out tonight, tomorrow would be too late. Come first light, he and the herd would be on the move, possibly to never see her again. His inner self was struggling to voice that which was in his heart, when a drastic change overcame him.

It was the moon that gave him the confidence to find the words that were so evasive. He looked into her eyes. The moon was reflecting in her beautiful eyes, the strength, assurance and love that he found there was just what the cowboy needed. "I reckon there is only one way to tell ya…so here goes. It all happened so sudden, and was unexpected too. I reckon I have fallen for ya Lynn, real hard in fact. Dog-gone it all, I'm head over heels in love with a trader's daughter from the Powder River."

The gasp that she gave was real, and so was her happy giggle. She flew into his arms, looked shyly at his handsome face and said, "Matt Brannon, I love you too…more than you will ever know!"

The cowboy wasn't through talking but the girl's kisses were keeping him mighty busy. Though visibly shaken, he gently moved her back so he could look in her eyes once more. "Dog-gone it all Lynn, I could go on like this forever but, but ya must let me finish what I've got to say. Lynn darlin', would ya consider becoming the wife of a Texas cowboy?"

Once more her lips found the cowboy's. She stopped long enough to answer his question. "Yes, yes I will marry a Texas cowboy…but on one condition. The condition is that the cowboy's name must be Matt Brannon!"

The cowboy and the girl were transformed into a heaven of their own choosing. Nothing else mattered at this time in their young lives; they had found what they had both been seeking. The girl was so happy she could hardly speak. It took awhile, then she settled down and told the cowboy of her Mom's death when she was only a child, that her Dad had raised her, loved and cared for her all these long years. She talked of the French trapper from Belle Fourche, the one who wanted her for his own. How she had kept him at bay, so far, but had feared she would be unable to resist his advances much longer. His was a relentless pursuit that was gradually wearing her down, weakening her resolve to wait for someone she could love.

Lynn Riley was so thankful she had found Matt Brannon. Someone who loved her for what she was. Someone she could talk to, to share her fears and desires. Most important of all, was someone to love, someone she could honour and respect, someone she knew was honest and good.

Out of the south he had came on his line-back dun, down the valley of the Little Powder River he rode. He just walked into her trading post and rescued her from her fears and dread of the unknown. The cowboy had sat at her table, ate her doughnuts and loved them. Matt's eyes had looked deep into her eyes, and in them she could detect nothing but truth and right and love. Lynn had known from that first meeting, as had the cowboy, that it was a love that would last if but given the chance.

Matt told her of his life as a cowboy, that it was all he had ever known. That on occasion he was called upon to use his guns to uphold that which was right. He had no use for those who took advantage of the defenceless, weak and downtrodden. To harm a woman or child was an unforgivable sin in his eyes, one that had to be avenged and made right.

He told her many things. That he had been a wanderer, seeking for he knew not what. Now he knew! It was Lynn Riley he had found at the end of the rainbow, worth far more than a pot of gold. It was this lovely girl from the Powder River whom he had been seeking, to share his love and his life. It would be she who would be his saviour, point him in the right direction and settle him down.

The moon now settled beyond the distant breaks. It was a lover's moon for Matt and Lynn, a moon the two would remember for the rest of their lives. "It's sure a getting' late darlin'," the cowboy said. "Reckon it's time we head back to the store and tell old Tom and yer Dad our plans.

"They must be a wonderin' what has happened to us...I sure don't want Ben Riley a huntin' me with his scatter gun."

Hand-in-hand they entered the store. Lynn was chattering excitedly and hanging on to her cowboy. She was radiant and happy as she told the two oldsters the exciting news. The news came as a surprise to old Ben and Tom, but it was a happy one. They had both been thinking the same thing.

Lynn would have it no other way. She sat the men at the table, put on a fresh pot of coffee and brought out a plate of doughnuts. It was time for a medicine talk.

Old Ben appeared in a daze. The news of Lynn's coming marriage would sure wreck his plans with the traders from Belle Fourche; he just had to chew on it for awhile. After a bit he found his voice. "Matt Brannon, I will be honoured to have you for a son-in-law…it's sure enough sudden, but I too believe you're a good man." But tell me this! How are you going to take care of my daughter?"

Appearing at a loss for words, Brannon was plumb nervous until he felt Lynn's hand slip into his own. This was all he needed, his confidence returned, he replied to old Ben's question. "Well sir, Lynn and I haven't talked it over yet. But if God's willing, and Lynn's willing, I would like to head up into the Canadian territories and start us a spread of our own. I hear the grass is good up that way, with plenty of water. The best part of the whole plan is the land is wide open for the taking!"

Lynn squeezed her cowboy's hand; she was looking into Matt's eyes and smiling. "Father Ben, I love him with all my heart…I will go wherever Matt takes me."

With tears showing on his cheeks, Ben Riley gave his daughter a loving hug. "That's good enough for this old hombre. I'm going to miss you my daughter, I'll always love you."

The excited foursome talked long into the night. A decision was made that old Ben would deliver his daughter and her belongings to Miles Town, on or about the same time as the trail herd arrived there. Matt and Lynn would be married before the Texans headed back down the trail. Old Ben reckoned he would sell the trading post to the fur-trading bunch from Belle Fourche. It was only about a month back that they had stopped by and made an extremely generous offer. An offer he had refused because of the uncertainty of Lynn's future. Now that had all changed.

This past winter of 1876/77 had been hard on his old bones. A cold spell that about done him in and 40 below temperatures that just would not go away were the last straws. Ben Riley's interest in this harsh climate of the northern plains was no more.

"Ben, come back to Texas with my outfit," suggested Lynch. "I'd be mighty pleased to have you along."

And so it was decided. Lingering over their coffee, the two oldsters were figuring out the details of their southern journey when Matt and Lynn slipped out the door. The cowboy walked over to the dun, tightened the cinch and swung into the saddle. Bending slightly, his arm encircled the girl's waist and lifted her into his lap. Reining the dun away from the hitch rail, they rode off into the darkness.

Lynn was thrilled and deeply moved. She rewarded him by finding his lips with a kiss. The trader's daughter and her Texas cowboy once more vowed their love to each other. Old Ben and Tom soon left the store. Tom tightened the cinch on his saddle and old Ben was sure becoming worried. "Wonder where those two love birds have gone," he said. "I have never seen Lynn act this way before. It's the strangest thing! Lynn sure seems a goner, reckon she's plumb wrapped up in your trail boss,"

"Don't worry none'bout them two Ben!" replied Lynch. A finer pair of youngsters couldn't be found. You can be mighty proud of that little gal my friend. I've never met a more kind, gentle, and graceful lady in my life…and she's a beauty you know!"

The remarks of Lynch were all that old Ben needed to settle him down, he relaxed some and with a hint of a smile replied, "Why thank you Tom, she's just like her mother…a spittin' image of my darlin' wife."

"Matt Brannon's a good man Ben. Lynch continued, the best there is. He'll take care of her, don't you worry none!"

It was then the two in question rode back to the trading post out of the darkness. Brannon assisted Lynn to the ground, speaking to her father he said, "I reckon it was fate that brought me here, to Riley's Post…and to yer daughter Lynn. I love her ya know, will do my best to give her a good life. Thank ya Ben Riley, for yer daughter's hand."

Lynn was standing beside her Dad. She was holding his work-roughened hand, they both had tears in their eyes as they watched the cowboy rein his dun horse off into the darkness.

Tom Lynch and his trail boss rode back across the Powder River to their camp on the big sage flat. Brannon rode out to check the longhorn cattle; spoke with the nighthawks…all seemed quiet. Then back to his blankets for a few hours rest.

At first light the drive would continue on into the uncertainty of the northwest.

* * * Chapter 4 * * *

The herd was once again on the move, the longhorns strung out for a country mile as they left the Powder River behind. Lead by the two trail-broke steers, Tom Lynch pointed the herd for the Yellowstone River country. Matt Brannon was earning his pay as trail boss, riding from the point to the rear, and around the moving herd positioning the cowboys on flank and swing. Then back to the rear to assist those unfortunates who had been assigned to the lowly position of drag. The bunch quitters were lively this morning, forcing the cowboys and their cayuses to muster all the cow sense they had in them.

It was fun when the trail boss came back to help out. The cowboys respected Brannon for taking a turn on drag, for showing no qualms in eating dust with the rest of the crew. The noise of the bawling herd was intense, the dry choking dust a curse to those working back there. Take their turn they must, or answer to the big trail boss they knew as Brannon. The drag riders reckoned if ever there was a living hell, this must be what it was like.

The last stragglers had been hurrahed and chased back with the herd, the drag riders were now settled in for a long, scorching day ahead. Brannon was riding in the din and confusion of it all when a rider reined in along side. He turned to speak to the cowboy, and here in the hellish Powder River dust rode a grinning Lynn Riley.

"Howdy, Mr. Trail Boss...need another hand?"

Brannon flashed a grin of his own, side-passed the dun horse close to the pinto mare and gave his wife-to-be a hug. "I'm a takin' ya up on that ride ya promised me," she drawled, mocking the Texan's talk.

"Reckoned maybe you'uns might need another ha-and." The young couple, soon to be wedded, laughed in unison amidst the longhorns and the dust.

"I sure enough can Lynn darlin'. The pay around these parts is not up to much...but the company is the best there is." They were still laughing and holding each other's hand when they emerged out of the dust and galloped ahead to be with old Tom.

Leaving Brannon and his Powder River girl riding point. Lynch, accompanied by old Ike at the reins of his chuck wagon, travelled on ahead to prepare for the mid-day stop. When the herd caught up and were settled for a rest, Ike had a hearty meal prepared of baked beans, fried meat, and scalding coffee. Not to be outdone, Lynn went to her saddle and returned with a bulging bag of her doughnuts. These she shared with the awe-stricken cowboys.

Though they appeared shy over the presence of a dusty-cheeked Lynn Riley, the camp cook treated her like a queen, as did all the cowboys. It was an honour to have her at their fire and they absorbed every minute of her stay. Her contagious giggle and big Powder River smile, they would never forget.

With a wink old Tom drew his trail boss aside and spoke to him in confidence. "After that young filly of yourn has finished her meal, I reckon you should escort her back to the tradin' post. Could be that some of them hostile Cheyenne are hangin' around...a spyin' on our herd. Be a cryin' shame to lose her, after you just got her lass-ooed!" Matt Brannon was only too happy to be allowed the opportunity to be alone with Lynn again.

Once again they were with each other. Matt and Lynn knew that there was no place on earth that they would rather be than right here, riding together across the prairie.

* * *

Trouble started two days north of the Powder River. The route was swinging northwest into a region of strange time-eroded hills. Massive up-thrusts of ancient volcanic origin shattered and eroded into a sinister landscape of nothing but fractured rock.

Matt Brannon had a tough decision to make. As trail boss, he had left the herd behind and rode ahead to scout the area, to see if the longhorns could be driven through this maze of broken landscape. After checking things out, weighing the pros and cons, he reined his dun horse back towards the advancing herd. He must have a medicine talk with old Tom.

Lynch was sure enough relieved when Brannon returned. They both reined in their broncs, the two lead steers and the herd closing in behind them. Tom Lynch fired up his pipe, concern heavy upon his whiskered face. "Whatta you think Matt—reckon we can pull this off?"

Matt looked long at his good friend, recognized the turmoil he must be having. "I'll tell ya like it is Tom, no beatin' around the bush—the chips are

45

sure enough in the fire this time. Yer longhorns can be driven through, but it will take tricky manoeuvring and excellent horsemanship by the cowboys to avoid a wreck. It won't be easy, but there is a passage through, reckon old Ike's rig can make it too." Brannon continued, "It's either push them through the hell-hole, or a fifty-mile drive to get around...I found good grass and plenty of fresh water on the other side."

Brannon appeared confident that it could be done. For the big cowboy to be here at this time was money in the bank to the old Texan. "Let's give it a try Tom," he advised. "These young Texans of yours are up to it, best cowboys I ever rode with...plumb full of cow sense and savvy."

Old Tom was worried sick about pushing the herd into these desolate badlands that lay ahead. It appeared a natural barrier for travel of this kind— for a herd of 2500 head of longhorns. Yet, with no water or grass for fifty miles, he knew they'd be in one hell of a fix. "All right Matt, I reckon you know best...let's give it a try," replied Tom. Brannon answered, "Follow this old buffalo trail Tom. It will take you to the other side, shouldn't take more than a couple o' hours...three, maybe four at the most. I'll stay back and help out where I'm needed."

A suffocating heat-saturated breeze moaned through the arid maze, a breeze sent here from the depths of hell it seemed. Large heads bobbing this way and that to prevent their yard-length horns from banging on the ledges, old Tom's lead steers trailed closely behind the cattleman's bronc. The steers were trail-broke; they knew their place was behind the point rider.

Though the steers weren't considered pets by any means, the entire crew respected them and knew old Tom treated them to a generous portion of oats now and then. A bit reluctant at first, the herd settled in and trailed behind the two leaders.

Though young in years, the cowboys were at their best, their wiry mustangs performing as if they were cutting horses entered in the show rings of San Antonio, perhaps even Mexico City. This was how cowboys played on their day off, training their mustangs to work cows. It was cow horses they rode...there were no better.

The crossing was going smooth enough, the herd was mostly through the hellhole and the badlands would soon be behind them. There were, however, a few stragglers still on the far side, perhaps fifty or so. The two cowboys on drag had performed an awesome task. Though they and their horses were trembling with fatigue, they were able to keep the stragglers headed into the hellhole. They had ridden for the brand this day, old Tom and Brannon would be proud of their drag riders.

From out of the gloom and dust all hell broke loose. It was sudden and final, the twang of a bow string, the smack of an arrow driven deep into human flesh, and a rider known as Colt McGraw was in trouble. He slumped in the saddle, tugging at the hand-honed, arrow head which had penetrated his thigh.

Whooping and yip-yipping a frightening tune of the wild places, a small band of Cheyenne appeared from their hiding place in the shattered ledges. Even though mounted on half-starved ponies, they were able to cut out about twenty head from the drag bunch and head them into the badlands.

Chick, the remaining rider, gave chase, but was tumbled from his saddle, an arrow driven deep into his chest. The attack on the drag had been well planned and executed.

Colt McGraw was Tom Lynchs' horse wrangler who had been assigned to drag. He was reeling from shock and pain. Hanging on to the horn of his saddle, he allowed the bronc to follow the last of the longhorns into the hell-hole. Once on the other side, he hollered for the trail boss as he tumbled to the ground.

Brannon spotted the youngster as he fell, stepped down from the dun and ran to the downed rider. He propped him into a sitting position, cursing at the arrow still in Colt's leg. "It was Injuns Matt...took us by surprise. A bunch of 'em hit the stragglers and the remuda." With a groan the boy continued his talk, "Got me and Chick both, he's down and hit bad—took a direct hit in his chest!"

"Take care of him Tom," Brannon managed to say, he was furious and getting more so by the minute. "I'm a goin' back after Chick." Old Tom was white as a sheet. "You boys take care, Matt," He appeared weary and burdened with a heavy load. "Don't get yourselves killed...you hear?"

Mounted on their broncs, Brannon and three of his cowboys rode back through the hellhole. He spotted Chick right off and was soon by his side. The boy was in bad shape, the Cheyenne arrow driven deep in his chest. Blood was seeping from his nose and mouth. He was silently crying and alone.

"I'm here now Chick...hang in there boy," the big trail boss told him. "We're a taking ya through to the herd. You'll be a ridin' in the chuck wagon with old Ike, headin' to Miles Town in fine old style."

"Ga-wd a mighty, it hurts...I'm hit bad Mr. Brannon...not gonna make it!" The young Texan coughed up blood. He was just a teenaged boy. This cattle drive was his first time up the trail.

Gently Brannon took the cowboys outstretched hand. "Chick, ya hear me? Cut out that kind o' talk…no sense to it! Fight boy! Fight, I know ya can do it!"

"We was a doin' our best Mr. Brannon. Didn't see'em for the damn dust, nuthin we could do." Chick's body shook in a convulsion of coughing, moaning in fear and pain, gripping Brannon's hand tighter, and tighter. "Gawd a mighty, it hurts. Sorry I'm such a bo-ob, Mr. Bra—!" The young Texan's body convulsed once more. His hand loosened, his body lay still, his eyes wide open staring at the blue Montana sky.

Brannon was shaken. He was proud of this Texas boy who had ridden for the brand. He never knew Chick's last name or his hometown. Tom would know if he had friends or relatives who should be told. Matt felt that Chick had died a hero's death. He had given his all, his very life while riding for old Tom Lynch's brand. They tied the boy's body across his saddle and sent the mustang back through the hellhole to be picked up on the other side.

As shown by a cloud of boiling dust, the cattle thieves weren't that far from the site of Chick's death. The ways of the Cheyenne were foreign to the longhorns who were putting up a stiff resistance at being driven from the herd. Choking back a lump in his throat, Brannon roared, "Let's go get'em!"

After a brief skirmish in which one of the hostiles was shot from his horse, the Cheyenne rode out of range of the Texan's guns, leaving the longhorns behind. They appeared half starved with no rifles he could see. Brannon reckoned the bunch was a small family clan foraging for food.

Before returning to the herd, the cowboys cut out several old bunch-quitters, the same ones that had given them trouble all the way up from Fort Worth. "Leave'em for the Indians," Brannon roared, watching one of the cagey old moss-horns charge a mounted Cheyenne, upsetting both the horse and rider. "These cattle rustlin' devils will be mighty hungry'fore they get them critters over their fire!"

The remaining longhorns and Colt's remuda were bunched together, then hurrahed into the hellhole and taken through.

* * * Chapter 5 * * *

In awed silence the young cowhands dug a grave for their fallen comrade and then they lowered his blanket-wrapped body into the hole. The entire crew stayed close by to pay their last respects to a fellow cowpuncher they knew only as Chick. "Matt, I would like you to say a few last words over Chick," Tom Lynch asked, "before the boys cover him up."

Brannon agreed and stepped forward so he could look down at the young boy's body. Crowding in close, the cowboys too, wished to be part of it all. The trail boss appeared hesitant to begin with, then, after brushing a tear off his cheek, he began to speak.

"This young cowpuncher known to us as Chick was proud to be a cowboy. I just know he was! From the time he was old enough to talk, this must have been the boy's desire. It was chance that brought him to Fort Worth that day, the right time at the right place. He was hired on with Tom Lynch's cattle drive, up the trail to Montana we were headin'. Chick was proud of his spurs and rawhide lasso, his sweat-stained hat and an ol' well-used six-gun in a cow-hide holster. Though his slick-forked saddle and clothing were patched, and showed much wear, he was still proud. "He learned, learned well; it is the cowboy way!" the big Texan continued, "His body is now laid to rest in this Montana soil, a Cheyenne arrow driven deep in his chest. His fate has not been the first, nor will it be the last of its kind. The pain he suffered no longer shows on his sun-bronzed face, instead, a trace of a smile on his wind-chapped lips. Chick died well…riding for the brand, doing that which he loved so well. There is no other place he would rather have been at the time of his death than here in Montana Territory, riding his bronc up the trail, earning his pay as a cowboy with Tom Lynch's longhorn drive!"

Brannon's eulogy touched the young rider's, there wasn't a dry eye in the bunch. Somehow they now felt closer to Chick, a comrade who had given his all while fighting for the brand. This experience would change their outlook on life, they reckoned. It would make each one of them proud to be a cowboy.

Although Indian sightings were now a daily occurrence, there were no more troubles to speak of. The herd arrived in Miles Town a week later. Another day was spent in crossing the Yellowstone where the cattle were scattered far and wide across this new grazing country. It was at the buyer's request that they do so. As a bonus to the buyer, were a couple of dozen buffalo from the big stampede on the Little Powder. They had made themselves at home with the longhorns, trailed along as if they were cows.

During the last half of the 1870's, the railroad continued to push towards Montana Territory. The cattle business picked up briskly. Montana ranchers and Texans too, were following the lead of the early trailblazers. Thousands of longhorns from the over-stocked southern plains were driven north into this lush grass country. By the end of the decade, ranching in the territory was on the verge of a boom. The most enduring of the early ranchers were prospering to no end.

Beginning from a small trading post, similar to Riley's Post a 100-miles to the southeast, a thriving settlement came to life along the Tongue River. With ranchers advancing into the area, a town developed and flourished, assuring a long and bright future.

Even now the settlement was experiencing a flurry of activity, growing rapidly, supplying many of the needs of a U.S. Army fort taking shape near by. It would serve as a base of operations for the rounding up of the Indian tribes who were defying the government and avoiding the reservation life that would be their lot. The fort was planned as a strong bastion for the region, from the advances of the unruly Sioux and Cheyenne.

Cattle would be needed, great herds of them, to feed this influx of white men and the Indians that were pouring into one of the last of the great grass regions of North America. Miles Town was doing its share in satisfying the hungry bellies of the soldiers, settlers, and Indians alike.

Near the Tongue River was a clutter of pine-pole corrals that passed as the local stockyards. The Lynch outfit was camped here awaiting the arrival of Ben Riley and his daughter Lynn. It was here in this frontier settlement that Tom Lynch paid off his cowboys. They were now free to go their separate ways, or accept an open invitation to ride back to Texas with the outfit, still eating Lynch's grub and still bound to obey his orders.

With gold pieces jingling in their jeans, the young punchers went shopping at the local business houses. Some bought a new ten-gallon hat, maybe a pair of boots or a much needed saddle. Others carefully tucked the hard earned wages deep in their pockets for loved ones back home. It could have been for a young wife or perhaps needy parents struggling to keep food on the table back at their rundown shacks on the plains. There was one or two who blew their gold pieces on wine, women and song. A few nights of hell raising and they were broke again. This has always been an inevitable trait of human nature.

The cowboys cleaned up in the Tongue River, donning their best duds, some fancy and brand new, some plain and patched at the knees, then, as a group headed up the main thoroughfare of this oasis of the plains to see the sights and sample the wares on offer. It wasn't hard to do in Miles Town, a town where most doors swung both ways.

After the long, dusty journey up the trail, one that consumed six months of their lives, the Lynch outfit was ready to party and have a good time. Forgetting is what they wished to do, to forget about their downed amigo, Chick. To escape the hellish heat, the dust of the trail. The damn dust that seemed embedded in their very souls.

Another day had come and gone and the shadows of night were closing in on the northern plains. The cowboys that worked for Tom Lynch had left for the saloons earlier on, most of them mere boys, a first time sampling of the diversions of the night. Matt Brannon and his boss located a small log cabin diner a home-grown venture ran by a widow of the Indian wars. Delicious home cooking was her drawing card and she never lacked for business.

The two best friends were quietly eating a late supper when in limped Colt McGraw, old Tom's horse wrangler. The lad's arrow wound was healing nicely, but he would have an obvious limp for months to come. He appeared excited and out of breath when he spoke, "Brannon, Mr. Lynch...old Ike's been shot!"

Pausing to catch his breath, Colt spoke again, "The boys are set to bust loose...looks like a fight with them two gamblers,'twas one of'em who shot old Ike." "The Marshal hustles right in, calls us a bunch o' Texas trouble makers, says he's gonna throw us all in the calaboose!"

Three angry cowpunchers left the back-street diner and strode down the path to the Bull's Head Saloon. Brannon and old Tom were two abreast as they slammed into the bat-wing doors and entered together. Old Tom might have been getting a bit long-in-the-tooth, but he was plumb salty when riled. "What's a goin' on here?" he roared. "Stand back! Back off from my cowboys, you hear!"

Advancing towards the tin star, he glared in anger as he spoke, "What's this I hear about you lockin' my boys up in your two-bit jail?" Brannon hurried over to old Ike, who sat slumped in a chair, blood seeping from a bullet hole in his shoulder. "What happened here Ike? Which of these hombres shot you?"

The old cook's face was as white as if he had seen a ghost, he was drifting into shock as he nodded toward a sneering, fancy-dressed gent, obviously the gambler in question. "It was that slick-fingered son-of-gun," he mumbled. "I caught him a dealin' off the bottom of the deck!" "I called him on it, the tin-horn up and shot me...I never even drew my .45."

Appearing in a near panic, the Marshal was quick to reply, "Now hold on here, that's not the way I heard it...this cowboy of yourn was stirring up trouble."

Brannon was fighting mad, intense rage and disgust crackling from his eyes. Turning from old Ike, he roared so all in the room would be sure to hear, "Back off Marshal, you're bitin' off more than ya can chew. Old Ike doesn't lie. He's the best camp cook who ever tossed dish water under a chuck wagon, stand back and let's hear what the tin-horn's got to say."

The Marshal seemed transfixed, plumb rooted in his tracks. Across the card table stood the gambler and one of his cronies, both armed to the teeth. The stage was set, the curtain ready to be drawn. It happened faster than a blink of an eye. With an obscene oath the tinhorn's hand flashed for his gun. The roll of gun fire was harsh and final, a biting presence of burnt gun powder hung in the air; a deathly silence filled the Bull's Head Saloon.

Brannon shoved his smoking Peacemaker back in its holster, a blood-raw gash was slashed across his cheek. "The son-of-gun was fast," he murmured, "Too damned fast for his own good!"

No one had moved, the onlookers seemed in a trance, they just couldn't believe their eyes. "You seen what happened Marshal," Brannon said, looking at the old lawman. "They drew on me. I'm a hopin' you and me don't have any trouble over this!"

The whiskered old law man was still stunned, his mouth opened wide in disbelief when he replied, "I seen it all right...and still can't believe it! You just out-gunned Wild Deuce Smith, the fastest gun north of Dodge City."

Sprawled on the floor in a pool of his own blood lay the unscrupulous tempter of fortunes, a bullet hole had replaced his left eye. Standing in a state of shock, staring at the blood oozing from his bullet-torn shooting hand, Wild Deuce's partner watched his own blood drip to the bar room floor near his shattered derringer.

"It's all over boys," old Tom told his cowboys. "A couple o' ya help old Ike get outta this hell hole. Head back to camp...pronto I say!"

The old cattleman was still shaken from the drama he had just witnessed. He looked at his trail boss with awe and respect. "Matt are ya all right? Thar's blood a drippin' off your chin."

"That hombre was fast Tom. First time I bin near enough to hell to smell the brimstone," replied the big cowboy, dabbing at the wound with his bandana, as he followed Lynch and the crew out of the saloon.

The Texas boys would never forget this fight! It would become a famous gunfight. The saga of their trail boss would be retold time and time again to family, friends and those they would meet on the trail where only cowboys wander. Brannon was their hero now, an example of a man they could proudly envision themselves to be.

Sleep was hard to find for Brannon that night. Rousing early from his blankets, he stirred up the fire and put on a fresh pot of coffee. It would take time he reckoned, time to unwind, time to ease off from the gut-wrenching tension brought on by the gunfight. He poured himself a cup of his life-saving elixir and watched old Tom wander in out of the darkness.

"I couldn't sleep much either," Lynch greeted. "Here's something I want to give you 'sides your wages," and offered Brannon a plump bag of gold coins.

"No! No Tom. I don't want ya to do this...it's too much," exclaimed the big cowboy.

"Fiddlesticks. I want you and Lynn to have it as part of your wedding present," insisted Tom. Smiling now, he continued his talk, "Well, seein' as how you two young'uns are a headin' up to the northern territories, I also want to give you the covered wagon and the four hosses that pull it." "Save me a draggin' it all the way back to Texas...'sides, your Lynn will need a warm, dry place to sleep until you folks get settled."

"I'll never forget ya Tom," Brannon said. A tear was trickling down his sun-bronzed cheek.

"I'll never forget you either Matt Brannon. And thanks again for last night. I can only shudder as I think of what would have happened if you hadn't been there to handle Wild Deuce Smith," old Tom continued, "Some of us would be a takin' off our spurs at the Pearly Gates, that's for sure."

The old Texan wasn't through his talk, he had began to relax, he was smiling when he drawled, "This wagon I'm a givin' you and Lynn was our supply wagon, carried the camp gear, supplies and what not. As you'll remember, near the back end is where we kept the oats for the hosses. Them two moss-horn steers, our point leaders, bedded-down by the wagon every night...waitin' for me to slip'em a bait o' oats each mornin'. Seems as if them two critters have become downright attached to this here wagon. They swam back across the Yellowstone and came back to camp," old Tom said, "I found'em bedded down behind the wagon, a waitin' for their mornin' oats!"

Pausing to stoke his pipe, Lynch looked Brannon in the eye and grinned. "I'm a thinkin' they're going to follow when they see this wagon headin' north...don't you fret about'em. Them two will keep up, and be darn good company too. "Beats havin' a watch dog around any old day."

* * * Chapter 6 * * *

Lynn and Ben Riley were finally ready to roll. Their life possessions were carefully packed in the covered wagon. Lynn's possessions didn't amount to much though, several canvas bags, and they weren't large ones either.

Amid the preparations for turning the trading post over to the new owners, the Riley's were putting the finishing touches on packing the old freight wagon with their personal possessions and the supplies they were taking with them. The task finally finished with tears in their eyes, they bid farewell to their old home.

It had taken longer to get away than they had planned, resulting in a days delay in leaving. Lynn was irritated and upset. She knew that Matt would be concerned she just knew he would be. She also knew that like her, he would never be happy until they were married, and together as one.

It was late in the day before they crossed the Powder River and pointed into the northwest. Old Ben was at the reins of a four-horse hitch, Lynn Riley was riding her mare Evening Star, and in her own way was acting as the outrider, the only one. Twilight was upon them before they pulled in and made camp.

It's sure a nice camp, Lynn thought. There are only two things wrong with it, we are camped on the wide-open prairie, and my big cowboy, Matt Brannon, is not here to share it with me. She sure missed Brannon. She could hardly wait to get to Miles Town where they would hunt them up a preacher.

Old Ben slept real good, was tired and plumb worn-out from all the hustle and bustle of packing up their roots and storing it all in a wagon. Lynn was different. The tedious struggle to wind things down was wearing on her. Her nerves were on edge, the excitement of her coming marriage was turning into a worry, and she was a bit frightened of being alone with her Dad here on the open prairie. It was nearing midnight before the girl finally dozed off. A pair of yodelling coyotes and her Dad's snoring lulled her into a deep sleep.

By first light of the next morning they were on the move and making good time, when the Crows showed up. Crow Indians were usually friendly, but then one never knew. They had moved in and were quietly stalking the Riley wagon, flanking the wagon one line on each side. They were one hundred yards out riding single file. Lynn counted nine riders on one side, and seven on the other. She was riding close to the wagon now. "Oh! Father, what should we do? Do you think they will harm us?"

"Don't rightly know Lynn. The Crow have always been a friendly bunch—we've traded for their fur many times—treated them fair too," Old Ben replied, "The Crow trappers are the best there is, brought us some mighty fine pelts while we was at the trading post!"

Old Ben kept the big wagon rolling, Lynn stayed close by, never straying far from the wagon.

"Tell you what Lynn," old Ben thought a moment, and then continued, "I think our Crow friends are escorting us across the prairie. Reckon it's their way of telling us good bye—a token of respect."

Come time for the noon break, old Ben pulled in the teams, built a roaring fire and in no time had several pots of coffee brewing. Along with a huge bag of Lynn's doughnuts, he prepared a feast for his Crow friends.

The scent of the coffee drew them in. "This will be our way of telling them goodbye—them red-skinned critters will go on the warpath if necessary, for the chance to drink coffee and eat your doughnuts Lynn," said old Ben.

After ravenously devouring the coffee and doughnuts, the Crows slipped away to continue their escort duties. They continued this vigil until they were within sight of the soldier fort at Miles Town.

It was nearing sundown when Ben Riley and his daughter arrived in Miles Town, old Ben was at the reins of a four-horse hitch, the big freight wagon loaded with supplies of every kind. Lynn riding Evening Star trotted alongside the wagon as they rolled into the roundup camp situated along the Tongue River. She looked lovely in the fading sun, excited and ever so happy. In no time at all, she spotted her big cowboy, and was wrapped in his arms before the wheels of her Dad's wagon even stopped rolling.

"Your cheek, Matt!" she exclaimed. "What has happened to you?"

"Ah, it's nothin' much…just a scratch," he replied.

Old Tom could hardly wait to tell them about the gunfight, and how Brannon had handled the notorious Wild Deuce Smith. His words were full of praise for his trail boss, and he never lacked for words in the telling.

"You still want me after all this?" Matt murmured in her ear.

"Of course I do!" Lynn moaned, her arms wrapped around him. "You might have been killed," and hugged him all the tighter.

Brannon wouldn't let her out of his arms, and it was just fine with Lynn. The long week they had been parted seemed like an eternity, much too long. She kissed her cowboy again, and again. She just could not let him go, and it was just fine with him.

The cowboys were green with envy as they watched their hero, and his beaming, happy Lynn Riley. They were happy for him and wished him the best, yet they were human, couldn't help it they reckoned. They all wished it was their trail boss's boots they were walking in instead of their own.

After the stock and gear were secured for the night, Matt escorted Lynn and old Ben to a back street rooming house. The rooming house was owned by the same widow of the Indian Wars who owned the small log cabin diner that Matt enjoyed eating at. It was part the of the widow's thriving business venture.

Brannon gave his beautiful gal time to freshen up, then took her on a tour of this up and coming crossroads of the west. Lynn had been here before, but this time was different she reckoned, this time she was with the man she was going to marry.

There wasn't much to see, several log cabin saloons, a log cabin diner, the rooming house and a large trading post that was stocked to the rafters with goods of every description. They also saw the livery stable, stockyards and a couple of dozen log cabins scattered at random along the trail that led to the crossing of the Yellowstone. Several more buildings were under construction, including another trading post and saloon. Along the Powder River a small outpost of tents, U.S. Army tents, were located.

Hand in hand, the cowboy and the trader's daughter entered the trading post it was a wedding ring for Lynn they were searching for. Try as he may, the old whiskered trader could not locate one. Brannon was devastated, right put out with the outfit for not having a ring for his girl. "I'll find ya one darlin'," he vowed. "The next chance I get."

Lynn wasn't upset, and offering one of her special smiles, told him that she loved him, ring or no ring.

He did buy her a colourful Mexican serape. It was made of woven sheep's wool and was dyed an eye-catching red. "It will keep you warm as we travel," he told her. A vial of perfume was next, one of sufficient size to last her for some time to come. Lynn was happy with her gifts, and told him so.

Then it was Lynn's turn. She found her cowboy a fancy shirt and a cowboy vest, with a silk scarf to match, a cowboy necktie for the man she loved.

Brannon was equally as pleased with his gifts, and could hardly wait to wear them.

With a blush or two, Lynn excused herself she wished to make a few purchases, on her own, for their wedding day. Her gallant cowboy stepped into the background as his little gal shopped. To finish up she bought herself a pair of divided riding skirts. She just loved them she told Brannon, they will be so comfortable to ride in.

Their arms were bulging with packages when they returned to the rooming house. Waiting for them in the lobby was an elderly gentleman. He wore a white collar and was dressed in black. He informed them he was the Reverend W.W. Van Orsdel, a travelling preacher who just happened to be passing through the Territory.

He was the one and only 'Father Van' a highly respected Montana territory pioneer preacher who rode horseback hundreds of miles over mountain and prairie taking the gospel to isolated ranches and mining camps.

He greeted them with a cordial handshake and a friendly smile. "I hear there is to be a wedding here tomorrow," he said. "It will be my pleasure to tie the knot for you two youngsters."

"The good Lord up above and the great Territory of Montana will look with favour upon this sacred union!" This welcome offer was gladly accepted by the cowboy and his excited Lynn Riley, who was beaming with happiness and hanging on to her husband to be.

Brannon arranged lodging for Brother Van, and then escorted Lynn to her quarters. The big trail boss had a tough time leaving his soon-to-be wedded bride. "We just have this one last night to sleep alone darlin'," he promised her. "Then we'll never again be parted...this is my promise!"

Lynn kissed him one last time, and reluctantly watched him leave. There were tears rolling down her cheeks as she whispered, "It is a promise I expect you to keep Matt Brannon...parting like this is hard to do, mighty hard! I love you Matt Brannon. You come back to me, you hear!"

At high noon of the next day, under the porch awning of the widow's back-street rooming house, Matt Brannon and Lynn Riley were married, the knot tied securely by Brother Van.

Old Ben gave away his beautiful daughter who was radiant in her Mother's wedding gown, as she took her place by her new husband's side. Ben was drawn back in time remembering Lynn at six years old when her Mom died from typhoid fever. At old Ben's request, Matt placed the wedding band that had been her Mother's onto Lynn's finger.

Brannon was beaming and his chest was all puffed out. He looked great in the new shirt and vest that Lynn had given to him and the fancy cowboy tie as well. Tom Lynch, his beloved friend, stood by him as best man. To a man, Lynch's cowboys were there to support their fellow Texan and his new bride. They as well stood in line for a wedding kiss from a happy Lynn Brannon.

As expected it was the French trappers from Belle Fourche who purchased Riley's Post back on the Powder River. The one who desired Lynn for his wife, the same one who had wooed her at every opportunity, was enraged when he discovered the trader's daughter was to marry a cowboy. He packed his gear and headed for the Big Horn Mountains never to be heard from again.

The old Powder River trader held back a wagon loaded with supplies from the deal, enough to last his daughter and her new husband for a long time to come. These supplies were being transferred to the Brannon wagon.

"My wedding present to you newlyweds," Ben Riley told them. "Before you get settled in Canada you'll be a needin' these supplies and trade goods."

As they were finishing up loading the Brannon wagon, old Ben brought out two special gifts, one for each of them. "Lynn, darlin'," Ben said. "Bring that husband of yourn over here and see what I want to give you. You'll be a needin' these here long guns in Canada…I hear the Blackfoot and Bloods are mighty tough hombres, savage as all get out!" "Son," he said to Brannon, who was now standing close by, "I want you to have this here rifle. "It's a .44-40 calibre, made by Winchester…one o' the best guns I ever seen. Ol' Charles Goodnight himself owned one o' the first to come into the West. He said it was this rifle that helped him to survive the Comanche wars…wouldn't part with it for all the longhorns in Texas. You take care o' my Lynn now, you hear?" Accepting the shiny new .44-40, Brannon assured the old trader that he surely would, and thanked him with a big cowboy smile.

Ben turned to his daughter and said, "Lynn darlin', now it's your turn. I want you to have this here 'Yellow Boy' border rifle that you have been a shootin' coyotes and prairie wolves with. I have watched you shoot it and you handle it well.

"It ain't as heavy as Matt's .44-40, uses a .38 cartridge and only weighs a tad over nine pounds…a real ladies gun if I ever seen one. This here Yellow Boy was the first gun to carry the Winchester name, 'fore that they were known as Henrys. I reckon the Yellow Boy is just right for you darlin', the twenty inch barrel makes it nice and handy as a saddle carbine too." "And here's plenty of ammunition for both them guns."

The perils and unknown of Indian country were a constant worry for old Tom Lynch. He was an orphan of the Indian wars in Texas. Comanche and a wagon train were all that he could remember, but it was enough. As the time of departure drew near, he beckoned Brannon aside and explained to him of an Indian situation that appeared to be getting out of hand. It was increasing in intensity and not that far away.

Lynch had been chatting with some of the Miles Town locals in the widow's diner that morning. Over breakfast he was told of the flight of Chief Joseph and the Nez Perce. He even had the chance to read a three-week old Virginia City newspaper that was playing it up in grand style.

"Matt, thars big trouble a brewin' west o' here, word is some Nez Perce tribes from the Idaho country are in trouble with the Army, a land squabble of some kind. The Nez Perce crossed the Bitterroots into Montana, and then pushed on to the Yellowstone. The Blue Coats a crowdin' 'em, the Nez Perce a runnin'...stoppin' every now and then to fight. They bin a whippin' the britches off the Army at every stop."

Old Tom had to pause to catch his breath, and then continued his story, "The latest word in these parts is that them Nez Perce have crossed the Musselshell...a headin' for the Missouri River and to Sittin' Bull's bunch in Canada. You young'uns be on the watch for this bunch, ya hear?"

The inevitable had arrived sooner than anyone had expected, it was now time to leave. The wagon was packed, the teams impatient to get under way. Standing at the rear of the outfit were the two mossy horns, lowing in anticipation of the long journey ahead.

After the goodbyes by one and all, Lynn was sobbing, tears as well showing on old Ben and Tom's whiskered cheeks. Old Tom's crew of cowpunchers were saddled and ready to ride, they would see the Brannon outfit safely across the Yellowstone.

"You two take care, Matt Brannon!" Tom Lynch warned for the umpteenth time. "Watch out for them Nez Perce, you hear?"

* * *

From the south shore of the river the Texans could see Lynn waving her red serape, as a farewell gesture. The Brannon outfit grew smaller as it travelled in to the distant prairie. Secured, one on each side of the lead team, Buck and Evening Star trotted along side. Plodding behind came the two longhorns, the same two who had followed the point riders up from Texas influencing their headstrong clan to follow. Perhaps the two were pets perhaps they were not; only time would tell. Little did the young couple know that never again would they meet up with old Ben Riley or Tom Lynch.

Several miles to the northwest of the river they knew as the Yellowstone, Lynn was sitting beside her husband on the wagon seat, snuggled as close to him as she could get. Shyly, she looked at him, and with a come-hither smile spoke his name. "Matt Brannon! I just can't wait another minute longer. You stop this wagon right now and...and give your new wife some hugs and kisses and—!"

"All right darlin'," Brannon replied, a smile spread across his face as wide as the prairie they were travelling on. "I've been a dreamin' about the same thing ever since we crossed the river." He was grinning as he reined in the teams, applied the wagon brake, secured the reins around the brake lever and turned to face his new bride.

"I love ya darlin' Lynn," he told her. Eager arms embraced each other in a bear hug, one that toppled them both off the seat into the soothing comfort of Lynn Brannon's blankets.

* * *

A lonesome prairie breeze ruffled and soothed the long blue stem grasses. A bobolink hovered above the disturbance created by the breeze, whirring to his mate below on her nest, singing and courting in the ways of those that were free.

Vanishing into the mysterious horizons of the great northwest, Matt and Lynn Brannon were at the outset of a new beginning.

* * * Chapter 7 * * *

The sun was setting beyond the western prairie before Brannon reined in the team and made camp beside a small stream. The Yellowstone River, Miles Town, and the Texas cowboys were far behind them now, nothing but memories in the minds of Matt and Lynn Brannon. Old Tom and Ben, they would never forget. Lynn's father and Matt's good friend would remain forever in the memory of the cowboy and his Powder River girl.

While Matt was caring for the stock, Lynn prepared the first meal for her new husband over a campfire. They were both hungry, and the way Matt carried on about her tasty supper pleased her immensely. Later they sat around the fire drinking coffee and basking in the happiness that was theirs to share. Near by in the shadows, large eyes reflected the firelight, and each placidly chewing his cud, lay the two longhorns as content as could be.

"Tom Lynch was right," Lynn said with a nervous smile. "Them two big critters he gave us…haven't let us out of their sight all day. You sure they're not going to hurt us, with those big horns, and all?"

"Shucks no," replied Matt, "These two are as meek as lambs. They sure do like ya Lynn…your scent and all. Ya now have a pair of friends to guard ya when I'm not around, just wait and see."

"Are you sure of this Matt?" continued Lynn. She still wasn't too comfortable with the big animals in such close quarters.

"Ya see darlin', a longhorn is like nothing else ya ever did see. If a man thinks he knows cattle, he should look over a longhorn first of all. The longhorn developed from cattle turned loose on the plains of Texas, growing up wild and carin' for themselves; and for the country they were in, no finer or fiercer critter ever lived," Brannon explained. "There were some tough old mossy-horns in Lynch's herd that weighed sixteen hundred pounds or better, and when they held their heads up they were taller than our hosses. They could be mean as all get out, and ready to take after ya if they caught you afoot. Believe me darlin', a man needed a six-shooter and needed to get it into action fast if one of those big steers came a stalkin' him," continued the big cowboy.

Glancing over into the shadows Matt shook his head and said, "Reckon these two are different somehow, must have been Old Tom's influence, treating them to oats and all. Don't ya worry none, these two are your friends...will give their lives for ya if need be," added Brannon. "Lynn I reckon it will be your chore to feed them their daily oats, they'll love ya forever for it!"

Rising from the fire, Matt sauntered over to the wagon. "It's way to hot to sleep in the wagon," he said, as he returned with an armful of blankets and prepared their bed in the tall grass.

"But Matt, exclaimed a surprised Lynn, "I've never slept on the ground before! There must be spiders, and rattle snakes, and what not, a crawlin' all over on this prairie!"

"These northern snakes won't bother you none," he was grinning as he spoke, "They crawl in prairie dawg holes and curl up with the gophers to keep warm, come morning time the snake will gobble a praire dawg up for breakfast. Now if we were in Texas it'd be a different story...them ol' sidewinders wander around at night some." The big Texan carried on with his snake tales while Lynn got ready for bed.

With their blankets spread in the lee of the wagon, they bedded down under the stars. Lynn had never experienced this kind of roughing it before and was nervous to start with, but she grew to love the sounds of the night. The howl of a coyote, the hoot of an owl, and the lonesome cry of a mourning dove were the three sounds that Lynn decided she liked best.

She was also thrilled with the millions of stars in the sky, and begged her husband to tell her all about them. Matt sure didn't mind and relished the chance to talk to his wife. He explained how the big dipper rotated around the pole star on a 24-hour basis. He told how the cowboys, while riding nighthawk, knew when to come off shift by locating the position of the big dipper as it rotated around the pole or North Star as most folks call it

Then it was Lynn's turn. She told her husband of the evening star. It was her favourite star which she looked for each night after the sun went down. Somehow the star reminded Lynn of her long dead mother and helped her feel closer to her mother when she could see this brightest star in the heavens. "See Matt!" she said, rising off her pillow, "there it is, over near the horizon!"

"Ever since I was a small girl it has been a comfort to me, in my loneliness." A tear rolled down her cheek as she continued to speak, "I named my pinto Evening Star, in memory of my mother." As if the little pinto mare had been listening, she gave a whinny from the other side of the wagon where she was staked out eating the lush Montana grass.

To be together in each other's arms would be the most fulfilling time either of them would ever experience. They were sure thankful to have found each other.

The Texas cowboy and his Powder River girl planned on a journey to the eastern front of the Rocky Mountains, far enough to the east to pioneer a cattle ranch. Here, in a much cooler climate, they planned to sink their roots deep and live a lifestyle of their own choosing. Matt had had his fill of the damn heat, dust and drought of his homeland. This was just fine with his new bride as long as she could be with her husband.

After talking with some of the Miles Town boys, including Father Van, Brannon had decided on a course into the northwest, crossing the Missouri River where it was safe to do so. After listening to old Tom's warning of the Nez Perce tribe's desperate flight to Canada, he reckoned on a slight change of plans. He'd point his outfit a bit north of northwest, hopefully missing the guerrilla warfare that was heading north at a rapid rate.

The slight change would take them through the badlands of the Missouri breaks and onward to the Milk River. After crossing over the Milk River he would rein his outfit into the wind. Keeping the west wind in their faces, it would be much like following a pointed arrow to their destination.

The crossing of the Missouri was touch-and-go, scared the britches off them both. After considerable scouting of the south bank, Brannon picked a spot with an easy descent into the ominous, mass of silent, moving water. The team wanted no part of it, stubbornly balking and refusing to step off the bank into the swift flowing water. They had never crossed anything like this before. No amount of persuasion by Brannon and his whip would induce them to step into the water.

"Oh, Matt, don't whip them anymore," Lynn pleaded, "I've got an idea that might work." Matt tried to ease his cowboy temper some and Lynn's calming influence won out.

"Let me drive them Matt I've driven teams many times before—going to Miles Town for supplies," Lynn pleaded.

Brannon was silent for a spell, just staring at the river, a challenge that had him buffaloed. After a bit he turned to her and said, "Reckon your husband is a failure at crossing rivers, best I listen to ya and settle down before I get us into worse trouble."

Lynn thanked him with a hug and told him her plan. Matt listened, and listened well. Then he set out to do the tasks that she had laid out for him. Fetching Buck from the rear of the wagon he led him around to the front of the teams and lashed one end of his lasso to the neck-yoke of the lead team and the other dallied around the horn on his saddle. Lynn freed Evening Star to cross over on her own. "She will follow me," Lynn said. "She always does."

Brannon was to lead the way on Buck giving the team the confidence they needed to follow. Lynn was in the wagon now, reins in hand, still talking to her husband, when they both could not believe what they were seeing. The two big longhorns old Tom Lynch had given them, sauntered past the wagon, entered the river, and struck out for the opposite shore.

"Let's do it!" Lynn shrieked. "Follow them longhorns Matt, I'll be right behind you." Lynn's plan was working she was as thrilled as could be. The horses were chest deep and nearing the half-way mark, when the big wagon slewed to the side. It appeared as if the mighty current of the Missouri River might win out after all—roll over the wagon and drown them all. Matt put the spurs to the buckskin dun. The Texas mustang lunged and scrambled to get footing but was being pulled back into the current by the team and the wagon.

Determined, Lynn was screaming and hurrahing the team, struggling to keep them moving for the opposite shore, all the time praying in her heart for a miracle to happen.

They never could say why perhaps a freak eddy caused by a sunken tree, or the deepness of the river was abating, but the current eased some and the wagon began to swing back in line with the team. The small caravan strung out in a straight line again with the horses scrambling for the bank. The longhorns waited on the shore as the rest of the outfit pulled onto dry ground. Lynn Brannon leaped from the big wagon, ran to her husband and threw herself in his arms.

She was a frazzled wreck, her nerves were completely shot and she was shaking like a leaf. "Oh, Matt—we made it," she sobbed, "I reckoned we were goners for sure, that was one of the toughest thing I've ever had to do!"

"Ya did just fine Lynn, you're the finest teamster I've ever laid eyes on," Brannon told her, "Ya sure saved our outfit Lynn."

"Oh pooh," she replied. "You did just fine on Buck, kept us a headin' in a straight line and gave the teams the confidence they needed to keep swimming."

Things were starting to settle down when Brannon remarked, "Reckon them longhorns are worth a whole bunch to us now Lynn. Saved our bacon sure, striking out on their own like they did—leading us across this here Missouri River." The two Texas longhorns were lying behind the wagon now, chewing their cuds. They were waiting for Lynn to give them their oats and Lynn made sure that tonight they got double rations.

After a few days travel, they entered a region where a dominant wind blew from out of the west. Day after day it blew, often a raging force, other times a soft caress on the cheek. The wind was to become a constant force to be reckoned with the farther west they travelled. The long prairie grass was forever bowed to the rising sun because of the persistence of the west wind. It was a natural clue to help them keep their bearings. After dark the trustworthy North Star worked just fine as a guide.

There were times when Matt would caution his wife into silence, his wilderness-honed hearing sensing an alien sound in the night. Crawling from the blankets he would pull on his boots, put on his hat, strap his shooting iron over his long johns and prowl the camp checking on the stock. "To better hear and feel the night," he told Lynn, "is one reason I prefer sleeping on the ground."

The big Texan was an early riser, he would pile fresh fuel on the fire, put on the coffee pot to simmer then he would tend the stock. Returning to the fire, he would have bacon frying before he woke his darlin' Lynn. She would scold him for allowing her to sleep so long. Yet he reckoned, for her to maintain her health in this harsh environment, she would need all the rest she could get.

To live out of a rolling wagon on the prairie wasn't an easy task for women folk, Lynn was no exception. It took some getting used to. She had always shown pride in her appearance, just could not stand to be unkempt. Each and every morning she would bathe as best she could, faithfully brush her long auburn hair, care for her beautiful complexion, and always look great in her ankle-length dresses. She loved her divided riding skirts, and the red serape Matt had given her. There was an enticing scent about her. Matt had made sure of this with another of his gifts given to her back in Miles Town.

Every morning before the day's journey began; it became a ritual for her to practice the finer points of shooting her rifle, the lever-action Yellow Boy that her father had given her. She became an excellent shot, even mastered with ease the art of shooting from the hip. Matt was pleased, and with a big hug and a grin told her, "I'm mighty proud of ya Mrs. Brannon…you'll sure do to have along. I couldn't ask for a better partner to share my fire."

"And don't you forget it Matt Brannon." With a flirtatious smile she spoke again, "I sure do love my wild Texas cowboy."

Antelope are a natural part of the northern prairie. Lynn became as adept as her husband in bagging the elusive creatures. She was rapidly learning plains lore from her husband, and was totally amazed how he could lure the inquisitive pronghorn into rifle range. All it took was a red bandana tied to a stick, or the end of a rifle barrel, oft-times just a piece of rag hanging on a stick. The fresh meat was a welcome addition to their food supply.

On a two-day stop to rest and graze the horses, they were able to smoke and jerk an abundant supply of the delicious meat for future use. Lynn took advantage of the stop, and a clear pool of spring water, to give their soiled clothing a good scrubbing.

The miles and days rolled by as they crossed rivers, skirted hill spurs and buttes, and faced the challenges of the ever changing landscape. Lynn gave Evening Star a workout each day, riding along side the wagon, her husband up top at the reins of the four-horse hitch. Stopping at mid-day to rest and graze the teams, he would join her riding his dun horse, Buck. Together they would ride ahead, checking trail conditions, Indian sign and the like. It was always a welcome break to be able to ride together across the vast Montana prairie.

Their noontime meal was usually coffee and biscuits, whatever was handy would do. Lynn was a fine cook and was rapidly learning the secrets of campfire cooking. It was when supper time arrived that she ruled the roost, exposing her husband to her talents every chance she got.

* * *

The equinox of autumn had arrived, the westerly breezes becoming stronger as they cooled off the land. With each passing day the breeze turned into a steady blowing wind, bringing with it a reminder of snow-capped mountains, glaciers, and ice-chilled water; the western horizon was now filled with the awesome Rocky Mountains.

On one of Matt and Lynn's scouting expeditions, they were riding together when Matt turned back and spotted a group of riders off in the distance. The bunch was burning up the prairie, riding straight towards the Brannon outfit.

Matt gesturing a warning to Lynn as they touched spurs to their horses and streaked back for camp. They reached the wagon several minutes ahead of the riders. "Indians," Matt shouted, "climb in the wagon…use your rifle if ya have to darlin'."

Lynn scrambled up behind the wagon seat, positioned her Yellow Boy where it was handy, then anxiously awaited her husbands orders. Matt had just finished hitching the team and had Buck and Star secured along side the wagon when the visitors arrived.

There were eight of them riding seven hard-used ponies. Riding double behind another, a wounded warrior was barely hanging on, blood oozing from a bullet hole in his gut. Though the ponies were sweat-stained and as grimy as the Indians that rode them, they appeared strange to the cowboy. A distinct aura surrounded them, which gave him a start. He looked closer, now he knew—Appaloosa! He had heard tell of the breed but had never seen one before this time.

The connection came to him like a bolt out of the blue; Nez Perce! This bunch must be Nez Perce Indians from Chief Joseph's flight to Canada. The ones Tom Lynch had warned him about.

Freeing the Peacemaker, he edged toward the rifle he had left leaning against the wagon. Glancing at Lynn he said, "Show them your Yellow Boy…lay it across your lap…pointing towards them. If ya sense trouble, back my play darlin'. Like I showed ya, remember?" Lynn needed no urging, and though she was frightened, she did as her husband had asked.

Lifting his big hand high in the air, Brannon signed the plains tribe's token of peace, still edging toward the .44-40. Although not native to the plains, an old one who appeared to be the leader signed back. Brannon was relieved the old one seemed to understand this sign language.

The old Nez Perce then jabbed two fingers at himself, and spoke in a guttural tone, "Nez Perce." Gesturing toward the western horizon, he again spoke, "Joseph. Blue Coats!"

Glaring at the Brannon's, the old warrior gestured more forcibly. It was the easy to understand symbol for hunger, a rotating, open hand on his paunch, followed by a two-fingered jab towards his mouth; signing at his companions as well.

Even Lynn could understand and, watching her husband take another step toward his rifle, knowing his Peacemaker was ready for a fast draw, she quietly spoke, "They're starving, perhaps if I find them some food?"

Brannon's attention was on the old one, he nodded to his wife in agreement. The Indians watched Lynn disappear under the tarp cover and began to sign and mutter in protest. Though they were in possession of four rifles, the cowboy reckoned they were out of bullets or would have used them by now.

His attention was quickly diverted to another Nez Perce. This one was a hot head, edging his Appaloosa closer to the wagon, jabbering to the others and brandishing a filthy rust-pocked rifle. It was a single-shot U.S Army issue, the fortunes of war no doubt.

Slinking low along side the pony, the hothead uttered a chilling scream and buck jumped the frenzied horse forward, his arm outstretched for the cowboy's Winchester. The others never moved, just watched and waited. The cowboy drew and fired one shot. The wild one fell at his feet, blood gushing from a bullet hole in his throat. The Peacemaker swung slightly, covering the remaining seven. His hunch had been right. They had no cartridges or there would have been a war on by now.

Brannon's inner self was in turmoil, struggling to comprehend between right and wrong. This had happened only once before, now it was happening again. The first time was back in Texas when he had gunned down the killers of old Hugh Arnett and his good wife from the Medicine Pipe ranch. He knew in his heart the turn-coat cowboys had it coming, after robbing the Arnett's of their life savings and leaving them dead on the ranch house floor. And later, he would never be able to forget, gloating about it over a bottle of booze. The strangeness was with him then, and now here on the Montana prairie he was struggling with it again.

It was a strange sensation, a gut feeling to gun them all down. He just could not believe what was happening to him, his head was ringing and his heart was telling him to finish the job, gun them down and be done with it. The big gun fighter was struggling, all set to give in to his intuition when Lynn stepped out from under the canvas with a bag of food. It was now much too late, an intuitive moment had passed.

Brannon passed the food to the old buck. Lynn handed her husband another bag; she was frightened, but brave. "I found them some doughnuts Matt." Then perhaps an apology, but well said for the time and the place. "It is no matter...I saved back plenty for my husband!"

Forcing a smile, Brannon held Lynn's doughnuts for the old one to see, and slowly ate one. Licking traces of sugar from his lips, he signed a symbol meaning good. The Nez Perce accepted the bag, withdrew a doughnut and stuffed the whole thing in his mouth. His eyes opened in wonder as he tasted this strange food, then he ate another and another. The others dismounted and crowded around Lynn's Powder River treats.

With his rifle finally in hand, Brannon wasted no time in stepping up into the wagon and driving away. With a sigh Lynn looked back and smiled. "The Indians are sitting on the ground devouring my doughnuts...as fast as they can."

"I'm proud of you darlin', your doughnuts saved us a bunch of trouble and some Nez Perce lives." Tucked far back in his mind the urgent plea was still with him—*gun them down...don't let them go!*

"The one on the ground...the dead one, you had it to do, didn't you Matt?" remarked Lynn, as the reality of the situation set in.

"He was plumb loco," her husband replied. "Given the chance, they'd a killed us both and thought nothin' of it. It was our guns and supplies they were after."

"I was impressed how well you handled them," Lynn replied. "Your sign language was just wonderful...I am so proud of my husband!"

The hostile Nez Perce warriors were just a dot in the distance back on the prairie. Lynn's husband, her big cowboy was beginning to unwind, the crisis was over. He put an arm around his wife and hugged her close. "We handled it together darlin', we handled it together!" Matt murmured as the wagon bounced along the prairie.

Sign language was perfectly understood on the Great Plains. The various tribes, mountain men and plainsmen alike had little difficulty in conversing with each other. They were highly skilled in the ways of this pantomime of the mountain and plain, they had to be to survive.

Brannon told her of the mountain man, and plainsman alike, squaw men they were called, taking Indian maidens as wives. Though neither could speak the other's language, they got along just fine for the remainder of their lives.

Travelling from first light until the shadows of night forced them to stop, another day was behind them. Matt Brannon was attempting to outrun the Nez Perce and their war. The incident at their doughnut camp, as they both referred to it, had him all riled up. He now reckoned the main body of the fleeing Nez Perce was somewhere ahead, possibly closer than he realized. He did know that he would have to dig deep into his knowledge of survival to keep from becoming mixed up in the big fight. The Brannon outfit must be on guard night and day.

In a shallow draw in the hills that would conceal the wagon, they camped for the night. It was becoming much colder; an essence of a coming storm was in the air. Not chancing an open fire, Lynn prepared a cold supper. For the first time since their marriage they slept in the wagon. Their plans were to take turns, one sleeping while the other kept a vigil over the wagon and teams. Lynn had strict orders to wake her husband if she heard anything out of the ordinary.

Sleep was hard to find for Brannon. It was long past midnight before he finally dozed off. Lynn was awake, and had been for several hours. Her husband needed the rest, she reckoned, she loved him dearly and would have it no other way.

It was nearing first light when she was startled by a sound alien to this bleak northern prairie. Somehow it reminded her of sporadic rifle fire. Then, faintly at first, off in the distance bouncing around in the turbulence of an increasing wind, she could hear another sound more startling than the first.

Lynn turned to her sleeping husband and gently woke him. "I can hear the sound of guns shooting Matt…and, and another sound that reminds me of a Cavalry bugle signalling a charge," she continued, "When Father and I were last at Miles Town, we watched the soldiers training near the new Fort, the bugle calls and all. It is a Cavalry bugle Matt, I just know it is!"

A weather front had moved in with a vengeance, a cold wind blowing in rain that was fast turning to snow. Above the draw that concealed the Brannon wagon, a ridge of broken sandstone thrust across a saddle back of rolling hills and off to the west was the Bear Paw Mountains.

Brannon pulled on his sheepskin coat, picked up the .44-40 and prepared to go. "I'm a climbin' up to the rocks and see what's a goin' on. Stay in the wagon Lynn and keep a sharp lookout, ya hear," he told his wife.

You're not leaving me here Matt Brannon, alone and all. I'm going with you!" Lynn quickly retorted.

Realizing that it was not worth debating the issue, Brannon relented. He gave her a hug, bundled her in warm clothes and took her hand in his. Together they climbed up to the ridge top to see what was happening.

As they neared the crest, the din and violence of a terrible battle greeted them. Brannon spotted a natural enclave amid the eroded stone. He then built a breastwork of shattered stone to protect them from the biting north wind. Protected from flying bullets, the Brannon's settled in to watch as a one-sided battle raged below.

The Bear Paw battlefield was a scene of chaotic action. The incessant norther had eased some allowing them to hear the terrible noise, and it was blood chilling to listen to. The enraged war cries of the warriors, the hoarse curses of the soldiers, and then there were the Nez Perce women. They were shrieking and wailing, attempting to protect the children and babes who were screaming in terror. The death song of a people was strong upon the land.

Intermingled in all this was the sporadic cannon explosions, constant rifle fire, and the pitiful scream of dying horses. Over the entire Snake Creek Valley lay an impending atmosphere of doom.

Peering over at the chaos, Lynn was stunned at what she saw. After a bit she murmured, "It is so terrible Matt. To see those poor people fleeing for their lives...the Calvary chasing after them, slashing at them with their swords, riding over tents; and killing little children!"

"I just can not bear to look any longer!" Sobbing, she covered her eyes with her scarf and slid back along side her husband. The sound of stray bullets ricocheted off the shattered ridge top above where they lay. "We're a lookin' at a massacre darlin'," the big Texan told her. His arms were around her trembling body holding her close. "Don't watch if it upsets ya so," Matt said, "I reckon there's nothing we can do to help those poor folks."

Scrubbing tears from her eyes, Lynn spoke again, "I'm sorry, I shan't watch any more."

It was much later, near nightfall before the fighting died down. The Brannon's returned to their camp, they were hungry and cold and sick inside. Tucking Lynn into her blankets, Matt risked a fire, brewed coffee and prepared supper for them both. Lynn dug right in and enjoyed the meal. "I'm mighty proud of you and your cowboy cooking," she said with a smile. "You are welcome at my fire any old time." They were both laughing now and hugging each other. Matt was relieved, Lynn seemed her old cheerful self once again.

Down from the time-eroded saddleback blew an ominous wind. The big freight wagon was rocking like a ship at sea. The canvas top was tugging at its mooring until they felt it would break loose and fly away. As they snuggled in their blankets, the savage gale howled and moaned throughout the long night. Could this be an eerie protest to what took place on the nearby battlefield? Perhaps it was a protest of the ghosts of the dead!

Come morning, Matt returned to the ridge crest for a last look. The soldiers and their prisoners including Chief Joseph were no longer there. Even the bodies of the dead were gone. A heart-breaking litter was strewn across the Snake Creek Valley. Scattered remnants of the camps, destroyed equipment and gear were all that remained. Then there were the slaughtered horses, the Texas cowboy felt a twinge in his heart for all the appaloosa mustangs that lay dead across the valley before him.

Uttering a harsh croak, a raven flew over the battlefield. An eagle, reluctant to drift near this scene of carnage and despair, was soaring high above the Bear Paw Mountains. A clan of magpies chattered their greed as they gorged on the dead horses. Except for the ghosts of the dead, the Bear Paw battlefield was now quiet and deserted.

Lynn had a hot meal waiting when Matt returned to camp. They sat by the fire eating and relaxing in the welcome warmth, relieved the big fight was over and done with. The past twenty-four hours had left them both with mixed feelings. They could travel safely now, they reckoned. On the other hand their hearts were saddened, a sadness over the defeat of this proud people. Never would they forget the cruelty that was shown to the women and children? It was a harsh chapter in history as far as the Brannon's were concerned.

"The fighting is now over Lynn...the battlefield is deserted. The Nez Perce people have suffered a terrible lickin', I reckon," Matt explained, "Let's vamoose outta this place while we can. Our hosses are fresh and a rarin' to go."

"Those are the words I have been waiting to hear my husband. The farther away from this spooky place, the better I will feel," replied a relieved Lynn Brannon. Treating her husband to one of her special smiles, she spoke again, "I've already packed the wagon and saddled Buck and Star."

With a grin as wide as the northern prairie, Matt gave his wife a hug and went to hook-up the team.

* * *

Skirting the hill spur that had sheltered them from the battlefield, the young settlers continued their journey north for the Milk River. Evidence of those fortunate enough to escape the slaughter, on the run for the Canadian line, were strewn along the trail. Many had made it, there was no doubt. It had not been easy as witnessed by the Brannon's.

There was blood in the snow, and there was plenty of it. Tattered clothing and blankets scattered along the way. Here and there a useless rifle and an empty par fleche told the story. Matt spotted a dead mother and child, whom he never pointed out to Lynn, and a crippled Appaloosa pony, whose agony was ended by a bullet from the cowboy's Peacemaker. Stumbling along the trail of mud and slush were two old Nez Perce women. One with a baby in her arms, the other clutching a blood stained blanket and a par fleche to her breast.

They were starving and freezing and chanting a strange tune. "Oh!! The poor wretches," Lynn exclaimed. "Stop the wagon, there must be something we can do for them!"

The two old ones were survivors of the battlefield. The approaching wagon driven by two white-eyes presented a new danger to them. They screamed and wailed, staggered off the trail and collapsed in the snow. The baby was dead, had been for hours. Expecting to be killed, one was chanting a Nez Perce death song, the other lay speechless in fright.

"I reckon we can spare some food and a blanket," Brannon said. "Be careful darlin', there may be more around…could be they're armed."

Lynn crawled back under the canvas, in a moment she returned. Before Brannon realized her intentions, she jumped down from the wagon and walked towards the two old ones, her arms outstretched offering them her gifts. Brannon was taken by surprise; he hadn't expected Lynn to act this way. He drew the Peacemaker and covered his wife as she came closer to the Nez Perce women.

As Lynn approached them with the packet of food and a blanket, one of them drew a knife, gave a savage shriek, and lunged upward from out of the snow; attempting to stand.

Her intentions were clear to Brannon; she would kill Lynn if given the chance. His six-gun in hand, he jumped to the ground, plumb upset over the safety of his darlin' Lynn. "Stand back!" he roared. "Don't go any closer…these two will kill ya if given the chance."

This attempt on her life had him all riled up, yet he reckoned he had been expecting it. He roared once again, "Drop the blanket Lynn! Come back to the wagon…leave them be! These two are like rattlesnakes, they'll strike and kill you'fore you can blink an eye."

Back on the wagon seat Lynn Brannon snuggled close to the big cowboy known as Brannon. Following behind the outfit trailed the two longhorns, big eyes rolling in wonder as they passed the Nez Perce women. One of them came to a halt, shook his massive horns, a challenging bellow rising from deep in his throat. The strange scent of the two old ones, a scent of blood and death, enraged the beast. He was set to attack when the sound of Lynn's voice drifted back. Viciously swinging a lethal set of horns, the brindle steer turned and followed after the departing wagon.

Lynn was silently weeping. Her cowboy drew her near, his free arm wrapped around that which he cherished more than anything else in the world. "I was sure a fearin' for your life, had a hunch the Nez Perce squaws would react as they did," Matt muttered, "The old one would have slit your throat and thought nothing of it."

"You would have shot her if, if—?" stammered Lynn.

Nodding his head, Matt spoke again, "She would have been dead before her rusty butcher knife touched ya."

An intense shudder coursed through the body of Lynn Brannon, she wept like her heart would break. Later, after her tears were spent, she gave a sigh. She felt ashamed of her boldness now, yet, she couldn't help it, she reckoned, it was her way. She was only offering kindness to the poor starving wretches. After all, she reasoned, they were women like her.

"I never dreamt they would be so savage...I won't be so careless again," promised the girl from the Powder River.

It turned into a long, tough drive through the mud and slush that day, at least twenty miles to the river, Matt reckoned. The horses were tired and hungry; they needed rest and the nourishment of a good graze.

He swung the wagon off the trail into a small grass clearing surrounded by river brush. Before stepping down from their canvas-covered rolling home, he took Lynn in his arms. He told her how much he loved her, how proud he was of her, and how thankful he was that she hadn't been harmed or killed. That soon they would be far away from this scene of carnage and despair.

Lynn loved her wild Texas cowboy. There was no place she would rather be than right here in his arms. Though her tears had returned, they sealed their love and forgiveness with a kiss.

* * * Chapter 8 * * *

The day was long spent, the shadows of the coming night were rapidly moving into Milk River country. Matt was caring for the trail-weary stock, watering them and securing them on good graze. The draft horses were put on stake ropes, Buck and Evening Star were hobbled, the two longhorn steers free to graze at will; always bedding down near the wagon.

Bouncing across the frozen, slushy trail that day had been hard on Lynn, leaving her stiff and weary. While her husband was doing the night chores, she was prowling the edge of the river brush, looking for firewood and stretching her legs after the long ride from the Bear Paw. She was packing her rifle; Matt had told her to never leave the wagon without it. What happened next to Lynn was like a terrible nightmare.

Finding a set of fresh cottontail tracks in the snow and, giving in to her woman's inquisitive nature, she followed them deep inside a willow thicket. Thinking only of fresh rabbit for supper, the hunt was turning into a challenge.

Nearing a large clump of birch, her attention solely on the rabbit tracks, a ghostly figure appeared out of the gloom and lunged toward her. The unexpected movement startled her. The figure looked bloody and wild, and in the dimming light she could detect a knife in its outstretched hand.

Lynn Brannon was terrified. Uttering a scream, she swung the Yellow Boy to her hip and pulled the trigger. It was an impulsive action, drilled into her by her husband's long hours of training. The hostile apparition was almost upon her, but was dropped at her feet by Lynn's little gun. Screaming with fear that there may be others she turned and fled for camp.

Lynn's screams and the sound of her Yellow Boy came as a shock to Matt. He knew the shot had been from her little gun and that she was in trouble and needed him right now. Charging towards the brush, he was met by his fleeing wife who wound up in his arms, terribly upset and plumb out of control.

"Oh, Matt!" she wailed. "I've done something awful...I have shot someone, an Indian I think!"

It took some doing to calm her down, and after drying the tears from her cheeks, he said, "take it easy darlin'. Crank another bullet in that gun of yours and follow me, cover me from behind Lynn."

Matt followed his wife's tracks back to the birch thicket. There lay the body of an Indian, shot through the heart, a rusty butcher knife still clutched in his outstretched hand. The cowboy signed his wife into silence, frozen in his tracks, listening and sensing. She was by his side now, he whispered in her ear, "We're not alone; I reckon there's still someone here."

Pointing into the shadows, he whispered again, "See that pony standing over yonder? Follow me Lynn."

Though she was badly shaken from her nearness to death, Lynn was in awe at her husband's silent approach to the little horse. Not a twig snapped, not a sound could be heard as he walked in the frozen snow. She followed as best she could, panting and trembling like an aspen leaf.

A flick of motion caught her attention. "Matt, over there," she whispered. "Something is moving in the snow."

"Looks like a scrap of blanket, tangled in the brush," he whispered back. Stay close darlin', we'll go over and check things out." Brannon's six-gun was ready for action, and so was Lynn's rifle.

A small Indian girl lay on the ground under the willow brush. She wore a soiled buckskin dress, a small portion of a filthy trade blanket lay across her trembling body, and the remainder was snagged in the brush. She was suffering from hunger and exposure, a bloody rag hung from a wound on her leg. "The little one is still alive Lynn, but just barely," Matt reported.

He lifted her out of the snow and they returned to the wagon. Lynn removed the filthy bandage and shuttered at what she saw. "Oh Matt, come see! The poor thing is sick, and maybe dying," she moaned. "And her leg, I can't bear to look."

"The little one's been shot. Clean the wound as best ya can," he told her.

Lynn gritted her teeth and was doing as her husband had asked, while he returned to the river to see about the pony. The little appaloosa was trapped. A shank of grass-woven rein was effectively snagged in the brush. It appeared the starving animal had been grazing on the lush grass that grew in this damp place when it became entangled.

A blood-caked wound was slashed across the spotted pony's shoulder, a bullet wound Brannon reckoned, must be the same bullet that struck the girl. Fleeing to escape the Blue Coat soldiers, a flying bullet had struck them both.

Only great pluck and grit allowed the Nez Perce child and her pony to cover the 20 miles from the Bear Paw.

He led the pony to the river for a drink, then back to the wagon for a handful of oats. "We're sure gettin' us a remuda," he muttered, as he secured the Indian pony where it could fill up on grass.

Brannon packed the Pony's bullet wound with tree moss, covered with river mud to hold it in place. Then he crawled up in the wagon and placed the same concoction on the girl's wound, covering it with a strip of cloth from Lynn's petticoat.

Sleep wasn't easy to find that night. The cowboy and his girl lay awake for hours reflecting on the experiences of this past day. Held tight in her husband's arms, Lynn said, "The one I killed in the willows was the wounded Nez Perce from before...you remember...our doughnut camp?

"I must tell you now my husband. I-I hid a handful of my .38 cartridges under the doughnuts that day."

The cowboy reared out of the blankets and almost roared at her, for the second time that day. "Why? Why Lynn? Why in tarnation would ya do a thing like that?"

His darlin' Lynn was silent, so silent that he almost could not hear her reply. "I don't know. It was an impulse that came over me...I cannot explain it," Lynn said, "Please don't be cross with me!"

And then it happened again. For the second time a strange sensation gripped the cowboy's soul, the same impulsive urge that had tempted him back at the doughnut camp; as Lynn aptly called it. It had been an urgent whispering to gun down the Nez Perce hostiles. Shoot them down to the last warrior and be done with them.

He tossed and rolled in the blankets, sweat was pouring off his body, the invincible one, the big Texas gunfighter was frightened; frightened over what lay ahead. What is wrong with me?" Matt wondered, "I must be a comin' down with the river fever, or crackin' up, one of the two."

"I love you so much my husband," Lynn whispered. "Help me to be strong...and brave, like you would have me be."

Matt Brannon groaned and turned to face Lynn. She gave him a hug and drew back in surprise. "What is wrong?" she gasped. "You're all sweaty—and burning up with a fever. Don't get sick on me, please don't!"

"I reckon I'm just tired, can't seem to settle down," Matt muttered.

The small Indian waif tossed and moaned in her blanket. Her lips were fever-cracked and moving. The Brannon's were sure she spoke the words, Nez Perce, Joseph and Sara.

"What about the little one Lynn?" Brannon asked, "We shouldn't take her with us. Why, she's an Indian, a Nez Perce Indian, she belongs with her own kind."

"Matt Brannon! I'm surprised at you." Her husband's question was answered in no uncertain terms. "We cannot leave her here in the snow, alone and all. The poor thing will perish, die all alone, and she is lost you know!"

The big cowboy known as Brannon was easily riled. Right now he was ready to erupt at Lynn who, for the second time this day, had championed the Nez Perce people. For the second time she was offering compassion to those who had been humiliated and driven from their homes. He was sure in a fix; he knew that if given the chance, the Nez Perce would slaughter them like animals. What could he do about Lynn's attitude?

The Nez Perce girl survived her ordeal thanks to Lynn's compassionate care. She discovered the waif could understand English, but was reluctant to speak it. The little girl was timid and shy. Using her husband's sign language of the plains, Lynn was able to converse with, and win her over.

Lynn discovered the girl's name was Sara, she was twelve years old, and the powerful Chief Joseph was her father. It was he who boosted her on the pony and sent her from the battlefield that fateful day. Much to the surprise of the Brannon's, the child recovered rapidly, although she would walk with a limp for the remainder of her life.

Sara would remain shy and backward around Lynn's cowboy husband; she was frightened of his strength and roar. Yet, she worshipped Lynn and never left her side.

Due to the arrival of the cold and the snow, Matt and Lynn were now sleeping in the wagon. Sara would have no part of it. Come bedtime she would spread her blankets under the wagon. In the severest of weather she was right at home sleeping on the ground.

* * * Chapter 9 * * *

As unerring as the flight of a bird, the Brannon camp on the Milk River was located 30 miles south of the 49th parallel. Chief Joseph's followers who had fled the Bear Paw had passed this way. Their intent, to cross north of the Medicine Line that divides old Grandmother's Land from that of the great White Father; whose Blue Coat soldiers were attempting to nullify their very existence.

Not wanting to risk any Indian encounters if he could help it, Matt Brannon reined his outfit toward the west. This would delay their entry into Canada by a few days, which was fine with him. All the young couple wanted at this time was to vamoose from this region of grief and despair. Tom Lynch had been right. The old Indian fighter had warned them of what might happen, a premonition perhaps, and he had repeatedly voiced his concern.

It was the Old North Trail the Texan was seeking. A well-used trace used by the ancient ones, running north and south along the eastern front of the Rocky Mountains. It was sacred to the Old Ones, and though parts of it were hidden by the influx of grass and trees and later travel, it was still there just the same.

"It should be easy to find," told an old wanderer, a mountain man whose path they crossed one day, and who stopped and enjoyed one of Lynn's meals. He described the perils that lay ahead—militants all of them, the Blackfeet, Peigan and Blood.

He told of a determined group of traders, using freight wagons pulled by bull cattle, and a thriving business moving supplies from Fort Benton on the Missouri to Fort Macleod on the Old Man River in the Canadian Territories. Bull train after bull train headed into Canada, transporting goods to those who inhabited this isolated frontier, prospectors, a few scattered ranches; and of course the Canadian tribes.

"Watch out for the whiskey smugglers," he told them, "A group of renegades, dishonest as sin, crossing north of the border, their pack trains loaded with rot gut whiskey." Highly sought after by the natives, the Missouri

River booze was bartered for fur, horses, anything of value the whiskey-crazed natives might have in their possession. In desperation, the Indian would even swap the favour of their wives for a bottle of booze.

"The old rutted trails are there," continued the old mountain man, they shouldn't be hard to find, just use the big mountain as a landmark... the Big Chief it is called."

"Set your course for Old Chief Mountain," he said with a smile. "You young'uns will wind up in Canady'fore you know it...it is a land of Her Majesty, The Queen of England, they say!"

The old wanderer, seeker of gold and prime fur, left the Brannon camp as silently as he came. One minute he was there, the next he was not.

Tucked in a pack on the back of a little gray mule, was a packet of coffee, beans, and flour, given to him by Lynn Brannon. They were richer for his cordial visit to their camp, by the trail of information they received from a real live purveyor of the moccasin telegraph.

After his departure, a birch-tanned mink pelt was found on a rock beside Lynn's cooking fire it had been left there by the old mountain man—Liver Eating Johnson.

The Brannon camp was peaceful, the time of the morning when the eastern sky was softening, the light and energy of a rising sun soon to arrive on the desolate plains.

Matt and Lynn were still in their blankets, still sleeping, storing up the reserves that would see them through the coming day. A small shadow flitted through camp, towards the horses to blend in with the darkness that was still there. This tranquil time before dawn was suddenly shattered. A shrill shriek echoed out of the darkness, a startling noise that grew louder, and louder, until it became a steady wail. From their habitual bedding ground by the wagon, the two longhorns lunged to their feet, awesome horned-heads swinging this way and that to discover what was disturbing the quiet of the night.

Awakened by the strangeness of it all, Matt scrambled into his jeans, donned his Stetson, and with six gun in hand was ready to find out what in the blue-blazes was going on. Lynn, clad in her nightgown, was by his side, her little rifle ready for action. She was learning, the ways of the frontier well.

Striding through camp, they met a frantic Sara who was jabbering in her Nez Perce lingo and signing toward the horses. It was now light enough to see that Lynn's saddle mare was missing.

Lynn was devastated. Bursting into tears, she begged Matt to go find Evening Star. Her cowboy needed no urging, he reckoned there was a good chance of never seeing the pony again. "Guard the camp," he told her. "Keep that shootin' iron of yours handy."

He was cinching the saddle on his dun horse when Lynn shouted, "Matt! Star is coming...see, over by the aspen coulee!"

"Oh my," she said, tears were flowing once again, "My Evening Star is coming back to me."

Reaching the camp, the pinto was snorting and blowing, a piece of grass-woven rope dangling from her neck. Lynn's pony continued to buck and kick like a playful colt—upsetting the whole camp.

Brannon felt plumb foolish. It had been four a.m. when he last roused and checked the camp, all was safe and secure as near as he could tell. Between then and now, he reckoned, a hoss thief snuck in and made off with Star. Whoever it was, was good at it, very good.

Not caring for the strange rider, or his scent, she must have thrown a fit. Brannon reckoned she bucked off the thief and raced back to camp. "It had to be a Blackfoot," he said. "Indians of all tribes love stealing hoss flesh, a challenge the rascals can't resist."

"For a redskin to own a hoss as well put together as Evening Star is the same as striking gold to a white man."

Lynn's pinto mare never forgot the incident, or the feral scent of those who had stolen her.

* * *

The Brannon outfit broke camp and headed into the west. Late the next day they came upon a well-used trail heading into the northwest. It was rutted and worn showing signs of frequent travel. The Texan reckoned it was a trail used by the Missouri River smugglers while freighting their illicit wares north of the Medicine Line. They would soon find out the old visitor to their camp was right, the trace was indeed a segment of the Old North Trail of ancient times; which would cross into Canada through Whiskey Gap.

Off in the distance an eye-catching range of snow-topped mountains reared skyward above the bleakness of the prairie. One of them stood out from the rest, a bulky slab-sided monolith that imposed its strength and might. It was the landmark they had been seeking—Old Chief Mountain. The wanderer of the plains had sure enough known what he was talking about, the land known as Canada lay just ahead.

Lynn was tired and she knew that her husband was too, the trek through the Whiskey Gap country had been long and tedious. She was riding Evening Star, scouting ahead along the north fork of the Milk River—on the hunt for a campsite for the night. Brannon was following in the wagon, the Nez Perce girl sitting by his side.

In a way it was a challenge, a pleasant one though. "Your turn to find us a campsite," Matt had told her, a large smile spread across his whiskered face. She knew that it was his way, one of his lessons in plains lore that she looked forward to each day. And though she was weary, she never let on and accepted the challenge.

She knew her husband was testing her, to see if she remembered what he had taught her. So the trader's daughter from the Powder River was determined to do just that. She reckoned water would be of little concern; the North Fork would take care of that. It was grass for the stock, shelter, and firewood she must find. Lynn rode by several likely spots that might have worked, but somehow she was not satisfied and on she went.

Star's ears were suggesting caution; Lynn was alert as well when they rounded a horseshoe bend of the river trail, the Brannon wagon not far behind. Here in a clearing sheltered by river brush, and set back from the fast flowing stream, was a perfect spot for a night camp. There was only one thing wrong as near as she could reckon; it was occupied.

It was nearing sundown, a large campfire was blazing brightly. Walking over to the trail was a lean, moustached frontiersman. He was clad in buckskin clothing. Just above a holstered six-gun he wore a bright red Métis sash. Lynn reined in Evening Star and waited for her husband to catch up.

The presence of this man and his camp alarmed Lynn. Why, she reasoned, he could be an outlaw, or one of the whiskey smugglers the old wanderer had told them about. She reckoned she should heed Matt's council.

Reining the pinto ever so slightly, she positioned the carbine across her lap. Then, with a finger hovering over the trigger, discreetly shifted the barrel in line with the stranger. She was shaking and frightened, but this was her husband's way, the way he had taught her to handle this type of situation.

Brannon pulled the outfit along side Lynn. He had watched her getting set, her rifle ready for action if needed. He was proud of her, so proud of his Powder River girl.

"Ya did just fine darlin'," he spoke so only she could hear his words. "You'll sure do to ride the river with."

Lynn gave a big sigh and relaxed in the saddle. "Well thank you Matt Brannon. I was frightened and did not know what else to do."

"Couldn't a done better myself," he replied with a big smile. I'm sure enough proud of my wife, mighty proud!"

Lynn was pleased with the praise her husband gave her. She flashed him one of her special smiles and a contagious giggle for good measure. It was her payment to him for his kind words. She spoke once more, and she meant every word of it, "I sure do love you Matt. I surely do."

The buckskin clad stranger hesitated. He had not missed Lynn's defensive actions, a hand hovering near his own gun. He waited for Brannon's wagon to roll in. He saw the cowboy talk to the woman; he could hear her laughter and noticed the smile on the cowboy's face. It was only then he relaxed his vigilance, it appeared all would be well.

He approached the wagon, flashed them a smile and doffed his hat to Lynn. "Good evening strangers. Pull your outfit off the trail and camp with us…you are welcome to share our fire."

Pausing to puff the embers of his pipe into a usable condition, he continued, "I am John George Brown." Signing toward the fire he spoke again, "My wife Olivia and our youngsters." An attractive Métis woman walked over to stand by her husband. She looked to be in her late twenties and offered the Brannon's a wisp of a smile.

"Reckon we'll take ya up on your offer amigo, we'll be happy to share your fire. Matt Brannon they call me, my wife Lynn on the hoss, and our little friend Sara," indicating the Nez Perce girl sitting beside him.

John Brown tipped his old campaign hat to Lynn once again, gave them all a smile and turned to go. "When you folks get settled come on over and enjoy our fire. You must call me Kootenai…most folks in these parts know me as Kootenai Brown."

In the lee of a willow thicket, camp was made along the North Fork of the Milk River. They hurried their night chores so as to have more time to visit this interesting frontier family. It had been several long weeks since they had been around friendly people, this night would be a welcome change.

Sara was too shy to go to the Brown camp; she preferred to go to her blankets under the wagon. With tears in her eyes the Nez Perce girl lay awake watching the flickering of the campfire. Bedded down nearby were the longhorns, the firelight reflecting from their watchful eyes as they calmly chewed their cuds.

Arriving at the Brown camp, Lynn had a bag of doughnuts in one hand, the other hanging on to her husband's arm. He was toting a large pot of coffee, and it was hot. Sitting on driftwood logs that some previous traveller had brought up from the river, the newly found friends drank Matt's coffee, ate Lynn's doughnuts and began to talk the night away.

Kootenai accepted the Brannon's as friends. He admired Lynn's stand on the trail and knew that she would sure do to ride the river with. He was a jolly sort, seemed at ease with the younger couple and inquired, "Where is it you folks are going?"

"We're a headin' for Canada," Brannon said. "It is good grass we're lookin' for, a ranch to build and stock with cattle, a land to settle down in and call our own."

The cowboy's words brought a wide grin to Kootenai's face. "Why, this is Canada my friend. You Yanks crossed the 49th parallel about two miles back, you are now in Her Majesty the Queen's country!"

A whoop came from the cowboy's lips. almost a rebel yell so common to the Texas drovers. "Did ya hear that darlin'?" he said, giving Lynn a bear hug. "We're in Canada...we made it, we sure enough made it with our hair intact!"

Kootenai was a talker, appeared to be just warming up, and the young couple sure didn't mind. This is one night they were content to be listeners, they would have it no other way.

"The North West Territories are vast and cover thousands of miles," he told them. "Why, you can pick almost any location you choose for your ra-unch. For my money, and I have covered as much country as Anthony Henday himself, the best ra-unching country in the world is right here in these foothills east of the Rocky Mountains.

"Fact is," his talk flowed as smooth as the stream by which they camped. "I ran across a smashing place about ten-miles west of here, along the St. Mary's River. I was riding through one time on my way to Fort Benton on the Missouri, and chanced across it. The spread has water, shelter, good grass, and some timber for building up your ra-unch."

Lynn had to smile, it was all so clear to her now. This very day her husband had been instructing her on how to locate a suitable campsite. She could now realize how important it was to survive in this wilderness country. Brannon was excited, bubbling over in fact. An infectious grin was on his face, he turned to Lynn and said, "Sounds great, don't it? Just like what we're lookin' for.

"Reckon we owe ya our thanks Kootenai Brown. You and your family will be welcome at our fire any old time," exclaimed an excited Brannon.

Helping himself to another of Lynn's doughnuts, Kootenai said, "By jove! These are delicious little beggars; you will have to show Olivia how to prepare them."

"I will be happy to show Olivia how to prepare them," Lynn replied, she was pleased with the frontiersman's praise of her doughnuts.

While their host was catching his breath, Brannon did manage to tell them of the cattle drive up from Fort Worth, of meeting Lynn at the Powder River, their marriage in Miles Town, and their experience at the Bear Paw battlefield.

"As I recall," Kootenai interjected, "them Nez Perce are a right salty lot...will not back down from no one. I met a few of the Nez Perce west of the Rockies, in the Stud Horse Creek country it was. The bandits sure love to steal horses."

And though quite comfortable just listening, Lynn told of the sighting of a bull buffalo at the crossing of the Missouri. The old patriarch of the plains appeared stunned at the loss of the once great herd he had been a part of. It would be only a matter of time until wolves or hungry Indians would find him. The evidence of an uncaring genocide was appalling, the magnitude a sight to behold. Thousands of carcasses—bones and skulls scattered across the Montana plains, and it was the same up the trail from Texas.

Kootenai's jug was partly to blame. Not to accuse him of bragging, it appeared he was desirous of sharing his experiences and accomplishments, which were many. The Brannon's did not mind, they were satisfied to just listen. His talk was a living testimony of the history and lore of the Great Plains. The information he was exposing them to would be a treasured asset for the rest of their lives.

He just could not be stopped. "It was in 1865," he reminisced. "I was in company with a group of gold hunters heading to Fort Edmonton by way of the North Saskatchewan. We came across the Rocky Mountains from Wild Horse Creek—through the South Kutenai Pass, a summer route used by the Kutenai Indians. They would come this way to hunt buffalo for food, you see."

Tossing a log on the fire, which was a first for him, since Olivia had left the fire to tuck the children in their blankets, he continued to talk. "The party I was with came down the Pass into the foothills near the mouth of Pass Creek. It would be here, stretching as far as the eye could see, we discovered this country, a smashing good grass country. The Great Plains of Canada begin right there in this valley of Red Rock."

He told of the prairie to the far horizons, as one vast herd of buffalo. Thousands upon thousands of the shaggy beasts scattered at random across the boundless prairie, over yonder, foraging along the flanks of Old Chief Mountain and beyond. Everywhere you might care to look was a living mass of the great bison of the plains.

"I have stood at the summit of the Cypress and Sweetgrass Hills...two hundred miles east of here, and it was the same," he continued. "The buffalo were everywhere!"

The abundance of this native of the plains would not last. In a sense Kootenai was partly to blame. He had ridden with the hide hunters, had engaged in his share of harvesting the beasts for their hide only. Sometimes a hump or tongue was taken for food. More often than not the rich, nourishing meat was left for the wolf, buzzard and crow.

Following a winter of light snowfall, the prairie was tinder dry, water was scarce, and the grass was short. Famished, the herds migrated south into the United States. American hide hunters set grass fires behind them to deter their return to the Northern Territories.

Native Indian hunters stripped the Canadian prairie of any remaining game by the summer. The tribes suffered to no end; the great herds had been their bread basket for hundreds of years. They were obliged to eat seeds, mice, carrion, and eventually their camp dogs and ponies.

Kootenai Brown was enchanting to listen to, rugged and wild as the West he chose to live in. He had a twinkling eye and a charming wit that was hard to beat. The campfire talk drifted back to himself and his family. Before he began he requested his wife to fetch more refreshments, the kind that came in a jug. "Look under the wagon seat," he instructed. "This blasted crock must of sprang a leak...not a drop is left Olivia."

The Métis woman vanished in the darkness, returning with her husband's whiskey. "Here Matt Brannon," he offered. "Have some of this Missouri River barleycorn. A good stiff jolt will do you good...take the kinks out of your sinews!"

Brannon hadn't had a drink since Miles Town and could not refuse the friendly offer. Hoisting the jug in the crook of his arm, he managed several hearty swallows. It was firewater at its finest, unrefined gut warmer. Never in his life had he came so close to choking to death. Tears streamed down his cheeks, as he was struggled to regain his breath when Lynn said, "Matt Brannon, look at me! Are you all right? That awful stuff of Kootenai's has poisoned you," she moaned. "And your eyes—they look terrible!"

Their host thought it was a big joke and, after regaining possession of his jug, he imbibed several hearty swigs which seemed to have little effect on his person. Then, smoothing the unruly hair on his upper lip, Kootenai began once more to reminisce.

He told of fur trading in Manitoba with the Chippewa and Cree, buffalo hunting with the Métis in North Dakota. It was here with the Métis in 1869 that he met his bride, Olivia Lyonnais, a French/Cree maiden. She was a comely girl and always dressed as her Métis forbearers. She kept herself neat and tidy, smoked a pipe and hoisted her husband's jug for a few modest sips now and then. Though Lynn Brannon never smoked a pipe or hoisted a jug, she and Olivia became good friends.

After another snort of river whiskey, which Brannon refused, the jolly frontiersman continued his story. He told of accompanying American wolvers, so called from their vocation of poisoning wolves for the pelts, to the Cypress Hills country. Each fur brought them two dollars. Then south of the 49th parallel he had travelled, dispatching mail to the isolated Army Forts that were scattered up and down the Missouri River.

Pausing while Olivia put more fuel on the fire, Kootenai fired up his pipe again and, in a more meditative mood, continued to spin his yarns. "I found myself in a deuce of trouble with the American lawmen, you see. Over in the Dakotas it was. It began with a difference of opinion over the quality of my furs. A buyer was cheating me on price—the blighter challenged my word, came at me with a knife, so I drew my Green River!" Kootenai continued, "Well anyway, I survived with a minor wound, the cheating half-breed never made it. They charged me with murder and locked me up; I thought I was going to swing from a Dakota gallows. At my trial at Last Chance Gulch I was acquitted on grounds of self-defence. I immediately rounded up Olivia and the babies and we headed home to Canada.

"We're heading up to the Kutenai Lakes—about forty miles west of here, in the Rocky Mountains. We have a good cabin there and a few head of cattle. We're thinking of starting us a rau-nch of our own."

The Brannon's were ready to call it a night, the hour was late, both were tired and could use a few hours sleep. But still this man, known to them as Kootenai Brown, was reluctant to stop his talk. "You folks get settled, come spring time drive over and camp for awhile. The fishing is good; there are some big whoppers living in the Kutenai's."

Kootenai had really taken a liking to the young settlers. They were his kind, pioneers in the truest sense. Seeking new horizons, always an urge to see what was over the next dip in the prairie. He could see that Brannon was capable, a frontiersman like himself. The big Peacemaker in the well-worn holster was an indication of this, and the man known as Kootenai respected him for that. Matt and Kootenai had become friends that night, a friendship that would last for all their days.

Matt and Lynn were finally able to excuse themselves and slip away to their wagon. Lynn's arm was wrapped tightly around her husband's waist. She was concerned about her cowboy, who seemed unsteady on his feet and stumbling in the darkness.

"Matt, darling, are you all right?" asked Lynn, "Your eyes have looked bloodshot ever since you drank that awful stuff Kootenai gave you. And your voice—it doesn't sound like my husband's!"

Though it was still pounding something fierce, Brannon's head was clearing some. He managed a grin in the darkness and spoke, "That was the worst poison I ever tangled with."

"Rot-gut whiskey in the raw I reckon. Lucky I never choked to death," changing the subject he continued, "Did ya notice Kootenai's wagon? It was plumb full of the stuff."

Lynn tucked her husband into bed and gave a sigh. She was relieved they had finally arrived in Canada, it was here, she reckoned, that she would live out the rest of her days.

At first light of the next morning the two outfits left the North Fork of the Milk River together. Ten-miles down trail Kootenai reined in his outfit and approached the Brannon wagon. "You folks head west from here," he said. "The St. Mary's River is not far, there is a smashing good site for your raunch. You will see it when you cross over to the big grass flat."

"Olivia and I are going down river, cross at Indian Ford, and then cut across country to the old Lee Trading Post on Lariat Cross Creek. We'll camp there, then go on to the Rocky Mountains and home."

"Lariat Cross, ya say. That's sure a name that strikes a cowboy's fancy," Brannon remarked.

"Well you see, Matt Brannon, when I came across the Rockies the Blackfeet referred to the creek as 'Banks Roped Together'; after translation that is. The clever natives would stretch a line across the stream secured to a tree on each side. The rope was a useful means of crossing over in the season of high water." Kootenai continued, "Early trappers and the Red Coats renamed the stream Lariat Cross. I figured it was easier for them to remember."

"Now I reckon that's a plumb interesting story Kootenai Brown," Brannon replied, "I always did like to know the workings of a name. We are in debt to ya for sharing your fire and the kindness of ya-all to a pair of strangers."

Kootenai Brown was beaming when he replied, "We've got to be on our way now, been a pleasure camping with you Yanks. We really enjoyed your doughnuts Lynn Brannon…right tasty they were."

* * *

"Oh my, isn't that big mountain beautiful," Lynn exclaimed. "Sitting in front of the rest, beckoning us to come and find our new ranch. What did Kootenai Brown call it?"

Brannon was equally impressed and with a grin answered his wife, "He called it Old Chief Mountain, our own landmark in this new land called Canada. Always there on the horizon like a good friend!"

It was but a short drive to the river, and after a safe crossing, the cowboy wheeled the wagon on to a well-grassed basin, protected from the elements by a horseshoe bend of this glacier-scooped stream.

The long journey from Miles Town was behind them. After six-weeks of continuous travel there would be no more of the big wagon rolling westward into the unknown. Brannon assisted his wife to dismount from Evening Star. For the first time on their long trek she appeared tired and not her vibrant, tireless self. It was a long tedious journey for her he reckoned.

He was proud of his wife and held her close in his arms, just would not let her go until they danced a happy jig. "We're here Lynn," he whooped. "This will be where we build our new home, in Her Majesty the Queen's land of Canada."

Sara the Nez Perce girl stared at them in awe and muttered strange things at their antics. She was fond of them both. It was Lynn who had saved her life back at the Milk River. She knew that Lynn loved her big husband, therefore the waif was obliged to love him as well, it was the way of her people.

The weather turned warm, Indian summer at its finest. For a few days they relaxed and took it easy, they had earned the rest they both agreed. It would be a time to sense and absorb this new land of plenty. Plentiful water and grass, abundant shelter and firewood—a ranch of their own; what more could they ask for?

Kootenai had been true to his word. Sheltered in the lee of the Deerhorn Hills the ranch was an oasis on the great northern plains.

Cottonwood and poplar were abundant, with an occasional stand of pine and spruce. Sharp tail grouse and sage hens, were right at home in this river environment. Deer and elk were sighted browsing high on a wind-blown hill. As pointed out by Sara, there were antelope here as well.

Pooling at the mouth of a sandstone coulee was an abundant supply of cool spring water. And the grass, the grass was unbelievable, belly-high to Lynn's saddle mare. A sight the new settlers had never seen before.

Lynn worked by her husband's side night and day. Wherever he went, or whatever he was doing she was there to help. She would have it no other way and he sure enjoyed her company and help. The cabin site was chosen with care, ensuring easy access to the free-flowing spring. They located suitable timber and began dragging in pine and poplar rails. Together they worked, building a small stable to protect the horse gear from the weather, a shelter for the stock when the northers blew, and even a much needed corral. Heavy timber was found, building logs for the erection of a cabin. Hitching a team to a makeshift drag, Brannon began hauling river rock to the building site for use in the foundation. Day after day they worked.

This was a new experience for Matt Brannon, who just a short while ago had lived by a different philosophy, if a job could not be handled from up-top on a saddle—then it wasn't worth doing. It was the cowboy way he had reckoned. But with Lynn by his side, and their combined determination, there was nothing they could not do.

One morning they were down at the river prying loose a large flat rock that would serve as a doorstep for their cabin. Both were wet to the knees, laughing and giggling as they struggled with the cumbersome stone. After much hard work, it was eventually loaded on to the drag. As they sat in the sun to dry off their clothes, Lynn became serious and exclaimed, "I just love it here Matt Brannon...I just wanted you to know. This splendid river, the St. Mary's, is alive and excited. It is talking to us day and night as it travels over the rocks. Don't you think so?"

"I reckon you're right darlin'...I surely do," Matt replied, "It is strange to find these northern riverbeds covered with rock and boulders. Why, I swore the wheels on the wagon were gonna bounce right off the axles when I crossed over."

He was grinning when he spoke again, "It came near to chatterin' the teeth right outta my mouth. You were lucky darlin', Evening Star carried you across" Brannon continued, "I'm a thinkin' the closer to the Rocky Mountains, the more rock and gravel that is deposited on the bottom of these rivers. Down south when crossing the Brazos, we were ever mindful of mud and quicksand and snakes. Crossin' a river was a plumb serious undertaking that took much care and attention."

* * *

Brannon was sitting by Lynn's cooking fire drinking coffee, watching the girls prepare their noontime meal when suddenly he froze. "Hush you two! Did ya hear something?"

"I'm sorry Matt," Lynn replied, "I was making too much chatter myself to notice anything."

"I heard a gunshot," he told her, "and what sure sounded like whoopin' and hollerin'."

Lynn could now detect the sound of gunfire and the faint bellowing of cattle. She quickly placed the Nez Perce girl in the wagon and gave her strict orders to stay there. With her Yellow Boy in hand, she returned to the fire to stand by her husband.

"If I didn't know better," Brannon said, "I'd say some mighty thirsty cattle caught a whiff of our water, and someone is tryin' to stop them.

"Act natural like Lynn...I reckon everything will be all right."

The unseen clamour was closing in. As if out of nowhere a horde of longhorn cattle, showing the strain of a long run staggered over the far bank and plunged into the river. With them came two cowboy riders, one who fell at the water's edge, the other found himself in the river with the cattle; buck-jumping a near-spent bronc across. Both the horse and the rider went down near Lynn Brannon's cooking fire.

In mere seconds, a howling mob of Blackfeet Indians, all decked out in war paint and feathers, appeared on the far bank of the St. Mary's River. Several carried old trade rifles and were taking pot shots at the Brannon camp; the rest jumped their lathered ponies into the water right after the longhorns.

Brannon took one look and yelled, "If we plan on a keepin' our hair intact...we've got to start shootin'. Ya pick off those on the skyline Lynn; I'll take the ones in the river."

Together, standing side by side, the Texas cowboy and his Powder River girl stood off the crazed Blackfeet, sending four of them to the happy hunting ground. The deadly barrage was too much for the attacking warriors. They gathered their dead and departed, keening a fearsome jargon over those who had been killed. The Blackfeet had had their fill of the deadly shooting of Matt and Lynn Brannon.

Heaving sighs of relief, Matt and a distraught Lynn turned to the cowboy rider who had made it across the river. Lynn's face was ashen; she was shaking like an aspen leaf. "I have killed again with my rifle," she moaned. "Do you think God will forgive me for what I've done?"

"Of course He will darlin'," Matt replied, "We were defending ourselves…this ya must understand!" He continued, "Given the chance, the savage devils would have slaughtered us like animals. Your pretty hair and mine as well, would be hangin' on a war lance by now. I'm sure proud of my Powder River girl, ya hear, mighty proud."

Her husband's words were like medicine to Lynn; she knelt by the fallen rider while Matt moved the dead horse off his leg. "Can ya shift him some Lynn," Brannon asked, "the boy's in bad shape. Without our help he's gonna cash in his chips."

"He's so young," Lynn said, "just a boy, and terribly hurt. See—this broken arrow in his side—and the blood!"

"I'll cut the arrow out of him while he's still unconscious." Brannon said as he doused his long knife in a pot of water that was boiling on Lynn's fire. Kneeling by the boy, Matt peeled back his blood-caked shirt, and with several deft incisions and a stout pull he popped out the flint-carved arrowhead.

The boy stirred, a groan escaped his fever-cracked lips. Lynn's countenance was pale and unsteady, yet she cleansed and bandaged the wound as best she could. "I reckon the youngster's a lucky hombre," Brannon said, "and so are the Brannon's!" Brannon continued, "I'm a hopin' he'll wake up soon and tell us how he got himself in such a wreck."

The longhorns were now making their way across the river, ravenously feeding on the Brannon grass. More were coming all the time. The big Texan was surprised at the tally he was ticking off in his head. Tallyin' cattle in your head is a God-given talent for those who are range born, a talent of Matt's that had impressed old Tom Lynch, Hugh Arnett and others whom the cowboy had worked for. "Must be close to a couple o' hundred head," he said, "and more a comin' by the sounds of it, there's bound to be stragglers showin' up for the rest o' the day."

Lynn and Sara were never far from the boy, Brannon had just returned from a scout across the river bringing with him a small bunch of stragglers. "Come quick," Lynn shouted, "the boy is waking up—and wanting to talk.

He's going to make it, I just know he is." Unknown to her, Sara had treated the boy's wound with a concoction of secret herbs she had hidden in her par fleche.

Grinning from ear to ear, Brannon poured a cup of coffee, raised the boy's head and gave him a good stiff jolt of his wonder medicine. "Take it easy lad," he said, "You're safe now; drink some o' this here cowboy coffee," Brannon continued, "I reckon it's sure enough cowboy medicine, will put good red blood back in your veins. Why, we'll have ya as good as new in no time at all!"

Greedily the boy drank, then looked up and saw Lynn hovering by the big cowboy's side. "The angels must be with me," he murmured. "I must have made it to heaven after all...reckoned I was headin' to hell for sure. Ma-am, please tell me this is heaven that, that I'm not just a dreamin'."

Lynn's countenance turned a rosy red; she was blushing and did not care. Together she and her husband roared with laughter. Sara, the Nez Perce waif, looked aghast and muttered her strange talk. "No, you're not a dreamin'," Brannon told him, wiping a tear from his eye, "and you're not in heaven, but on the Brannon ranch where we've just saved your hair from that war party of Blackfeet. Soon as you're able, ya must tell us how ya came to be in such a fix."

The boy was now fully awake and appeared to relax some. The young cowboy rider saw the cooking fire and said, "I could sure use another cup o' that coffee and, one o' them sourdoughs I see there by the fire. I haven't et any grub for three days now."

Brannon's coffee and Lynn's food made the boy sleepy. He would talk some, then fall asleep; rouse and continue his rambling talk. As the evening progressed he unfolded a heartbreaking tale of his family's flight to save their five hundred head of longhorns.

"Billy Marshall, they call me," said the young boy, "my Dad and seven of us brothers started out from Johnson County, Wyoming with our herd. It's a heck of a ways south o' here, other side of the Montana Territory," he continued, "Johnson County was a troublesome place. The neighbours, such as they were, weren't friendly...then there were outlaws and the cattle rustlin', and what not. My Dad wanted to get away from it all and start fresh. He'd heard there was grass up this way so we headed north."

Billy's dad, old Bob Marshall and his boys made it into Montana Territory without mishap, from there on it was a running fight to save the herd. First it was the Crows, who rustled about a 100 head and killed one of his sons. He buried the boy near the Yellowstone River, and then continued pushing the herd north. In the Judith Basin country they were attacked again. Billy never could figure out what tribe these Indians belonged to, but he saw first hand that the bloodthirsty devils were savage as all get out. It was here old Bob lost two more of his sons.

"Tommy drowned when we pushed the herd across the big river," Billy said, "I reckoned it was the Missouri. We were having a bad time, our cows were drowning and getting swept away. The longhorns went plumb loco in that big river, reckon we picked a bad place to cross, but there wasn't much choice with them blasted Injuns everywhere!"

Somehow they made it to the Sweetgrass Hills. Half of the herd was lost and four of the Marshall brothers had been killed. The chuck wagon was last seen rolling end over end down the Missouri River. All that was left was old Bob, three sons and about 250 head of cows. The grass was fair, so they laid over a few days resting the herd and themselves. They hoped that their troubles were now over. They could see the Rocky Mountains in the distance and continued onward.

Sixty miles west, along the North Fork of Milk River, trouble struck them again. A blood-chilling band of savages attacked the herd, scattering them to the far winds. It was here old Bob and his oldest son went down, Blackfoot arrows driven deep in their chests. Billy and his remaining brother, Jeb, fled for their lives.

Late the next day the boys began finding small bunches of Marshall cattle. The boys hazed the longhorns together and continued into the west. As they continued on the herd grew larger, more of the scattered cattle showing up all the time. Spying a large square mountain through the distant haze, they hoped that perhaps they could find safety. Across the plains they rode, pointing the longhorns towards Old Chief Mountain.

It was this very morning the Blackfoot struck again. Billy and Jeb were hit with arrows right off, but stayed with the cattle and stampeded them toward the big mountain. It was the only landmark they could see.

"Them Blackfoot devils were vicious and mean," Billy murmured, "plumb loco. The cusses would ride up along side us and shoot their arrows at close range," he continued, "we were out of bullets…never had much of a chance."

Determined to finish his story, Billy Marshall struggled to keep his eyes open. He gulped another cup of coffee, shuddered and spoke, "I reckoned Jeb was in bad shape when we made it to this river o' yourn…that's 'bout all I can remember'til I woke up here by your fire," Billy looked at Brannon and asked, "Did Jeb make it Mister? What happened to my brother? What happened, anyhow?"

The boy's fearsome story of the destruction of his family and their dream was a repetition of hundreds of such incidents. All across the Great Plains this had happened, from the Texas panhandle to the prairies of Canada, and all points in between.

Brannon shuddered as he remembered an incident similar to this, the slaughter of his family by a Comanche war party. The big cowboy was shaken, Lynn sat by the fire silently weeping. Brannon took a deep breath, reckoned he should tell it like it was. "No, Billy. He never made it; he died as he was riding, with a Blackfoot arrow in his back! He died brave, son. Jeb hung on to the saddle horn long after he was dead—I buried him across the river where he fell. Brought his saddle and trappin's back, they're layin' right here by the wagon." Brannon continued, "Your brother's six-gun was missin', he was riding with an empty holster!"

Billy Marshall's tears couldn't be stopped, but he was brave. He had proven it many times throughout the ill-fated journey. "I've lost my Dad and all my brothers," he sobbed, "I just don't know what I'll do now. Guess when I'm able I'll ride back and hunt up my Mother to let her know what happened. It will break her heart...but I reckon I've got it to do."

"Yes Billy," the big Texan replied, "it's a man's chore to do such things. It's the cowboy way."

* * * Chapter 10 * * *

The Marshall cattle, not counting those that were gut-shot with Blackfoot arrows, amounted to 179 head. Brannon offered to buy them from the convalescing boy, offered him four-dollars a head in gold coin.

Billy gladly accepted, and with nothing more than a handshake, a deal was struck. The longhorns with the BL connected brand were now the nucleus of the Brannon ranch in the Deerhorn Hills.

Billy was still on the mend and could do no heavy lifting, yet he was willing to assist the big cowboy as best he could. Together, they built a modest, but sturdy log cabin near the banks of the St. Mary's River. It was a comfortable structure, one that would keep the women folks safe and warm during the approaching winter.

The cabin was furnished with a plank table, a plank bench, and wall mounted shelves. The welcoming front door was hung with leather hinges and there were two windows covered with swinging wooden shutters. A loft at one end of the cabin provided sleeping accommodations for Sara. A metal flat-topped stove complete with a pipe, was set at one end of the main room. A pallet of Lynn's blankets at the other end would serve as the Brannon's bed.

Indian summer was now behind them. Ice was forming along the river's edge, Canada geese and green-head ducks, were filling the skies—heading south to some winter retreat. Winter was closing in on the Brannon ranch in the North West Territories.

When Billy Marshall had recovered sufficiently from his injuries, he saddled the horse that had belonged to his brother Jeb. He was worried about his Mom, wanted to ride back to Wyoming and give her the gold that Brannon had paid for the longhorns; tell her what happened to her husband and six of her sons. The Brannon's tried to persuade him to wait till spring, but his mind was set. Lynn loaded him down with food for the trail; Brannon gave him a warm coat and a blanket.

"Take these cartridges for yer gun," Brannon offered, "and this bag o' jerked meat. Remember not to flash any o' that gold around...keep it out o' sight, in that money belt I gave ya.'Til ya make it out o' Blackfoot country son, ride at night, hole up and sleep in the daytime. Hide yer camp like I showed ya."

Billy replied, "Thanks a whole bunch Matt and Lynn Brannon. I'll never forget ya…ya saved my life ya know. Ya saved my Mom's life by buying them longhorns that were left. She'll be mighty thankful fer the gold I'm a takin' her."

"Adios Billy, have a good ride. There's a job a waitin' here for ya anytime ya decide to come back," exclaimed the big Texas cowboy.

Struggling to hold back the tears, the young cowboy doffed his hat to the woman folk and headed down the trail south toward the Wyoming Territory to return home to his mother.

It was shortly before the snow came when Lynn found her husband digging a hole in the woods near the horse corrals. She watched and waited, finally asking, "Are you hiding something from me Matt? What are you putting into that hole in the ground?"

Brannon looked up and grinned, then lowered a well-wrapped packet into his cache. "Shucks Lynn, its nuthin' much—a six-gun and some cartridges, a bag o' jerked meat and part o' the gold coins Tom Lynch gave us." He then explained, "This cache will be an ace in the hole. Never know when we might be in a fix and really need it."

A norther moved in whispering of the land of the midnight sun, the northern lights and other strange things. Snow covered the land, ice formed on the river, winter was settling in. However throughout the changing season the settlers were busy and happy, living life to the fullest.

Sara had overcome the trauma of the Bear Paw because of Lynn Brannon's loving care. Lynn's friendly nature had won over the Nez Perce girl. She was filling out and growing like a weed, her teenage years now upon her. Back in the Nez Perce camps many of the girls her age were wed as it was the custom of her people.

One day she signed to her crippled leg, smiled and spoke, "– Lame Deer— Sara Lame Deer!" From that moment on, and for the remainder of her life, the daughter of Chief Joseph would be known as Lame Deer.

At night as the young settlers lay in their blankets, Lynn would snuggle close to her husband. "Keep me warm," she begged, "I've been freezing all day—I can't seem to keep my feet warm."

"You'll get used to it darlin', this climate sure beats the damn heat and dust of the southern states."

Outside the cabin the norther howled and moaned, Lynn snuggled closer to her husband, and closer. Deep inside herself she could sense changes in her body that almost frightened her. Yet, she was as excited as could be; it would be her secret for now; for a while anyway.

The Brannon's kept busy surviving the cold and the snow, the below zero temperature that they sure weren't accustomed to. Lynn and Sara stayed mostly inside the cabin, while Brannon dragged in load after load of firewood. "It's gonna take a heap of firewood to last us'til spring," he told the girls.

"I found some coal in a coulee up-river a ways, reckon I'll dig some out and try it in our little stove—reckon I'll call the site Coal Mine Coulee, a right fittin' name, don't you think?" On one of Matt's scouting excursions, he returned with a sack of surface coal from the coulee. He gave it a try and found that it worked just fine in their little stove. The log cabin along the St. Mary's River kept snug, and warm, that long, cold winter in the Canadian Territories.

Lynn and Lame Deer prepared a bounteous feast for Christmas dinner. Among the usual trimmings were roast prairie hen, venison ribs, and even a can of peaches that Lynn had put aside. The peaches and her doughnuts were their dessert.

For Christmas Brannon gave Lame Deer a small belt knife with a tanned ermine-skin sheath. Lynn gave her some red ribbon and an ivory-handled brush for her hair. The Indian girl had never received such generous gifts, only after brushing her hair and tying it in a ponytail with the red ribbon would she go to bed.

Much later, Lynn and Matt were in their bed, watching the flames flickering from the fire in the little stove. "Merry Christmas," she told him, turning to face her husband, "The only present I can give you is my love."

Lynn's chatter continued, hoping her husband would join in, but Brannon appeared on edge, as if he just could not settle down. "Merry Christmas, Lynn." he finally replied, "I've never had reason to celebrate the Christmas holiday before, never knew what it meant until I met ya. I reckon if I had a gift for ya, it would be a wedding ring, one that I picked out especially for ya. Remember Lynn, at the trading post in Miles Town I was unable to find a ring for ya? The traders had plumb run out of them."

"Is that what has been the matter with you?" queried Lynn. "I have been puzzled as to why you have been so quiet lately. Don't worry about it Matt, I'm sure not."

"You do have a present for me though," she giggled and snuggled close, "and I also have another gift for you. It is a gift we are going to share with each other…a special one!"

"We are going to have a baby!" Lynn exclaimed.

Brannon was somewhat shocked with her announcement, reckoned he had been too busy to give the matter much thought. Yet he was happy and proud that he was going to be a Father. It took a few minutes for him to find his voice, and then with a whoop he said, "Why, that is wonderful news…best Christmas present yer cowboy could've ever hoped fer."

The cowboy whooped once more, embraced Lynn in a bear hug, one that tumbled them both out of their blankets on to the cold cabin floor. "I've known it for some time, darlin' Matt, our baby will be with us sometime this summer." Lynn explained. Laughing and giggling the happy pair remade their pallet and crawled back into bed.

Peace and security reigned at the cabin along the breaks of the frozen river. The Brannon's schedule of unending daily chores ensured their survival on this lonely Canadian prairie. They loved every minute of it; they were putting down roots, planting them deep for a long stay.

As the weeks rolled by the winter of 1878 became that much shorter. One day Brannon sensed a change, the daylight hours became longer, the intense chill of the land was broken. Spring was getting closer he reckoned, he could feel it in his bones.

Matt saddled Buck and rode up river scouting for the longhorns. It was time to get the cattle rounded up and brought back to the home place where the cattle could drop their calves and where Matt and his long gun could protect the little calves from prairie wolves, coyotes and other dangers.

Calving time is harvest time on a cattle ranch. The baby longhorns are valuable, because they were the only harvest Brannon would receive from the ranch. As replacements these calves assured the health and survival of the herd and as grown steers they provided a means of receiving cash money. Cash was needed to keep the BL a viable and financially fit ranch.

The big Texan located the horse herd in a secluded basin about five miles up river. They were pawing aside the deep snow to reach the rich grass that lay beneath. The cattle were also there, living with the remuda, eating the grass the horses were uncovering from under the snow.

Brannon gathered the remuda and started them back for the home ranch. The longhorns appeared at a loss, and soon headed down the trail after their winter-long friends.

The snow began to melt from the warm sun. An abundance of rich meadow grass was showing across the aspen clearing. The cattle were content to stay here throughout the birthing of their new babies. The remuda and the presence of Brannon gave them a sense of security. After the calves were dropped they would be back to their former God-given temperament. When venturing too close, the lives of man or beast would be in peril from these long-horned denizens of the Lone Star State. Brannon was never far from the calving grounds, prowling the outer reaches of the meadow, his .44-40 Winchester always with him. On several occasions he shot coyotes that snuck in too close. The ringing report of the .44-40 sounded a dire warning to the wolves, who were never much of a problem.

There were times though, when an old mossy-horn cow would take offence when spotting the cowboy and his horse. She would viciously shake her massive spread of horns in warning and would stalk the rider; bellowing a challenge to one and all. Brannon reckoned she had a calf hidden in the grass, or was all set to drop one; and he would discreetly ride away.

Matt Brannon was doing chores around the corrals when a rider approached the cabin. From the looks of the uniform he was wearing, the Canadian military must be paying them a visit. Brannon reckoned he must belong to this new mounted police outfit that he had heard tell of .

With his Winchester in hand, he sauntered over to greet the visitor. "Howdy amigo," Brannon spoke, "stomp that mud off yer boots and come on in. Some hot coffee will do ya good."

The Corporal, as the stripes indicated, dismounted and jauntily replied, "Sounds smashing good old chap, but I would prefer a spot of tea."

The big Texan escorted the North West Mounted Police officer into the cabin, muddy boots and all, and seated him at Lynn's plank-hewn table. Brannon called to his wife saying, "We've got a visitor a callin' Lynn, some coffee and doughnuts would sure hit the spot—says he wants a spot o' tea."

"Never heard o' the stuff myself," Matt mentioned. "Where I come its coffee or else go without!"

Lynn subdued an urge to giggle and turned to her stove. Brannon gave the Corporal a questionable look and said, "This young Corporal here looks to be all tuckered out...appears he's been on a long ride from somewhere."

Clearing his throat, and making a show of stroking his moustache the lawman began to talk, "I am Corporal Henry Stokes, assigned to river patrol out of the Fort—Fort Macleod that is.

"When I inspected the Outpost six miles down the bloody river, I was told some Yanks were squatting up here. I had to ride all the way up here to check you blighters out."

His opening remarks were like a slap in the face to the cowboy, an aura of arrogance and self-importance lay heavy in the Brannon cabin. The cowboy's dander was rising fast; he was tempted to bounce the sharp-tongued rascal out, but strangled the urge and said, "Now hold yer hosses stranger...no need t' talk like that! We settled here just before winter hit us. We're gonna run longhorns in these parts—start us a ranch."

Brannon continued his talk; he was struggling not to roar, "My wife Lynn and I are making this our home, putting down roots! Reckon we plan on becoming a part of yer Canada." Lynn could tell her husband was becoming hot under the collar, very hot, and discreetly brought the coffee and doughnuts. She sat them down in front of the Corporal and stepped back. The Englishman pitched right in, drinking cup after cup of the scalding liquid, eating a lion's share of the doughnuts, all the time glaring at the big cowboy.

Lame Deer sat in the far corner muttering strange things.

In an authoritative voice Corporal Stokes began speaking, "You Yanks must come down river to the Outpost! You must register your livestock and yourselves, including that savage over there, nodding towards the Nez Perce girl. For the rest—your land and cattle brand—will have to be officially recorded at the Fort, Fort Macleod that is." Stokes continued, "Jolly well make it soon, old chap! It should have been done two weeks after entering Her Majesty the Queen's Colony of Canada, you know!"

With that said the trooper drained another cup of coffee, stuffed the remaining doughnuts in the pocket of his tunic and departed.

Lynn had never seen her husband in such a mood as this before. His face was as red as the serape that had graced her shoulders all winter long, she sensed he was fuming mad. Rather than face an open rebellion in her home, she sat down beside him, took his big hand in her own and looked him in the eyes. It was her special look, a look that could settle her husband down with a single glance.

She squeezed his hand and said, "The Englishmen is an impudent rascal...not worth getting into trouble over! We must not judge Canada by the actions of an uncouth law man like this, a discredit to the uniform I would say!"

This was their first meeting with an official of the Canadian government, and the Brannon's were not impressed with the welcome he had shown them.

It took some time for the cowboy to simmer down. He finally relaxed, his countenance still showing the strain, but easing. "Reckon yer right Lynn, he wasn't worth the trouble. I was'bout set to read him from the good book!" exclaimed Matt. "Thanks a bunch Lynn," he grinned. "Fer a holdin' me back."

The next morning he rode across the river, and on down country to the small North West Mounted Police Outpost the Corporal had spoken of. It was located south of the Blood Reservation, a clan of the mighty Blackfoot.

He was greeted warmly by a young trooper who bade him welcome, and assisted him with the paper work. The Constable wished him a sincere welcome to the Territories and warned him of the Corporal's dogged stubbornness. He advised Brannon to ride to the Fort as soon as possible.

Brannon thanked the friendly trooper, swung aboard the dun horse and headed back up river. He was within a half mile of the ranch when the sound of a rifle shot echoed along the bottom lands of the river the Brannon's referred to as their own.

"Lynn! Lynn must be in trouble." A jolt of fear throbbed through him; the goading of spurs urged the dun into a frantic race for home. Rounding the last bend in the river, Brannon could see a strange group of riders milling around the cabin, Lynn and her red serape were right in the middle of it all. As he closed in he could see his brave wife, and was fighting mad.

A tall rider on a bay horse had Lynn pinned against the cabin door, attempting to take away her rifle. She was having no part of it and was striking him with her weapon and yelling at him. Another rider wearing a dirty-grey hat, blood streaming from a slash across his cheek, had Lame Deer draped across his saddle. She was fighting like a wild cat, screeching and brandishing her little knife. There were two more riders lurking in the background, one slumped low in the saddle nursing a gunshot to his gut.

Like a Comanche raider, Brannon charged into the ranch yard with his buckskin horse sliding on its back legs, a wild rebel yell of his Texas forbearers gushed from the cowboy's lips. Hot, deadly lead was slashing from the Colt Peacemaker.

Lynn's assailant heard the chilling sound and, uttering a violent curse, pivoted the bay horse—his six-gun swinging towards Brannon. He never made it, his reflexes were no match for the Texas gun fighter, and a bullet from the Peacemaker tumbled him to the ground.

Ramming his horse, Buck, into the horse that held a fighting Lame Deer, Brannon roared, "Lower the girl to the ground or you're a dead man." The alarmed rider dropped Lame Deer as he was told, his arms reached for the sky.

"No need to butt in stranger," the rider said with a sneer, "Kinda stickin' your nose where it don't belong, ain't ya?"

Matt's answer to the assailant was quick in coming; there was no need for words from the enraged cowboy, as he struck the assailant to the ground with the barrel of the Peacemaker. Covering the other two, Brannon stepped to the ground. Lynn could not hold back her tears and was quickly in her husband's arms. Lame Deer was hanging on to him as well, jabbering hysterically in her Nez Perce lingo and scanty English.

"I'm so glad you came back Matt. They were taking our cows—I tried to stop them but they were just too much for me!" explained Lynn, "they were determined to hurt us. I shot one...they just would not leave us alone."

Matt Brannon was a terrible sight to see. It even scared Lynn some to see him challenge the two in the background, "You two miserable skunks want any more gun play?"

Attempting to raise his hands, the wounded one, the same one Lynn had gut-shot, moaned in pain. "Nothin' doin', Mister, that gal of yourn with the rifle outgunned me right smart, reckon I'm going to bleed to death."

Brannon could see what was set to unfold. The two riders in the background could not. Old Silver, one of the longhorn steers that Tom Lynch had given them, came from behind the corrals. He was moaning a fearful tune, a tune that originated from deep inside his massive self. Trotting close to the far horse and rider, he lowered his horns and with little effort upended the unlucky pair. Then in a bloody, feral manner, began to destroy the outlaw and his mount.

"Don't look darlin'," Brannon said as he covered Lynn's eyes, "Old Silver is helpin' us out I reckon. It's the critter's way of avenging the way these owl hoots were treating you and Lame Deer."

"Good thing ol' Dollar isn't with him, else we'd have one he-ell of a slaughter on our hands."

The two longhorns had become Lynn's friends. They were almost pets to the kind-hearted girl who was slipping them a handful of oats each day. It was Lynn who had named them Silver and Dollar.

The sharp scent of gun smoke lay heavy in the dooryard of Lynn Brannon's cabin. Lynn and Lame Deer were clinging to the big cowboy; Lynn's attacker was dead from Brannon's well-placed shot. The single shot from her rifle had found its mark; the outlaw was in rough shape from loss of blood, barely conscious, hanging on to the horn of his saddle.

Lame Deer's abuser, the one in the dirty grey hat, was out of it; huddled on the ground with a broken jaw and missing his front teeth. Silver, was standing in the background, still enraged over the smell of blood.

"Are you all right darlin'," Brannon was quick to ask Lynn.

"They never hurt us bad," Lynn replied, still sobbing as if her heart would break, "you got here just in time my husband."

It was then another group of riders arrived at the scene in a cloud of dust. Matt pointed the women toward the cabin, as he quickly threw some new cartridges into the Peacemaker and said to his wife, "Lynn darlin', take Lame Deer inside...we've got us some more trouble a showin' up!"

"What's going on here?" one of them roared, walking his horse ahead of the rest, "Looks like you've shot the hell outta my riders! I'm the ramrod of this outfit, riding for Three Peaks, a ranch south of here a ways. We're hunting strays, found this bunch on the meadow here, gonna take them back to the ranch."

"You're a rustling liar," Brannon replied, advancing steadily towards the spokesman, "a thieving bunch o' skunks. There's nothing south of here but mountains and Blackfoot Indians. These longhorns belong here, branded with the BL iron, savvy?"

Brannon sensed the gunplay wasn't over with yet, he could feel it in his bones. The owl hoots appeared enraged, yet one of them remained cool, a gloved hand hovering near his holstered pistol. The Texan never hesitated, continuing his advance toward the outlaws, his attention now on the quiet one—a swarthy looking half-breed of questionable origin. Brannon surmised that this one was different from the rest, a gun fighter if he ever saw one, the most deadly of them all.

"You're riding with a bunch of cowards," Brannon told those that could still listen, "I found these here owl hoots a roughin' up my women folk...had to read'em from the good book—teach'em some manners!"

Lynn was lurking near the cabin door, her little rifle loaded and ready for action. "I've got the rest covered Matt," she murmured, although she knew that he could not hear her. "Be careful my husband, please don't get yourself killed."

The half-breed was fast and mean, snarling as he drew on the big Texas cowboy. Brannon had issued the challenge and now had to face up to it, gun to gun. His gun hand was hovering, and then it was not. The Peacemaker was true to its maker, the half-breed collapsed in the dust, a run-down boot heel kicking a last farewell to his outlaw ways.

Brannon's gun swung on the outlaw leader, he roared again, "Now pick up the dead ones and vamoose. The first one who tries for the longhorns gets a taste o' this here .44-40."

It was only then that he noticed his brave Lynn. She had been covering him from behind, her trusty little carbine never wavering. A lump came to his throat, a tear to his eye. He strode to where she stood—an ashen-faced, beautiful, expectant lady. Who had faced down the intruders threatening the ranch.

Matt took Lynn in his arms and together they watched the remnants of the Three Peaks gang leave the valley. The border outlaws had been beaten by the skill of a Texas gun-fighter, his sharp-shooting wife, and an old brindle steer known as Silver.

Brannon took Lynn inside the cabin, gave her some coffee and tucked her into bed. She was exhausted and suffering from shock, the mauling from the outlaw had almost done her in. "Never leave me again Matt," Lynn pleaded, "I do not think I can handle any more of this fighting." With tears in her eyes she took her husband's hand and said, "I can feel it in my heart, right here Matt," and placed his hand upon her breast. "Another fight will do us in, me and the little baby whom is so close to being with us."

Moving his hand, she moved it over the plumpness of her belly where the baby lay. "Do you feel the baby kicking Matt?" asked Lynn, "it is upset as well, wanting to be with its Mom and Dad—wanting to be born."

Brannon was deeply moved. He had never thought of it this way before. He promised himself that he would never leave her again; he would always be close by. The big cowboy comforted his wife as best he could. She finally settled down, with her husband's arms holding her close, she knew that Matt Brannon was all the medicine she needed. Her eyes closed, sleep overcame her.

* * * Chapter 11 * * *

Brannon knew he had one chore left undone, the long ride to Fort Macleod to legalize their land claim and brand; however he was hesitant to leave his expectant Lynn. He hoped the matter could wait until after the baby came. He remembered his promise to Lynn and knew that he had no other choice.

Two weeks had passed since the gunfight with the border outlaws. Lynn was feeling much better now, not once had she mentioned the terrifying experience that had been forced upon her. The big cowboy was true to his word, never strayed far from the ranch, was always close by in case that she needed him.

One morning he was tending the saddle stock when he noticed a uniformed rider trotting up the river trail. "It's that blasted Englishman again," he muttered to himself, struggling not to curse. "Wonder what the Red Coat's up to this time?"

"Ho, the corrals," the Corporal shouted. "I was riding by and decided to check on you Yanks."

Brannon knew why he was here, and once again suppressed an urge to curse. He greeted the rider rather coolly, never invited him in for coffee and doughnuts as before. He left the corral to meet the Red Coat, whose sweat-caked horse was reeling from fatigue, blood dripping from the goading of the lawman's military spurs. The thoroughbred was jigging on the spot, pawing the ground, defenceless against the Englishman's cruelty. "Settle that hoss of yourn down," Brannon warned, "So's ya can hear what I've got to say." Brannon spoke, "Appears you're a checkin' on me...I rode down river the next day after ya were here before. The longhorns and my family are now registered, just as ya asked."

"Yes, I know!" the Englishman replied. "I checked it out this very morning. I am here about the rest, your land holdings and the brand. Tardiness will not be tolerated you kno-ow!"

"So that's what you're up to," Brannon drawled, "I never figured ya for one to come a visitin', might rub against your grain."

By now the Red Coat was red in the face and shouted, "I do not pay social calls on Yankee squatters, you kno-ow. I am in the service of Her Majesty the Qu-ueen!"

Brannon's temper was ready to erupt; he struggled to hold himself in check. Yet, he couldn't help it he reckoned. It was his way when facing an impudent rascal like Stokes. A steely edge came to the cowboy's voice, one that was not that hard to detect. Brannon talked, the Englishman listened.

"I'll tell ya this just once, you cocky fool…crawl off that hoss yer abusin' and I'll give ya a taste of Yankee welcome!"

Not mincing words, Brannon told him that Lynn's baby was due any day, that he couldn't leave her in her present condition, and that he would not ride to the Fort until after the baby was born. "Until then ya arrogant fool—there's the trail. Get outta here while yer still in one piece!"

"No Yankee exile can talk to me like that," Stokes screeched, "I am the law here you know! I'll give you three days to be at the Fort, otherwise you Yankee outcasts will be charged with squatting on Crown land…your brand will become null and void."

Brannon grabbed hold of the bridle of the frenzied horse, was set to drag the Englishman from the saddle when a biting slash from the Red Coat's quirt struck him across the cheek. Stokes then rammed his spurs into the staggering animal and went streaking down the river trail, a trill of laughter hanging in the river breeze.

The blow staggered the big Texan; he shook his head and sensed the blood dripping from his face. By instinct, and with a curse, he drew the Peacemaker and was set to down the Englishman when a scream stopped him from pulling the trigger.

"No! No, don't do it Matt Brannon!" Lynn screamed from behind him.

Lynn and Lame Deer had been watching the confrontation. She called to her husband once more, "Please don't shoot him Matt. He is not worth destroying our new life in Canada."

With that said, Lynn and the Nez Perce girl returned to the cabin. Lynn gave a sigh and was thankful she had stopped her husband in time. Brannon stayed away from the cabin the rest of the day. He was upset and mad, damn mad. What could he tell Lynn? How could he leave her at a time like this? Especially after his promise to himself that he would never leave her alone again. He couldn't take her along in the wagon, he reckoned. The baby was due any day now; the roughness of the ride might kill them both. "Hell's fire, what should I do?" murmured the big Texan cowboy.

This land, this ranch in the Territories, is why they were here, what they were seeking. It would be 640 acres of deeded land—homestead and pre-empted—with hundreds of acres of Crown land available for lease; all of this in a package that would belong to them but for the signing of legal papers in Fort Macleod.

It was nearing sundown before Brannon returned to the cabin. Lynn and Sara had prepared a fine supper, even fried a fresh batch of doughnuts. Lynn was teaching the girl the finer points of cooking on a stove, and she was learning well. Lynn's cheeks were as crimson as a prairie rose, flushed from the warmth generated by her cook stove, otherwise she was feeling fine. She greeted her husband with a warm smile and said, "It's about time you showed up Matt Brannon. I figured my husband must have ridden away and left us!"

Brannon scrubbed the blood from his face and seated himself at the table. He was uncomfortable, just could not settle down and enjoy the meal. Matt hesitated to look at Lynn, eye to eye, as was his custom. She could sense something was wrong, she felt his strangeness and could see the ugly slash across his cheek.

"Oh Matt, your face—I did not know, I am so sorry. "What is wrong my husband?" asked Lynn, "It is something I should know about, isn't it?"

Brannon was at a loss how to tell her, and then with a covert groan of anguish he began to talk. Lynn listened to what he told her, she listened well, and didn't appear upset.

Her mind was in turmoil; she was struggling to control her emotions and did not want her husband to think that she was afraid. She realized the urgency of the legal matters, that in her condition she could not ride Evening Star the 50 miles to the Fort. Bouncing across the prairie in the freight wagon would be even worse.

Yet, deep inside her soul, she somehow knew that a crisis was entering their lives. That life as they knew it would never again be the same.

Although it was hard to do, she forced a smile before she spoke, "Do as the lawman asks Matt. Ride to the Fort; let us put this land matter behind us once and for all. Leave in the morning, I will be fine. Lame Deer is with me and I'm not afraid."

The next morning at first light, the horse saddled and ready for the trail, Brannon entered the cabin for a last cup of coffee. Lynn was clinging to her husband trying to be brave. Deep inside herself, hidden from her husband, her soul was shattered as it wept bitter tears. "I cannot bear to have you leave me.

Please hurry back…I need you so much!" she finally told him through clenched teeth.

"Dog-gone it all, this is a tough decision for me too," he said, comforting her in the best way he knew how. "Time's a runnin' out the Red Coat told us. I reckon I should go and get this blasted chore over and done with," Matt said.

He gave his Powder River girl a final kiss, a long passionate one, which left Lynn shaking like an aspen leaf. Then with a hug for Lame Deer, swung in the saddle and headed up the trail. "Bye Lynn Brannon, bye Lame Deer. I love ya both; take care of Lynn for me, Sara Lame Deer!"

Lynn took several steps after her departing husband. "Matt!" she screamed, "Matt darling wait up!"

The cowboy reined in the dun horse and turned once more to his sobbing wife. She moved a few steps closer, the Nez Perce girl right beside her. "I love you Matt Brannon, come back to me…you hear?" she called.

"Adios, my beautiful Lynn," he replied.

After climbing the long grass-ridge north of the home ranch, he paused on top to give the horses a blow. Brannon was leading a packhorse to haul back supplies. Turning in the saddle for a last look, he doffed his Stetson and waved it to Lynn who was standing far below.

Lynn was watching her husband. She took the red serape from her shoulders and waved it in return, long after he had ridden out of sight she waved the beloved serape. An intense chill rippled down her spine as the rebel yell of her Texas cowboy echoed down from the ridge top.

Travelling north, Brannon crossed through Blood Indian country, then on to Fort Macleod situated along the banks of the Old Man River. This was the first North West Mounted Police fort in the Territories, erected in 1874. The modest frontier town, the Fort's namesake, was the seat of government in this far western region.

From the Brannon ranch to the river that ran by the Fort was a fifty-mile ride. Brannon made it in a day and half of the next. He accomplished most of his business before nightfall, even found Lynn a diamond ring. It was apparent the land papers needed the signature of a federal land commissioner, who was somewhere between Fort Calgary and Fort Macleod, riding south on a stage. This meant a delay of at least a day, maybe two. Brannon was visibly upset over the delay, driven by an over-powering urge to return to the St. Mary's River and Lynn Brannon.

The shadows of night were heavy upon the Old Man River country. Randomly situated along the wheel-rutted trailhead, the business houses of the Fort town were stirring with activity, preparing for the lucrative trade of the night. The twinkling of kerosene lamps drew them to the doors that swing both ways, the melancholy strains of a fiddle and the revelry from inside was an added incentive.

Matt Brannon was hungry and entered a log structure that boasted 'Whiskey, Dancing and Eats'. He reckoned that a meal and some hot coffee might settle him down, help ease the tension that had been his for so long.

Saloons served the same purpose wherever they might be located, in Miles Town or here in the Northern Territories, they all were the same. A saloon was a meeting place, a club, a place where business deals were made and a handy location for neighbour to meet neighbour for a friendly drink and exchange information. The saloons were always outfitted with poker tables and a roulette wheel, or two, for those so inclined. The old trail saloon was alive with the humanity of the plains. Filling the room were off-duty Red Coats, a few ranchers and cowboys, the odd fur trapper, and drifting half-breeds. Wandering through the crowd were girls offering their wares to the takers of which there were plenty. As far as Brannon was concerned, the denizens of this crossroads of the West were all here and accounted for.

The St. Mary's River rancher was sitting alone, a pot of steaming coffee on the table, minding his own business when his attention was drawn to a nearby table. Playing draw poker were a pair of Métis hide hunters, a young rancher, and one other, who by his fancy duds appeared to be in the gambling profession.

By his talk the rancher was an Englishman, just in from his ranch in the Porcupine Hills for a night on the town. He was protesting the gambler's questionable way of playing the cards.

"By Jove, old boy," He exclaimed, "you appear to be as crooked as a Zimbabwe snake! Are you pulling a fau-ust one on us? Show your cards, you bloody rotter!"

The gambler's face grew as red as the fancy tie he wore. The rancher's hand revealed a full house, Queens and Jacks. "The good Queen and her Knaves hau-uve you beat you know," the Englishman added, forcing the issue.

Snarling an oath, the card-slick flipped a derringer from his sleeve and shot the young cockney in the shoulder. Not content with wounding the fellow, the enraged gambler cocked the remaining action of the little .32 calibre double-action and aimed at his victim's heart.

Brannon was gritting his teeth, struggling to remain neutral, determined to stay out of the drama that was unfolding before his eyes. "Damn my luck," he muttered.

This wasn't his fight; he was determined not to interfere. Yet, it seemed no one cared, even the off-duty Red Coats standing by the bar were unconcerned over the plight of the young rancher. But the big Texan could not stand for the unfairness of it all. This was something beyond his control, it was the cowboy way.

The harsh sound of a chair sliding on the rough-hewn plank floor distracted the murderous intent of the gambler, his insatiable urge to kill diverted for the moment. Brannon was now standing, the big Peacemaker in hand. He pulled the trigger and was content to watch the results.

The numbing shock of a .44-40 slug smacked into the slick's gun hand, the red-hot lead diverted by the little gun ricocheted into the man's rib cage and he tumbled to the floor howling in pain.

The Porcupine rancher turned to face the big cowboy. He was unsteady on his feet, his face was ashen, the realization that he had been shot was sinking in. Several bystanders, one of them Kootenai Brown, assisted him to a chair. Kootenai grinned at Brannon and winked.

Still eyeing the cowboy who had saved his life, the rancher spoke, "Thank you, old chap. It was jolly decent of you to step in like you did."

"I'll be damned, what next?" Brannon muttered as he eyed three uniformed members of the North West Mounted Police who had just entered the saloon—one of them was Corporal Stokes. Though there were a room full of witnesses, including several off-duty Red Coats, Stokes insisted on arresting the cowboy for attempted murder.

"You bloody Yanks must obey the laws of Her Majesty the Queen," he bawled.

Brannon felt boxed in. His options were to fight or to follow Stokes like a lamb to the slaughter. He had decided on the former until Kootenai Brown spoke, "Just hold your horses Corporal! My friend here has just saved your brother's life. He needs a medal pinned on his shirt, not a lock-up as you suggest."

Pointing to the howling tinhorn, who no one had given the time of day, Kootenai Brown continued to press his advantage. "This card playing crony of yours has been in and out of trouble ever since he arrived at the Fort, as you are aware of. He has shot several unfortunate chaps and got away with it, thanks to your influence and the bilge water you offered as testimony."

"The strange gambling blighter, as your brother aptly quoted, is as crooked as a Zimbabwe reptile!"

The plainsman from the Kutenai Lakes had the Red Coat where he wanted him and wasn't about to slacken the pressure. "As you know, you young blighter," Kootenai's words sliced with an edge of steel, "The half-breed, Potts and I, are the Colonels chief scouts on the eastern plains. We scout the land from Fort Macleod to the hills that are known as Cypress and on to Métis country. I will take charge of the cowboy, and post his bail—if any. He has a big rau-unch to run you know."

Stokes was not used to being spoken to this way and it made his blood boil. His face turned bright red and the veins in his neck and temples pulsated as though he was suffering from apoplexy. His mind was numb as he listened to the murmurs of agreement growing stronger throughout the crowded saloon. He knew Brown was highly favoured by the Colonel, and hated him for it. Colonel Sam Steele valued Kootenai's advice and expertise, whether they were on the trail or at the Fort.

Stokes was now boxed in and he was frantic to find a way out. He searched the cowboy's eyes, eyes that were cool and collected, yet cold and deadly. The Englishman's ego-inflated mind whispered of feral danger and urged him to back off. He knew the Yank would use his gun again, and this time he would be the one to feel the sting!

Gaining confidence from the Corporal's hesitation, Kootenai spoke again, "Colonel Steele's scout to the gold diggings at Stud Horse Creek has been successful, and word is he'll return in a fortnight. Until then Matt Brannon will be my responsibility. I want you to leave him be, before you young chaps get yourselves shot to pieces. There will be no other fodder for the buzzards on my watch."

With that said, Kootenai took Brannon's arm and guided him from the smoke-filled room; the impending shoot-out was now a Mexican stand-off. Dressed in buckskins from head to foot, a huge bear of a man met them near the door. He was Fred Kanouse, Kootenai's drinking companion whenever he was laid over at the Fort.

"Cover our backs old chap," Kootenai said, "we are going to the cabin for a medicine talk."

The three of them entered the darkness of a back street shack. Kanouse was groping for a match to light an oil-burning hurricane lamp that was hanging near the door. "Hurry old chap," Kootenai urged, "before the young blighter changes his mind. These remittance blokes are as unpredictable as sin. Stokes might come a gunning for us yet!"

The burly Rocky Mountain trapper, Kanouse, went to fetch Brannon's horses and gear, which were corralled on the far side of town near the Old Man River. While he was gone, Kootenai and his cowboy friend shared a pot of coffee laced with river whiskey. The whiskey loosened their tongues and they began to talk.

Brannon received a brief run down on remittance men. They were male offspring of wealthy British families who, to get them out of their hair, so to speak, sent them to preferably a British Colony. Here they were to live out their lives sustained by financial remittance from home.

Stokes and his brother were remittance men from Britain, sent to the North West Territories. A ranch had been purchased for them in the Porcupine Hills and, presumably they were to make their fortunes and live out the rest of their lives here. Most remittance men were honest God-fearing chaps, as Kootenai described them, but there were a few who were not.

Stokes had many vices and was prone to nipping at the bottle, wasting time at the card table, and indulging himself in the favours of the half-breed girls along the river. He soon caroused away his share of the ranch. Even with a known reputation the Englishman was accepted into the North West Mounted Police as a non-commissioned officer. "No doubt political influence from the homeland," Kootenai remarked, "Stokes hates his brother, you see, who now has full possession of the rau-unch. The demented fool is a constant drinking crony of the gambler, the one you tangled with Matt Brannon. Kootenai continued with his story, "The spiteful devil will never forgive you for saving his brother's life you know!"

"Stokes has been a burr under my saddle blanket for some time now." Brannon told the old Scout. He went on to tell him of the harassment he and Lynn had endured from Stokes and the urgency that he felt to return to his expectant wife, who he should be with at this very moment. "By Jove," the old plainsman bristled, "the blighter needs to be caned and banished to the outback. My sympathy is extended to you and your charming maker of doughnuts, give her my best regards. The arrogant bloke will be reported to Colonel Steele, I'll see to that." Kootenai concluded.

The night was near spent before Kanouse arrived with Brannon's outfit. The corral had been under close surveillance by Stokes' men. Kanouse was able to use the wiles of his profession as a Rocky Mountain trapper to outwit the Red Coats under Stokes command. "The hostler was sure dry," Kanouse grinned, "the glutton drank a bottle o' me best grog before he keeled over."

Gripping Kootenai's hand, Brannon thanked him, secured his possessions and swung aboard his dun horse. As the fort faded away into the darkness he could hear the voice of Fred Kanouse loud and clear saying, "The bloody trooper was a haw-wg. I reckoned the blighter would never pass out. "Let's get outta here Kootenai, afore we get our necks in a sling."

The St. Mary's River rancher rode hard and fast, stopping only to give the horses a chance to catch their winds. Into the dark shadows he rode, south across the rolling plains, past the sand hills along the Big Belly Buttes. He was able to avoid a brief skirmish with Blood warriors at the Belly River. The warriors watched in awe as he vanished into the south. Crazy man they gestured, pointing to one of their fiercest warriors sagging on his pony, a bullet hole through the brave's shooting hand.

As day light approached, still he rode like the wind. The sun was swinging into the west as he arrived at Lariat Cross Creek, where it forked with the St. Mary's River. Brannon stopped for an hour's rest; the horses were spent and needed the break. He built a small fire and heated a bit of coffee. Rest wasn't easy for the cowboy to find, his mind was in turmoil, concerning the welfare of Lynn.

Matt had completed his chore of the land claim and was secure in the knowledge that the ranch now officially belonged to him. The obstacles he had conquered were behind him and his family and ranch waited ahead.

* * * Chapter 12 * * *

Matt Brannon knew the Red Coats would be after him, that he would have to answer to them sooner or later, but he just didn't give a damn anymore. His one and only purpose in living at this time was riding home to Lynn and to the possibility of a new baby.

With the ranch just ten-miles up river, he could see Old Chief Mountain, the massive silhouette showing through the southwest hills. Yet, somehow, the mountain appeared different today. Ominous storm clouds were attacking the Chief, intermittently concealing it from view. At times the mountain could be seen above the invading clouds only to submit to their onslaught again, and again.

The cowboy was struggling to hold himself in check, sober faced and worried sick over his Lynn he galloped onward. Strange emotions were tugging at his soul; emotions that whispered of fear and dread. Was it the mountain talking to him?

It was as if a message borne on the wind emanated down across the hills from Old Chief Mountain. It sent a message the cowboy was unable to grasp.

The horses were ready to drop, and so was Brannon before he reached the ridge-top high above the home ranch. A chilling yell, the wild rebel yell of a Texas cowboy boomed down from the ridge-top to alert Lynn Brannon of his arrival home.

The strange sensation returned and overcame the cowboy. Long hair prickled on the back of his neck warning him that something was wrong! For a brief instant, just an instant mind you; Brannon heard Lynn's voice speaking to him. It was faint, and far away, a sorrowful cry from far off in the southern sky.

"I love you, Matt Brannon...come back to me...you hear?"

* * *

Lynn Brannon watched her husband ride away, then turned and entered the cabin. She was devastated and felt as if her heart would break, she feared she would never see him again. Lynn remained in her blankets throughout the long day, not even Lame Deer could console her. The Nez Perce maiden brought her beef broth and coffee. She spoon-fed Lynn, like Lynn had done for her back at the Milk River when they had found her.

The third day after her husband's departure she began feeling like herself again. She knew Matt should be home soon, he had told her that he would be gone for five days at the latest.

Lame Deer was out at the corrals fussing with her Appaloosa. The little horse from the Bear Paw was now healed from its wounds; however, both Lame Deer and the pony would bear the scars of the Massacre for the rest of their days. Lame Deer was now a teenager, rather comely and maturing rapidly. She spoke fluent English when she wanted to. She had been taught the white man's talk back at the mission school in the Southern Territories, but due to her shyness was reluctant to speak it with strangers.

Lynn was feeling like her happy old self, the haunts of her depression cast aside. She was singing as she prepared supper, and as she walked to the door to call Lame Deer in for the meal. The weight of the baby she was carrying was causing spasms in her hips. As she neared the door, Lynn stopped for a moment. She sensed someone outside the door. She heard a faint knock and her heart soared, Matt must have returned from the Fort.

She swung open the door and there stood Billy Marshall. He looked in terrible condition; his clothes were blood-stained and torn. A strange, frightened look was upon his face as he stepped inside and collapsed in a chair. He was supporting his arm, a broken arrow shaft embedded in the flesh.

Billy was soaking wet from wading across the river. He appeared to be in a daze as he spoke, "I never made it Ma-am! A bunch of Indians jumped me again, strange looking devils they were! Them murderin' devils are not far behind...seems like they bin a chasin' me forever—!" Billy uttered a groan and shifted in the chair when he spoke again, "The devils shot my horse and'et it. I seen'em do it...they wouldn't let me be."

Lynn gasped as she listened, then poured coffee for the boy and set a bowl of stew in front of him. He dug right in like he was starved, gorging the food to start with, not taking the time to chew before he swallowed. Lynn moved the bowl away and gently chided, "Don't eat that way Billy, you need to take your time! You'll make yourself much worse gorging yourself like you're doing."

In a way she was glad Billy was here, he gave her something to think about besides her own worries. She would be all right now she reckoned. Lynn put water on the stove to heat; she had to clean Billy up and remove the dreadful arrow from his arm. She remembered the way Matt had taken the last arrow out of Billy. She knew she had to give it a try. Pushing the stew back in front of the starving boy, Lynn moved towards the door to call Lame Deer in to help her take the arrow out.

As she opened the door a terrible noise and confusion greeted her. Lynn was met by the screaming of Lame Deer, lunging horses, whoops and savage yells. As Lynn took in the scene of mayhem she could hear the Nez Perce girl shrieking her name, "Ly-nn! Ly-nn! Ly-nn!"

Slowed by the weight of the baby inside her, Lynn was out of breath as she picked up her little rifle. She gasped as she realized the trusty Yellow Boy was not loaded. Matt would be cross with her she reckoned. He had given her strict orders to never leave her gun without cartridges in it. She now realized the wisdom of his words; she was so sorry and hoped her husband would understand.

She punched a cartridge into the gun, cranked the lever action and swung wide the door. Lynn was terrified but forced herself to be brave. The words of her husband took control of her mind. "Lynn darlin', it's just like pointin' your finger, much simpler than you might think."

"I must be brave," she whispered, "I must be brave for my husband and do as he has taught me."

She could see Lame Deer scrapping with a mounted warrior, who was attempting to lift her on to his horse. She was kicking and screaming, waving the little knife Brannon had given her for Christmas. Blood was streaming from a slash across her captors' evil jowls. He was treating her badly, slapping and mauling her in a feral manner. Old Silver, bellowing loudly, came charging from the far side of the corrals in the young girls' defence. The longhorn swung its head and the little horse was knocked to its knees dislodging the warrior from his mount and freeing Lame Deer. With a twist of its neck the other horn impaled the appaloosa. The little horse screeched in the agony of its death throes as the Indian warriors put arrow after arrow into the big long horned beast.

Lame Deer picked herself up and ran towards Lynn, all the while shrieking and jabbering in her native language. The Indian warriors quickly gave chase. Lynn Brannon swung the little rifle to her hip and pulled the trigger. The warrior in the lead was almost upon Lame Deer when he tumbled to the ground, a .38 bullet driven deep in to his paint-smeared chest.

Lynn was desperately trying to put another cartridge in her little rifle when the butt end of a war lance struck her alongside the head. She collapsed by the open door as a pulsating darkness swept over her, her lips were moving, "Matt—where are you Matt?"

The combination of Lynn's hot stew and the warmth of the cabin was a strong inducement for Billy Marshall to become drowsy. He was struggling to keep himself awake when the sharp bark of Lynn's rifle penetrated his fever-wracked mind. He arose from the chair and staggered towards the door. His six-gun was in his hand as he watched Lynn Brannon go down. The raiding warriors were close, screeching and howling near the open door where Lynn lay. The young cowboy was able to shoot one intruder before he too went down, a war spear driven deep in his chest.

Billy Marshall died where he lay next to an unconscious Lynn Brannon.

The big Texan was frightened of what he might find below; a sense of emptiness engulfed his soul. Harsh words and cursing filled his mind as he urged his weary outfit down into the valley. From this distance the ranch appeared deserted.

As Matt Brannon neared the cabin a frightening scene greeted him and an intense shudder convulsed through his body. The door to the cabin was hanging from only one of its leather hinges, the slab-hewn shutters were torn off leaving the windows gaping open. Their family possessions were strewn about the yard.

Matt saw the carcass of a ragged appaloosa pony laying about twenty yards out from the cabin. Its body displaying lethal gore wounds which were a stark testimony to the violence which had taken place at the ranch. Moaning in agony, old Silver lay close by the pony carcass, his shaggy hide riddled with arrows. One of the arrows was driven deep into his rib cage. Silver's long horns were stained with dry gore, and fresh blood was seeping from his nose and mouth.

Brannon leaped from the saddle and raced to find his wife. "Lynn! Lynn darlin'!" he roared, "Are ya here?

Bursting inside the trashed cabin, a pack rat scurried out of his way. He found his log home to be empty and in a shambles. Once again he felt the strangeness, as if he were in another time, another place. The big rancher, once a Texas gun fighter having been invincible to any and all, was now shaking, frightened and alone.

One more time on the breath of the wind he was sure that he heard a faint cry from off in the southern sky. "I love you Matt Brannon, come back to me...you hear?"

3

33333333

Leaving the cabin, a long anguished wail erupted from his tortured soul, one that could be heard from the river-bottom brush to the tops of the wind blown hills.

"Lyy-nnn!"

Matt walked over to old Silver and using a bullet from the Peacemaker, he put an end to the longhorn's suffering. Brannon spoke to the trusted pet, "Reckon you gave your life," he said, "defending a gentle friend. Sorry I was late a getting' here Silver...I'm so sorry!"

Long after the sun had vanished behind the Deerhorn Hills, another terrible gut-wrenching roar echoed throughout the lonely basin. It was a chilling sound, the wild yell of Matt Brannon, the Texas gun fighter.

The renegade savages that attacked the Brannon ranch were members of the Nez Perce tribe, the leavings of Chief White Bird's bunch who had fled the Bear Paw battlefield in an attempt to reach Canada. They sought safety from the relentless pursuit of the U.S. Bluecoats.

It was north of the Milk River that the Nez Perce had been scattered by a band of hostile Assiniboine, who had chased them far to the east. There, on the open plains to the east, the Nez Perce had encountered Matt and Lynn Brannon's outfit and her doughnuts. During this first encounter, Brannon had shot one of the Nez Perce Indians. The wounded one that had been riding double that day was killed by Lynn in an attempt to attack her with a knife at the Milk River camp. Lynn had shot another at the Brannon's cabin door at the ranch on the St Mary's River and Billy Marshall had killed one before he fell. These killings had pared the Indians' numbers down to four; the old chief and three warriors.

It was chance, possibly fate that had brought them to the Brannon ranch that day. Not fully aware of Chief Joseph's lot, the small band was wandering the border country, foraging and stealing to survive. Buffalo were scarce on the northern plains, game of any kind was sparse, and the Nez Perce were starving; striking at anything or anybody they happened to meet.

After several one-sided encounters with the Blackfeet, old White Bird was ready to vamoose from this country. Their encounter with Billy Marshall and his subsequent flight to the St. Mary's River led them to the Brannon Ranch. They were on the prowl for provisions enough to last them on the long journey back to Lapwai in Idaho a place where they could settle.

After killing Billy Marshall and subduing Lynn and Lame Deer, the remaining Nez Perce pillaged the Brannon cabin. Anything of value was heaped in a pile and a longhorn was butchered to be used as food on the trail. They used one of the ranch teams, which were easy to handle, and packed the booty securely for the long trip ahead.

Little Elk, one of the remaining four Indians, was a teenaged warrior wise in the ways of battle. He listened with interest to Lame Deer's outbursts in her native language, and championed her from their first meeting. When he discovered she was the daughter of Chief Joseph, whom he had admired since he was a small boy, Little Elk protected her from the advances of the other warriors. He protected Lynn Brannon as well, because he sensed that Lame Deer loved and adored her. During the frenzy of the Nez Perce looting and destruction of the Brannon Ranch, Little Elk obtained Lynn's little Yellowbird rifle. He had also found a stash of cartridges in the cabin.

As Lynn had lain unconscious on the doorstep of her log cabin home, Lame Deer had covered her with a blanket, comforted her and never left her side. Cowering in fear, she watched as the old Chief rode near to them. Quickly she covered the body of her dear friend with that of her own. "White squaw must die...killed Nez Perce warrior," she heard him say. His war spear was held high. "Big in belly—no good to take!"

Before he could release his lethal blow, a shot rang out; a bullet from Lynn Brannon's Yellowbird rifle clipped a portion from one of the chief's hairy ears. Little Elk had fired the shot.

Chief White Bird gave a terrible shriek, swung his plunging horse around and faced Little Elk. With the smoking rifle still in his hand he signed for the Chief to stay back. Little Elk made it plain that the two women were in his possession. Chief White Bird knew that Little Elk was holding the winning hand; he was the only one with bullets and a gun.

The Chief calmed down, his killing rage thwarted for now. A decision was made to take Lame Deer and the white squaw with them to Idaho. Lame Deer and her new friend Little Elk rigged a travois. It would be pulled by one of Brannon's saddle mares. One of the saddle mares had a suckling colt that never left its' mother's side.

Using Lynn's trade blankets, that her father had given her as a wedding present back at Miles Town, the Indian maiden fashioned a snug bed on the travois. Little Elk gently moved Lynn Brannon on to the travelling bed and the caravan left the scene of carnage and headed up river.

In the St. Mary's River country along the Deerhorn Hills, the Brannon ranch lay in a piteous state of ruin. Brannon could read the sign and was enraged at what he discovered. It was all too plain to the big cowboy that Lynn had fallen near the open door. The threads from her red shawl were snagged by the rough-hewn boards of the cabin floor, and blood was spattered on the door frame.

Brannon found an empty .38 shell casing from Lynn's rifle and saw many hoof prints in the dust indicating that a wild fracas had taken place. Behind the cabin he found Billy Marshall's body, scalped and stripped naked. There were the remains of a butchered longhorn and it appeared the cattle had been driven across the river and had been scattered into the emptiness of the plains.

And then there was the carcass of old Silver, Lynn's pet longhorn. The same steer, along with his partner, Dollar, had been in the lead, pointing the herd up the long dusty miles from Texas. He cursed as he stood there looking at the remains of the big steer and wondered where old Dollar had wound up at. It was all here, the sign was as plain as reading a chapter in a book.

Out behind the corrals was his next stop, the cache he had left earlier would now be put to use. The cache contained a six-gun, some jerky and a bag of gold coins, these items would be a most welcome addition to his scanty possessions.

As the shadows thickened along the river he could not find his darlin' Lynn. The signs told him that she had put up a valiant fight and had been overpowered by the hostiles. A frightening feeling left him thinking she hadn't survived the fight. Where was she? Where could she be? Had the murderin' devils taken her away? Though he could not find her body he had a strange feeling that she had been killed defending their home.

Brannon built a small fire near the river and he spent the long night grieving, sobbing and cursing. He blamed himself for breaking his promise to Lynn and for not being at home when she needed him. Lynn had begged him not to leave her, had done everything but get on her knees. Brannon had not heeded her simple pleas; he had crawled on his bronc and rode away. Somehow, no matter how hard he tried not to, his rage became centred on the North West Mounted Police and the arrogant Corporal Stokes.

At first light he returned to the cabin, gathered up the litter, tossed it into the cabin and set the whole place ablaze. Securing his few possessions on the packhorse, and without a backward glance, he reined his dun stallion, Buck, up river. He was on a scout to find the sign that would lead him to Lynn.

Brannon found travois tracks. They were simple to follow, yet, they puzzled him. He wondered, "What, or who was on the travois?" Continuing south, he neared the 49th parallel and discovered a fresh heap of brush and ground litter that had been disturbed by prairie wolves. Among the brush lay the remains of two dead warriors that had been shot. Cursing bitterly he set the brush and bodies ablaze and continued on his scouting expedition.

The sign was possibly a day old but Matt Brannon would not give up. In the rocky soil near the mountains the trace became scarce. It would take most of a day, sometimes longer, before he could locate a nicked rock, a bruised twig or a horse dropping, that would enable him to continue the hunt again.

In the rolling country south of the Hudson Bay Divide, he picked up a soil-stained piece of Lynn's red serape. He dropped to the ground; and held the treasured reminder of his wife close to his breast; his grief was almost more than he could bear. He now assumed that Lynn was the one who travelled on the travois.

Tucking the poignant reminder of Lynn in his saddlebag, Brannon continued onward. The trail sign was heading across an isolated portion of Blackfoot country, swinging southwest into the Rockies. He followed the trail into the high country, winding through a lodge pole forest and into the Marias Pass region. It was late spring when he rode high into the pass and he was greeted by a late snowfall. The higher into the pass he rode the deeper the snow became. "It's no matter," he reckoned, "I must find my darlin' Lynn."

Two long, gruelling days had passed and the Nez Perce caravan was now high in the Marias Pass country along the Continental Divide. Lynn Brannon began to stir from the deep sleep brought on by the vicious blow she had received. Her head was pounding something fierce, she was sick and in pain. The blow to her head had fractured her skull.

As she stirred the throes of childbirth began in earnest. An ancient instinct known only to expectant mothers, one that dated back to Mother Eve was rousing Lynn Brannon from her deadly sleep. It was time for the birth of her baby.

Lapsing in and out of consciousness, pitiful screams escaped her fever-cracked lips. "Are you here Matt?" she murmured, "I'm hurtin' bad...hold my hand darlin' Matt."

Lame Deer was never far from her beloved friend. When she discovered Lynn was awake, she held her hand and insisted that Little Elk stop the travois. With the assistance of Lame Deer and Little Elk, Matt Brannon's Powder River girl gave birth to her baby. Heavy snow began to fall as the new babe entered the world. It appeared to be healthy and strong. The Nez Perce maiden had performed an excellent job as midwife, invoking a God-given talent that she had been blessed with.

The plucky little Indian maiden, the same one who had escaped the Bear Paw battlefield wounded and struggling for her life, cleansed Lynn Brannon's baby by rubbing it with a piece of blanket. She then swathed the baby in another piece of blanket, and smiled with pride as she noticed it was a little auburn-haired girl. She tucked the baby in the blankets beside Lynn on the travois. Lame Deer coaxed and soothed her beloved friend. The terrified cries of the baby finally penetrated Lynn's clouded mind. She could hear Lame Deer talking to her, "Take your new baby, Lynn. It is here with us now! Little Lynn...all right! Feed her! Little Lynn hungry...need suck!"

With the assistance of Lame Deer the new baby, she had named after its mother, was soon suckling at her mother's breast. Though she was deathly ill Lynn roused to look at her baby, smell her scent and snuggle her close. She even managed a wisp of a smile before sinking once more into a merciful sleep.

Lynn Brannon roused one more time to feed her baby. She was coherent for only a short time and begged Lame Deer to care for the child as her own. She gave the Indian girl the bag of gold coins old Ben Riley had given her. These gold coins were her back wages that her dad had saved up and given to her when she and Matt had headed for Canada. The coins had been hidden in a leather pouch that she had sewn into the folds of her dress. Lynn pleaded with Lame Deer to find Matt Brannon and return his daughter to him some day. She wanted Lame Deer to tell him that she loved him and their baby daughter very much.

As her scant talk diminished and her voice became muted, Lame Deer detected a faint whisper from her dying lips, "I love you Matt Brannon, come back to me...you hear?"

Her happy, loving spirit was set free, the pain-wracked body of Lynn Brannon settled into the lifeless void. The void that was too deep for the girl from the Powder River to ever return from.

* * * Chapter 13 * * *

Along the Great Divide of the Rockies, at the area known to the natives as the 'Medicine Line That Divides The Waters', Lynn Brannon's spirit was taken away and the life of her new baby began. Lame Deer reverently wrapped the body of Lynn Brannon in blankets, smoothed the lines of fatigue from her face, and muttered her last goodbye to her dear friend. With the help of Little Elk, she laid Lynn's body to rest in the lee of a spruce thicket.

Large fluffy snow flakes fell on the disturbed soil of the grave site. The late spring storm, so common to these high places, moaned through the forest, perhaps it was an omen of things to come.

Evening Star, Lynn Brannon's beloved saddle mare, would have nothing to do with the Nez Perce warriors. She couldn't stand their scent and would not allow them to touch her. Star had stayed near to the caravan as it moved away from the pillaged ranch on the St. Mary's River, following the travois into the high mountains. One of the Nez Perce braves made numerous attempts to catch her though she craftily eluded each of his efforts. In disgust he gave up and let her be.

The pinto stayed near the travois night and day, close to her unconscious mistress. Star's velvet nose constantly sniffed the mountain breeze. She was puzzled that Lynn never moved from the swaying travois, her voice and enchanting laughter never sounded. Star sensed that something was wrong. She stayed near the travois, laying her ears back and guarding Lynn from the hostiles. Only Lame Deer was allowed to come near.

As the storm worsened, old Chief White Bird became restless and would not wait for the birth of the baby or for the burial of its mother. He and the remaining two Nez Perce warriors loaded most of the supplies onto the horses and continued towards the west. Little Elk was left alone with Lame Deer, the baby, and the mare that had been pulling the travois. Evening Star was always close by but remained just out of reach of human hands.

The storm had maddened, howling and moaning through the high places. Lame Deer cuddled the baby in a blanket to keep it warm; Little Elk gathered the few provisions left behind by the fleeing warriors. They had to continue on and get away from this place of bad spirits.

Out of the storm a large snow-covered apparition appeared. The apparition stopped for a moment, its head showing a set of massive horns, swinging this way and that. Its nose was searching for scent that was so elusive in the raging gale. It then strode to Lynn Brannon's grave and began pawing the snow with huge cloven-hooves. It began to rumble and bellow in rage.

Little Elk was terrified and picked up Lynn's little rifle. He was determined to protect Lame Deer and the baby from this evil spirit. "No! No," screamed Lame Deer, "it is all right. This is the one with long horns that is named the Dollar. Do not kill it Little Elk—this one will be our friend."

Wrapping the blanket tight around the baby, Lame Deer approached Lynn Brannon's old longhorn steer. She was chanting a strange song and clutching her medicine bag. Recognizing her voice, Dollar ceased his fit of rage and swung around to face the Indian girl. "Ho, my big one," she cooed, "smell the scent of this little one...it belongs to your old friend. Lynn will be happy to know you are with us!"

The longhorn, Dollar, shook its mighty head as its spear-shaped horns glistened through the gloom of the storm. A deep rumble came from within its chest. Its nose stretched out and sniffed the bundle that the Indian girl offered. The scent was good; there was much about the smell of the babe that reminded it of Lynn Brannon. Dollar relaxed and followed Lame Deer back to the camp. Dollar, in the company of Evening Star, never strayed far from the baby known as Little Lynn Brannon.

As the storm abated the small caravan moved on. Lame Deer rode Evening Star. Star accepted Lynn's friend as a rider now that the warriors were gone and the baby was with Lame Deer. The baby was wrapped warmly in a blanket and tied to an improvised cradle-board that was secured on the maiden's back. Old Dollar followed closely behind Evening Star. Bringing up the rear was Little Elk, riding the Brannon mare, with the suckling colt tagging along side. The travois had been discarded near Lynn Brannon's grave.

The baby let them know when she was hungry, her vociferous shrieks echoed down the forest trail. Lame Deer would sing and coo to the little one, comforting her as best she could in these extreme conditions.

Little Elk secured the foal with a piece of rope while he stripped the rich mare's milk into a wooden bowl. Lame Deer would then soak a cloth in the nourishing liquid and allow the babe to suckle this elixir of life. Little Lynn was eager to suckle anything that came near her mouth. This nourishment was needed in order for the baby to thrive sufficiently and to survive.

With the baby's hunger satisfied, they continued their journey out of the pass. The shadows of night were thickening through the pine forest before they arrived on the valley floor. It was much warmer at this lower elevation. As they travelled further down the valley, they left the snow behind. The snowbound pass and Lynn Brannon's grave were nothing more than a sad memory.

Little Elk stopped the little caravan in a grove of cedar trees by a cold mountain brook. He knew that the ancient trees would give them protection against any rain or snow that would fall during the night. He went through the chore of obtaining milk from the mare again for little baby Lynn. Lame Deer knew that they were in need of more supplies. The old Chief and his warriors had left them only meager rations when they abandoned them at the summit of the mountain pass.

The Nez Perce Indians primary staple food was fish. They would rarely hunt big game. After they had been pushed out of their homeland, the Nez Perce had been forced to include other foods into their diet in order to survive.

It was midway through the next days travel when Little Elk called to Lame Deer to ride up beside him. As she did, he pointed to the smoke rising up through the Ponderosa pines. The smoke was coming from what appeared to be a trading post further down in this valley of the Flathead.

The Nez Perce usually avoided such places, but Lame Deer and Little Elk knew that they were in dire need of supplies. Lame Deer was aware that the Nez Perce people would not be welcome here. This was the land of the Kalispell, Kutenai, and Flathead tribes. These tribes were not friends of the Nez Perce. Her father, Chief Joseph, had told her that this was the way of the Indian people. You were either a friend or an enemy, there was no middle ground.

The trading post was situated at the crossing of several trails and catered to the needs of the local tribes. Little Elk did not speak any English so Lame Deer had to go into the trading post. She was afraid because she knew the risk, she could get into trouble, be taken captive, or even be killed.

A cry came from the bundle on her back. The hunger of the baby gave her the courage to go inside. Leaving the baby with the young brave, Lame Deer carefully removed a gold coin from the pouch that Lynn Brannon had given her and emerged from the timber walking toward the trading post.

The young Indian maiden bravely stepped through the door and was greeted by an old whiskered trader. He eyed her with interest, and asked her what she was doing there.

Although Lame Deer could speak fluent English, she replied in broken English as if she were struggling to communicate. She placed the gold coin on the counter and told the trader that she needed milk for a baby, salt, flour, bacon, coffee, and a can of hard tack that she noticed on a shelf nearby.

The trader brought the goods, including a case of canned condensed milk. Condensed milk had been used as early as 1861 by the union army in its field rations for its troops. Since that time it had made its way further into the frontier and was found on the shelves of many local trading posts. Crafty and sly at his trade the whiskered trader offered the Indian girl no change from the gold coin.

Loaded down with her purchases, Lame Deer quickly left the old log building and scurried into the timber across the clearing. The trader stood in the doorway holding the gold coin, his mind was churning as he watched Lame Deer disappear into the shadows.

Speaking loudly the old trader summoned a flunky that was in the back room of the trading post sucking on a near-spent bottle of booze. "Follow that there Nez Perce girl, ya hear?" the old timer said. The trader had recognized that Lame Deer was from the Clearwater tribe to the south and west of the Flathead Valley. He continued to speak, saying, "After they bed down, sneak in and bring her back here. Get the baby too!" Still fingering the double eagle he muttered to himself, "Reckon there's more of this here gold where this one came from."

Little Elk was waiting in the thicket for Lame Deer. He realized that he may not see her again; sending an Indian girl alone into a white man's trading post was not a safe thing to do. He had seen what white men did to Indian girls, keeping them from their own people and enslaving them. He had even heard of young girls being bartered or sold amongst the white men.

As these thoughts were running through his mind he came to the realization that he had feelings for Lame Deer. He gently rocked the baby hoping that it wouldn't make too much noise. Old Dollar, the longhorn, lay close by Little Elk eyeing him intently as he cared for the baby. Dollar watched out for the little bundle that smelled so much like Lynn Brannon.

Little Elk was relieved when Lame Deer finally approached the waiting horses. He was glad to see that she had been successful in obtaining the supplies. They quickly strapped the baby onto Lame Deer's back and secured the supplies on the horses so that they could distance themselves from the trading post.

Lame Deer and Little Elk continued to ride to the south and eventually made camp by a large lake known as the Flathead. They made a fire, ate a filling meal, fed the baby and settled in for the night, exhausted from the adventures of their day.

Sleep came easily to the weary travellers. All was quiet when the horses became uneasy at their pickets. Little Elk was awakened instantly. He levered a shell into the Yellow Boy rifle and like a ghost vanished into the Ponderosa pine forest. The young Indian warrior located the intruder and was moving in close when an amazing scene unfolded before his eyes.

As silent as a shadow, the big longhorn, Dollar arrived at the scene. Brutally it attacked the screaming intruder. In mere seconds the unfortunate victim, the flunky from the trading post, was sent to meet his maker. Dollar looked long at the lifeless heap, grumbling and shaking its massive horns, and then it turned and vanished into the shadows.

Little Elk returned to camp and told Lame Deer what he had witnessed. The giant of a steer emerged from the darkened forest. "Look!" exclaimed Lame Deer, "it's Dollar." Blood and gore still dripped from its horns, "he was protecting us, and our Little Lynn!"

With a sigh, the old longhorn lay down in the shadows of the firelight and began to peacefully chew its cud.

Lame Deer, Little Elk, and Little Lynn travelled south and west skirted wide of Fort Missoula, then headed west up the Lolo Trail into the Bitterroot Mountains. Sad memories returned to haunt them in these mountains as they both remembered their Tribe's frantic crossing here. It had been nearly a year since the bluecoats had chased Chief Joseph and his people from their homeland and north toward Canada.

The keen sense of Evening Star gave them warning, and even now, so much later, they were forced to leave the trail and hide in the forest as a boisterous troop of Blue Coats passed by.

When they finally reached their people in the Clearwater River country, they were warmly welcomed back. The two young Nez Perce had grown to love and respect one another and were married. The Brannon baby was adopted by Little Elk and Lame Deer; they would raise her as their own. Lame Deer gave the baby the tribal name of 'Cries in the Night', in memory of her birth in a forest glade high in the Rocky Mountains. This reminded the maiden of her Father's name—"Thunder Rolling in the Mountain".

* * * Chapter 14 * * *

Head hanging low, the weary rider on his rangy dun horse moved steadily into the west. Up a mountain trail he travelled following a faint trace, a trail that remained close to a noisy mountain stream rushing down from a high saddleback on the mountain. Though it was tough to find at times, the sign was there—the travois tracks, even the cloven-hoofed spoor of old Dollar could be seen following along behind.

The big cowboy's conscience wouldn't let him be. His anger consumed him. He was humiliated and ashamed of himself for losing the most precious treasure of his life—his darlin' Lynn. In his mind, he blamed himself for not being with her when she needed him. He knew that he would feel this guilt for the rest of his days.

"What has happened to Lynn?" he would roar to the heavens. "Where is she? I must find her, so's I can put this matter to rest." Then his anger would cloud his mind and he would curse the arrogant Corporal Stokes and the savages who he blamed for destroying his life with his darlin' Lynn at their St. Mary's river ranch.

Looking behind him to check on the trailing packhorse, he noticed the travois tracks, the sign that had drawn him to this place, he now had hope that he could catch up to the fleeing caravan. Matt Brannon reckoned he was only a half a day behind, maybe less.

The high pass ahead was covered in clouds, storm clouds he reckoned, a spatter of snowflakes lit on his whiskered face. He looked again at the darkening sky, cursed his luck and continued on. He sure didn't need a snowstorm to cover the tracks he was following. An eerie wind began to moan down from the high mountains and the snow became heavy as the wind drove it into his eyes.

He had reached the summit. He could tell because the horses were no longer struggling up hill through the knee deep snow, the trail had levelled off into a small clearing. Matt had ridden into the howling blizzard and he could no longer see the tracks that he had been following. The travois tracks gave him the faith that Lynn could still be alive. The hope of finding her kept him struggling to follow the trail.

The Rocky Mountain snow storm had been sudden and unexpected. High on the summit of this unknown pass, he reined in his big buckskin and the packhorse. "The storm is too fierce. I can't go any farther!" he reckoned, talking to his horse and the wind, "I sure can't see nothin' in this confounded blizzard—not even your ears Buck!"

Both Buck and the trailing packhorse were exhausted, as was Brannon. Fatigued and chilled to the bone he knew he had to stop, he booted away the snow close to a large spruce tree and prepared a small camp. Here he sat over a scanty fire, blankets wrapped around his shivering body, in a forest clearing surrounded by spruce and fir.

Soaked to the hide and struggling to keep warm, he sat huddled by his small fire. The wet, heavy snow continued to fall, an eerie moaning wind continued to sweep down from the high places.

Presently the wind eased some, though the heavy snow continued to fall piling deeper by the minute. Here in the lee of the giant spruce tree, a feeling of calm came over the cowboy. He almost felt warm again and marvelled at the change. It was a peaceful warm feeling that soothed his tortured soul. He was able to rest, even sleep for the first time—since riding away from his darlin' Lynn back at the St. Mary's ranch.

A sound born to Matt's wilderness honed ears by a gust of wind brought him to his feet. He was straining to make out the sound as he grappled to become wide awake. It was a sound that he hadn't heard since he was a small child. He swore he had heard that sound before; it was the cry of a baby.

"I'm a losin' it for sure!" he muttered, to his faithful dun horse who was never far from his good friend, Matt Brannon. "Must a bin a mountain cat a squallin', possibly a lobo wolf a huntin' some o' his own kind."

"Sure sounded to me like a baby a cryin'—a cryin' for its mama!"

Morning brought more snow, increasing in depth by the minute; Brannon was reluctant to move on. He delayed his departure, lingering and absorbing the strange, yet peaceful aura of this clearing in the forest.

For an unknown reason, he could not comprehend, he removed the remnant of Lynn's red shawl that he had found and hung it from a branch of the spruce tree—on the lee side sheltered away from the wind. Brannon knew he would always remember this special place, and the peaceful feeling that was here. It was if his darlin' Lynn was standing there beside him.

Brannon knew that it was time to continue his search. It was urgent that he be on his way. The snow had piled up stirrup-high on the Buck's saddle, putting a boot in the stirrup he swung aboard and reined his dun horse into the driving blizzard. There was no longer a trail to follow and as he started to descend the west side of the pass, the snow began to deepen; it was well above the stirrups of his horse. The big buckskin and the packhorse began to flounder and the situation had become desperate. Unable to continue his pursuit of the caravan the cowboy let out a wild Texas yell because he knew he had been beaten.

Due to the weather it became urgent that Matt get down off this mountain. He turned the horses back to the east as he picked his way back across the summit and began the descent that would take him back the way he had come. Buck, the packhorse, and Matt Brannon followed the noisy little mountain stream out of the snowbound pass.

He felt relaxed as he rode, the feeling just would not go away! Somewhere from a far place came a ripple of sound, a mere whisper that penetrated his soul, "I love you Matt Brannon...come back to me, you hear?"

The heavy wet snow continued to fall. High up the pass a lonely forest glade was silent once again.

The site of the grieving cowboy's camp and the grave of his darlin' Lynn were so near, and yet so far apart!

* * * Chapter 15 * * *

Following a faint trace of the trail of the ancient ones, a lone rider on a line back dun rode along the eastern front of the Rocky Mountains. Matt Brannon had become a wanderer, sentenced to a life of always being on the move. Alone on the trail with only his memories haunting him night and day—old Tom Lynch's cattle drive, Riley's Trading Post on the Powder River, meeting Lynn Riley; his darlin' wife, ranching at the St. Mary's River, and the desperate chase into the mountains.

He preferred the high country, riding the trails of the ancient ones, stopping now and then at mining camps and isolated ranches to replenish his supplies. When his coin ran low he would hire on with some outfit, didn't matter what brand, then with money in his pocket he would be off again on his endless quest.

From the Porcupine and Highwood country he rode, along the eastern front of the Rockies and out onto the plains as well. Deep into Milk River country he travelled, always a loner, always seeking some peace for his soul.

Working cows was his chosen profession. It was the profession that he knew the best, if only he could leave his past behind him. The burden of his past was hard to bear. He was a changed person, the man who rode the big dun buckskin known as Buck. Brannon's personality had been transformed; he no longer had a reason for living. He did not want a life that was without Lynn Brannon. His was the life of a lonely wanderer now.

From the Kutenai Lakes along the 49th parallel to the banks of the Klondike River he travelled, stopping at all points in between. Occasionally he would stop and contribute to the history of the old Northwest, then quietly disappear into the void of the frontier.

Matt Brannon remained a loner, a rough salty one, championing the cause of the under dog. It would be hell to pay for those he caught mistreating women or children. Most folks let him be, shaking their heads in wonderment when big Matt Brannon passed by.

At Kootenai Brown's ranch in the Kutenai Lakes country, with its beautiful setting of alpine lakes and majestic peaks, Matt was able to find a moment of respite. Even though Brannon's visits were rare, his old friend Kootenai would greet him warmly and would invite the cowboy to share his fire.

On one of Brannon's visits Kootenai and his wife, Olivia, were hosting a group of her Métis relatives, including a pretty young maiden quite suitable for marriage. The old mountain man, Kootenai attempted to use his power of persuasion on his big bearded friend. Kootenai said, "You know Brannon, she is yours if you want her. She is quite capable of hunting and cooking and…breaking wild horses! Métis women make good wives. The little lasses can sure keep your blankets warm on a cold winter's night!"

With anguish in his soul, Brannon thanked Kootenai for his good intentions and rode on. Kootenai shook his shaggy head, reflecting his opinion of the cowboy. "By Jove, Brannon is a conundrum!" Kootenai stated, "The grieving bloke is going to mourn forever!"

It was late summer when Brannon rode away from the Kutenai Lakes. On an impulse he reined his dun horse into the west crossing the Rocky Mountains in an endeavour to see what was on the other side.

Matt was incredulous over Kootenai's attempt to marry him off to Olivia's niece. It was true that she was a pretty girl that could cook, hunt and break wild horses. He could not dispute the fact that she would make a desirable companion, one that would be an enticing resource to his lonely blankets. Matt was still tormented from losing Lynn he could not take another woman until he first found closure.

On he rode, up the Kutenai Pass trail to the medicine line that divides the waters. From the continental divide, it was a long ride into the Flathead country. At the end of each day he would spread his bedroll under the lodge poles and at first light continue his journey into the unknown country that lay ahead.

The 49th parallel was as good a trail as any he reckoned. Along the 49th parallel was another medicine line which divided old Grandmother's Land from that of the great White Father. He travelled along the border until he met the Walla Walla trail, deep in the Tobacco Plains country. It was an easy trace to follow, well defined ruts made so by the travel of countless freight wagons pointing into the northwest. The wagons were all headed northwest to the Canadian gold fields at Wild Horse Creek.

Brannon rode his dun horse, and though Buck was showing his age, the wiry mustang from the Brazos was still sturdy and dependable. To make life easier for his old friend, Brannon traded the pack mare for another buckskin saddle horse. This was a three-year old that showed a lot of promise and a bunch of talent. As he rode, he would alternate the two horses, which gave the colt the experience he needed, as well as pampered his old Texas friend.

It was long into the day when he rode out of the ponderosa forest into an expansive river valley. In the open country before him was a Fort surrounded by a bustling community. It was a Police Fort flying the colours of the Union Jack. Fort Steele, it was known as, erected and manned by the North West Mounted Police.

Brannon was hard pressed to believe his eyes. It seemed everywhere he rode he was running into the blasted British Police. The idea of the North West Mounted Police riled him. His memory was not short, he was still bitter and deeply scarred by the memories of Fort Macleod, the arrogant Corporal Stokes and the subsequent loss of his darlin' wife.

He rode past the fort and located an extensive tent community near the outer woods. Matt staked out a campsite, cared for his horses, and took a stroll up front street of the boom town on Wild Horse Creek. The town was known as Stud Horse Creek and was born with the gold strike in 1863.

Since the gold strike, millions of dollars worth of gold nuggets and gold dust had been found in the area. It was apparent that a good share of the treasure had been taken out of the community. There was still a lot of gold circulating in the town especially on the night life. It was a wide-open town, which needed the North West Mounted Police for influence in the region.

Brannon was amazed at the crowds of people. Scores of miners, gold seekers, and wanderers like himself, all mingled together. This mix of humanity was a first for Matt Brannon, not even Fort Worth could compare to this spectacle of a boom town in gold country. There were gamblers and outlaws, lawmen and preachers, Indians and Chinamen, rich men and poor men, painted ladies of the night and dancing girls.

Brannon entered a saloon and found an empty table where he could sit with his back to the wall. This old habit, of days gone by, positioned him where he would have an edge on any trouble because he could see what walked in off the street.

It had been a long spell since his feet had been under a table, he figured, he was extremely hungry for a meal that wasn't cooked out on the range over an open fire. He ordered himself a big steak with all the trimmings, and he planned to enjoy every bite.

The Saloon was hopping, jam-packed with a boisterous crowd that had gathered to eat, drink, dance and have a good time. The big Texas cowboy was doing justice to his well cooked meal when a stranger approached his table carrying a plate loaded with food. The stranger asked Brannon if he would mind some company. The big cowboy was happy to have someone to talk to and warmly welcomed the stranger. The stranger appeared a jolly sort and began to talk, "Me Sainted mother gave me the name of Robert O'Neil…she has." With an infectious smile on his face, the Irishman settled at the table and spoke again, "While a workin' the docks of Dublin town the name of Paddy was given me, and Paddy it is."

Brannon was amazed at how the Irishman could eat his meal and talk at the same time, he managing the feat with little difficulty. He told Matt of the many gold strikes he had been a part of and that he felt Wild Horse Creek was about played out. A syndicate of rich bankers had taken over here. The bankers financed powerful hydraulic equipment that was used to rip, gut and rape the creek beds of the gold in the banks, mile after mile. "It is a terrible sight to see," he told the cowboy.

Paddy ordered a round of warm beer and they began to visit like two old friends. He told of an exciting new strike in the Klondike, far to the north in the land of the midnight sun. Paddy was searching for a partner he could trust, someone to share the expenses and the profit of a gold expedition.

"Tell me more Paddy, your talk sounds mighty interesting," Brannon said, a surge of interest took hold of his lanky frame. He suddenly knew that he wanted nothing more at this time than to accompany this Irishman to the Yukon.

The journey would be just what he needed, a reprieve from his relentless search for Lynn, a chance to see new country, and to stash a little cash. "How much to buy in?" he asked, "I would like to go north with ya…be your partner if ya figure ya could trust me."

With his thick brogue and winning smile, the Irishman replied, "Faith and begor-ra Matt Brannon, ol' Paddy would be delighted to have a cowboy for me pard. Aye lad, the worth of passage on a steamship out of Victoria harbour is not that bad. Four hundred Yankee dollars will outfit us, land us on the beaches of Nome in fine ol' style, it will." And so a deal was struck with the shake of a hand.

Paddy O'Neil was uniquely different, fresh, dashing and most of all appeared to be openly honest. His quaint Irish brogue was a mockery of the Queen's English. He was a mercenary, turned adventurer, wise in the ways of the world. This unusual fellow from the land of the shamrock excited Brannon, gave him something to think about besides his shattered life. He was thankful to Paddy for finally giving him a reason for living.

After so many months Brannon finally started to relax, and amazingly, was at peace with himself. He laughed at Paddy's gift of the blarney. Nursing a fresh cup of coffee in his hand Matt suddenly froze. The cowboy's manner completely changed, it was if an unseen force had taken control of the big man known as Brannon. Paddy looked into his eyes and gasped.

Never had Paddy witnessed such a change in a person. A frightful spark of disgust, revulsion and pure hate gushed from the cowboy's eyes like static electricity.

Staring at Brannon from across the crowded Saloon was the arrogant Corporal Stokes. He was the same corporal who had arrested the cowboy that long ago night in Fort Macleod. Brannon's mind was in chaos—'You bloody Yanks must respect the laws of Her Majesty the Queen', the Red Coat's words were reverberating in his mind. Lynn's bloody red shawl, a spectre haunting his soul, flashed before his eyes. Paddy O'Neil shuddered at the sight of Matt but could only watch.

Stokes, unchanged, shoved his way through the crowd, and swaggered up to Brannon's table sneering, "It is you, isn't it? The bloody Yank who got me into trouble at Fort Macleod!"

Brannon was fuming mad, blue flame crackling from his eyes. He shoved aside the table, arose and faced the transplanted Englishman, eye to eye.

The Corporal's chest puffed out, his eyes were glazed, he nervously stroked his stringy moustache, and blurted out, "I arrest you in the na-ame of Her Majesty th—!" His words broke off, as quick as a flash of lightning a rock-hard fist cold-cocked the Red Coat lifting him off his feet and sending him skidding far across the floor. "Keep outta this," Brannon roared to the crowd, "I have a score to settle with this pompous ass. His high and mighty arrogance was to blame for the loss of my…darlin'wife!"

Offering the Peacemaker into Paddy's care, Brannon spoke again, "Cover me friend. I'm gonna give this stubborn spawn o' Satan a lesson in the code of the West."

Robert Paddy O'Neil was in a state of euphoria, this was his element; rough and tumble on a bar room floor. Shouting so everyone could hear, the Irishman replied, "He's a disgrace to'is bloomin' uniform'e is, needs a good tunin' up'e does. Paddy O'Neil will watch your back Brannon. Go get'im my boy…go get'im!"

Grabbing the stunned Englishman by the collar of his tunic, the cowboy drug him out on the street, and there in front of a spell-bound crowd, gave the Red Coat a terrible beating, a flailing the Englishman would be unable to forget.

Paddy was finally forced to pull Brannon away. "Easy does it Brannon me boy," he warned, "don't go a killin' the miserable skunk, it is a har-rible beating that ye have given him already!"

Several in the crowd that followed them out of the saloon were betting on the outcome, including several young North West Mounted Police recruits who made no effort to interfere. It was obvious he wasn't one of their favourite Corporals; the new recruits were enjoying the rascal's demise.

The Irishman was still holding Brannon's Peacemaker, covering the onlookers as the hapless Mountie slumped to the ground. "Thanks Paddy," the cowboy said, and took the gun in hand, "Anyone else wants a part o' this?" Brannon asked the crowd, there were no takers.

Brannon was flexing his battered hands when Paddy quietly whispered, "We better get outta here, me boy. The old Colonel will be back from patrol in a couple o' days...be the devil himself to pay...if we still be around!"

* * *

Following the Dewdney Trail, Matt Brannon and Paddy O'Neil rode away from the North West Mounted Police Fort and Wild Horse Creek. Their destination was the sea harbour at Victoria town in British Columbia, 700 miles to the west. After a fortnight of steady riding they arrived at Fort Langley on the Fraser River. Here they secured provisions and arranged for the disposal of their horses.

They had been told it was impossible to take horses aboard the river boats, the stock would have to stay. Brannon was upset about leaving his horses, especially old Buck, but there was no other way. After so many years of companionship Matt hoped he could find old Buck an owner who would let the horse live out its days lazing in a sunny, grassy meadow.

Scouting the area, Matt located a Chehalis Indian village up river. Here he was able to leave his horses in the care of an old timer and his grandson. The Chehalis elder seemed to be honest, and with a twenty dollar gold piece from Brannon's poke a deal was struck.

Paddy O'Neil was a trader from way back. He carried traces of gypsy blood in his veins from some wandering ancestor. It was a God-given talent of which the Irishman exploited to the fullest. Paddy started to deal with a French-Canadian adventurer and seeker of fortune for the trade of his two horses. His name was Francois Duval and with his two Chehalis wives they were embarking on an overland journey to the Yukon.

After hours of intense haggling, using adjectives that neither could fully understand, the trade was near to being concluded. Paddy was at his finest, "The har-rses would not be for bar-rter," he told the wily Frenchman, "If it weren't for the sea captains. The scurvy-ridden lot will not allow the passage of four-legged beasts, you see! Paddy continued, "Their teeth have no holes, even a thick coat of hair they have, to keep them war-rm in the season of rain and sleet."

Paddy knew the Frenchman desperately needed the horses; it was now time to close the deal. His praise for the two broom-tails he had swapped from a Flathead brave was now at an end. The haggler now moved in for the kill.

"I'll tell you what, my good Monsieur, Ol' Paddy will throw in the saddles and that genuine tanned otter pelt—outta the goodness of me Irish heart. I must have that crate of tobacco and the car-rn cob pipes to go with it." Along with the tobacco and pipes, Paddy received six cases of canned meat, two rifles plus a case of cartridges, and a tanned buffalo robe.

Brannon and his Irish friend boarded a small packet boat on its run to Victoria Town. In Victoria Town they boarded a steamship out of Seattle plying the inside passage to Alaska which provided them with transportation for their trip to the Yukon.

It took some doing, but with Brannon's pluck and grit, and Paddy's gift of the blarney, the two seekers of gold made their way to the Klondike River.

* * * Chapter 16 * * *

To be in Dawson City at the height of the gold rush was an intoxicating influence on a man's soul. To have reached this El Dorado of the north safe and sound was an achievement in itself. The goal would be to survive here and make a fortune.

The glitter and excitement was in Dawson City. Life in the gold fields was harsh and pretentious. It became a stark gut-wrenching routine of wielding the pick and shovel, drilling and blasting, and protecting their claim from invaders who would try to run them off.

One cold autumn day, Paddy O'Neil dropped his pick, crawled out of a deep, mucky hole and exclaimed, "Brannon me boy, ol' Paddy has had enough of the pick and shovel. This devilish muck and cold is no good for me bones!" The two seekers of fortune had been in the gold fields for six strenuous months making less than survival wages.

Brannon was quick to agree. "I've always reckoned anything that can't be done from the back of a hoss, ain't worth a doin'," he said with a grin, "I'll take ol' Buck and a herd of longhorns any ol' time."

Up until now the spoils from their hard labour had been lean and hard to come by. Had it not been for Paddy's constant trading, Brannon felt sure they would have starved to death. "What do ya have in mind?" he asked, "I've had my fill of this gold mining too, I sure enough have."

"Back to Dawson City we should go," answered a beaming Paddy, "find us a pack string! "Hawlin' in supplies to these starvin', frozen devils will put the jingle back in our empty money pokes."

No time was wasted in breaking camp and heading back to Dawson City, a boom town made up of 30,000 fortune-seeking souls, located at the fork of the Klondike and Yukon rivers.

Most evident was the glory and excitement of being where the action was taking place. Hundreds of souls were coming and going, tramping up and down the frozen streets, bartering for supplies and claims; and just absorbing every minute of this exotic adventure as it unfolded.

As with most boomtowns, surprises were in store, astonished gasps and protests were evident over the exorbitant prices being charged for merchandise. Innocent people were victimized by the vultures of business, the swindlers who made their living off of the gullible and unwary.

The Irishman Paddy was at his best, trading at every opportunity that arose. Before they reached the city, he had bartered for a dozen pack-mules along with all their rigging. It cost the two partners their mining claim, most of their supplies, and Paddy's buffalo skin coat.

After the cowboy's long years as a loner this bustling hub of the north was going to take some getting used to. He was plumb uncomfortable around the thousands of miners, speculators, and seekers of fortunes here in the land of the midnight sun. Matt reckoned he could put up with the noise and confusion of it all and give Paddy's scheme a chance. Their new venture just might pay off in a big way.

Brannon leased a small office, with a warehouse and corrals out back for the mules. It was decided he would stay in Dawson handling the banking and arrange for supplies. Paddy would become a muleskinner; packing supplies to the camps that were scattered across the gold fields.

It was a sight to see the Irishman arrive back in Dawson for a fresh load of supplies. Mobs of people would line the streets to watch the spectacle, some wagering on who, or what might be lashed to the mules. Paddy's mules were always loaded, bringing in the miners who had quit, were broke, homesick, or just plain cold. Disgruntled wretches were the lot, willing to barter their souls to the devil himself just to get out of this lonely, desolate place. Paddy O'Neil would haul in the losers. Business was business and he didn't mind where it came from.

More often than not, lashed on the mules would be a corpse or two, stiff as boards; those who had succumbed to the harsh, unforgiving land. Many, before their death, pleaded to be sent back to a warmer place. A last request was heard, "send my frozen body south," they pleaded, "At least my bones will be warm again."

The winter had been terrible, a cruel and deadly season in the gold fields. Paddy's mules, all twelve of them, were packed with frozen corpses. Several of the unfortunates had perished from starvation; others had simply frozen to death. Two were killed while defending their claim; others had succumbed to a broken heart. They all had been defeated by the frozen north.

Paddy's outfit paraded down the main street of Dawson City destined for the warehouse located at the far end of town. One of the cadavers, lashed to his mules, was sitting upright, extended arm at the square, the frozen hand gripping an empty bean can; clutched in the other was a wood-carved spoon which had never made it to his open mouth. A spectacle it was, swaying with the rhythm of the mule's gait.

"The poor frozen devil was perched beside the trail, he wus," "Paddy exclaimed, "frozen solid, he wus…while a eatin' 'is last supper."

Paddy's eyes were wide as saucers as he continued his yarn, making the sign of the cross as he spoke, "'tis enough to give this Irishman the banshee creeps, it is!"

In this frozen land there were those who toiled from daylight till dusk in the muck and cold, with nothing to show for their efforts except a few tiny flecks of gold in their pan. The yarns that they had heard back home of fortunes waiting to be picked up off the ground were not true. Gold was not everywhere that one may care to look. The stark reality was harsh and it was more than most people could handle.

The people just kept streaming into Dawson though, the prospectors, the speculators, those that had conceded defeat, and the dead. It was not fit for humanity out there; the weather was just too damned cold. Months rolled by, a new year turned over and the two partners' business was booming. Matt and Paddy scrolled away their money. The combination of Brannon's level head and Paddy's gift of the blarney made the pair well-to-do businessmen.

Above his ethereal good fortune, Brannon could not help but feel the deep hurt that was still embedded in his soul. He still pined for his lost Lynn. Periodically he would become lonesome, irritable and depressed. In the niche of his soul lay a hidden torment that would not release him.

Brannon consoled himself by spending a considerable amount of time at the various saloons, eating places and the theatre. Frequenting the poker tables, he played for modest stakes. This behaviour served as a diversion from his emotions, a method of passing time.

One night in the old saloon, boasting a dance hall and a stage, the cowboy was given a start when a beautiful young lady came out to perform. With the accompaniment of the piano, that was said to have been packed on a mule's back over the Chilkoot Pass, she crooned a repertoire of sad melodies. The lyrics of her melodies reached out to the lonesome audience of gold seekers. Tears were flowing freely throughout the crowded old saloon reviving memories of the loved ones that they had left at home.

A crowd of boisterous admirers elbowed their way to the plank-hewn stage and showered it with gold coins, pokes of dust, paper money and various baubles of the north in a show of appreciation.

This charmer of lonely souls was known throughout gold country as the angel of Bonanza Creek; there were some who preferred to call her Yukon Nell. From the first night Brannon heard her perform he never missed one of her performances. The big cowboy and Yukon Nell spent considerable time together and often shared a friendly drink. Despite their age difference they grew to be good friends. Yukon Nell helped Brannon to heal the pain of his past miseries. He treated her like a queen, and in her gentle way, Yukon Nell adored Brannon for his cowboy ways.

* * *

It was a cold night in Dawson City, forty degrees below at least. The wood smoke and ice crystals at these temperatures created an eerie haze. Above the haze the northern lights beckoned across the heavens in a timeless, exotic display.

With his sheepskin collar turned high, Brannon walked up front street to his favourite haunt. He often met Nell here for supper and tonight he was eager to get out of the cold, to relax and to forget his worries. The dance floor was crowded with patrons, miners who were in town for the winter, new arrivals to Dawson, and those who were waiting for spring so that they could take a passage back to the south.

The din was pounding in his ears. He walked through the thick tobacco smoke eye-watering haze shouldering his way through the milling crowd to his usual table. He was surprised to find Nell standing near the table with another man. The stranger was dressed as a gambler, and he had a swarthy countenance. Matt noticed that Nell was sobbing. He could see that the stranger had a firm grip on Nell's arm as he stood there and berated her.

A fiery rage took control of Brannon; his face turned a deathly white. Advancing steadily, he peeled back his sheepskin coat, allowing easy access to the Peacemaker on his hip. He did not know this low life who was manhandling his gentle friend. No one mistreated Yukon Nell or any woman when the big cowboy was around. With his hand on the butt of his Peacemaker Brannon moved in close to the table.

"Hands off the lady," he roared, "I mean pronto ya cowardly pole cat."

The sound of Brannon's voice brought relief to Nell as she wrested free from the stranger's grip and ran to her curtain-covered dressing room. Ignoring Brannon the stranger, acting crazy and out of control, snarled and swaggered after Nell.

The commotion had alerted the crowd and a hush fell over the room. One more time the cowboy roared, "Stay away from the lady!"

The stranger hesitated but a moment, then with six-gun in hand; he spun on his heels and fired point blank at the cowboy. Brannon's draw was a split-second slower, but proved more deadly. With blood oozing from a bullet hole in the chest, the big Texan slumped to his knees, then on down to the bar room floor. A few yards away, the strangers boot heels kicked a last farewell, a bullet hole between his sightless eyes.

Nell heard the shots. With an anguished scream she came running, tears flowing as she knelt by the cowboy's side. "Oh, Matt," she sobbed. "Matt Brannon you've been shot!

"Please! Please someone help me get him to a doctor. He's been hurt bad!"

A tall stranger, with a dark moustache that showed more than a trace of gray, stepped up and beckoned to a burly miner. "You there, give me a hand, let's do as the little lady asks."

Then turning to Nell he said, "My name is Earp, Ma'am, Wyatt Earp. I saw the whole incident unfurl. I was getting' set to help you out when this friend of yourn took over. I never reckoned he would catch a bullet like this."

Gesturing toward the dead one, Wyatt Earp spoke again, "That scoundrel was fast...mighty fast and tricky too. Had his gun drawn and cocked before he swung around. The advantage was all his."

Earp and several miners packed Brannon across the street to a small log building that housed the doctor. Inside the office, Earp turned to Nell and asked, "What's this gent's name, Ma'am? He's sure no slouch with a six-gun, heard tell of a fast gun that might be showing up around these parts seems he's a Texas gunfighter, Matt Brannon is his name, from down in the Canadian Territories."

"This is Matt Brannon, Sir," Yukon Nell replied.

It was touch and go during that long, cold night in the Yukon. The bullet was lodged near Brannon's heart and took a firm hand and a delicate touch to remove it. When she wasn't performing, Yukon Nell spent her time at the cowboy's bedside. He was in serious condition, his mind wandering from the terrible shock to his body. In his delirium he sensed a young woman by his side and rambled on to her as if she were Lynn Brannon. He was reliving the vivid details of a life he had tried to put behind him.

After several days Nell knew the complete story of Brannon's life. She wept long and hard for her anguished friend. When Paddy returned to

Dawson City and heard the news, he too kept vigil by his partner's side, giving Nell the chance to rest and unwind.

After a month of sickness, on another chilly Yukon night, Nell and Paddy were with the cowboy when he finally aroused from his long sleep. Paddy's constant Celtic chatter had penetrated the darkened void that had been Brannon's lot.

His eyes opened, his face looked haggard and pale. He was still weak and sick as a dog. Nell spoon-feed him hot broth and a bit of tea. It would take time, yet she knew that Matt Brannon was going to recover.

* * *

One morning a North West Mounted Police officer came to the doctor's modest infirmary. He introduced himself as Superintendent Sam Steele, said he was here to question Matt Brannon about the shooting.

Though still not fully recovered, the cowboy fired-up at the presence of this Canadian lawman. Where were the Red Coats when he and his family needed them? Why wouldn't they listen to reason when he told them of his expectant Lynn, alone and suffering at the river ranch. His mind was in turmoil. When he looked into the clear piercing eyes of this law man, he sensed a caring person.

With a silent groan Brannon settled into his blankets. "I'd best hear this gent out," he reckoned, "find out what he's got to say." Matt had nothing to lose, just as well tell it like it was.

A long silence followed before he could bring himself to talk. Eventually he looked the Red Coat in the eye and said, "The shooting was self defence! The man was a cowardly bully, offending...roughing up a lady! Yukon Nell is her name."

After fidgeting a bit, Brannon was finally able to continue. "I called him on it. He turned and shot me, they tell me the shot I fired downed him for good!"

With a hint of a smile, the moustached officer said, "Yes, you killed him and it was self defence. There was an entire room full of witnesses, including Wyatt Earp—a retired U.S. Marshall up from the Dakota Territories."

Then a stern look came to Steele's face. "I am required to charge you with carrying a sidearm inside the city limits," he said. "The fine will be a hundred dollars in gold, then you must turn in your weapon until you leave town!"

The cowboy was struggling hard to understand. He stared the Red Coat in the eyes for a long time before he spoke. "The Peacemaker's a hangin' on the wall over yonder," he said. "Are you the same Sam Steele from Fort Macleod and Fort Steele?"

"Aye, I am he. Are you the same Matt Brannon from Fort Macleod and Fort Steele? We've been looking for you, you know!"

Once again Brannon peered long and hard at the North West Mountie, he was different from Corporal Stokes. Steele gave Matt confidence of his sincerity and honour. With a sigh the cowboy settled on his pillow. He related the shooting in Fort Macleod, how the untimely journey to the Fort and Corporal Stokes threats resulted in the fact that his wife and unborn baby were missing. He related his version of the showdown at Fort Steele with the same over-bearing pompous ass, Stokes.

The old Mountie smoothed his moustache, cleared his throat and spoke, "I thought as much, Matt Brannon. Kootenai Brown told me your side of the affair, and I believe you both."

After firing his pipe, Steele continued, "That trooper, Stokes was a rascal, a remittance man. Young hell-raisers sent over from England by their wealthy families. A family embarrassment I suppose. The families were happy to get them out of their hair, so to speak.

"Stokes was given a share of a ranch in the Porcupines, and then gambled it away. The chap in question enlisted in the North West Mounted Police. The force is always in need of recruits, so he was hired on. Henry Stokes was a troublemaker and given a dishonourable discharge. As far as we have been able to find out, the man returned to England."

"As far as the rascal you shot in the saloon is concerned we have been on his trail for a long time Matt Brannon. He was a confidence man who was wanted back in the United States.

"He was a former husband of Yukon Nell whom he treated quite savagely. Yukon Nell had come here to the Klondike to get away from him."

A freshly filled pipe in hand, the old Red Coat had more to tell. "Matt Brannon," he said, clearing his throat before he could continue. "On behalf of the North West Mounted Police, I offer you an apology for what has happened to you and your family. We will never be able to compensate you for your terrible loss!"

The cowboy's emotion flared, he was reticent as he struggled to accept the old lawman's sincerity. It was at this time a soothing influence settled him down. From some far away place he could almost hear the words, "I love you Matt Brannon. Come back to me, you hear?"

The harsh lines of tension left his face. Matt Brannon had something to admit as well, "I was wrong too," he said. "I blamed the Canadian Police for the loss of my family. This Stokes ya speak of, the one who is responsible for it all, I reckon we will meet again some day. The son o' bitch took away my life!" Brannon continued, "I too must apologize for my actions, for my thoughts against your North West Mounted. I reckon Canada is a better place to live and raise one's family because of ya hombres. I would like to shake your hand, Sam Steele."

Nell had been listening and heard the entire story. As Brannon's weakened condition returned, she entered the small bedroom and told the old Red Coat he would have to go.

"He's a wonderful man Mr. Steele. I know that he saved my life that night...I don't know how I will ever be able to repay him!" Nell spoke.

Holding Brannon's holstered Peacemaker in the crook of his arm; Sam Steele paused at the door. "Yukon Nell, there is a way, you know?"

Nell gave the old lawman a hug, and then returned to the bedside of Matt Brannon, a heart-broken cowboy from the St. Mary's River country where the Old Chief Mountain keeps a lonely vigil over the western sky.

After his brush with death in the Dawson City saloon, Matt Brannon was no longer the same. He had come face to face with his own mortality and, since recovering from the gunshot, had an urgent feeling that was pulling him away from the gold fields wanting him to return south to his old stomping grounds. He knew that he had to follow this feeling.

Spring was now upon the land; the mighty rivers were free from ice and fit to travel. Brannon packed his gear and was ready to go. Paddy wanted to return south as well but agreed to stay until he could manage a suitable sale of the business.

"Ye can't be rid o' me that easy," the Irishman told Brannon, "I'll be a joinin' ya in no time at all...we're pards ya know!"

Nell was devastated when she heard the news that Matt Brannon would be leaving. She begged the cowboy not to leave her behind. She told Matt that she would be willing to go with him anywhere. Their friendship meant so much to her that she felt she needed to be together with him.

"It wouldn't work Nell," Brannon said, "I am honoured and pleased that ya feel so strongly and reckon I could love ya forever, but there's a part of my life that is calling me to go back. I feel a sense of urgency that I just can't shake!"

At the dock on the day of Matt's departure Nell cried as she showering him with hugs and kisses. "I'll never forget you Yukon Nell," Matt said. "Take care of her for me Paddy," Matt exclaimed to his Irish partner as he turned and walked up the gang plank of the Queen of the Yukon. The paddle wheeler was crammed with people and gear as it slipped quietly into the main stream of the Yukon River. A heavy fog shrouded the vessel and an intense chill rippled throughout the crowded decks. Penetrating the river mist echoed an alarming sound, the rebel cry of a lonely Texas cowboy.

* * * Chapter 17 * * *

Far back in the darkened woods, on the western rim of the continental divide, a small female mule munched on the seasoned plants that grew there. Methodically her head would raise, long ears pointed towards a man seated on a log beside a blazing fire. The faithful mule adored the big transplanted cowboy, so out of his element here in the snow and ice. He had saved the mule's life on numerous occasions and in its own stubborn way it had repaid him in kind.

The nose-tickling scent of cedar smoke drifted throughout this niche of the forest. As a small, yet cheery fire chased away the shadows. The campfire sure looked inviting, aromatic boughs crackled amid the flames. Strips of bacon spattered fat in the skillet and the scent of fresh brewed coffee wafted in the air. Matt felt his spirits lifted as he was roused from his daydream.

The cheerful flames of the fire were partly to blame for his reverie. They supported his determination to continue on, to solve this blasted enigma that was constantly tugging at his heart strings and gnawing at his soul. He had unfinished business, there was more adventure out there for him to be a part of.

Later as he lay in his blankets, watching and tending the small fire, a horde of memories confronted him. Memories of his past, memories of the Yukon, memories of how he found himself here in this snow locked basin he had christened Wall Lake. Tossing more fuel on the fire, the old cowboy settled back in his blankets and let fate play its hand. He recalled leaving the Yukon, leaving Paddy and Yukon Nell behind, sailing away on a journey to find his destiny.

Matt Brannon's journey back to the lower mainland had been by water. It was a troublesome time for the old cowboy when the big boat entered the inside passage of a storm-tossed Pacific Ocean. The steamer paddled on down the mighty Fraser River and finally docked at Fort Langley. Brannon heaved a sigh of relief when he stepped on to dry land at the fort. He never did care much for travelling by boat. For one who had been raised in a region where heavy dew was a rarity, all of this water was an unnerving experience.

He went directly to the Chehalis village for his two saddle horses; it was his old friend Buck he was anxious to see. After struggling to communicate with the Chehalis Indians in their strange language he got the jest of what they were trying to say. The old Indian that he had left his horses with had died. He was told by the Chehalis' that the oldster was in the happy hunting grounds, spear fishing for salmon.

The old Indian's grandson was now a husky lad who had grown like a weed since Brannon had last seen him. The boy signed to the cowboy that he would bring the yellow horse. Brannon was concerned and signed for two horses. The Chehalis again indicated one horse only. It was true, all the cowboy could see was the younger buckskin, and his old dun friend was not to be seen in the small paddock.

Sitting the boy down in the grass, Brannon signed one more time for two horses. From the young brave's limited vocabulary of sign language and a few words of broken English, he was able to piece together what had happened to Buck.

"—old horse, sick. Big cat…long tail—eat um up!" the boy stammered.

The cowboy was horrified; he shook right down to his boot heels. Not old Buck, his beloved friend of the last twenty years. The Chehalis boy showed him where the dun's bones lay. They had been picked clean by the cougar and by the scavengers that followed.

Motioning for the boy to leave him alone, Brannon sat for a long time at the scene of old Buck's death. Near a tuft of bunch grass he discovered a small scrap of weathered horsehide. A long ago brand was still plain to see, the horse brand of the Medicine Pipe ranch.

An eerie sound disturbed the Chehalis villagers a sound that struck awe and fear into their superstitious minds. "—devil noise…bad medicine…!" one brave said.

The fearsome sound that upset them so was the wild blood-chilling yell of a Texas cowboy!

Brannon rode back to the Fort to purchase supplies for the long journey. He needed a pack animal, one that was dependable and able to carry all he needed. He found the corrals empty; horses were selling at a premium price and selling faster than the horse traders were able to replace them. The only animal Matt could find was a small female mule. She was in the far corner of the big corral staring at the distant mountains, lonely and bored.

A horse trader hustled right out anxious to make a sale. "She doesn't look like much," Brannon said, "What'll ya take for her?"

The old bearded trader was all a flutter, brushing off the mule, showing Brannon all her features pointing out that she could lead and stand. "Why this here mule is well trained, never kicks, or bites...hardly ever gives any trouble," explained the horse trader, "Let's see now, I'll have to have forty-dollars worth of dust for her at least, should be askin' fifty... but I'll give you a deal today."

A frown had appeared on Brannon's bearded face. "Sounds mighty steep amigo," he said. "Tell you what; I may consider forty if ya throw in that pack saddle over yonder, and a bag of oats to boot."

The trader hummed and hawed, scratched his chin whiskers and finally said, "You're sure a tough one to deal with...guess it will have to do. You found yourself a bargain today stranger."

Pointing his horse and pack mule towards the rising sun, Matt Brannon travelled across the valley of the Fraser River. He was heading for the Rocky Mountains and to the wide-open plains on the far side.

It was late autumn; the valleys looked beautiful in a gorgeous array of colours. Great wedges of water foul were flying south, their chatter echoing throughout the land. The fur of the cottontail and weasel was turning a snowy white. Matt knew that this close to winter it would be a risky venture to head into the Rockies. He would have to make good use of his time and not waste a precious minute.

Brannon grew attached to the little pack mule, she was very dependable on the trail and a comrade in camp. He was learning that she had her own way to alert him to danger. This little companion had proven that she was invaluable so Matt dubbed her Jenni, Jenni the Mule.

The old cowboy was making good time, he was happy to be back in the saddle with the long miles falling behind him. High above the Flathead Valley, near the tree line, troublesome clouds hung low and a howling, freezing norther struck his little outfit. He retreated to a subalpine thicket of stunted fir and began searching for shelter. Shoving his blankets ahead of him, he was able to squirm beneath the gale-ravaged branches and create a snug shelter away from the elements.

Jenni and the buckskin stood down wind of the thicket with their rumps to the blizzard. As the temperature dropped far below zero the cowboy knew that it would take all of his survival instincts to stay alive. He ate jerked meat and quenched his thirst with the snow that he melted in his mouth.

The sun arose in a blue sky to a vast sea of glistening white snow. It had taken forty-eight hours for the blizzard to howl itself out. Matt crawled from his shelter and discovered the two animals missing, there were no tracks in the blinding mass of white snow.

Brannon knew he was in trouble; this scenario was a life-threatening crisis that would test his mettle as never before. He knew he would have to improvise to stay alive. He was thankful for his sheepskin coat, with its pockets stuffed with jerked meat, and the six-gun on his hip. His belongings and gear were in Jenni's pack and the rifle was in the saddle-scabbard on the buckskin. He cursed himself for not securing the animals properly he never reckoned they would drift away in the wild blizzard.

Using the long knife that was secured in the steer-hide scabbard on his belt, he went to work fashioning a set of snowshoes from fir boughs. He lashed the makeshift snowshoes to his boots with strips of leather cut from his coat. He cut two holes in his bandana to make an eyeshade, of sorts, that would protect him from the brilliance of the sun that reflected off the snow. He reckoned this might save him from the fatality of snow blindness.

Tying his bedroll to his back, Brannon shuffled forth to find his lost animals. He would check the high pass to the east he reckoned. "They must have headed that way," Brannon thought, "there was no place else to go."

It was tough walking, but the fir boughs were working and he was thankful for that. He had to stop often to ease his cramping leg muscles, as he continued onward into this high saddleback of the Rocky Mountains. An eternity of time had passed before he spotted a dark object far ahead. The object could be a lobo wolf, a hungry bear or it could be a mountain cat. The big Texas cowboy continued onward, climbing and shuffling ahead with his makeshift snowshoes. Closing in on the strange object he released the leather whang from the Peacemaker in case he needed to protect himself.

The object of his concern turned out to be Jenni! She was perched on a cliff staring into a bottomless void. Her lead rope had snagged in a fractured slab of rock and was trapped. Unable to turn her head, Jenni sensed Brannon was coming to save her and greeted him with a pitiful bray. The cowboy talked to the mule praising her as he untangled the lead rope and backed her away from the crumbling precipice.

She had been without food since the blizzard began, and was starving. He dug in the pack and found her some of oats. He also removed his field glasses from the pack and used them to peer over the edge. Far below he could make out his dead buckskin, the saddle, the gear and the Winchester .44-40.

Groping their way through the gloom of the howling blizzard, Jenni and the buckskin had drifted with the storm. The buckskin in the lead had walked off the cliff to its death below. Luckily Jenni was stopped when the lead rope snagged in the rock.

After back tracking from the cliffs, Jenni brushed past her cowboy friend and took the lead. She was breaking trail for the big cowboy, who had saved her from starving to death on that wretched crag. She led Brannon down a long pass into a secluded basin that was surrounded by high-walled peaks. Far below, encircled by pine and spruce, lay a lonely alpine lake.

Matt Brannon was worn out and freezing, his leg muscles jerking with agonizing cramps. The little mule would not stop until she reached the deep woods on the far side of the lake. She came to a stop; a feeble groan escaped her shivering body, perhaps a sigh, as she waited for the struggling cowboy to catch up.

Brannon struggled with every step as he staggered into the small clearing and collapsed in his tracks. As he lay in the snow recovering from the terrible ordeal, he looked around the area and marvelled as he took in the sights. "This is an ideal campsite!" He thought. Jenni was drinking from an open freshet of spring water, surrounded by downed timber. The timber lay scattered in the lodge pole forest. Water, firewood and shelter—everything a campsite needed was right here. He thought of Lynn Brannon and how proud of the Jenni mule, she would have been.

Brannon roused himself from the snow, pulled the fir boughs from his frozen feet and built a roaring fire. He put the coffee pot over the fire then fashioned a shelter from his blankets. He pulled the pack from Jenni's back and fed her a generous handful of oats. "I'm lucky to be alive," he mused, "I was sure lucky to have found Jenni and these supplies."

Later that night, beneath a sky full of a million twinkling stars Jenni lay close to the old cowboy's shelter in the Wall Lake basin. One of Jenni's long ears pointed towards the southwest, the direction from which they came down from the pass. The howl of a timber wolf echoed down from that high place, from the vicinity of the dead buckskin saddle horse.

The mule spent most of the daylight hours pawing in the snow, searching for something to eat. To sustain her meagre pickings, Brannon rationed the few oats that were left, mixing them with aspen bark shavings from a nearby thicket. Jenni also loved Matt's sourdough biscuits, which he willingly shared with her.

The winter was long and cold and posed a deadly challenge for the cowboy and the mule. They were alone together and relied on each other to get through the cold. The cowboy figured that he would have perished from loneliness without his mule. Jenni became Matt's guardian. The mule was constantly alert; her long ears would pick up even the slightest rustle of a vole beneath the snow pack.

One morning the little mule was missing from camp. Her tracks led down a spring-fed stream beside a series of small cliffs and a waterfall. In a small clearing in the forest were several mountain goats that appeared to be wintering in the area.

Jenni stood back in the trees intermittently staring at them as she gnawed on aspen bark. It wasn't long before Brannon, who was on her trail, spotted the little mule. Silently he came toward her with the big Colt Peacemaker ready for action. He caught sight of his wandering mule and noticed one of her long ears pointed towards the clearing. The ear would then straighten as if it was pointing toward something. That was when he noticed the goats.

Brannon crept in closer and was able to drop one of the goats with his trusty weapon. The goat meat meant that his rations would last until spring.

Late in April the warm Chinook winds blew melting the snow and opening up the passes to the east. Crossing over the Continental Divide, Brannon and Jenni plodded down through the valley following a creek that was overflowing from the melting snow. Now this was familiar country to the cowboy. The trail was the same one that he had he had followed on his westward journey to the gold field. They followed the trail down to the shore line of the Kutenai Lakes and continued on to a river by the same name. Here they were able to cross over and be on their way to Kootenai Brown's ranch. Matt Brannon was sure eager to see his old friend Kootenai again.

The old scout was not at home but his new wife, Isabella, greeted Brannon and fed him a meal. Matt was saddened to hear that Olivia had died from childbirth complications. He was pleased that his old friend had found another mate. Remarrying was something that Matt had not been able to do. Isabella's Cree name was *'Chee-nee-Pay-Tha-Quo-Ka-Soon'*, she informed him, meaning 'The Blue Flash of Lighting'. Kootenai called Isabella *'Nitchamoose'* which meant 'my good woman' Brannon thanked her for the meal and continued his journey for the plains.

Giving in to a strange feeling that influenced and beckoned him on, the old cowboy and his mule drifted south into the Chief Mountain country high up the drainage of Lariat Cross Creek. It was here that Jenni balked and refused to take another step. Brannon unpacked and prepared a camp. He reckoned this would be a good place to hang his hat while he wrestled with his future plans.

He knew Paddy would be bringing more gold with him when he returned from the Yukon, however, Brannon intended to prospect for more here. It did not matter that he had plump pouches full of the Yukon yellow, already, to look for more would help him pass time.

For several mornings in a row Brannon awoke to find Jenni lying up next to an eroded ledge next to the mountain cliffs. Finally deciding to see what the little mule was up to, he pulled on his boots and climbed up through the shale cluttered gulch.

"What in tarnation are ya doin' here?" He asked the mule, "beats me why you're a layin' up in these rocks every mornin'"

With no human contact for months on end, Brannon would talk to his mule as if she was able to understand him. He also would ramble on to himself at times, a habit developed by loners of the vast wilderness.

Jenni watched with interest as the Texan scouted around on the shattered ledge. Brannon's muttering suddenly ceased when something caught his eye it was a glint of colour, a reflection, from the eroded ledge that was caught by the rising sun. After scratching around, he returned to camp and hauled up his prospecting tools.

It wasn't long until he realized that Jenni had discovered a ledge of gold-laced quartz. As the weeks rolled by he had made a small cavern, following the vein into the rotten shelf. The gold he was taking was out of the small cavern was considerable it compensated him for the time that he spent mining.

"Think I'll call this here area the Mule Dung Diggings," he said one day to Jenni, "Your sign is scattered all around here and it was ya who found it, ya know. I've got all the gold I'll ever need right here. We've got ourselves a mine my long-eared friend, the Jenni Mine!"

The loneliness of the nights was hard on Matt Brannon. It was during the night that the demons of his past came to haunt him. The demons of his past life caused him to mourn for his wife, Lynn Brannon, and the unborn child that he never knew. "Why? Why was she taken from me?" he would shout to the heavens. "Why? Why—?" As the demons abated a fierce guilt fire would engulf his soul as he blamed himself for not being with his family when they so desperately needed him.

He was happier when his memory would recall the more recent times, Yukon Nell, the beautiful entertainer from the land of the frozen north. Her singing had soothed his soul and her companionship had nursed him back to health.

The strange enigma, that began in the Klondike and had caused his constant unrest, was urgently tugging at his soul. It was as if something or someone was beckoning him leading him into the unknown. Even here at his camp at the headwaters of Lariat Cross Creek, Matt Brannon found no diversion from it. This powerful sense of urgency took control of his mind. It left him emotionally drained, frightened and alone. Always alone!

Giving in to the enigma he broke camp, loaded Jenni's pack and headed down the valley following the winding Lariat Cross Creek. Heeding the pull of his soul, the plaintive cry urged him to continue his quest. His goal seemed within his reach as if it were closing in on him.

"I'm a losin' it for sure," he drawled to himself as he led the little mule along the faint deer trail, "don't know what in the dickens is wrong with me, must be going loco!"

* * * Chapter 18 * * *

After the surrender of Chief Joseph at the Bear Paw battlefield in 1877, the Nez Perce wars came to an end. The old Chief's esteem and influence with his people were still highly regarded, forcing the powers in Washington to exile him from his native land. Never again was he allowed to return to the land where he was born.

In recognition of the mighty Chief and his valiant struggle for the freedom of his people, the Nez Perce gave Joseph's daughter and her husband a tepee in an honoured site in the village. It was here that little Lynn Brannon, Cries in the Night, grew and flourished. When Little Lynn was old enough to sit on a horse, Lame Deer would boost the child on to the bare back of her mother's pinto pony.

Evening Star could sense a part of her old mistress emanating from this child. When the youngster would become unseated and tumble to the ground. Star would stay by Lynn, her soft velvet nose comforting her until someone came and boosted her on again.

Years rolled by and Lynn Brannon developed into a beautiful girl, an exact replica of her mother. She loved to ride the old mare into the countryside far from the Nez Perce camp as she searched and explored the land. Lynn felt a strange urge to ride to the north and east. She was determined to find what was out there.

She often rode to the trading post on the far side of the reservation to purchase supplies for Lame Deer and Little Elk. She revelled in the strange smells of the place, and enjoyed shopping for the goods it had it offer. Most of the items at the trading post she had never been exposed to before. Lynn enjoyed meeting people and visiting with them. She would listen to and marvel at their yarns of strange places and exotic adventures. Her wanderings were taking her farther from the Nez Perce village yet she always returned to her family's tepee before nightfall.

One day when Lynn was out exploring she met a dashing young French-Canadian adventurer. He had noticed her riding the old pinto mare and admired her grace and beauty. On his own horse he had accompanied her back to the village, spinning her enticing tales of strange people and stranger places. He had many thrilling tales of romance, adventure and gold.

Lynn respected and loved Lame Deer and Little Elk. She knew that she was an orphan and that her real parents were dead. The stories of Matt and Lynn Brannon were often on her mind.

One night the girl experienced a strange dream, a dream in which she saw an old prospector and a mule standing on the brink of a high canyon. As plain as if she had been standing with them, she noted the man was bearded and appeared lonely and sad. As the impression began to fade, she was sure she could see tears in his eyes, and then she heard a frightening sound, almost a roar. It was a long echoing call, so lonely and sad.

As the dream faded into an endless void, she felt a faint gnawing at her soul, she heard a woman whisper, I love you Matt Brannon, come back to me...you hear?"

Lynn awoke from the experience tossing and turning. She was soaking wet with sweat, frightened and terribly upset. What did the dream mean, she wondered? Why was this happening to her?

It was not unusual for Nez Perce maidens to enter into wedlock at an early age. Having been raised in Lame Deer's tepee since a small babe, she was fully aware of the Nez Perce customs, one of which was that maidens were expected to marry shortly after puberty. Many nights she lay awake in her blankets because she did not want to get married. She wanted to follow the urgent desire that was tugging at her soul. Lynn knew that she had to leave the Nez Perce village and travel into the northern territories that Lame Deer had spoken of, to search out her roots if possible.

Lame Deer had discovered that the tribal elders were watching Lynn with much interest, discussing which of the young men in the tribe should take her as his wife. The word of the council was law so the white protégé of Lame Deer would have no choice but to do their bidding. This predicament was an added incentive for her to leave the encampment.

This would be the solution she had been seeking. A decision was made as she lay in bed; she now knew what she must do to satisfy this constant searing of her soul, there was no other way.

She appeared to be captivated by his swashbuckling charm, the charm that was taught to him by his voyageur ancestors. Little Lynn allowed the dashing French Canadian adventurer, whose name was Francois Duval, to sweep her off her feet. She was fourteen years old when she fell in love and was married in the Catholic mission near the reservation.

The Frenchman promptly took his young bride to the Canadian Territories so he could prospect for gold. Following the Old North Trail along the eastern front of the Rockies, he struck colour north of the 49th parallel in a lonely creek valley where the foothills tumbled into the Rockies.

Francois built Lynn a small cabin that was nothing more than a shanty in the creek brush. Lynn Duval appeared happy as she fought the constant tugging at her soul the impulse that was always urging her on.

One morning, months later, Lynn Duval awoke to find her husband gone. He had just ridden away taking all their possessions including gold he had found. She had an inkling that something like this would happen. He was a wanderer who had ridden away in the night to chase another exotic dream.

Lynn was heavy with child when her husband the French Canadian Francois Duval had left her. Searching around she found that he had left little food and had only left her with the clothes on her back and the blankets she slept on. Outside she found her old mare, Star, and a young colt. The only other useful things she found were an old axe and a broken rifle.

Being raised by the Indians, survival skills were second nature to the young girl. Lynn survived and actually thrived by catching fish from the stream, and small mammals and birds close by her cabin.

The mysterious shadows of the night were softening along the creek valley. Inside the humble cabin Lynn Duval's time for birthing had arrived. She was exhausted as she struggled to meet the challenge of bringing her baby into the world unaided.

The door of the little shack slowly opening and in stepped an Indian woman with a pack on her back. Lynn was terrified and thought that her time had come to die. Pulling the old trade blanket over her head, she began to chant a death song that Lame Deer had taught her when she was a small child.

The woman spoke as she walked towards Lynn's pallet bed. Lynn gasped when she heard her adopted mother's voice. The Indian woman was Sara Lame Deer. Lynn hugged her happily and was delighted with the food and provisions Lame Deer had brought with her. Sara gathered wood for the fire and prepared a simple meal for the frightened girl. Lame Deer then helped Lynn Duval to deliver a healthy baby girl into the world as the sun was showing above the breaks of the creek known as Lariat Cross.

The Nez Perce woman talked as she worked. She told Lynn the Great Spirit had sent her to help Cries in the Night have her papoose. "—dream say, little Lynn in this place. Lynn is alone, and hungry…no one to look after her!"

Lame Deer talked for a long time, telling the girl many things. Although she had told parts of it before, she now repeated it again, filling in the gaps. She told of Lynn's parents, Matt and Lynn Brannon. How Lynn had found Lame Deer wounded and alone at the Milk River, saving her life. Most of all she told how happy and in love they were.

"A big cowboy with gun and your mother Lynn much love for each other, much love for Lame Deer too!"

The Nez Perce woman still carried the knife Brannon had given her for Christmas so long ago, and the hairbrush from Lynn. She told of the fight with the border outlaws, of Lynn shooting one from his horse with her little rifle. How Brannon came to their aid with a howl and a roar, shooting the bad men with his devil gun. He had scared everyone with his wild Texas yell. Lame Deer would never forget the yell from the Texas cowboy.

"Lynn's big white warrior, howl like wolf—make scary noise!"

With tears in her eyes, Lame Deer told of the Nez Perce raid on the St. Mary's River ranch. Lynn Brannon had shot one of the raiders with her rifle, and then she was struck down by the old Chief's war club. They were captured and taken into the big mountains that are white on top. There the birth of little Lynn occurred in a spruce thicket, while a bad storm, that talks, raged about them.

After Lame Deer finished the history lesson of Lynn's parents, she went to the door, reached outside and brought in a rifle and gave it to Lynn Duval. It was a bit battered from years on the trail, but it was Lynn Brannon's famous Yellow Boy carbine. After all these years it still worked just fine.

Lynn wept over the history of her mother and over the story of her birth in a raging blizzard high in the Rocky Mountains. She was saddened to hear that her injured Mother had died only a short time after her birth. To hear of the trials her Mother had suffered through, made Lynn appreciate her even more.

Lynn enquired about her Father, Matt Brannon. Lame Deer shrugged and said, "Matt Brannon, good man to Lynn and Lame Deer. Maybe dead…maybe not! Maybe big warrior that roars will come here to find you. Much noise like a wolf—Lynn will know."

Lynn was somewhat surprised at the Indian woman's lengthy talk. She could never recall hearing Lame Deer speak of the Brannon's at such length. Lynn Duval remembered Lame Deer telling her that her mother had asked

Lame Deer to care for her baby, Lynn Duval was grateful to this kind lady who had saved her life and cared for her all these long years. Sara Lame Deer was her mother; she was the woman who had raised her. Lynn heaved a thankful sigh now that she knew the whole story of the events that occurred so long ago.

Lynn thought about her lost parents, her mother who had died while giving life to her baby and for her big cowboy father. No one knew where he was, or if he was even alive. Little Lynn Brannon, the name Lame Deer had given her, prayed that her Dad was still alive and that she and her new baby could meet him someday.

Lame Deer stayed with Lynn Duval for a year, and then one day stood at the door with her par fleche in hand. "Lame Deer must go now," she spoke in her Nez Perce tongue, as Little Lynn was fluent in this language she also understood. "Little Elk need...dream say, he sings in the night for Lame Deer!

"Lame Deer will come back after five snows! To see if little Lynn is still all right."

Having said her goodbyes, the Nez Perce woman stepped out the door and was gone.

Lynn Duval turned to her sleeping baby, and gasped with pleasure. There beside her baby girl on the Hudson Bay trade blanket, which Lame Deer had brought for her, lay the hairbrush that had belonged to her mother, Lynn Brannon.

* * * Chapter 19 * * *

Deep in the foothills of the Rocky Mountains, hunkered low in the shade of a pine thicket, the big Texas cowboy was intently scanning the creek bottom below. The stream was Lariat Cross which formed the nucleus of this rugged canyon in the shadows of Old Chief Mountain.

He squinted long and hard into the void searching the contour of the big country below him. "Dog-gone the luck anyhow," he muttered. "Hope I haven't come out below the tradin' post ,that would be just my luck to have to travel up country agin."

Matt Brannon was on the move because his provisions were running low. He was lonesome and yearned for someone to talk to beside his little mule. The mysterious force was still chipping away at his soul. He vowed to settle this feeling once and for all and to save his sanity.

Brannon was travelling from the Mule Dung Diggings in the Chief Mountain country to a little known trading post on Lariat Cross Creek. When Matt last saw Kootenai Brown he had mentioned the place in his conversation. His old friend had told him of a trader by the name of Lee, who had opened for business along the creek.

Stirring from his roost under the pines, Brannon picked up his rifle and went to find the Jenni mule. This was the same gun given to him as a wedding present by old Ben Riley, the same Winchester .44-40 that went over the cliff with his buckskin saddle horse.

He had made his way to the remains of his saddle horse at the bottom of the cliff once the weather had warmed up. Matt retrieved the saddle that was beat up and the rifle that was weathered some but with a little tinkering he was able to get it to work just fine. He was also glad to find his pipe, and the possibles pouch full of Kinnikinik tobacco from the Flathead, that was in the saddle bag.

Jenni delighted in irritating her old friend. Every time he stopped for a rest to smoke a pipe of tobacco, she would wander off. This time he located her not far away, in a small hollow munching on the tender plants that grew there. A small trickle of cool water was flowing out of a rocky ledge.

"How come every time I stop, ya wander off?" he asked the mule with a twinkle in his eye. Brannon would cuss the mule for being a contrary beast, in reality though he would not swap her for all the gold in the Yukon.

"What in the name of thunder is wrong with ya...anyhow?" he added. With her lead rope in hand he led her out of the hollow. Pausing at the top of the hollow he looked back and spoke again, "How ya do this sort of thing...I'll never know. Ya always find us such fine places to camp Jenni. Ya and my darlin' Lynn would have got along just fine."

Jenni's countenance did not change, one long ear pointed toward the hollow, the other toward Brannon. "You'll always be welcome in my camp," he said. "I reckon you're the only pard I got left!"

Back at the canyon rim, Brannon settled once more in the lee of the pines. He crushed some kinnikinik leaves and stoked his pipe. He had never smoked a pipe until he went to the gold fields where he picked up the habit out of boredom.

At ease in this welcome haven away from the afternoon sun, Brannon gave a sigh. He could not explain the turmoil that he was suffering from. He felt peaceful here in this place though. Jenni had drawn him to this place, like a horse heading home for hay.

Brannon did not view himself as growing older. He was physically slowing down, his crisp speech had eroded but his mind remained active and alert. Rest is what he needed. His eyes closed and he fell asleep. In his sleep the wanderer appeared troubled, stirring now and then to mutter at his mule.

Tossing and turning on the ground litter, traces of tears showed on his whiskered cheeks. In his dream his sub-conscious was in control, placing him in a scene in which he was talking to Lynn Brannon. "Lynn! Lynn darlin'...I had to go. I know now I shouldn't have left ya alone with the baby comin' and all. Darlin', we were between a rock and a hard place I reckon. The confounded land deeds and, the English lawman—! Your ring, Lynn! The ring I was never able to give ya at our wedding, I've got it right here, Lynn. It's a beauty too and, and I'm sure it will fit your finger."

Twilight had now consumed the high canyons, the chatter of Lariat Cross Creek could be heard far below. Jenni was lying beside her cowboy friend. She had been back and forth from the hollow several times as Matt slept. She sensed something was wrong with Brannon. He tossed, turned, and muttered strange words.

An unnatural sound penetrated to the very depth of his conscience. He awoke with a start and sat up. "Wus that ya makin' that noise?" he asked Jenni, "I swear I could hear laughter...sounded like a child a laughin'."

163

Rising from the pine needles where he had spent most of the afternoon, Brannon spoke again, "Don't reckon it was a child though, not way out in these here mountains! Yet, dog-gone it all, it was the sound of laughter that woke me!

"Why, it's a gettin' dark on us...and me a layin' here sleepin' the day away, we got to get us a camp set up Jenni."

Matt Brannon stretched and worked the kinks out of his back and continued talking to his mule. "Funny thing though, I don't feel rested at all... I feel kinda hazy like, all washed out. Reckon I'm a gettin' old!"

Brannon pulled the pack off Jenni, laid a fire and began to prepare a meal. He shoved the coffee pot on the fire, than suddenly he stopped in his tracks. "Ya hear that Jenni?" Matt exclaimed, "Dog-gone it I was right. I do hear a child laughin'"

He returned to the canyon rim, a peal of laughter came wafting up from the shadowy depths below. This mysterious laughter had him on edge; he was really unnerved by it. Coffee cup in hand he paced between the fire and the canyons edge peering off into the darkness. In the distance, he reckoned he heard a dog barking.

Jenni bedded down in the far shadows of the camp, she stared towards the canyon too, her long ears on the alert. Someone or something was down there!

Brannon could not determine what he had heard. "Could a bin a mountain cat I heard. Them big cats can sure scream and yell sound just like a woman screechin', or a child hollerin'," Matt thought, "Sometimes one o' them coyotes reminds ya of a dog a barkin' but it weren't no wolf though."

Brannon could just not explain it. He returned to the canyon rim and surrendered to an impulse that he was never able to control; the wild rebel yell of a Texas cowboy escaped his lips and echoed down through the darkness below.

After returning to the fire he noticed Jenny was staring at him. She flipped a long ear and attempted a feeble bray of her own. Brannon had a slight grin on his face when he spoke to her, "Ya must think I'm crazy, Jenni. Don't know what cum over me, I really don't! Come first light, we'll head down to the creek...find out what in blue blazes is a goin' on."

Matt Brannon crawled into his blankets and stifled a yawn. It was rest his body craved; a restful night's sleep would do him good he reckoned.

* * * Chapter 20 * * *

The man known as Matt Brannon was never quite sure what woke him that morning. It may have been the noisy clan of magpies or maybe it was the laughter from the night before. He glanced towards Jenni's bedding ground and discovered that she was missing. He followed her tracks in the dew-soaked grass and they led him to the canyon's rim.

"The little wanderin' cuss has left me again," he said to himself. "She's turning into a mysterious rascal; never know what she's up to lately."

Far down the slope he could see her long ears showing above the canyon grasses. Brannon rubbed his eyes and peered more closely. He wasn't quite sure, but it appeared to be somebody in the grass beside the Jenni mule.

The old prospector of gold started down the steep slope. He had to stop now and then for a breather. Jenni was aware of his arrival at the bottom of the slope; she had one long ear pointed towards Brannon, the other towards her newfound friend. A small girl was petting and cooing over the mule bedded-down in the grass. When the child noticed that Brannon had approached, she flashed him a smile and a happy giggle. That happy giggle drove a pang of emotion straight to his heart.

The small girl was barefooted and dressed in skimpy clothes. She was a beautiful girl with curly, auburn hair fluttering in the morning breeze. Her face was radiant with an ever present happy smile. There was something about her that appeared familiar to him.

Brannon stopped a few yards from Jenni and the youngster, unable to control his trembling body. The strenuous downhill trek was partly to blame and he had left camp without his morning coffee. These weren't the only reasons for this intense jolt of peace he felt.

The main reason was this happy little girl. She was the enigma that had drawn him to this rugged canyon. It was she who had not allowed him a minute's peace for a long, long time!

"Hello Mister," she greeted, "my name is Lynn…what's yours?"

The old gunfighter was trying to stay calm the tears were heavy in his eyes. Did he hear the child say her name was Lynn? He was overcome with emotion as he wrestled to answer the child's question. Her chatter continued, "Sure is good to see you Mister. Is this mule yours? She likes me I reckon—could I ride her?"

Brannon didn't know what in the deuce was wrong with him. His voice was gone but somehow he managed to stammer, "Matt, Matt is my name."

"I'm sure glad you're here Matt. Come down to our cabin and see my Mother. She gets lonesome, awful lonesome Mister Matt."

His voice had returned to a workable condition and he was able to answer this little Lynn, "Reckon I could go and see your Mother, child...I mean L-Lynn."

Matt nudged Jenni to her feet and boosted little Lynn up on to the mules back. With the lead rope in his hand they continued on down to the valley floor. They stopped here so that Matt could have another breather. Lynn slid to the ground and squatted in front of Jenni so she could watch her crunch the tender plants that grew on the valley floor. "She's sure a nice mule Mister Matt, I think she likes me," exclaimed the young girl. Changing the subject she said, "I don't have a grandpa, would it be all right if you were my Grandpa?"

An aura of mysterious emotion enveloped the old wanderer. The question she had asked left him rocking on his boot heels. Echoing in his mind he heard the familiar refrain, "I love you Matt Brannon, come back to me . . . you hear?"

With a shrug of his shaggy locks, Brannon turned to face little Lynn and answered her urgent plea. "Reckon I've never known anyone like you before. You can call me grandpa if you like...I reckon it will be all right!"

Their breather was over so Matt boosted the child on Jenni's back, and they strode off up the creek trail leaving Brannon standing by himself. He pulled off his old sweat-stained Stetson, scratched his shaggy locks and muttered to himself, "The blasted long-eared critter has taken up with a child...I never seen the likes."

Lynn was chattering and giggling as she called back to Brannon. "Follow us Grandpa Matt. My Mother's cabin is up ahead...around the next bend." A peal of happy laughter resounded through the creek-bottom brush of Lariat Cross.

As he muttered to himself, Brannon strode off down the trail. Around the horseshoe bend he could see Jenni and Lynn nearing a small lean-to cabin. There was smoke coming from the chimney, a floppy-eared dog lounged on the door step and a pinto horse was tethered on a rope near the creek brush. Matt knew that horse. It was Lynn Brannon's horse, Evening Star, he was sure of it.

The old cowboy's heart was pounding something fierce, he stopped in mid-stride, as he gazed at the mare, and he was stunned. Though she was showing her age, it was for sure his wife's saddle pony. He could never forget that great little pinto horse.

"I just can't believe what I'm seeing," he managed to mutter, somewhat over the shock, "If I don't tip over with a heart seizure, reckon it'll be a miracle."

The cabin door opened and out stepped a young woman. She was beautiful in the morning sun; a red shawl was around her shoulders. She had long auburn hair, a flawless complexion and a slim well-built figure. In the crook of her arm, as natural as the sleeve of her buckskin dress, was a little saddle carbine.

Brannon gasped as a groan escaped the lips of his sun-bronzed face. His complexion turned a sickly gray as he looked intently at the gun. He knew that it was his wife's old Yellow Boy even though it was battered and worn. It was Lynn Brannon's old carbine from so many long years ago.

With a great shudder he managed to whisper, "Is that you Lynn? It has been such a long time...such a long, long time. You were taken from me at our ranch at the St. Mary's River!"

Wondering what was wrong with him, the small child and her mother approached the old wanderer. With a giggle, the little girl said, "This is Grandpa Matt, Momma. He let me ride his mule."

Lynn Duval was now smiling as her big brown eyes worked him over, eyes that seemed to penetrate his very soul. "Why this has got to be my Lynn," Brannon reckoned, "It has just got to be." Her smile, her eyes, every aspect of this charming lady was as Matt had remembered. The red shawl, the little carbine, that he had cleaned and polished for her, and had trained her to use. With his help she had became one of the fastest and most accurate shots with a long-gun he had ever seen. The Evening Star mare, it was Lynn's pinto, the same one she had loved so much.

Lynn Duval appeared to be somewhat hesitant then she flashed him a smile. "Sure good to meet you Grandpa Matt. My name is also Lynn, Lynn Brannon Duval," she said in heavy Nez Perce accented English.

Brannon was shaking like an aspen leaf as an intense shock battered the old gunfighter; he struggled to fill in the pieces of the puzzle. He laboured to comprehend what was unfolding before his eyes.

His countenance was deathly pale as he faced this phantom of the past! "You've got to be my darlin' Lynn. You've come back to me after all these long years. Why, you're as beautiful as ever Lynn just as I remember ya. I thought ya died at the hands of them murderin' savages, back at our St. Mary's river ranch! And our baby, Lynn! What happened? Were ya able to give birth to our little one without me there to stand beside ya? I did the best I could to be there Lynn, the very best darlin' Lynn!"

A long silence followed his talk; his shaggy head was hanging low. Brannon's mind returned to the present, his powers of reason had been restored. The pieces of the puzzle were falling into place. His eyes cleared and he looked closely at Lynn Duval.

Lynn Duval had grown numb as she listened to this strange man talk about her mother. "How did you know my Mother?" Lynn inquired, "Sara Lame Deer told me that my Mother died giving me life, her name was Lynn Riley Brannon.

Brannon interrupted her and very quietly he spoke, "Ya see, Lynn Riley Brannon was my wife. She saved Lame Deer's life after the big fight at the Bear Paw, a long time ago. The girl lived with us and Lynn treated her as our own until—!" Brannon's voice broke, he could not continue.

Lynn Duval was starting to understand, sorting out the history of her life. Tears overcame her. This old wanderer had to be her Father. She felt he was from the bottom of her heart. Her soul soared as she cried.

The old cowboy was equally touched by emotion as his large frame shook. "Yer red shawl and the rifle fooled me Lynn Duval. Ya look exactly as your mother did nearly twenty years ago.

"My name is Matt Brannon, ma'am, I lost my darlin' Lynn at the St. Mary's River and now I've found two Lynn's I never knew about."

Nearby a robin chirped a happy tune as the strange music of the mourning dove came out of the creek brush. In the clearing Lynn Duval embraced her father. She hugged him a long time nestling her head on his shoulder.

Little Lynn was hanging on to her Grandpa's leg as they all embraced. The old cowboy had been reunited with his long lost family!

Lynn Duval stepped back and looked the old whiskered wanderer in the eyes. Matt noticed that she had the same big brown eyes as her Mother's. Those eyes that could wilt a man with a single glance and could bring down a Texas gun fighter without firing a single shot. All Brannon could do was remember.

"Oh, Father Matt, is it really you? Lynn Duval asked, "My prayers have been answered, you have finally found us Matt Brannon, and I have found you."

"You really are my Grandpa," little Lynn exclaimed, "I knew it all the time…Jenni told me so." The three surviving members of the Brannon clan hung on to each other for along time.

The inhuman yell that had frightened Lynn Duval last night had haunted her for hours. She had wondered if it was a mountain cat until she recalled Lame Deer's words, "Big howl…Lynn will know!"

After all the long lonely years of wandering, Brannon had found the answer to the mystery that had been tugging at his tortured soul. He was now at peace, now that he had found his family. He would never be able to fully understand this turn of events. He had lost his Powder River Lynn and had found two new Lynn's. He was thankful for the little family his wife had left him. His wandering days were behind him now and he felt complete.

Over yonder in the willows, the Lariat Cross creek sang a happy tune as the family reunited in the shade of a cottonwood. Lynn told of her life on the Nez Perce reservation with Lame Deer and her family, of her marriage to Francois Duval, and about how she had come to live at Lariat Cross.

Brannon told of his memories of Texas and his cattle drive north, of meeting Lynn Riley and their journey to the St. Mary's River Ranch and of his fateful ride to the Fort Macleod. He told his daughter Lynn how he had wandered like a lost soul seeking what only his heart knew, following the strange enigma that beckoned him to return to the Lariat Cross country.

"I prayed for you Grandpa Matt," piped up little Lynn. "Every day I prayed that you and Jenni would come and find us!"

At this late morning hour, with the turmoil of his old heart settled, Brannon was in need of his morning coffee. All three of them climbed the ridge and moved his camp down by Lynn's cabin. He was shocked at the condition that the two girls were living in. They had only meager furnishings in the cabin, daylight beamed through the roof, and there was a lack of anything to eat. Matt could not see any food at all.

Though his own supplies were mighty skimpy, Brannon brewed a pot of coffee, stirred up a batch of sourdough biscuits and opened his last can of peaches. As he poured himself a cup of hot, strong coffee, he watched his two Lynn's relish the food he had prepared for them. He could see by their ravenous appetites that they had been without food for some time. The hot biscuits and peaches were manna from heaven to little Lynn.

"How have ya been getting by," he asked, "without much food or supplies?"

"It has been hard, we've had no money," replied Lynn Duval, "Little Lynn and I pick berries, and snare cottontails, capture grouse and catch fish in the creek. We also dig for roots of plants that are good to eat. I know all about edible plants because as a small girl growing up in the Nez Perce village I learned how to survive." She continued, "I have been able to shoot a deer now and then but I have run out of bullets for my gun. I saved two bullets back for emergencies... in case we—, we're over-run by hoodlums. You know what I mean Matt!"

"Yes Lynn, I know what ya mean and I'm proud of ya for it," Brannon replied.

"This past while I've been cooking at a lumber camp, an hour's ride north of here, it belongs to some Mormon people from Lee's Creek," Lynn explained.

"Mormons ya say," mused Brannon, "I've heard of 'em, never run across any though."

"Why, they're people just like us," Lynn was quick to reply, "good, generous people, and kind too. Someone had left us food for two years; I would find it on the doorstep, when Lynn was still a baby. I discovered it had been a Mormon family from down country who had helped us, the same ones who operate the big lumber camp over in the Pole Haven country."

Brannon became fuming mad when he thought about Francois Duval. He remembered seeing a fellow named Duval at the Fort on the Fraser River and couldn't help but wonder if it was the same fellow who had left his daughter Lynn here alone, near deaths door. He shuddered to think what might have happened without the timely arrival of Lame Deer.

"How far is it to the trading post, the one on Lariat Cross Creek, Lynn?" asked the old cowboy.

"There isn't a trading post on the creek anymore," replied Lynn, "that old site has been vacant for years. It was known as Lee's Trading Post named after a trader by the name of Lee but he shut down and moved away, no business to speak of. The Post was located down the valley near a Mormon settlement."

"Well I'll be horn-swaggled," he replied, "This is Lariat Cross Creek, ain't it?"

"Yes, that was its original name," she giggled, her eyes were sparkling like stars in a cloudless sky, "Early Indians gave it that name, each season of high water they tied ropes from one bank to the other, which made them a safe place to cross over, but it hasn't been known by that name for years."

Scratching his shaggy locks, Brannon asked, "Well if that's the case, what is this creek called now?"

"It is hard to explain, but I will try," Lynn replied, "after the old trader settled here, the name was changed to Lee's Creek. This is the South Fork of Lee's Creek. There is a Mormon settlement down stream about twenty miles it is known as Lee's Creek, most folks know it as the town named after the trader Lee. Talk is it will soon be known as Cards Town, after a man by the name of Card. He is the leader of the Mormon people here in the northern territories."

Brannon was frowning and in deep thought, he never was one for change. "To me it is Lariat Cross and it always will be. I think it is a better soundin' name—more fittin' and proper!"

Still amused his daughter replied, "Matt Brannon, you can call it whatever you like it's all right with me. Lariat Cross will do just fine."

"Tell ya what," Brannon was grinning himself, "Come mornin' I'm a takin' ya two girls down to this Mormon town ya been tellin' me about. This little spread o' yourn could use some supplies. A man could starve plumb to death around these parts."

The shadows of night had softened in the Lariat Cross valley and an eerie mist was rising above the creek brush. The old cowboy and the two girls were on their way to Lee's Creek, the sun still below the Milk River Ridge as they rode through the Dugway Crossing country heading east.

Brannon rode a young pinto, Evening Star's colt. She was a handful for him, and reminded him of Evening Star when she was young. The old saddle he was using was a beat-up old California with its leathers curled and worn. The tree much too small for his large frame, he sure missed his Texas saddle. He muttered an oath as he remembered that he had stashed his Texas saddle up by the Jenni Mine. He wished he had it now because even in its state of disrepair it would be much better than the torment he was enduring. Lynn Duval rode her Mother's old Evening Star mare. Though Star was slowing with age her spirit still showed and she was willing to do her best. Lynn rode bareback as she was accustomed to doing from growing up in the Nez Perce village in Idaho. Little Lynn was happy as a lark riding her Grandpa's mule. As long as she was with her old cowboy Grandpa she was the happiest girl that could be found.

They made several stops along the way to give Grandpa Matt's backside a reprieve. The trip turned into a twelve-hour ride before they finally checked in at the Kearl Hotel in Lee's Creek. Matt Brannon could see that this was a popular stopping place for this region. All three of them were tired and sore from their long ride. "That confounded saddle galled me something fierce," Brannon groaned. "Take a coon's age'fore I dare sit down again."

The hotel was like a palace to the two girls. They were impressed by the ornate furnishings, crisp linens, fresh bedding and over-sized rooms since neither of them had ever stayed in a hotel before. While they were freshening up, Brannon located a livery stable for the stock. At the barns he purchased a large canvas-topped wagon and the teams to pull it. No way was he going to ride back to Lariat Cross on that confounded saddle!

Over supper that night Grandpa Brannon ordered coffee, a pot full of hot coffee, and was gently chided by his daughter. "You know," she said with a grin, "these people do not believe in drinking coffee they will serve it, but only if they have to."

"Well, I've never seen the likes," the old Texan fumed. "What kinds of people don't drink coffee, anyhow?"

Lynn flashed him a big smile. She had caught on quickly to his temper and was learning that a simple smile could settle him down in no time flat. When his urn full of coffee arrived he took a big swig and eyed his daughter, she was still smiling and he gave her a big grin too.

After a good nights sleep with feather ticks, pillows and soft mattresses, they were well rested and in good spirits. Brannon escorted the two Lynn's to an establishment known as H.S. Allen and Company they were dealers in anything and everything. You named it and it was there. Grandpa Brannon was going to enjoy this shopping expedition as he patted out a sack of gold dust in his pocket.

He assigned Lynn the task of picking out clothes for her and for little Lynn. He also suggested that they pick out bedding and anything else they might need. This was going to be fun he reckoned, a spending spree the likes that hadn't been seen for a long, long time. Brannon left his women folk and went on the hunt for some larger items.

His first purchases included two beds, a cook stove, and a table and chairs that matched. Then he purchased a copper bath tub for the women, the creek was good enough for him. He amassed grub and supplies, in great quantity, enough food to last for a year at least, maybe two. He would ensure that his daughter and granddaughter were never going to starve again.

Matt Brannon was on a roll, he collected tools, saddles, horse gear, nails, barb wire and ammunition. He bought several cases of cartridges for all their guns. He located tobacco for his pipe which would be a welcome change from the harsh, tongue-biting kinnikinik that had been his lot. He also purchased two hefty bags of coffee beans and a grinder to boot, and of course oats for the horses. As a surprise he picked out a lever-action .22 rifle for his granddaughter. After adding the gun to the list of purchases he snuck it out of the store and tucked it secretly into the wagon.

The bearded old Mormon proprietor was rejoicing he had not received an order like this in all his years. He was kept busy hustling back and forth as he packed the Brannon's supplies in the big wagon.

Grandpa Brannon wasn't finished shopping yet. He picked out new clothes for himself, and bought a long buffalo coat to replace his old sheepskin which had seen better days. He found a pair of black Stetson hats for the girls and insisted they try them on for fit—and wear them right now!

When Brannon noticed that the wagon was overflowing with goods he tossed his plump poke of gold dust on the counter and told the Mormon storekeeper to start his ciphering. Lynn gasped when she saw the tally of the spending spree. The trader weighed out four hundred dollars worth of dust and handed the remainder back to Brannon. The buying spree had lightened the plump poke a little.

With a big Matt Brannon grin, he offered the remainder of the gold to his daughter. "My family will never go hungry again, darlin' Lynn. This is yours...use it as ya see fit."

She replied, "Thank you Father. We would sure like you to stay on with us back at the cabin."

* * *

Back home in the high valley Matt Brannon referred to as Lariat Cross; the new furnishings were all in place in Lynn Duval's cabin. The food and supplies were unloaded and packed away.

Brannon backed the big wagon into the lee of an aspen thicket, this would be his home now, a place where he could sleep and stow his belongings. The new team was put out in a pasture with Lynn's pintos. Jenni had the run of the place, always bedding down as close to Brannon's wagon as she could get.

Though tinkering around a homestead was not the work he was accustomed to, Brannon spent considerable time fixing up the shanty cabin and land; patching the roof, building a corral for the stock, and even putting up some fences. He branded the horses with B-L. Lynn was thrilled to see the Brannon brand for the first time. It was the same brand as the one that was on Evening Star. The brand had been registered so many years ago in the name of Matt and Lynn Brannon.

Early one morning several riders arrived at the ranch on Lariat Cross. They were bearded, pleasant fellows mounted on well-bred horses. Lynn greeted them warmly. She told Brannon that these men were the Mormon woodcutters from the lumber camp back in the mountains, the ones who had given her a job cooking for the crew.

Brannon greeted them warmly and thanked them for their kindness to his family. He told them how overjoyed he was to have found the family he had never known. From now on, he would be here to look after them and care for their needs. He invited the visitors to come on into the cabin, insisting that they stop and set a spell.

"Lynn's got coffee all brewed and a waitin'...best tastin' coffee in the Territories I reckon." Matt bragged.

The younger of the riders would have willingly accepted, he was all for doing what Brannon asked. With a slight smile the older Mormon replied, "Thank you for your kind offer Brother Brannon but we've got to be on our way. Sure sorry to hear Lynn will not be coming over to cook anymore. We're going to miss your doughnuts Sister Duval!"

As they wheeled their broncs to leave Lynn called to them, "I'll miss coming over. You Mormon people have been so kind and good to me and to my daughter as well. I'll never forget you!"

With a wave and a polite doff of their hats, the bearded riders rode up the valley of Lariat Cross and vanished in the aspen woods.

"I believe you," Brannon said. "These Mormons are good people. How can we repay them for their kindness to ya and little Lynn?"

"The Mormon people practise the law of tithing," she explained to Matt. "They are required to give one tenth of their earnings to the Bishop's storehouse. Would it be all right if we gave them some gold—to help them build their new meeting house down at Lee's Creek?"

"That's a splendid idea," Brannon was quick to reply. "The next time they stop by I will give'em some of this here gold."

"By the way," he said with a frown. "What's this I hear about doughnuts?

Have ya bin a holdin' out on me? One of the ways your Mother won my heart was by makin' me delicious doughnuts!"

With a tremor in her voice she spoke, "The Mormon woodcutters, the ones that were just here, brought me flour, sugar, and pig's fat and I would fry them doughnuts. They paid me for my time; the doughnuts helped us stay alive. Lame Deer taught me how to make doughnuts she said that my mother, Lynn Brannon, had showed her how to make them."

The old wanderer was settling down, he was happy and content to be with his family. Since his arrival at Lariat Cross, Brannon's mind had cleared; he was no longer bothered by the demons of the past. He was desirous to teach the girls his skills of survival.

He insisted that Lynn Duval learn to shoot like her Mother had. He was a hard-boiled teacher and consumed many long hours and cartridges teaching his daughter how to shoot her Mother's old Yellow Boy. As he had taught his wife, he now trained Lynn to shoot from the hip. "Shoot from the hip only in an emergency," he insisted. "Time and the element of surprise will be your means of survival! "Instead of a fast draw with a six-gun this is a fast draw with a rifle. Matt commented, "Why, it's just like pointing your finger...more accurate than most folks might reckon."

There was no denying the fact that little Lynn must join in the shooting lessons as well, following her Mother's example. He gave her the little gun that he had bought for her in Lee's Creek. He had reason to be pleased when his two Lynn's caught on quickly to handling a gun, following in the footsteps of the gun-fighting patriarch, Matt Brannon. Lynn Brannon would have been proud of her shooting daughter and granddaughter, Matt reckoned.

With all the recent purchases and tithes to the Mormons, Matt's poke was getting a little light. He decided to make a visit to the Mule Dung Diggings and dig a little colour out of the Jenni Mine. Lynn decided that she had too much work to do so she sent Little Lynn off on an adventure with her Grandpa.

After a long days journey, Brannon, little Lynn and Jenni arrived at the Jenni Mine to check things out, make sure no one had moved in on the claim. They found the diggings undisturbed, the place was as Matt had left it, and no one had been there except old Raven Wings, the Flathead Indian holy man.

Raven Wings, wandered the Rockies seeking visions for his people. He often stopped by at the mine, to see his white-eyed friend, to have a meal and get a chance to drink a pot of Brannon's coffee.

Matt Brannon knew the old Indian had been at the mine for tucked on a ledge near the mine entrance was a small bundle of black feathers wrapped with several strands of sweet grass and sage. This was the calling card of the old Flathead. Brannon took the medicine bundle and left in its place a bundle of store-bought tobacco and a gold coin. Chances are, mused the old cowboy, the rascal is sitting up in the crags watching us.

The journey from Lariat Cross to the mine under the crags of Old Chief Mountain, had a telling effect on Grandpa Brannon's old legs, equally tired were little Lynn and Jenni. They were ready to call it a day. Unpacking Jenni and preparing a scanty supper, they spread their blankets for a good night's rest.

Little Lynn was thrilled to be with her Grandpa Brannon, and as they lay under the stars, he told her many things. He described how Jenni had saved his life in a blizzard high in the Rockies and that it was she who had led him to this place and showed him the ledge filled with gold.

The young girl loved to hear stories of her Grandma. How fine and beautiful she was, and how he had met her at the Powder River, only to lose her again at their ranch in the St. Mary's River country. He continued to talk long after Lynn was asleep. Jenni was bedded down nearby, content as could be listening to Brannon's talk.

The moon had slipped behind the big Chief hours ago; the Big Dipper suggested that it was now past midnight when the girl roused from her sleep. She wasn't frightened and had no reason to be since her Grandpa's blankets were on one side of her and Jenni, her best friend was on the other.

Something had awakened her; it must have been her Grandpa's snoring! She turned in her blankets to watch the campfire. It had burned low, a hint of red embers still showing a vague glow. Then she saw what had awakened her. An eerie apparition appeared out of the darkness, picked up the coffee pot that was balanced in the ashes and raised it to its lips. It drank the scalding liquid without a stop then, stooping low, discovered a plate of sourdough biscuits which it promptly devoured. Wiping its mouth on the sleeve of its shirt it looked over at little Lynn knowing she was awake and watching. Turning, it looked toward Old Chief Mountain that filled the entire sky to the west, and then silently disappeared as suddenly as it had arrived.

Jenni had awakened too and watched the events take place. Her long ears were pointed straight up and her small legs were ready to spring into action. Lynn was a little spooked by what she had seen, but was otherwise okay. She soon drifted back into a sound sleep.

Grandpa Brannon was up and about, stirring up a fresh batch of biscuits. He had a fresh pot of coffee brewing and bacon was sizzling in an old seasoned skillet. Lynn sat on a log next to the fire soaking up its welcome warmth. She was so happy; there is no other place she would rather be than here with her Grandpa.

Little Lynn described the events that she had seen in the night, and asked him what, or who it might have been. "What was this thing wearing," he asked her. "Could ya tell in the darkness?"

"I am not sure Grandpa, it was so dark! I think it had on ragged buckskins and, a feather in its hair," replied his little granddaughter.

He appeared relieved to hear this. "It weren't no ghost then child…though some folks think it's such. It was old Raven Wings; the pot licker sneaks around at night a huntin' food. He can pick up the scent of coffee ten-miles away, then comes and raids your camp," explained the old cowboy. "The old scavenger is plumb loco. Why, I left the coffee pot here a purpose, reckoned he would drink it dry before mornin'."

Grandpa Brannon was now sitting on the log beside his little Lynn, coffee cup in hand a freshly lit pipe in his mouth. Gesturing towards Old Chief Mountain, which towered in front of them, he began to talk. "Many a mountain man of the Rockies, and I know a few of 'em, tells of strange things happening on this mountain. The higher you climb, the more this strangeness is present. Faint, mysterious music can be heard, almost like some long, lost people are a singin', reckon it must be the 'old ones' a worshippin' this sacred place. Old Raven Wings swears that Old Chief is a sacred mountain to all the Indian people, ya see. And I believe him! You have to listen real hard mind ya, but the music is there if ya will listen. Also an unearthly feelin' of not being alone…mutterin's and stirrin's is what impresses ya the most. Yer Grandpa knows Lynn; he has climbed up in these here crags many times."

Brannon lifted the crispy-brown biscuits from the skillet, now the big cowboy and his granddaughter were ready to eat their morning meal. "Here child, this is how ya do it," he said with a big smile, breaking a biscuit in half, soaking it in hot bacon grease and popping the whole thing in his mouth.

"Mmm-mmm, now this is what I call eatin' high on the hog," he exclaimed, and washed it down with a hearty swig of campfire brewed coffee.

Lynn giggled, picked up her plate, and ate her morning meal under the shadows of the big mountain.

The sojourn at the Jenni Mine was a fun time for them both. The long days were filled with camping out, gold mining and getting to know each other.

This time together was good medicine for both of their souls. Late one night, old Raven Wings, the Flathead vision seeker, snuck in to the camp again and absconded with the remainder of Grandpa Brannon's coffee.

With the theft of his coffee Matt became a physical wreck. Soon thereafter Grandpa insisted it was time to go back home. The happy pair packed their belongings on Jenni, faced the rising sun and returned to the home ranch in the valley of Lariat Cross.

* * * Chapter 21 * * *

An enchanting, calm twilight had settled across the valley before little Lynn and her Grandpa arrived back at the ranch. They were tired and ready for supper. Brannon was irritable and showing signs of wear, having endured the last twenty-four hours without any coffee.

The old cowboy was pulling the pack off Jenni's back when he suddenly stopped, and listened closely. A familiar burst of laughter was coming from his daughter's cabin. It had a bit of Celtic blarney that brought a big grin to his whiskered face.

Paddy O'Neil was back from the Yukon!

Bursting into the cabin, little Lynn just could not wait to tell of her exciting journey. "Momma, Momma, guess what? I slept with Grandpa Brannon and Jenni and an old Indian stole Grandpa's coffee so we had to come home."

Brannon came inside right behind her, and on seeing his old pard, Paddy stomped right over and grasped his hand. "Faith and beg-gorie Matt Brannon...you've been a holdin' out on old Paddy. This beautiful Lynn of yours is a sight for me sore eyes!" exclaimed the excited Irishman.

Lynn Duval was blushing and smiling and was ever so relieved to have her family back home. Little Lynn was chattering and giggling, as happy as could be. "Why that sounds like such an adventure," Lynn responded to her daughter as she went about getting their supper on.

"How is it you have been, Brannon me pard?" asked Paddy O'Neil, "It is sure good to be seein' you, it is."

Nursing his third cup of coffee, Brannon gave him a run down on events since he had left the Yukon, how happy he was to have found his family; how Lynn Duval had been left on her own. He told of Francois Duval, and the deliberate, dastardly way he had abandoned his young expectant wife.

The Irishman exploded, cursing a blue streak, shocking Lynn and even Brannon. "Why, the cowardly devil," Paddy finally said. "He made it overland to Dawson City...he did. The scurvied wretch wus too lazy to do any manual wa-ark, was a sellin' the services of his two Chehalis wives to keep from starving to death. The miners were a flockin' to them like honey bees returnin' to a hive!"

Packed in plump leather bags, Paddy brought with him a tidy sum of gold from the sale of their northern venture. He had divided it equally and shared it with his partner, the money from the leather bags made them wealthy men for the times.

Old Paddy was a handsome cuss in his own Celtic way, quite dashing in fact. He possessed an inborn gift of the blarney, and a personality that was hard to beat. Although he was in need of a bit of taming and sprucing up, he and Brannon's daughter became friends, good friends.

One morning, several weeks later, Paddy roused Brannon from his roost in the wagon. He told his old pard he was going up to the Mormon sawmill for a load of lumber. He was planning to build a new house for Lynn Duval and her daughter.

"Lynn and the child shall have the new home. The cabin will then be yours, me friend….ol' Paddy will roost in this wagon, he will," he said and then with an infectious laugh he drove away.

"Don't ya harm those people none!" Brannon roared. "Or trade them the gold fields. They have been good neighbours to my two Lynns." He expected the worst and was uneasy until his Irish friend returned. He knew the rascal only too well, and feared for the Mormons.

Flanked by several bearded riders, the Irishman's freight wagon was bulging at the seams with fresh-cut lumber when he returned. Paddy O'Neil was standing ten-feet tall as he reined the big work team into the ranch yards. Waving at Brannon he shouted, "Don't be a worryin' me friend. These Elders want to help build a new home for your Lynn too.

"I told'em I guessed ol' Paddy would join the Mormon Church—if they would!"

The Mormons were talented craftsmen, constructing Brannon's daughter a fine log home. Paddy was kept busy hauling in logs and split lumber from the mill, then he would travel down to Lee's Creek for supplies; nails, glass windows, and shingles.

The day Lynn's house was finished called for a celebration. Paddy had bartered a jug from an old bootlegger he had run into on one of his trips to town for supplies. One and all partook of the illicit brew, except for the Mormons, who politely declined, and little Lynn, who just pulled a funny face.

Several months after the house warming Brannon now lived in Lynn's old cabin. There was room for him in the big house, but his wishes were to live alone. In the shanty cabin Brannon and Paddy would meet each morning and imbibe their first cup of coffee of the day.

One morning Paddy walked in to have a medicine talk with his old pard, Matt. He appeared uneasy at first, he made small talk as he hummed and hawed. Brannon could tell that Paddy had something on his mind. He seemed to be at a loss for words, which was a rarity for the jolly Irishman; finally he was able to speak.

"That Duval devil that was Lynn's husband...well, you see, I shot him for you in Dawson City. Ol' Paddy killed him dead as a doornail, he did. The spawn of Lucifer himself was mistreating Yukon Nell, he was!"

Brannon sat digesting Paddy's words as he listened to the story. Paddy was ill at ease; he appeared a nervous wreck as he related the events. Brannon thought he had more to say about Francois Duval. He just couldn't figure out what the Irishman was getting at.

"What in blue blazes is wrong with ya Paddy?" Brannon finally asked, "Are ya coming down with something bad? Ya're actin' as crazy as a longhorn eatin' loco weed."

"Faith and begg-orie Matt Brannon, ol' Paddy's plumb addled and in a dither. It is that daughter of yours, your beautiful Lynn!" Then gaining courage he said, "'tis a big favour I have come to ask of you. I would like my old pard's permission to wed your Lynn Duval. She's accepted me if it be all right with her you." Still pacing back and forth and nervous as could be, he continued his request, "Lynn said if you agree, well...we'll get a Mormon Bishop to say the good words."

For a long spell Brannon stared his Irish friend in the eye, weighing the pros and cons. Finally with a grin he gave his answer. "If what ya tell me is true, Lynn has indeed agreed to tie the knot with ya, I'd be happy to have ya for a son-in-law."

Then with a roar that could be heard over at the new house, Brannon spoke again, "On these conditions my wild Irish friend, never mistreat her, love her, and take care of her for the rest of her days!"

Beaming with joy, Paddy grabbed Brannon in a bear hug and promised, "Aye, I shall me old friend. Aye I shall!"

Soon thereafter, Paddy mysteriously drove away from the ranch. His destination was the Mormon camp over in the Pole Haven country. The Bishop in charge was his unsuspecting prey.

When he returned he was beaming from ear to ear and talking non-stop. In the wagon were several pieces of elegant, hand-made furniture.

"The furniture is a wedding present to us from those Mormon people," he told Lynn and Brannon. "The bishop agreed t' tie th' knot for us Lynn darlin'. Told me t' be keeping th' Words of Wisdom, he did. Meanin' he wants me t' give up me pipe'n jug he does. If'n I did this th' furniture will nary cost us a Dublin penny."

Paddy was bubbling over with Celtic pride when he added, "Ol' Paddy slipped a pouch o' gold in th' ol' Bishop's saddle bag-just in case—!"

Lynn Brannon Duval was a beautiful bride on her wedding day. Her beautiful face beamed with happiness. Paddy O'Niel was dressed to the nines, sparkling like a new Double Eagle. Little Lynn wore a new party dress and stood by her Grandpa as he gave away his daughter Lynn. The Mormon Bishop who performed the ceremony told Matt that he would have to be the best man. When it came time to exchange wedding rings, Brannon, in tears, stepped forward and presented his daughter and Paddy with a beautiful diamond ring. Brannon explained, "This ring was to have been your Mother's, Lynn, I found it at Fort Macleod a long time ago!"

* * *

The months flew by, turning into a year. All seemed well on Lariat Cross. One warm spring day found Brannon and little Lynn at one of their favourite fishing holes, located not that far from the ranch buildings. Cutthroat trout were hungry and jumped around the pond like crazy. Little Lynn loved to fish with her big cowboy Grandpa; her happy laughter could be heard echoing up and down the valley.

Paddy was back in the forest cutting lodge pole pine. He was now a rancher, building a series of corrals for his expanding herd of crossbred shorthorns.

Lynn O'Neil was singing in her kitchen. She was frying a huge batch of doughnuts, knowing that Paddy and Matt would do away with most of them as soon as they saw them. She was hoping there would be sufficient doughnuts left to send over to her friends at the Mormon camp. Lynn was eight months with child, happy and looking forward to her new baby.

Suddenly the solitude of Lariat Cross was fractured with the sound of horse's hooves thundering past the home corrals of the Brannon ranch. Accompanying this intrusion was a blood-curdling chorus of whoops and scary yells.

Lynn was no stranger to this sort of thing, having been exposed many times to the Nez Perce outbursts of rage back at the Idaho reservation. She left her doughnuts and quickly snatched her rifle, the trusty Yellow Boy. The daughter of Matt Brannon levered a cartridge into her gun and opened the door to face the intruders.

When she saw the Indians she knew she was in trouble. Where were her Dad and Paddy when she needed them? Gritting her teeth with determination, she gasped in shock at the confusion that greeted her.

Amid the chaos, dust, and the terrible war whoops were a wild looking bunch of Indians. They brandished spears, war clubs, several rifles, and were filthy looking wretches, smeared with mud and paint, as were their mounts.

Astride a plunging horse one of them moved near and blocked the entrance to the cabin, he had a war spear raised high. Instinctively the little rifle swung to Lynn's hip and she pulled the trigger. The attacker tumbled to the ground, blood spewing from a bullet to his throat. Lynn's mind was racing, thinking briefly of her poor Mothers plight as she levered bullet after bullet into the carbine. Her dainty finger pulled the trigger again and again.

Brannon heard the sporadic gunfire as it drifted toward the fishing hole. He recognized the sound of Lynn's Yellow Boy and knew his daughter Lynn was in trouble. Freeing the Peacemaker, the old cowboy ran for the house. He yelled at Little Lynn to stay where she was and to hide. He now heard the blood-chilling fracas—his daughter's screams, the shots from her gun, the hoarse whoops of the savages, and the screams of a dying horse were loud and clear. Matt was frightened for Lynn's safety.

A long eerie wail, the yell of a wild Texas cowboy, ricocheted through the ranch yards at Lariat Cross. The savages froze in their tracks, gesturing in terror at what they were hearing.

An old grizzled gunfighter, his huge moustache fluttering in the breeze, emerged from out of the aspens. Hot, deadly lead streaked from a vintage Peacemaker resulting in two more raiders being tumbled from their ponies. Startled yip-yips cued the remainder of the Indians to turn and flee. Several of the intruders were sagging limply from the bare backs of the ponies they rode.

Little Lynn quickly made her way from her hiding place and ran to her Mother who sat on the doorstep sobbing in shock. Brannon checked the downed Indians. Four were dead, two were wounded and there was one dead pony. He knew he had only downed two, his daughter had accounted for the rest. The old Yellow Boy rifle was once again a means of protecting the Brannon clan from a deadly danger.

He went to his daughter, knelt beside her and held her close in his arms. Tears filled his eyes as he spoke, "This must've bin what your mother, my darlin' Lynn, went through! Only—she was alone! I'm sure enough proud of what ya did, my darlin' daughter, so very proud. Your Mother is too, I just know she is."

Within the hour a troop of North West Mounted Police rode into the ranch. They were in hot pursuit of the hostiles, who were a band of young hot heads that had been raiding and pillaging the area. The Mounties gathered the dead and continued after the rest.

This had been a rough experience on the daughter of Matt Brannon. She now understood how her Mother must have felt all those years ago at the ranch on the St. Mary's river.

* * *

As Lynn's time for the new baby drew near, Paddy was insistent he should take her down to Lee's Creek so that the baby could be born there. She would have no part of it; Lariat Cross was where she wanted her baby to be born. She told Paddy that this was where she would stay.

Two days later Lynn's labour started, it was time for the birth of the new baby. Her Irish husband was in a dither, ashen as a clean sheet, stumbling around interfering more than he was helping. "Paddy," Lynn ordered, "go find my Dad...I have things to attend to!"

The Irishman was only too glad to go fetch the big cowboy; anything to get out of the house was just fine with him.

Lynn was alone now as the pains came more frequently she knew the baby was not going to wait. She was bracing herself for the ordeal when the door to her bedroom opened. Lynn raised her head from the pillow expecting to see her cowboy Dad but there instead stood a smiling Sara Lame Deer.

After a swift glance at the scene Lynn's adopted Mom muttered to Lynn in her Nez Perce tongue, "Five snows gone now—Lame Deer come back—must help Lynn have...papoose!"

The new baby let out its first cry as Brannon and Paddy burst into the room. Paddy took one glance at what was going on and sprawled on the floor in a faint. Hand on his shooting iron, Brannon was on guard, puzzled over this strange Indian woman in Lynn's bedroom. On second glance he settled down, he noticed that she was assisting his daughter.

Lame Deer stepped back and looked at the old cowboy; there was a slight twinkle in her eyes. Brannon, somewhat puzzled, wondered who the woman was.

"Father Matt, do you remember Sara Lame Deer?" Lynn said with a giggle, she was snuggling her new baby, suckling it to her breast. After a long and hard look, Brannon smiled and said, "Why, it is you, Lame Deer! My how you've changed...I wouldn't have known ya."

He gave the Indian woman a hug, and then gently moved her back so he could look into her eyes. "I'm sure beholdin' to ya for raisin' Lynn all those years," he said, "and for helping her to birth her two babies."

It was hard for him to do, but somehow he found the words. "Thanks a whole bunch for helpin' my wife Lynn, for being with her when...when—!" Unable to continue, he choked back the tears and walked away.

Lame Deer who seldom smiled now had a slight upturn to her lips as she groped in her par fleche and brought out a ring, which she offered to her old friend. Brannon took one look and choked, he couldn't find the words to speak. It was Lynn Brannon's ring, the one old Ben Riley had given to her on their wedding day in Miles Town.

Paddy roused, though he was pale and still a bit shaky, he stood at the bedside of Lynn and their new son. "What were you doing on the floor Paddy?" she asked with a giggle. "Your new son needed you, and you were on the floor sleeping!"

It was a sheepish look that graced his face when he replied, "Faith and begg-orie darlin' Lynn. This birthin' business is enough to give an Irishman the shakes, it is. How you poor colleens manage it...ol' Paddy will never be able to know!"

The newest member of the Brannon clan was named Matthew Ben O'Neil. Little Lynn was so proud of her new baby brother. Lynn and the new baby were doing fine.

Hard times had come upon the Nez Perce people to the south. Lame Deer and her family had decided to travel to the Canadian Territories to live with her adopted daughter, Lynn. The small caravan consisted of her husband, Little Elk, three teenage children, four appaloosa horses, and several reservation dogs. At the time the new baby was uttering his first roar as a member of the Brannon clan, Little Elk and his children were setting-up a large tepee over near the aspen grove.

"Great Spirit tell Lame Deer, time to come back to this place," Lame Deer explained, "Little Lynn need...papoose is ready to cry in the night.

Paddy and Lynn assured Lame Deer and Little Elk that their family would have a home on Lariat Cross as long as the creek flowed, as long as the sun set behind Old Chief Mountain.

* * * Chapter 22 * * *

The South Fork of the Lariat Cross Creek, located in a region where the vastness of the plains is consumed by the foothills of the Rockies, was where the ranch was found. In this remote southwest corner of the Territories the families were thriving and doing well. With the turn of the Century drawing to a close, the rip-roaring 1800's were soon to be nothing but memories. Happiness was now a part of Matt Brannon's life, the great happiness that had evaded him for so many long years.

Up stream from the Brannon ranch lived a sizeable beaver colony. It was in this lonely corner of the Blackfoot Reservation, at the backed-up water of a beaver dam, that little Lynn, Matthew and their Grandpa came to fish for cut-throat trout. Brannon's grandchildren were growing like weeds, Lynn was thirteen now, and Matthew was seven. They worshipped there old cowboy grandpa more and more as the years flew by. He loved and doted on his little Lynn as if she were a Princess and was proud to see little Matt turning into quite a cowboy. The two children and their mother were the joy of Brannon's aging life.

The August afternoon was hot and sultry. The three fishermen had caught plenty of trout for supper and were preparing to return to the ranch. Jenni was with them, a small pack lashed on her back. The pack held their fishing gear, rain slickers, and of course their catch of trout.

To be walking cramped the old cowboy's style, even though the ranch was but a mile to the north. Brannon had never fully recovered from his hellish walk out of the Kishinena Ridge country, the site of the blizzard which had resulted in the death of his buckskin saddle horse. For some reason, Brannon had never got around to replacing either of his horses, old Buck or the buckskin colt.

Never one to admit it, Brannon enjoyed these walks with his grandchildren. He was packing his .44-40 Peacemaker on his hip. Little Lynn was armed with her mothers Yellow Boy carbine and Matthew carried his sisters .22 lever action rifle. The big cowboy was constantly teaching his grandchildren the ways of the backcountry and would never let them go into the woods unarmed.

The serenity of this peaceful fishing trip was suddenly shattered. Without warning Jenni threw a fit, it surprised Brannon to see her act this way; ears on the alert, eyes as big as saucers as she stared into the willow brush. The mule was a quivering bundle of nerves, nearly pushing Brannon into the pond. He staggered and gave a harsh pull on her lead line.

"What in tarnation is wrong with ya," he roared. "Act like ya seen an apparition in the brush! Must o' got bit by one o' these here pesky yaller jackets."

There was no stopping Jenni the mule. For the second time she went berserk, her eyes wide with terror as two small bear cubs trotted out from the creek brush in front of the fishermen. The two small cubs where followed by a grizzly sow who was roaring as she crashed through the brush.

In a blink of an eye the grizzly sow slammed into Brannon and Jenni, slashing, chomping and roaring. Jenni jerked free and raced away, blood flowed freely from a claw scrape across her rump. Brannon was knocked to the boggy ground, damp from the constant seepage of the beaver dam. The bear jumped on top of him, its feral jaws clamped onto his shoulder, as it shook and mutilated him.

Little Lynn was terrified at the sight of seeing the bear mauling her Grandpa, but she quickly sent Matthew up a nearby aspen tree and levered a cartridge into her mother's Yellow Boy. In one fluid motion she swung the little carbine up, firing from the hip. The 180 grain bullet smacked into the grizzlies shoulder. Roaring in pain, the big bear let go of its hold on the cowboy and swung to face Little Lynn.

The bear was coming at her, she could hear her Grandpa Brannon's words, "it'll be just like pointin' your finger darlin'', more accurate than most folks might reckon." Shooting from the hip, Little Lynn levered and fired repeatedly until her Mother's little rifle would shoot no more. With an anguished roar, the grizzly collapsed at Lynn's feet, blood gushed from its wide-open mouth. The feral roars ceased and the big grizzly lay still.

Little Lynn rushed over to her Grandpa who lay still in the mud, face up to the sky. The girl burst into tears at what she saw. Blood was gushing from the terrible fang wounds to his neck and shoulder. She was in shock but knew she must be brave. Stooping low beside him to see his eyes she spoke to him, "Grandpa! Grandpa Brannon can you see me? Can you hear me? Oh my, there is so much blood!"

LARIAT CROSS

Matthew scrambled down from his perch in the tree and stood next to his sister. Anxiously he asked, "Is he all right, sis?" He turned to Brannon and called, "Grandpa, talk to me Grandpa. Tell us what to do!"

The old cowboy from Texas was in serious trouble. He moaned and somehow cleared his head enough to mutter, "I can't seem to get out of this damned mud...I'm squashed in pretty deep kids. First time I ever tangled with a fightin' bear. See if ya can find Jenni, she can help pull me outa here."

Little Lynn attended to her Grandpa, as Lame Deer had shown her, taking handfuls of the clay mud and pressing it into the bleeding lacerations. Matthew ran over to the thicket where Jenni was pouting over her wounds. Reluctantly the little mule allowed Matthew to lead her back to where Brannon lay. The cowboy wrapped the lead line around his hand and yelled, "Back up Jenni. Back up an' pull me out of this here mess I'm in!"

Jenni, Grandpa Brannon's little friend, just stood there nostrils flaring, and stared at him. Matthew and Little Lynn were coaxing the mule to back up and were pulling on her halter when one of the cubs streaked out of the willows to sniff around its mother, the dead sow. When Jenni saw the little bear heading her way, she jerked her head back in terror and lunged almost over backwards, all the time braying in her mule lingo. This sudden burst of energy was enough to help Brannon turn on his side. Shakily, he was now able to kneel, and then get to his feet.

The old cowboy wasn't in his best form, swaying back and forth, bog-mud and blood from one end of him to the other. "Help me to get over by them quakin' trees," he said. "So's I can sit down, if I stay here I'll fall for sure. It's up to ya now Matthew, you'll have to go for help...pull that pack off Jenni's back and high-tail it to the ranch. Hurry now, please hurry!"

Brannon sat against an aspen tree while Little Lynn helped Matthew strip the pack off of Jenni's back. She legged her brother up, then gave a blood curdling hee yaw as she whacked the mule on the rump. The mule disappeared down the trail towards the ranch as young Matt held on for dear life.

Little Lynn turned her attention to her Grandpa. She quickly loaded the little rifle and placed it nearby. The bleeding had slowed down except for the stubborn gash on his neck. She scooped up a handful of mud, applied it to the wound, and held it tightly. She closed her eyes and talked to herself and to the old cowboy, "Everything will be okay, don't worry none cause helps on the way." She silently prayed that this was true.

Brannon knew he was in a tight spot. He didn't know how badly he was hurt but he did know he was weak and had lost a lot of blood.

After what seemed like an eternity, Paddy, Lame Deer and Little Elk arrived in one of the Irishman's wagons. With some expert horsemanship and cuss words that shocked all present, Paddy O'Neil reined the reluctant team in close to the beaver dam.

Shock was closing in on Matt Brannon's old body; he drifted in and out of consciousness, he was aware of his granddaughter's vigilance. The men carried the big cowboy to the wagon where Lame Deer took over and quickly cleaned up the wounds and applied dressings to help slow down the bleeding.

Lynn and Matthew O'Neil ran to meet them as Paddy's wagon pulled into the yard. Anxious to find out how her father was doing, Lynn yelled, "Is he still living Paddy? How bad is my Dad hurt?"

With a grin so characteristic of his heritage, Paddy answered his wife. "Aye, he's still with us, me darlin' Lynn. Ye daddy's a tough ol' rooster; take more than a grizzly bear get him to cash in his chips." He turned and looked at Little Lynn as he continued his banter, "Lynn, daughter o' me charmin' wife that was a superb bit o' shootin' you did out there in the bog. The leprechauns were a helpin' ya lassie, they surely were."

Paddy's work-hardened hand incessantly made the sign of the cross, he seemed as if he were unable to stop. "Saved your Grandpa's life, ya did," he said, "Ol' Paddy's proud of ya little Lynn."

Willing hands assisted the old cowboy to get cleaned up and into his bed. Lame Deer treated his wounds with special herbs and secret potions. The ugly neck wound was stitched tight with a long hair from Jenni's tail.

The men returned to the beaver dam. Little Elk skinned the grizzly and removed the claws for Lame Deer. Paddy attempted to capture the cubs. Though he was bleeding and covered with mud from head to foot, Paddy had captured the cubs. He lashed their legs together and tossed them into the wagon.

"Little bitin' devils they be. A month of Sundays will pass before ol' Paddy's hands heal, so I can be a doin' me work again!" exclaimed the Irishman.

After many nights of worry, Lynn and her children were relieved when their old cowboy called for his pipe and his coffee. Struggling to suppress a grin of his own, he glared at them and roared, "What's wrong with ya three anyhow? My nerves are plumb shattered, after fightin' at a ba-rr and all." Settling back on his pillows he continued, "All I asked for was my pipe and coffee, coffee so strong it will eat the handle off a spoon. What in the deuce are ya a laughin' at, anyhow? Matthew go n' fetch my pipe and tabacky," he bellowed.

No longer able to hold back his laughter Grandpa Matt laughed as the rest of the family joined in. Grandpa Brannon was going to be alright.

Wiping the dampness from his eyes, Brannon became serious with his granddaughter. "The next time I'm down to Lee's Creek" he said. "I'm buyin' you a new rifle just like your Grandma Brannon's."

Little Lynn managed to give her Grandpa one of her famous smiles. "I'm sure glad I was able to stop the bear in time," she said. "It was you who taught me to shoot like that...you know!"

Lame Deer who had been standing close by flashed a rare smile of her own. "Matt Brannon—big medicine," she said. "Big bear that roars!"

From that time forward the big Texas cowboy was known by the Indians as 'Big Bear That Roars'.

* * * Chapter 23 * * *

A sturdy team of horses plodded along pulling a tarp-covered wagon containing three happy women. Their destination was the Mormon centre at Lee's Creek, twenty-five miles to the east.

Clad in buckskins and long dusters, the women laughed and sang as they travelled. Chattering about new clothes they might buy, new people they might meet and the fun they were sure to have. The three of them had been suffering from a bad case of cabin fever; this trip would be just the medicine they needed to perk themselves up again.

Lynn O'Neil, her daughter Lynn, and Lame Deer were on a ladies only journey to the Mormon settlement. It was shopping they were planning on, stocking up on supplies and indulging in some new items for themselves and for the house. Although no one knew it yet, Jenni the pack mule was trailing behind. It was with some misgivings that Grandpa Brannon watched his family of head strong members of the opposite sex leave the ranch on this beautiful summer morning.

The travelling women were fifteen miles down the valley before they noticed a storm moving in. The western sky behind them had darkened; the ominous explosion of thunder could be heard above the rumble of the rolling wheels and scary lightning danced across the troubled sky. Seeking shelter Lynn O'Neil reined the team into an aspen clearing by the creek.

"Great Spirit say no stop this place," Lame Deer insisted, she was visibly upset, "keep going...up there!" Having said this she signed towards a high pass through the rolling hills.

Not heeding Lame Deer's protest, Lynn O'Neil jumped to the ground and began unhooking the horses. Little Lynn set about lighting a campfire in the howling wind. Jenni, the mule, was still about a mile behind the wagon trying to catch up. Lame Deer muttered and signed to the heavens. "Bad spirit here," she kept on repeating. "We must go away– Lame Deer knows!"

The late summer storm moved in fast. Before Lynn realized the severity of the storm, hurricane force winds struck the little basin. The campfire was blown out, the terrified horses jerked loose and took off for higher ground, the canvas top of the wagon was billowing like a sail boat at sea, and the three women struggled to keep it in place.

The savage tempest of the storm increased. Torrential rain gave way to hail stones the size of marbles. Darkness was that of a moonless night, broken by awesome lightning bolts—the heavens were a shattered wreck. The women struggled with the canvas top of the wagon and they screamed to speak over the storm. No longer able to hold the canvas in place, it flew away on the wind. They crawled on the ground and sought shelter under the wagon. Kneeling in mud and water, the luckless trio huddled together in terror.

Dulled by the din of the awesome storm, another roar was rampaging down the valley of Lariat Cross. Fed by numerous tributaries far back in the Chief Mountain country, a wall of raging, muddy water came smashing into the aspen clearing. It struck without warning, upsetting the heavy wagon, and continued on down the valley.

As the storm passed an ominous quiet settled over the aspen clearing. Far to the east sheet lightning still lit up the sky. Though still high and angry, the waters of Lee's Creek slowly receded. A large cottonwood tree, an aged patriarch of this place lay tipped out over the flooding waters, roots weakened by the awesome force of nature. The overpowering noise from the angry water remained constant.

Near the devastated wagon the sound of tiny hooves sucking through the deep, silt mud was heard. Jenni had arrived at the devastated campsite after wisely waiting out the storm on a sheltered knoll. She was looking for her human companions. She stared intently at the wagon, her long ears strained to pick up any sound of the women.

Eventually, in her own dignified time, Matt Brannon's mule turned and focused her attention on the downed cottonwood. Though it was faint, she detected a familiar sound, sobs and moans of fear. She plodded over to the tree and patiently waited.

The light of a new day revealed total devastation of the women's camp, a terrible sight to see. Jenni, the good friend of Lynn had not budged; she still stood staring at the tree.

Little Lynn stirred from her sanctuary on the top of the trunk of the downed cottonwood tree. She was battered, bruised, soaking wet, and shaking with the cold. Without releasing her death grip on the gnarled trunk, she raised her head and called out for help. Jenni's sharp ears picked up the girl's feeble cry, answering with a short version of her famous bray, which was almost a snort followed by a short silence.

It was a miracle that Little Lynn was able to recognize the familiar greeting through the noise of the rushing water. Her arms were aching fiercely, as she tried not to fall into the raging waters. Somehow she managed to turn her head and look back, but as she did so she felt her grip loosen. "Jenni, oh Jenni," she cried, "I am so glad you are here. Help me! Please help me Jenni, I cannot hold on much longer."

The mule's long ears still pointed toward her friend, it continued to stare at the cottonwood tree. After awhile, in Jenni's own good time, she stepped into the water and waded out to the girl. The water was surging around Jenni's shoulders when Lynn fell from the tree on to the mules back. Her arms were around Jenni's neck, her face in and out of the water, but she hung on. The mule turned toward the shore, the current pulled against them sending them down stream. The little mule's sharp hooves bit into the sandy creek bottom and she was able to pull them toward the safety of the shore.

They made it to shore and continued on to higher ground. When they were finally out of harms way little Lynn fell to the ground and lay still. Jenni lay down beside her, gave a sigh, and watched the cottonwood break loose and go bouncing down the flooded valley of Lariat Cross.

The heat of the suns rays warmed Little Lynn, she would survive her ordeal.

* * *

Fifteen miles upstream, the South Fork country had suffered a destructive pounding as well, including the Lariat Cross ranch. Paddy and Matt were worried sick over the fate of the women folk. They knew the women were in serious trouble, they could have possibly perished from the destructive force of the flash flood.

The following morning at first light, the old cowboy and his son-in-law started down the valley on a hunt for their loved ones. Matthew and Little Elk stayed back at the ranch to round up the loose stock. Paddy was at the reins of one of his big teams pulling a heavy freight wagon. The flash flood had erased all sign. All they could do is stay to higher ground and follow the contour of the creek valley, hoping for the best.

Hours later they spotted Jenni bedded down on a high knoll. She watched the approaching wagon, her ears signalling the fact, but she never stirred.

By now the old cowboy's nerves were on edge, he could sure use a stiff jolt of his coffee. "What in blue blazes are ya a doin' here Jenni?" he roared, "seems like you're always a wanderin' off somewhere." It was then he spotted his granddaughter snuggled as close to the mule's body as she could get, lying asleep in the sun.

"Why the little wanderin" devil, that she is! She's found my wife's daughter, that she has," Paddy was quick to emphasize.

"Are you all right Lynn?" Brannon roared again. "You sure look like you bin put through the wringer!"

Grandpa Brannon's roars awoke the girl. She stood up and saw him sitting in the wagon, and she began to sob. They wrapped her in a warm blanket and as she collected herself she told them of the terrible storm. She also explained how the little mule had saved her from the doomed cottonwood. She had no inkling of what happened to her mother or Lame Deer.

Brannon climbed from the wagon and approached his mule. His talk was full of praise as he talked to her as if she were human. "Thanks a whole bunch Jenni. I don't reckon I will ever be able to repay ya for savin' my granddaughter's life."

The Jenni mule, the one he wouldn't trade for all the gold in the Yukon, just stared Brannon in the eyes as if she could understand. Who is there to say she could not? "Why, you've saved little Lynn's life and for this I will be forever grateful," he said, trying to hold back his emotions.

"I know it's askin' a lot from ya Jenni, but I would like ya to go down and find my daughter. Go! Go find her," he roared. "I know ya can do it!"

Pointing into the valley below, Brannon stared his mule in the eyes and signed for her to go. Jenni did not seem to obey; she just stared back at her old friend, pleased with the attention he was giving her. Eventually, she uttered what appeared to be a groan, crawled to her feet and plodded down the hill into the creek brush.

"Paddy," Brannon said, the roar now gone from his voice, "I'll stay on top with the outfit—ya follow Jenni. She'll take ya to Lynn."

Without a word the Irishman was gone. Jenni's tracks led through the havoc of the women's camp, past the partially buried wagon and disappeared into the woods. As he passed the flood-silted wagon he spotted the women's two rifles. One was close by a wagon wheel, several inches of the barrel showing. The other had been washed against a downed tree, exposed on the surface of the boggy silt. He stood them against the exposed wagon wheel and continued on.

Jenni's tracks led back and forth through the cottonwoods and diamond willow thickets. When he finally caught up to her, she was standing in her tracks staring at a strange looking mound shoved above the muck and litter of the valley floor.

"Faith and begg-orie Jenni, is it one of the colleens that you have found?" screeched O'Neil. "Ol' Paddy's afraid to look, he is!" As he made the sign of the cross, the superstitious Irishman moved close to the mound in the mud that had caught Jenni's attention. He was convinced it was the shape of someone's shoulders and head showing above the muck, the remainder of the body must be buried in the silt. Uttering curses he dropped to his knees and began pawing away the mud.

It turned out to be Lame Deer; she was alive, staring Paddy right in the eyes. Digging feverishly, Paddy soon had her free. He lifted her into his arms and carried her back to the wagon. Delirious from her ordeal, she uttered strange words as if she were talking in her sleep. It was scary talk that had old Paddy O'Neil spooked out of his britches.

On his way once again to check up with Jenni, the Irishman passed by the wrecked wagon. What he saw made him freeze in his tracks. The two rifles that he had stood against the wagon wheel were gone. There were no tracks in the silt but his own, fear struck Paddy O'Neil. He made the sign of the cross many more times as he fell victim to his superstitious heritage.

"I can't believe me Irish eyes," he babbled. "The leprechauns are about...I just know they are! The little green devils would give a man the haunts, they would. A strange mystery it is they have created for the Irish this day."

Praying that he was not too late, Paddy was afraid of what might have happened to Lynn O'Neil. Striding off through the woods, he continued his hunt for Brannon's mule.

"I'll find the tracks of the Jenni mule," he said, still babbling and struggling to contain his superstitious thoughts, "the little wanderin' devil will find my poor Lynn, I just know she will."

He soon located Jenni's tracks. They led him down into the valley. Jenni's sign was easy to follow as he trailed behind her. He could see where the mule would stop and stare, always facing down stream. He continued to an area that had been a grassy meadow. He looked up from the clearing and spotted Brannon in the wagon moving down a gentle slope towards him. A long drawn-out bray from Jenni startled Paddy, she was signalling them.

"Have ya found her yet?" Brannon roared, after he spotted Paddy. "Lynn's got to be here somewhere."

"It is a strange thing that has happened," Paddy roared back, as he explained the missing rifles. "Jenni's up ahead...I kin hear her brayin' and carryin' on."

Matt Brannon ordered his granddaughter and Lame Deer to stay with the wagon as he joined Paddy in the search for his daughter. Paddy packed a double-barrel .12 gauge shotgun and Brannon packed his Peacemaker which was free and easy in his holster.

As it turned out Jenni wasn't far. They found her with her feet planted firmly staring at a blood stained coat snagged in a birch willow. It was Lynn O'Neil's coat. With tears in his eyes Paddy mumbled, "I'm afraid she is a goner, Brannon. I feel it in me bones, I do!"

"Nonsense!" replied Matt, "we'll find her soon, Paddy. Don't give up yet, Jenni's like a coon hound, she'll take us to my daughter."

Jenni waited patiently for Brannon to see the coat, and then she continued on her quest to find Lynn O'Neil. The search party followed closely behind.

The old cowboy was getting downright cross and upset, it was a long dry spell since he had consumed any hot coffee. The day was ending and it was close to sun down. Jenni was still in front leading the two men. The shadows of night were thickening and the little mule stopped. The wild yell of an old Texas cowboy echoed throughout the ravaged basin.

Above the roar of the angry creek, the crazy-sounding bray of Jenni could be heard answering her old friend; she was close by. The two searchers hurried on and finally found Jenni bedded down, long ears on the alert, staring across the creek.

It was now pitch black in the valley of Lariat Cross Creek, the scent of wood smoke laid heavy in the humid air. Across the troubled waters, in a secluded hollow above high-water line, sat an old, dugout cabin. A faint glow showed through a smoke-stained window.

Following his instinct, Brannon knew it would be suicide to attempt a crossing at this time. He knew better than to deny his feeling. Crossing a flooded stream in daylight was a risky venture but the idea of attempting a crossing after dark made his blood run cold.

"Let's head back to the wagon," he told Paddy. "Come first light, we're a declarin' war on this here place. Lynn's in the cabin, I reckon. To go after her now would do her more harm than good. It mighta bin different if there was a moon a shinin'."

The old cowboy and the Irishman returned to the wagon. They ate jerked meat and drank coffee around the campfire that Lame Deer and little Lynn had made.

* * * Chapter 24 * * *

In an awesome display of Nature's powers the flash flood had devastated the women's camp. Lynn O'Neil was carried away by the rampaging creek and swept away. Battered and gouged by flood debris of every sort, her limp body landed on the shore where she lay unconscious for hours. Long after the storm had swept away to the east, she aroused and staggered around in the darkness of the fearsome night.

Tripping on the root of an overturned tree, she once again fell into the creek and bounced and bobbed as the water carried her down stream. Nearing a horseshoe bend in the stream, Lynn was once again washed up on a gravel bar on the far shore. She lay lifeless near a well used path that led from the water line up to a weathered old structure dug into the side of a steep coulee. The place appeared deserted except for smoke curling out of the chimney.

Barber Jones was up and about at the crack of dawn; he always awoke at this time and was out back tending the horses. On his way back to the cabin he was checking along the creek for flood damage when he spotted a body lying at the waters edge. He walked down the trail to investigate and discovered that it was the body of a young, flood-battered woman. He knelt beside her and found that she was still breathing, but he knew that she was in bad shape.

He picked her up and carried her up to the cabin. He laid her on his bed and covered her shivering body with a dirty blanket. Her clothes were in tatters from the violence she had been through. Jones muttered, "Don't want those jaspers a pawing over her." He was referring to the two men who were still snoring on the cabin floor.

Jones stoked up the old stove, put on a pot of coffee, and settled back to try and make sense of his strange find. In his simple mind he figured that since the woman had been cast ashore at his cabin door she would be his to keep. He could tell that underneath the mud and the grime she was a beautiful woman. He presumed she would make a fine wife. He hoped she would stay alive, he wanted some company. Jones had lived here for so long without any companionship.

The two men on the floor were sleeping off a drunk. They had just walked in on Barber Jones the bootlegger, and they planned on hiding out here from the law until the heat was off. They brought with them a long history of robbery, violence, and murder. The men were on the run from the North West Mounted Police, for rustling horses at the Mormon settlements.

A survivor of the old Muleshoe Gang that was chased out of Virginia City by a posse of angry vigilantes armed with a rope, Jake Coe was an American outlaw chased north by U.S. Marshals. The other, Hank Henry Stokes former North West Mounted Police officer, had been retired from the force in disgrace. He was the same Stokes that Matt Brannon had a score to settle with.

* * *

Morning arrived but the sky was once again covered with big black storm clouds. Paddy and Brannon each climbed aboard one of the draft horses and were ready to find Lynn O'Neil. Paddy was packing his .12 gauge double-barrel shotgun and Brannon was never without his trusty Peacemaker.

"Please Grandpa," Little Lynn pleaded, "bring back my Momma…I know you can do it!"

"We'll do just that darlin'. Don't ya fret none, ya hear?" He assured Little Lynn that they would be back with her momma in no time at all. Turning to Paddy, Brannon roared, "Come on amigo, put the spurs to that hoss you're a ridin'…we're a burnin' daylight"

On their way to the mysterious cabin Paddy became uneasy because he knew of this place, though he would never admit it. On numerous occasions he had conducted business with Barber Jones, bartering various items for jugs of moonshine whiskey.

Riding down to the creek crossing, they discovered that Jenni had not moved from the night before, she was still staring across the creek at the cabin. Brannon dismounted and took a canvas sack from his coat pocket and gave his little mule a generous helping of oats.

He knew Lynn was in the cabin, he felt it in his bones. He had the reputation of becoming plumb salty when riled, and right now nothing or no one could stop him from finding his daughter. He was upset and in a fighting mood. If his daughter hadn't been treated with the respect that she deserved, there was going to be hell to pay.

Light was now returning to the valley, the flood-swollen creek was still voicing an angry roar. Brannon was ready; he cut loose with his cowboy yell. For a moment, over the din of the rushing waters, the old cowboy swore that he heard his daughter scream.

"Keep that scatter gun handy," Brannon called to Paddy, "we've just declared war on this here outfit."

Urging their horses into the water, they headed out into the current and after a short swim they plodded to shore.

"Ho, the cabin!" Brannon challenged, "askin' permission to ride in."

In return he could detect a muffled scream, some excited voices, a rowdy scuffle and a gun shot from inside the tiny cabin. The weather-beaten door opened a crack and a rifle barrel poked through the opening, it was pointed directly at Brannon and Paddy.

"Stop right where ye be," an unknown voice said. "Don't need ya a snoopin' around here, this is private property. You jaspers beat it'fore you git a taste of this here long gun!"

"Now hold your hosses," Brannon shouted back. "We're a huntin' a lost woman who got swept down the crik in the flood. We wuz a hopin' ya hombres might a seen her."

An ominous silence settled over the area. It was reason enough for the old cowboy to become uneasy. He knew what might be coming next; and that he would have to be ready.

With only the silence as a warning, the door of the cabin swung open, out charged Coe and the Englishman, their six-guns spouting hot lead. Paddy ducked on the far side of his horse, pulled the trigger on the old shotgun and was tumbled to the ground by an explosion of powder and flame. Jake Coe died on the spot, his chest shattered with buckshot.

Brannon's Peacemaker was at its best with the old cowboy at the trigger. He was up to the challenge getting off two shots, even though one would have been sufficient. The old gun brought down the Englishman, who died with a look of disbelief on his terror stricken face. The two outlaws had seen their last sunrise, as they kicked their death throes in the valley of Lariat Cross.

Paddy crawled to his feet and lunged through the cabin door. Brannon heard the sound of a gunshot! Paddy staggered out of the cabin, blood pouring from his side, and collapsed amongst the downed outlaws.

"Lynn's here!" he gasped. "Tied in a chair, she be—!

"Ol' Paddy be a goner, shot in me gut, I am—!" The shock of being shot and the sight of his own blood was too much for Paddy O'Neil, he collapsed in a faint.

"Come on out in the open, ya miserable skunk," Brannon bellowed, the instincts of his gun fighting past were coming back to him, "So's I can save myself from a sendin' ya to hell."

"Clear outta here," a voice replied. "The little woman will git hurt if you step inside the door! She's mine, d' you hear? I found her right here by the crik—that makes her my woman."

Though Brannon was enraged, he wasn't quite sure how to handle this one. He dare not risk Lynn's life with more gunplay. He reined the big horse around as if to leave. Then he slid to the ground on the far side of the horse and snuck in close to the cabin wall.

Several long minutes passed in silence. Footsteps sounded on the cabin floor then someone neared the open door. Barber Jones stood in the doorway, staring at his downed companions. Brannon stepped into view and roared a challenge, "Draw ya...miserable coward!"

The bootlegger froze then, pivoting on his heels, he fired from a crouched position. He was fast and took Brannon completely by surprise. The bullet branded an ugly slash across the cowboy's cheek, Paddy O'Neil revived just long enough to be a hero. Paddy used the remaining cartridge in his double barrel shotgun, and shot Barber Jones. Old Barber Jones had his spurs removed at the Pearly Gates.

Brannon was shaking like a leaf; he had blood streaming from the wound to his face. He was getting too damned old for this gun fighting business.

Matt burst into the cabin and was disturbed by what he saw. There sat his daughter tied to a chair, a filthy rag stuffed in her mouth. She was dishevelled and her clothing was in tatters. She was a poor, miserable looking soul. When she saw her father enter the room her eyes came alive, those big brown eyes, so like her mothers. She knew that the old cowboy would come looking for her and would save her. She had heard his roar the night before, it gave her the determination to hang on and endure.

He pulled the gag from her mouth, untied her and quickly wrapped her in his sheepskin coat. Picking her up, he carried her out into the warm sun, gave her a drink of water, and consoled her. She opened her eyes and smiled at him.

"I knew you would come," she said. "Your cowboy yell sure scared them last night."

Lynn sobbed quietly as she spoke once more, "They were drawing lots this morning to see who would take me first—!"

"Are ya all right Lynn? They never—!" Matt whispered.

"You came in the nick of time Father, and saved my honour...I sure thank you for that." Brannon snuggled the coat around her a little tighter, then went to check on Paddy O'Neil who was stirring amongst the blood and the gore.

Paddy, the mercenary and miner, was actually sensitive to the sight of blood. Lying on the bank of the creek with two dead men and the bootlegger's corpse draped across him, the Irishman would revive long enough to see and smell the blood, and then pass out again. Brannon grabbed him by the boot heels and drug him over by Lynn.

"Poor Paddy," she moaned, "He looks in bad shape, how is my poor wounded husband?"

Suppressing a grin, Brannon said, "The bullet just grazed his ribs a mite, reckon the sight of all this here blood is harder on him than the damage from the bullet."

Brannon turned his attention to the slain outlaws; he quickly identified the one that was downed with his Peacemaker, as Stokes, the ex-lawman from Fort Macleod. The same spawn of the devil who uprooted his life so long ago, and who was responsible for the chain of events that led to the death of his darlin' Lynn. The old Texan heaved a sigh of relief; as he felt he could now rest easy and forget.

"My beautiful Lynn from the Powder River is now avenged," he told his daughter. "I finally got the devil that took her from me!"

Then, as if he were talking to his wife in person, he spoke again, "I'm sorry that it took so long to avenge you darlin' Lynn. At least I gotta do it before I leave this here world to join ya in Heaven. I figure I'll be a joinin' you mighty soon."

The Irishman was once again struggling to regain his senses. He lay on the ground with his head resting in Lynn's lap, staring at the sky, watching a pair of prairie hawks circling in the warm thermals high above him. Their keen eyes searching the ground for prey, a juicy mouse, a ground squirrel, or perhaps…!

Paddy began to mutter, and then reared up crossing himself in a crazy manner. "Faith and begg-orie Brannon,'tis the vultures a flyin' in the sky—already they be a waitin' for ol' Paddy to die—so's they can feast on me bones!"

Then spotting the blood on Brannon's face, he gave a gasp and passed out. With a grin, Lynn said, "Father, your face…use your bandana to stop the bleeding, else Paddy will be like this the rest of the day."

"I'll be fine darlin'. I've got to round up the hosses, so's we can git us outta this place," replied Brannon, "The crik's a droppin, we're gonna be able to cross it a lot easier this time."

Though it was a struggle for old Grandpa Brannon, the boss of the herd was able to see everyone safely back to the wagon. Lame Deer and little Lynn helped load Lynn and Paddy into the wagon. They all headed back up the creek to their ranch, under the shadow of the big mountain.

* * * Chapter 25 * * *

It was on a trail used by the old ones, that the Flathead, Kutenai, and other western tribes travelled to the prairies to hunt buffalo. Early settlers widened the trail into a wagon road so that they could haul out timber to build their homesteads.

At the Dugway crossing the trail crossed the main stream of Lariat Cross, not far from the O'Neil ranch. A mile west of the crossing, running north and south, lay the eastern boundary of the Kutenai Lakes forest reserve.

Kootenai Brown had been appointed as the Game Guardian and Fisheries Inspector for the forest reserve. The beautiful lakes and preserve were named after the Kutenai Indians, who were driven from the area by other hostiles many years before.

The old campaigner, Kootenai Brown, was riding his best saddle horse and patrolling the eastern boundary, when he came upon Paddy O'Neil cutting lodge pole timber inside the sanctuary. Paddy had a mania for building corrals and the long slender poles were a temptation the Irishman could not resist.

Mormon wood cutters had told Paddy that this area was a game preserve. He never realized the forests were protected or that he would need a permit from Kootenai Brown to cut his corral rails. With fresh cut evidence of his larceny strewn all around, Paddy was sitting on a stump stoking his pipe when Kootenai rode into the clearing.

"I see you're cutting yourself some timber," remarked the old guardian of the Queen's trees, "the spindly trees make fine rau-nch corrals I hear."

"Aye that they do stranger, why ol' Paddy's been eye-ballin' this here stand for a coon's age, he has. Me father-in-law, Matt Brannon, says he reckons I'm a damn fool. 'e says, 'you shan't stop cutting till you've cleaned out the whole damned forest,' he did."

"Matt Brannon you say. I have not seen my old friend for years," queried Brown. "You folks live around here?"

Grinning broadly, Paddy replied, "Aye, down on the south fork we've got us a spread, we have. Light and set stranger. I'll dig out me jug and we'll hoist a few, we will." Paddy crawled into his lumber wagon and shoving aside a pile of gunnysacks revealed a gallon jug of moonshine whiskey that was stashed there.

The moonshine turned out to be Paddy O'Neil's cough medicine, brewed at a well hidden still along the 49th parallel. The formula, known only to the Irishman, consisted of various powerful ingredients that tested the unsuspecting drinker's mettle and grit. Brannon referred to it as Lariat Cross coffin varnish, others simply knew it as Paddy's gut warmer. One Blood Indian of high standing, collapsing in the dust, signed his description of the moonshine as, "heap...brave-maker."

The old lawman was a bit dry, not being one to pass up a chance to indulge in some moonshine; he decided to partake of the Irishman's generosity before he arrested him. He stepped down from his horse, made himself at home, and after a few swigs from the jug was rip-roaring drunk.

"Why you crazy Irishman, I should arrest you for hewing trees in the good Queen's forest," declared Kootenai.

The lawman's mental condition rapidly declined, as he staggered around the stumps in a daze, he said, "By jove, I'll tell you what. For two jugs of gut warmer," referring to the moonshine, "I'll let you off easy—!" With a bargain struck Kootenai collapsed to the ground, snoring peacefully in the wood chips.

Paddy realized he had been drinking with a lawman and tried to sober himself up. Then he loaded the drunken Englishman into the wagon, tied his saddle horse on behind, and headed down to Lariat Cross. Paddy knew that his moonshine was potent, and was somewhat concerned about the man's condition. He figured he would need help to bring this over zealous drinker to his senses again. Brannon's coffee, so strong that it would take the kinks out of barbwire, would revive the gluttonous Brown.

Though it was only a mile as the raven flies Paddy managed to stop several times and douse his head in the creek. He even mustered the energy to drag Kootenai from the wagon in an attempt to sober up the drunken chap by dunking his whiskered jowls in the chilly mountain stream. More than once he dunked the unfortunate lawman. If it hadn't been for the Warden's highly inebriated condition the Irishman attempts to revive Kootenai probably would have drowned him.

As the sun was going down, a somewhat sober Paddy reined the big team into the home ranch. The harsh jolting of the wooden wheels roused Kootenai from his stupor. He was sitting along side Paddy, still drunk as could be, with creek water dripping from his shaggy locks, and singing songs in Métis and Cree.

Lynn O'Neil heard them coming and came from the house to see what her headstrong husband was up to this time. Brannon was sitting on his pine-thatched porch enjoying the coolness of the evening. As Lynn approached the wagon, Paddy knew it was time for him to do some explaining.

"Faith and begg-orie, me darlin' wife," he greeted, a false look of sobriety about him, "I ran across this strange subject of Her Majesty the Queen a wanderin' around up in the big pine woods. Ol' Paddy has had a horrible time a getting' him here, he has. A stubborn man he is, who be drunker than an alley cat in the pubs of Dublin town."

Kootenai Brown was teetering on the wagon seat, still singing his songs. Lynn was suspicious that this might be one of her husband's shenanigans.

"Robert Paddy O'Neil!" she said, her voice was raised and he was sure she was angry. "What have you done to this poor man? Why, why he looks to be in agony and his mind seems unsettled." Shaking her finger at him, she would not let up, "And you, you big lug," she said in a strained voice, "You are as drunk as he is."

"Now hold your hosses darlin' Lynn," he spluttered. "Ol' Paddy be as fit as a fiddle, he be…this crazy Kootenai chap has'bout drove me to the loony bin, he has!"

By now, Brannon had recognized Paddy's passenger and strolled over to the wagon. "Why it is you Kootenai," he said with a smile, "It's been years since I've seen you last."

"What's a bin goin' on here Paddy? This man looks to have been roughly abused." Brannon too was suspicious of his old pard and spoke again, "Bring my old friend over to the cabin; we'll let him sleep it off."

The next morning Kootenai awoke very hung over, Paddy's moonshine had hit him hard. Brannon poured a gallon of strong black coffee down the old ranger. The old cowboy's coffee was sure to cure him, if it didn't kill him first.

"By jove, Matt Brannon,'tis a strange thing," he moaned, "last I remember, I was arresting an odd fellow for stealing the Queen's lodge poles. I think I can also remember my head being under water and, and—by jove, it is a strange thing that has happened to me, everything else is blank!"

Later, after Brannon and the Englishman had caught up on the gossip of the backwoods, Brown rode back to his obligations in the Queen's forest. As

Kootenai rode away Brannon began giving Paddy a lecture over his ill-mannered treatment of the old ranger.

The Irishman fired back, "The crazy blighter was a glutton...'e drank a jug o' me finest, he did! 'e took a big swig...and would not stop, seemed like me bloomin' jug was stuck to'is moustache!"

Struggling to keep from smiling over Paddy's yarn, Brannon glared at his old partner and roared, "This is the man who saved me from the calaboose in Fort Macleod so many years ago. He's been my friend since I came into these territories."

* * *

Sara Lame Deer drew the respect of many area settlers in her role as medicine woman, midwife, and spiritualist. The mountain folk travelled for miles to partake of treatments in her big Nez Perce tepee.

There were times when her powers of persuasion were not to be questioned. The Nez Perce woman convinced the superstitious Paddy to take her to the grave of Lynn Brannon, high in the Rockies.

"Lame Deer have a dream," she explained, "dream say: go bring Lynn home...to this Lariat Cross!" She patiently explained, "Go to snowy mountains—before white owl comes to fill belly."

Surprisingly, the Irishman agreed. He appeared awed by her request and went right to work building a coffin. When the coffin was complete he hid it in the big wagon. Then the pair, Paddy and Sara Lame Deer, slipped away in the night, mysteriously vanishing. Not even Lynn O'Neil knew of the events that were taking place. It would be two weeks before they returned.

Paddy's big team was grain fed and ready to go. It was no chore for them to pull the wagon up the boulder-strewn trail to the crest of the Continental Divide.

Lame Deer walked right to the gravesite that she and Little Elk had prepared so long ago in a howling blizzard. All that was keeping the blanket-clad remains from the predators of the forest was a pile of stones. Paddy was given the task of removing the stones and placing Lynn's bones into the coffin.

His manner appeared reverent and subdued when he spoke, "it is a creepy thing, it is...disturbin' the bones of this mother of me darlin' Lynn."

They were all set to return to Lariat Cross when two riders came up the trail from the west. They were in tow of a string of pack mules laden with surveying equipment. These government men informed Paddy that, starting early in the spring, this old Indian trail would be upgraded to the status of a stage road. On the summit of the Pass considerable grading and levelling would be necessary in order to allow easy passage of the top-heavy stage coaches that would be crossing over.

With his eyes as large as saucers, Paddy glared at Lame Deer and then he spoke, "Faith and begg-orie woman, ye must be a witch—how did ye know? The builders of this new road would a tore me mother-in-law's bones to smithereens, they would!"

Lame Deer, not understanding the Irishman's jargon, just grinned and said, "Paddy take Lynn and Lame Deer home now—to big man who roars like bear—!"

On the journey back poor Paddy was a nervous wreck. He was superstitious, he sat as far from Lame Deer as he could get. Sara Lame Deer gave him the willies sometimes. She would look at him and grin and the Irishman would make the sign of the cross each time she looked at him.

When Paddy finally reined the big team into the home ranch at Lariat Cross, all the members of the ranch were standing in the dooryard to greet them. The little crowd was agitated and appeared visibly upset.

"Where in tarnation you two bin?" Brannon roared. "We bin a huntin' all over the hills for ya. Lynn has worked herself into a tizzy; she's been worryin' for days."

Paddy O'Neil knew he was in trouble with the big cowboy and looked very uncomfortable. He was still wondering how he got himself in such a tight spot.

"'tis a sad state of affairs it is, Brannon me friend. This spooky Lame Deer would give an Irishman the haunts—it be she who made me do this thing," the Irishman explained. Paddy looked the worse for wear, he was not about to take the brunt of the old cowboy's wrath. Pointing toward the Nez Perce woman, he continued to talk, "It was she that did it, she hexed me into taking her to the bones of Lynn Brannon, she did. The remains of the mother of me darlin' Lynn are a layin' right here in this long box." He pointed towards the coffin.

A deathly silence enshrouded the ranch of Lariat Cross. Brannon's face was a sickly white, with a stunned expression, he gasped and stepped back.

Paddy had their attention now and wasn't about to lose the advantage. He made the sign of the cross and spoke, "Sacrificed ol' Paddy, I did, spendin' me days with this scary Nez Perce, Lame Deer!" The Irishman was becoming concerned over the old cowboy's appearance and stepped down from the wagon. "Take care, me old pard," he said. "Don't be havin' a fit on me. Tell me where you want your wife's grave, ol' Paddy will start diggin, he will."

Lynn O'Neil was overjoyed and could not contain herself. She understood what a feat her husband had accomplished. She also knew what he must have endured by doing the deed. She hurried over and gave him a big hug and a kiss that completely melted Paddy. He gave a sigh and relaxed, happy to be back in the good graces of his darling wife.

"Thank you Paddy," she told him. "This is a wonderful thing you have done for my family and me. I love you, you crazy Irish galoot!"

"I sure love ya me darlin' Lynn," he replied. "It wus me pleasure to fetch your mothers bones for a proper burial."

Brannon was in shock, this surprise was almost too much for him to bear. "Is it really my Lynn in the long box Paddy?" he finally managed to ask. "Why didn't ya take me with ya, the least ya coulda done was let me know what ya were up to."

"Great Spirit say—bring Lynn Brannon to Lariat Cross," Sara said. "Lynn Brannon happy now, Lame Deer happy now, Big Bear that Roars...happy now!"

She signed towards the Irishman and spoke again, "Crazy man...afraid of Lame Deer. Much chatter like magpie."

The old cowboy's roar was subdued as he spoke to Paddy in a quiet voice, "You can dig the grave up by the aspens Paddy, reckon we'll start a family graveyard up there. Leave room for me." He shook himself and gave a big sigh, "right beside my darlin' Lynn."

After her part in the rescue of the women of Lariat Cross, saving their lives in the flash flood, Jenni had become somewhat of a celebrity. She remained as aloof and mysterious as Lame Deer, just as silent, just as unpredictable; and always right.

With the completion of Lynn Brannon's grave in the new graveyard addition of the ranch, Jenni shared her loyalty between Matt Brannon's cabin and Lynn Brannon's grave. Each morning she could be found staring at the mound of dirt by the aspen grove. Little Lynn spent much of her time, along with Jenni, beside her Grandma's grave. Here she felt at peace and close to her Grandma Brannon. She would ponder on her namesake's short life, as she marvelled at the powerful influence this lady held over her Grandpa. It was balm for little Lynn's soul.

Here on the eastern front of the Rocky Mountains, Matt Brannon had settled in and was content to be with his family. He loved these secluded woods along Lariat Cross Creek and could think of no other place he would rather be.

Although Brannon was aware that the name of the creek had been changed to Lee's Creek, the old cowboy preferred to call it Lariat Cross. Folks figured he was tetched when they heard him talk of the creek, but the big Texan did not care. He would call the creek Lariat Cross for the rest of his days.

Matt Brannon was slowing down as the long years of heart ache and violence caught up to him. The bullet in his chest at Dawson City, the grizzly bear mauling, and the fight to rescue his daughter had taken their toll on him.

Often the family would gather at Lynn Brannon's gravesite paying their respects to Grandma Brannon. In the evenings as the sun faded into the west, a lonely howl was often heard, Grandpa Brannon's, wild cowboy yell.

"Faith and begg-orie," his Irish pard would exclaim. "The father of me Lynn does roar like a bear. I'm a fearin' of the leprechauns, I be. My old pard's roar will bring the little green devils down outta the dark woods, I can feel it in me bones."

* * * Chapter 26 * * *

It was early in the morning when Brannon arose, strapped on his Peacemaker and slipped out of his cabin with a sack of grub and his bedroll. He harnessed the big team, and smiled at the ruckus that was greeting him from out of the still darkened woods.

A coyote returning from its nightly hunt stopped a moment to yodel a farewell to a sinking moon. From a secluded den nearby, the coyote's mate yip-yipped an urgent reply. Out in the aspen woods a robin chirped, heralding the arrival of a new day, boasting of its family in a secluded nest.

The sad complaint of a mourning dove echoed from the creek brush, telling everyone that the long night was over—that morning is here—morning is here—morning is here. Brannon was often awakened by his forest friends the mourning dove, coyote, and robin.

As the wagon rolled down country it was getting light enough to see the winding trail. Brannon was still upset over the disappearance of the two rifles. The old Yellow Boy of Lynn Brannon's was a valuable keepsake, dating back to their marriage at Miles Town.

The old Texan could not believe his superstitious partner's yarn about little green men. He speculated that it was foolish to think as Paddy did. There had to be a reasonable explanation for the rifles disappearance. Besides he wanted them back. Lynn's gun meant a lot to him, it was part of the Brannon heritage.

The day was long spent when he arrived at the ravaged campsite. The wrecked wagon that the women had been using was still there. It was nearly buried in flood litter and silt. He would salvage the wheels after he searched for the guns. He planned on staying a few days that was why he had brought his bedroll and camping gear along. He needed time by himself to solve the mystery of the missing rifles.

Jenni wandered into camp, laid herself down by the big wagon and gave a weary sigh. She had followed her old friend, and would not allow Brannon to go anywhere without her. Kindling a fire, he put on the coffee pot and settled back to ponder out this confounded conundrum.

The old cowboy rose from his slumber with the sun. He enjoyed his first cup of coffee as he divided the team's oats with the horses and Jenni. This is just like old times he mused, when he was a wanderer, alone with the horses in the wild places he was so fond of.

* * *

A crisis had erupted at the home ranch; Grandpa Brannon hadn't shown up for supper. Grandpa, his mule Jenni, a team of horses, and a wagon had disappeared. No one had seen Brannon or Jenni all day. Paddy was unable to locate them and little Lynn and Matthew had not seen them either. Lynn O'Neil was worried sick and admonished her husband to find the old cowboy.

"'tis strange, me darlin' Lynn, ol' Paddy cannot figure out where they might be," he responded. "He's a takin' up with the little wanderin' devil, Jenni, he has. Might be a chinaman's chance he be at the Jenni Mine, under the big Chief Mountain."

Paddy, little Lynn and Matthew rode up to the Jenni Mine on the hunt for Grandpa Brannon.

* * *

Matt Brannon felt quite sure that the rifles were still here. He searched every nook and cranny of the old camp but luck was not with him. Returning to the campfire he sat down in the shade of a cottonwood and stoked his pipe. The tobacco relaxed him and he fell asleep. The old cowboy slept for an hour or two, and then woke up refreshed.

When he awoke from his nap, the sun at his back, he noticed an odd speck of light glittering across the clearing. He blinked his eye and the speck of light vanished. He was curious and walked over to discover a small spot of metal that appeared to be gunmetal.

With his belt knife he carefully scraped away the hardened silt. It was gunmetal all right, a rifle lay buried here. It was a tedious task, performed by a sweating Grandpa Brannon, that eventually uncovered little Lynn's lever-action rifle.

The rifle was sure a mess, but he would be happy to clean it up so that little Lynn could use it again.

* * *

Night was upon them before Paddy and the two youngsters arrived at the gold mine under the crags of the big Chief. They were tired from the long ride but prepared their camp before it was too dark to see. After a supper of biscuits, bacon and coffee, they settled in for a nights stay. They had discovered no sign of Brannon or Jenni at the Mule Dung Diggings.

Little Lynn was upset that they had not found Grandpa and Jenni here. She tossed in her blankets for some time before she could settle down. She recalled old Raven Wings and discreetly watched for him to sneak into camp. She giggled to herself when she spotted the bag of coffee sitting near the fire and the empty pot balanced on a stone of the fire ring. She hoped that she just might catch the old coffee-poacher in action.

Struggling to watch for Raven Wings, little Lynn could not keep her eyes open and fell sound asleep. A bird of the night voiced an eerie whistle, a faint rustle over near the cliffs as a figure appeared out of the darkness and moved to the tiny cooking fire.

The apparition took the coffee pot, lifted it up for a taste, and discovered it was empty. Spotting the bag of coffee it picked it up instead leaving a wee charm in its place. As silent as a ghost it approached Lynn's blankets and placed a small bundle of black feathers, wrapped securely with strands of sweet grass and sage, near the sleeping girl's cheek. Stepping back, it watched the sleeping family then vanished into the shadows.

The next morning at daylight, Lynn was roused from her blankets by the scent of sweet grass and sage, and by the sound of Paddy's Celtic cursing. She giggled at the sight of the medicine bundle on her pillow. It was old Raven Wings calling card.

Paddy was livid as he expounded to the heavens about the unholy virtues of the little green men that inhabited this place. They had stolen his bag of coffee, leaving only a wee shard of fossil rock in exchange.

In the daylight it became evident to Paddy that Brannon had not been here at all. The three broke camp and returned to the ranch on Lariat Cross hoping that Brannon and Jenni had returned in their absence.

* * *

Sweat was pouring from every pore of the old cowboy's body; he was bone-tired and plumb worn out. Stopping the digging and scraping, he took a break from his search for Lynn's old Yellow Boy. He stirred up the fire and brewed coffee, as he thought about how lucky he was to have found little Lynn's rifle. The other gun must be someplace near. He guessed it would take a bit longer to find Lynn's Yellow Boy then he would head back home to Lariat Cross.

He enjoyed the rest, even snoozed for an hour or two, then with his long knife continued probing the hardpan. He tired more often now but he would not give up.

The ten-inch blade touched something harder than the hardpan. "Could it be the Yellow Boy?" he thought. It was possible that he had just hit a creek rock. This was what he needed to continue his search. He was sure eager to find out if it was a gun. He was sweating more now; exhausted and ready to call it a day when, without warning, tightness gripped his chest. It was tightness that was followed by a dull ache. Then a sharp pain hit him that would not go away! The pain frightened him to the core, as it persisted without going away. His fright increased, he knew something serious was happening to his body!

"Oh God, not now," he prayed. "Just let me live a little longer...please! I'm so close, so very close."

The old Texas cowboy, a wild one in his day, was now stooped in stature with hair that was turning very gray. Brannon, the fastest gun fighter north of the Brazos, was now in trouble here in the valley of Lariat Cross, the kind of trouble that a fast draw could not fix. His breathing came in agonized gasps, as the intense pain consumed his chest. His entire body appeared to be on fire.

Even though he was in intense pain he would not quit, he stubbornly insisted on finishing his chore. It was Lynn Brannon's famous Yellow Boy that he wanted to find, her lever-action .38, the one old Ben Riley gave her back at Miles Town so long ago, the little weapon that she loved so much and could shoot so well.

"Why, Lynn could have faced the best there was and came out the winner," he mused. "When danger had confronted her, she had defended herself and her own. She had faced the danger so bravely."

Brannon knew that she was frightened each time she fired her gun but he also knew it was her bravery that had made all the difference. Lynn, the wife of Brannon the Texas gun fighter, had mastered the fast draw. The fast draw skill with a lever-action rifle was a hard skill to master.

Their married life had been so short. They had not had much time to spend together. Fate intervened and changed the course of their lives together.

With stubborn determination the old cowboy cleared away the baked soil and uncovered most of the gun barrel. He was pleased that it was Lynn's rifle he was uncovering. He was nearing the end of his quest.

Once again sundown arrived in this high country. Old Brannon returned to the fire and ate a small supper. He felt sick and his body was hurting, the damn pain would not let him be. A scary heaviness remained upon his chest and shoulders, moving down into his arms as well.

"Must be the bullet wound from Dawson City," he mused. "That must be it!"

The old scar had always bothered him, but now it was causing a much worse pain.

After a second sleepless night he crawled from his blankets. The heaviness remained in his chest and the pain refused to go away. He drank coffee, cup after cup of the stimulating brew he consumed. Why hadn't he thought of this before? Coffee is what he needed; the brew should fix him up right away.

All his life coffee had been Brannon's saving grace. He liked his coffee so strong that it could eat through barbwire. He used it as a cure for any ailment that might come along. This morning on the Lariat Cross creek his coffee let him down. His wonder medicine that had always helped him over the many long years, his elixir of the plains, was no match for this ailment that had befallen him. It didn't even taste good this morning, as the terrible pain throbbed in his chest.

He must uncover Lynn's rifle and then hightail it for home. His daughter and Sara Lame Deer would help him; they would know what to do.

It was touch and go, but the stubborn old Texan won out and retrieved the rifle. He tossed his gear slowly into the wagon and climbed up on the big front wheel. In the wagon seat was where he wanted to be. He would go back to Lariat Cross now, home to his family.

As the pain worsened, a terrifying pang penetrated Brannon's very soul, he collapsed on the wagon seat with sweat pouring from his brow. Oh, he was in pain; such agonizing pain! He spoke but no sound came from his lips, "I don't know what is wrong...must be a getting' old. The pain—if only the damned pain would let an ol' wanderer be!" he thought.

The wagon was moving; the horses were ready for the trail and started out on their own. The big draft team made a wide turn; they were uncertain where to go since no one was at the reins. Then Jenni moved out, in front of the wagon, leading the way. The team knew and trusted Jenni and they were content to follow her.

It was the middle of a dark night before Jenni and her entourage reached the home ranch. She never stopped at the corrals, but continued wandering up to the aspen grove. With a weary sigh she settled herself down by the grave of Lynn Brannon. The faithful team, following closely behind the mule, stopped and patiently waited.

Paddy had been roused from his sleep by the sound of the wagon passing the house. In his nightshirt he went to the door, looked and listened, but could detect nothing. Grumbling to himself, the Irishman returned to his bed.

Little Lynn was not sleeping well because she was worried sick over the disappearance of her grandpa. She wondered where he had gone and hoped that he was not hurt.

She arose early and decided to go up to her grandma's grave. As she rounded the big house and looked toward the aspen grove she saw Grandpa Brannon's team and wagon. Little Lynn also saw Jenni there as well; Lynn could see her long ears pointing towards the wagon.

Lynn's heart soared, she was so happy to see that her grandpa was back. She ran to the wagon, crawled up the big wheel and found the old cowboy sprawled across the wagon seat. His face was very pale and he looked dreadfully sick and in pain. She saw the two rifles and knew where he had been. There was something in his outstretched hand! She could see that he was offering an object to her. His voice was completely gone. Accepting his offering she recognized it as a gold wedding band. It was the same wedding band that had belonged to her Grandma Brannon. The ring had been given to Lynn Riley Brannon by her father, Ben Riley, on her wedding day so many years ago in Miles Town!

* * * Chapter 27 * * *

It was in the ranch graveyard, up near the aspen woods, that the old Texas cowboy was buried beside his darlin' Lynn. The two were together now, after all the heart-breaking lonely years; they were once again with each other. In this peaceful mountain valley their spirits could be content. They would finally be able to rest in peace.

From as far away as the rough breaks of Hell's Kitchen, the timbered slopes of Pole Haven, and from out across the prairie they came. Neighbours and friends stood by the grave, in a show of respect to the old Texas gunfighter, Matt Brannon.

The Mormon Bishop spoke at the woodland funeral. He gave a eulogy that comforted the mourners. It gave them the hope that after this life they would be reunited with Matt and Lynn Brannon.

The family of Matt Brannon were broken hearted but buoyed by their faith. Robert Paddy O'Neil was devastated. Matt and Paddy had been together for so long. They had gone through so much together. Paddy was subdued and forlorn; there was a void in his big Irish heart that could never be filled.

"Jumpin' Jehosophats," he moaned. "Why? Why me old pard? Lariat Cross will never again be the same, it won't!"

Lynn O'Neil was in shock over the loss of her father. She would sure miss him, especially his wild Texas yell, the smell of tobacco emanating from his pipe, and the taste of his freshly brewed coffee. Most of all she would miss the intense love that he showed for his family. She knew that Matt Brannon would always remain a powerful influence in her life, through her memories, and by his comforting spirit.

Sara Lame Deer, Little Elk and their family were shaken by the death of their friend. They did not show much emotion but grieved in their own way. Sara had always kept her feelings hidden to others, locked up inside her.

"Man Who Roars Like Bear—gone now!" she muttered in her Nez Perce language. She looked at the sky and mumbled again, "With Great Spirit now...with Lynn Brannon now!"

Little Lynn, his loving granddaughter was sobbing as if her heart would break, she just could not be stopped. He had left her so much, Great Grandma's gold ring, and the little rifle that he had taught her to shoot. But most of all, he had given her hope, courage, and pride in herself and a love for her family. Brannon had meant so very much to his granddaughter.

Brannon's little cowboy, Matthew, was devastated as well. He had never known a day that his Grandpa hadn't been there for him. The old gunfighter from the Brazos in Texas had spent many hours teaching young Matthew the ways of the cowboy. To Matthew, Grandpa Brannon had left the old Peacemaker 44-40.

Paddy and Lynn tried to console their children but it was as if their hearts had been broken.

Jenni the pack mule, Brannon's long-eared friend would spend any spare minute she had by the graves in the aspen grove. The two, Brannon and Jenni, had been inseparable, saving each other's lives on more than one occasion.

With the eternal music of the creek, Brannon knew as Lariat Cross, sighing in the background the mourners huddled together in their grief.

Brannon's wild friends, those of the forest and the plains, the coyote, the robin and the mourning dove sang him a farewell song, a chorus whose song was heard every morning just before dawn...the serenade of Lariat Cross.

* * * Chapter 28 * * *

The dawn of a new day was fast approaching the eastern front of the Rocky Mountains, and the wilderness canyon that was home to Lariat Cross creek. Several years had passed since the death of Matt Brannon. A pre-dawn darkness lay heavy in the wooded valley, a dense void that blocked out all sight and sound. Here, at the tree line, along the headwaters of this pure mountain stream, a lodge pole pine forest and a massive slide of fractured rock and shale became one.

Several hundred feet above the alluvial fan, a prominent ledge overlooked the valley below. A motionless apparition of the high places sat on the fractured ledge, legs crossed, peering into the intense blackness. The shadow was clad in greasy buckskins, had a black raven feather in its hair and a well-worn par fleche hung from its waist. It was keenly alert, staring intently down into a clearing where the pine forest and rock slide came together.

Probing the darkness below, the shadow perched on a ledge of Old Chief Mountain, watched another shadow moving about in a small camp. The apparition's keen eyes spotted the faint spark from a white-eyes fire stick, and watched with interest as a small flame spread through the kindling and ignited the cheery blaze of a camp fire.

A hawk-beaked nose reacted to the scent of seasoned pine smoke and to the scent of a young maiden as well. A slight smile took shape on a weather-tanned face.

The young female scent was familiar to the old Flathead holy man, and it pleased him. He was more than pleased when the aroma of fresh-brewed coffee came drifting up into the crags, carried there by a fitful canyon breeze. The coffee smell stirred old Raven Wings into action. A subdued croak of a night bird sounded from the ledge and then the old shadow of the wastelands was on the move.

Raven Wings knew the young woman belonged with his old friend, the one he knew as Big Bear that Roars, even though he hadn't seen either for several years. Her scent had been here at this camp when she was a young girl.

He also recalled that she had visited here more recently. She had been with the crazy white man who talked all the time. His mouth watered as he recalled the big tin of coffee the foolish white man had left by the fire. This time the young woman was alone.

Raven Wings was an unseen shadow on the move, invisible in the pre-dawn darkness, as he snuck in close to the camp of the white-eyed girl.

"It's a breakin' daylight...time we wus a movin' out!" The familiar phrase flashed through her mind. The saying brought a smile to the girl's lips and a pang to her heart. It was a phrase she had heard many times before from her Grandpa Brannon before he saddled his bronc and made that last ride across the great divide.

Wiping tears from her eyes, she stirred from the melancholy that surrounded her in this early hour. Mornings had been the hardest for her these past years since old Matt Brannon had died. She stood up from the fire, stepped back into the shadows and returned with an armful of dead branches.

Dropping the tinder-dry fuel on the glowing embers, she watched as the flames sprang to life and lit up the small clearing. The girl then settled back on the old windfall to relax and watch the fire.

Little Lynn Duval was out-of-sorts and couldn't seem to shake the melancholy that surrounded her like a shroud. She had been upset since she had a fight with Paddy O'Neil, her stepfather. He was the only father that she had ever known.

Their respective differences of opinion had worsened lately and she had finally blown her top. Lynn had a carefully controlled temper, but the constant badgering by the Irishman had been the last straw.

Unable to stand any more of his Irish blarney, and much to her mother's objections, she had packed her saddlebags and ridden away into the setting sun. Lynn had to get away from the Lariat Cross ranch and think the problem over. She also wanted to make plans for her future, which seemed bleak at this time in her life. Now she was here, at the Jenni Mine, in this beautiful, peaceful location at the lee of the big mountain, Old Chief.

This was a place where Lynn Duval could unwind, think, and plan. She could take her time to sort out her bleak future.

"'tis time ye wus a movin' out, lassie o' me darlin' wife!" Paddy would tell her, on a daily basis. Then an argument would erupt between her mother and Paddy.

"Faith and begor-rie Lynn, you're a big girl now. Find ye a man ye can live with lass – 'tis time ye wus a star-rtin' ye a life o' yer own—makin' and raisin' babies, and all the rest!" O'Neil had insisted.

Tears flooded her eyes as she remembered the fights. "Ride down to the Mor-rmon camps—latch on to the trader's son—a good catch he would be…he'd make a fine husband to ye Lynn Duval. Provide ye with a good'ome –and a warm bed too—Be a fool if he didn't!"

Paddy O'Neil's ancestry dated back to the infamous potato famine in Ireland, reason enough for his constant concern over food, shelter and a strong able husband for the lasses and widows of the family. These ideas were ingrained in his mind by the teachings of his parents when he was a small lad. Lynn was able to understand his feelings. She could forgive him for his constant badgering. Dog-gone it all she did want to have a strong, handsome husband, one she could love and cherish. She would be happy to bring forth strong sons. The trader's son was not the one for her. She would never marry him; he was not strong or handsome.

Brushing away a tear, Lynn Duval, the namesake of her mother and grandmother, shrugged away the memories and remembered she was hungry. It was sure enough time for some breakfast and a cup of coffee. A good strong cup of coffee would taste good and would help settle her jangled nerves.

Lynn smiled as she remembered her grandpa and his love for coffee. He had been addicted to the stimulating brew. It was Brannon who was responsible for her dependence on the brew as well. The drink was a comfort to her—she felt closer to him when the pot was bubbling and the enticing aroma was strong in the air.

Lynn kept busy around the camp, cooking her morning meal of biscuits, bacon and coffee. She giggled to herself when she remembered that this was the favourite food of her grandpa.

The fire blazed with a comforting brilliance, as its reflected light bounced off the bedroll and gear of the modest camp in the lodge poles. A trace of smoke spiralled upward, only to be caught by air currents plunging down from the big mountain in the background. This mountain is the old Chief of the others, Grandpa Brannon had told her.

The girl's saddle mare was tethered close by. Jenni, Brannon's old mule, was lying not far away at the mouth of the Jenni Mine, the gold diggings of her grandpa Brannon's. It was a real asset to the O'Neil family to know of this old mine and the gold that it contained.

She wondered if old Raven Wings was still here on the mountain, and if he was watching her now. Raven Wings and Brannon had been good friends, even though the Flathead holy man always absconded with Brannon's coffee.

To compensate for the theft of the coffee, the native of the Rocky Mountains always left a peace token, a medicine bundle of black feathers snugly wrapped with strands of sweet grass and sage.

"Perhaps he is dead now", she reasoned. While her back was turned in the shadows, her simmering coffee pot had mysteriously vanished! She found a peace token sitting on a rock of the fire ring, the calling card of old Raven Wings.

An eerie croak of a night bird sounded near by. The long ears of Jenni were standing straight in the air. Her pinto saddle mare, a progeny of Grandma Brannon's old Evening Star mare, was no longer grazing the long timothy grass that grew in the clearing. It had its head up and its alert eyes scanned the shadows.

Though an eerie chill rippled up her spine, Lynn was still in a good mood. She was happy Raven Wings was still alive and up to his mischievous ways. The swapping ritual was a token of honour and respect to the Flathead Indians.

As the sun began to show on the distant hills, high on the Chief that towered above her camp she spotted a trio of mountain goats perched on a rugged crag. These nimble, free spirits of the mountain were showing interest in the horse, the mule and the auburn-haired girl. Lynn secured her camp gear, walked over to the mine entrance and greeted Jenni with a warm hug. The little offspring of a donkey and a horse bounced to her feet and greeted Lynn with a bob of her head.

Though Lynn never noticed, Jenni's long ears were now pointing down through the lodge poles to some unknown sound emanating from the forest. Lynn thought Jenni must be thirsty as she watched the little animal ramble down the shale to a small stream of water.

The girl turned and entered the mine, nothing more than a modest tunnel dug near the down side of an immense alluvial fan. The precious metal was easy to find here at the Jenni Mine. It was found as small, irregular pieces of float and also modest-sized nuggets. The gold had never been smoothed by the action of swift-flowing water. Having filled a plump leather pouch with gold, she cached her mining tools behind a large slab of rock and turned to leave the little mine shaft.

Assisted by the mind-boggling intuition of his mule, Matt Brannon had discovered the Mother Lode here at the headwaters of Lariat Cross. That was the reason that he had christened the find "The Jenni Mine".

Besides the bag of gold she now carried, Lynn had another bag back at the ranch that her and her grandpa had mined years before. Her intentions now were to establish and stock a cattle ranch at her grandparent's old homestead on the St. Mary's River. She would get Paddy to build her a cabin on the old burned out site.

Paddy O'Neil and her Mother, along with young Matthew, her half-brother, owned Lariat Cross ranch and were working and living there. The old Nez Perce Indians, Sara Lame Deer and Little Elk lived at the ranch too.

The sun was now greeting the mountain tops; the birds of the forest were chirping a cheerful welcome to a new day in this high valley of Lariat Cross. Lugging the heavy bag of gold, sixteen-year old Lynn Duval retraced her steps back down to the camp. Out of breath, she arrived and dropped the gold by Jenni's packsaddle. Her mule would carry the gold back to Lariat Cross; it was her chore to pack the camp gear.

After taking a breather, she looked around for Jenni. A quick scan of the clearing indicated to Lynn that Jenni was not there. "The little rascal has taken of and left me again!" she muttered, as a sense of unease rippled through her. "Wonder where she might have wandered off to?"

She hurried over to the stream and found where Jenni had quenched her thirst. The dampness of the ground made for easy tracking. Her dainty footprints continued on down a swale into the forest of pine and spruce. With her saddle carbine in hand, Lynn tracked the Jenni mule far into a lonely niche in the forest.

"Jenni, Jenni, where are you?" she would call, stopping often. But there was no answer. After at least a half-mile of busting through windfalls and skirting around huge chunks of rock that had tumbled off the mountain, she stopped for a breather and once again shouted, "Jenni! Jenni, answer me...you hear?"

A mountain breeze was now teasing the tree tops as another breeze was worrying the plants that grew on the forest floor. The eerie croak of a raven sounded nearby. Then Lynn detected a welcome sound, an answer to her quest, the finale of a feeble bray from her little friend.

The girl from Lariat Cross prepared for danger ahead. She knew her Jenni mule was waiting for her to come to her aid. The forest was thick and scary; Lynn struggled to ward off a cold chill that attacked her senses.

Continuing on, the girl called and again an answer echoed back. This time the sound was much closer than before. When Lynn finally found the mule she was standing in a small clearing staring into the shadows of the forest. Lynn walked across the clearing, her rifle in hand. "Why did you leave me?" she chided, with caution in her voice. "What have you found here Jenni?"

The mule knew her friend would find her. She never moved, continuing to stare across the clearing. Remembering back to the flood on Lariat Cross Creek, when the little mule had saved the lives of Lynn, her mother, and Lame Deer, Lynn knew better than to question Jenni's intuitions. The girl knew her little mule was relaying a message, in her own way, and Lynn knew better than to doubt her warning. One of her long ears lowered in a greeting to the girl, while the other remained pointed ahead. A subdued sigh came from deep inside Jenni's chest, a sigh of relief that Lynn was now with her. Both ears were now pointed toward the forest on the far side of the clearing.

"Wait for me here Jenni...I'll go see what is upsetting you so." Lynn said.

The mule gave another sigh, almost a groan, ears still alert as she watched Lynn move to the edge of the trees. The girl's trusty saddle carbine was cocked and ready for action, her eyes intent on what lay ahead. She sensed something was here, and then she saw the body, or, what was left of a body!

Moving in close, the girl gasped when she realized this was the remains of old Raven Wings. Her missing coffee pot was here on the ground beside what had been a small twig fire. Raven Wing's mutilated body and the abundance of large clawed-tracks were stark evidence of a grizzly attack.

The corpse was still warm, wisps of steam rising from the remains. He had put up a stiff fight for his life but in the end the grizzly had won out. Following the tracks that the grizzly had left Lynn found drops of blood scattered on the forest floor.

Walking back to Jenni, she put her arms around her little friend's neck. She mourned for Raven Wings. This was a frightful reminder of the grizzly incident at the beaver dam on Lariat Cross when her Grandpa had been so badly injured. Grandpa Brannon and Jenni had suffered from the attack, and little Lynn, as grandpa had called her back then, shot the bear and saved old Matt Brannon's life.

For something like this to happen again was hard for Lynn to understand. Another grizzly bear attack had taken the life of old Raven Wings, her grandpa's good friend and a Flathead holy man who wandered the Rocky Mountains.

Once again unease overcame the little mule; she became downright fidgety and upset. Her ears were now pointing towards the shadows across the clearing. She was preparing to flee from this place.

"Take it easy Jenni," the girl told her little friend. "What is it that you see?" Lynn Duval was struggling to control her own jitters, she was frightened too. The girl and her mule stood together, facing the unknown of this silent glade in the forest.

The girl sensed a movement back in the lodge poles and could see a bulky shadow. As the shadow came closer she could see that it was a grizzly bear. It was moving back into the clearing where the remains of Raven Wings lay.

The bear snarled making a terrifying sound deep in its chest. Its fur was covered with blood that was streaming from an arrow deeply embedded in its side. Blood gushed from a neck wound too. The old Flathead's flint knife remained, buried to the hilt, in the neck of the bear.

The bear swung a shaggy head towards Lynn and her mule. It smelled their scent which was strong in the cool forest air. A blood-curdling roar gushed from its bloody jaws as it moved towards the mule and the girl who were only thirty-yards away. Jenni gave a terrified squall, spun on her hooves, and fled. Lynn was left alone to face this monster of the Rockies.

Panic was overwhelming her; she knew that she couldn't out run the beast. The only thing she could do was stand and fight. A calm peaceful feeling came over her and the fear abated. She sensed her grandpa standing beside her as his words came to her mind, "Stay calm little darlin', ya will do fine…remember…it's just like pointing your finger!"

The bear closed in giving Lynn no chance to aim her rifle. Bracing herself for what might be her last stand she swung the rifle to her hip and pulled the trigger. Ejecting the spent cartridge, she pulled the trigger again and again until the rifle was empty.

Lynn screamed as she leaped aside and watched the dying grizzly collapse at her feet. The terrible roars, the feral smell, and the blood were making her sick.

The grizzly lay dead at her feet, the danger had passed. Lynn Duval offered a quick prayer of thanksgiving that her life had been spared. She pulled Raven Wing's arrow and knife from the bear's carcass.

Turning to go, she picked up her coffee pot and headed back to camp. Jenni wasn't far ahead, and when she caught sight of the girl, she would wait patiently for Lynn to catch up and then continue on. Lynn had a tough time making it back to camp, her legs unsteady, her nerves jangled, and her emotions were very raw.

* * * Chapter 29 * * *

Sitting relaxed in the saddle on her pinto mare, Lynn headed back down the trail towards her Mom's ranch. It was hot and sultry with the midday sun bouncing off the shale and rocks that littered the trail.

Lynn loved the pinto horse that she rode, so full of spirit, yet faithful and ever mindful of the girl's wishes. She was a progeny of Evening Star, Grandma Brannon's old pinto mare; to have a horse with that lineage was icing on the cake as far as Lynn was concerned. The name she had chosen for her mare was Boots. The much darker shade of the pony's two front fetlocks reminded Lynn of a pair of boots. It was her mother who had suggested the name, and that was just fine with Lynn Duval.

She turned in the saddle to see if Jenni was still following. The little dun mule was trying to keep up with them as they all headed down the trail. With the little mule getting on in years, she often struggled to keep up and would often fall behind.

The day wore on, and soon Lynn reached timberline. She continued on to where a small stream crossed the trail, and reined back into the trees to a secluded spot in the shade of a balsam fir tree. A spring of cool water was close by, causing a rivulet to flow across the trail.

"This place will do for a rest", she mused, and stepped down from the saddle. The shade sure looked welcoming to Lynn Duval.

After she pulled the saddle from her mare's sweat-stained back, Boots drank from the spring and began to munch on the plants that grew nearby. The girl's trail lunch was a simple fare of jerked meat and spring water. It was enough to satisfy her hunger.

"Wonder what happened to Jenni?" she spoke to no one but her pinto horse. Her concern for the little mule became evident. Lynn consoled herself by thinking, "She will find us soon...she always does."

Time wore on, and still Jenni hadn't shown up. Cinching up the saddle on Boots, Lynn decided that she had better go back and find her little pet. "Jenni needs me." Lynn thought, "I just know she must be in trouble again."

All set to climb back in the saddle, with her booted foot in the stirrup, she detected a commotion back up the trail. She froze in her tracks and listened. A group of horsemen were riding her way. Loud hoots, laughter, and coarse language drifted in the still forest air.

Urging her pinto to be silent, she crept closer to the trail. From behind a thicket of birch willow she watched the rowdy bunch ride by. Luckily they paid no heed to the pinto's tracks. She counted six mounted riders and two packhorses. There was also a saddled horse with no rider along with it. Lynn was thankful her little mule was not included with their pack string. She waited for the ruckus to fade away, then stepped into the saddle and started back up the Chief Mountain trail to find her mule.

Often she would stop and call for Jenni, listening intently for a reply but no answer came. With the timberline in sight, the girl reined in the pinto. The little mare's interest was centred off to the right toward a thick stand of lodge pole. Immense chunks of rock were scattered through the timber, rocks that had tumbled from the Chief Mountain eons ago.

The horse became uneasy, and so did the rider. "Be a good girl Boots," Lynn said, trying to comfort the pinto. "Let's go and see what's back there...it might be Jenni."

The mare was reluctant to move ahead but gave in to Lynn's urging. Trembling, the pinto was set to explode, as if walking on thin ice, as she carried the girl back off the trail. Not far into the timber Boots gave a snort, almost a squeal, and stopped in her tracks. Her trembling continued as she stared at a huge cabin-sized chunk of rock, refusing to take another step.

Taking her rifle in hand, Lynn stepped to the ground and walked to the huge piece of the mountain with the pinto trailing behind her. Suddenly, the girl froze in her tracks; she thought she could hear one of Jenni's crazy sounds. It could have been a raven though; there were several of those around.

As Lynn manoeuvred around the rock, she gasped and stopped again. Across the small clearing stood a saddled horse; with its bridle reins hanging in the grass. In front of the horse lay the Jenni mule. The mule had one long ear pointed towards Lynn and Boots, and the other ear pointed to a figure lying beside her.

"I'm so happy that I found you!" Lynn shrieked. "I reckoned something bad had happened to you."

Jenni crawled to her feet and greeted Lynn with her usual mule garble; one ear was still pointed toward the ground. Trembling like a leaf, the girl crossed the clearing to the mule. As she approached Jenni, she saw that the figure in the grass was a body. "He must be a cowboy," she reckoned as she looked at the clothes he wore.

A cowboy hat lay in the grass beside him, his shirt was covered in blood and he appeared to be in bad shape. He was breathing, she could tell by the rise and fall of his wounded chest. Returning to Boots for her canteen of spring water, she propped the cowboy's head in her lap and managed to pour a few swallows of the life-sustaining liquid down his throat. She then soaked her bandana with water and cleansed his fevered face.

He stirred, attempted to rise, and then slumped back in the girl's lap. The only sound he made was a groan. "You have been hurt," she said, looking at his bloody shirt. "I'd better get you patched up."

Jenni was standing beside Lynn. Pleased that the girl had found her, though she kept her ears pointed toward the cowboy in the grass.

* * * Chapter 30 * * *

High up a wind-swept mountain, on a dim trail made by wandering sheep and goat, a horse and rider were finding themselves in trouble, as they struggled to reach the pass above. The game trail was nothing more than a trace in the massive shale slide. It was steep, narrow, and very treacherous. The shifting shale was prone to rock slides and a rider could never tell when one might occur.

The silence was broken by the harsh croak of a passing raven, and the sporadic and violent cursing of a young cowboy berating the posse that had been hot on his heels for the last three days.

The moaning of an incessant wind that blew high in the crags of Squaw Mountain swooped down now and then to pester the cowboy and the horse. Audible above the wind was the harsh clatter of sharp-shod hooves struggling for footing on the shifting, insecure trail. Though faint to hear, a poignant plea in the voice of the young rider was urging on his weary mount.

Eventually, they topped out on the windswept pass of Squaw Mountain. The trail worn rider reined in his sweat-lathered sorrel horse and took a long look back down the massive shale slide, cursing once more.

Young Will Bonner stepped down from the saddle, loosened the cinch and comforted his old friend. The big sorrel had given his all to get his rider here. The horse's head was hanging low, he was wheezing something fierce, ready to collapse on this shale-littered mountain pass. Will's beloved horse, Red, was in trouble.

Bonner caressed the sweat caked withers of the big gelding. "Reckon we'll make a stand here Red…give you a chance to rest and grab a bite to eat."

He knew that if he kept pushing the horse it would soon keel over dead. Weary as he was, the cowboy led his horse back into a copse of wind-stunted pine that was struggling to survive in this sub-alpine region. Unsaddling the horse, Will gave it a good rubdown with a scrap of sacking he kept tied on the saddle.

Then he gave his old friend a scanty handful of oats. That was the last of the oats that remained from the old stable keeper at Wild Horse Creek. Grass was sparse in this high country. Will was hoping the sorrel might find enough picking to help restore his fading energy. Rest was what the horse really needed, just a few hours of rest.

Over to the east, across a moonscape of shattered rock and barren shale, rose the backside of an old landmark that Will assumed must be Old Chief Mountain.

The big hunk of mountain is the one that stands alone, Will had been told by an old prospector while spending an evening by his fire. The big Chief Mountain is the gateway to the great grass country of the northern territories, a land that is ruled by the British Queen.

Will Bonner was comforted in the knowledge that he was nearing the northern territories known as Canada. At the end of this long, tedious journey, he hoped to find a new land and a new beginning. He would be leaving his shattered past and broken dreams behind him.

Glancing down the backside of the mountain, he cursed again as he watched the posse ride into view. He was sure it was them even though they were mere specks in the distance. At the timberline, the trail changed into a steep, shifting series of switchbacks. They were facing the same gut wrenching climb that had worn out his big sorrel horse.

The climb will slow them down, he thought. At second glance, he was stunned at the pace they were keeping, they were catching up. He had reckoned he was a good six, even eight-hour ride ahead of them but now they were closing in. He had only about two-hours he estimated.

With his rifle in hand, Will Bonner returned to the summit and hunkered behind a ledge of shattered limestone. No way was he about to allow this owl-hoot bunch to destroy his horse. They called themselves a posse yet they were nothing more than a gang of thieving killers banded together for revenge.

It was revenge against Will Bonner that they sought. Will was a down-at-the-heels cowboy riding a streak of hard luck that was destined to be his lot.

Munching on jerked meat, the young cowboy settled in to wait. He would lay low and wait for them to ride up the long exposed slope, which would put them in range of his Winchester long gun. Will planned on whittling them down some putting the fear of the dark place in their murdering souls.

Although Bonner had just turned twenty one years of age, he was still one tough hombre, as the Wild Horse Creek gamblers had found out. He was sharp-tempered and greased lightning with a six-gun.

Bonner fidgeted some as the strain of travelling through all the lonely places began to take its toll. His constant vigilance, sleeping in thin blankets, and eating like a foraging coyote were wearing him down.

His body relaxed some in the warmth of the noonday sun, his mind drifted back in time, reliving the events of the past several days.

He should never have stopped at Wild Horse Creek, the old gold town west of the Rockies. He should have continued on hunting for a spread of his own. He wanted a ranch where he could settle down, a place to stock with cattle and horses, with a sizable chunk of land. His goal was to establish the ranch and then add a wife and children to the picture.

Will Bonner was packing his small stake, enough for a start if he was careful. His luck changed when he entered that saloon in Wild Horse Creek for a meal and a bit of relaxation. He had just finished a hearty bowl of venison stew, when a woman approached his table to clear of the dishes.

As if on cue, three men stepped up to the table. With a deck of cards in hand, the oldest of the three spoke. "Care for a friendly game stranger? Could be your lucky day...Be a sport, and we'll play a foursome!"

Bonner sensed in his heart that the men were card sharks but like a fool had accepted their offer. He was eager for some company, and to participate in a friendly game of cards appealed to him right now.

Stud poker was the name of the game and after the first three hands, Bonner was down to his last fifty bucks. He had to sharpen up and win back his money so he could head on up the trail.

The fourth hand was going as poorly as the first three. Then he spotted the dealer sliding a card off the bottom of the deck. An intense emotion rippled through the cowboy's lean body. His emotion was two-fold, he was in shame at being taken for a bumbling fool and enraged that the crooked dealer of cards was cheating him. In a flash Bonner grabbed the gambler's closed hand and squeezed it with a vice-like grip, the hand opened and the ace of spades fell to the table.

"You damned cheating crook!" Will roared as rage swept over him like a thunderous storm. Swifter than a blink of an eye, Bonner grasped the gambler's fingers, crunching them until the bones cracked.

"My hand, my hand!" screamed the gambler. "You've broken my dealing hand—I'll kill you for this you damned border trash!"

The three gamblers and the cowboy stood up from the table. Bonner had released the dealer's hand, as he reached for his Colt .44.

"Reckon this here pot is mine," he said as he scooped up the coins. You ol' swindlers thought you could cheat me."

"Kill him! Kill the cowboy!" screeched the terrified dealer, as he cradled his broken hand.

"He has ruined me…I'll never be able to deal another hand!"

His two cronies in crime were ready to draw but hesitated as they looked into the cowboy's eyes. They could tell he was one salty cowboy.

Crazy with pain and shock, the dealer tried to make a cross draw for his gun with his good hand. Bonner's draw was smooth and fast, a red-hot streak of lead smashed into the dealer's partially drawn gun, knocking it to the floor. A neat bullet hole appeared in the palm of the crooked dealer's other hand. He now owned two useless hands.

Convulsing in horror the dealer screamed again, "Kill him!" The sight of his own blood dripping to the floor was more than he could handle. "Kill him I say…the saddle tramp deserves to die."

Recognizing the order, his two partners in crime went for their guns. Two more shots rang out in the saloon, so close together the Saloon patrons figured there had only been one. The two fell to the floor, with expressions of disbelief strongly embedded on their faces. The hush in the saloon was as thick as the smoke, no one dared to speak or even to breath.

"I had to do it!" Bonner broke the silence. "It was them or me, the miserable skunks drew on me—all three of them. Reckon it was self defence!"

With that said he walked out the swinging doors and crossed over to the livery stable. He needed to pick up his bronc and vamoose from this town. Paying the old timer in charge, Will was in the saddle ready to leave when the oldster spoke, "You had better clear outta here fast stranger, whatever your name is. The one whose hands you busted up has connections here. Blood kin, and what not. He'll have a posse hot on yer heels…string you up for sure!"

"Thanks old timer," Bonner said, and handed him another silver dollar. "That's for the oats you put in my saddle bags, I appreciate your kindness."

"Sure enjoyed the show you put on over there," the old one replied, nodding toward the saloon. "I'll side you with the law, it was self defence. I'll tell them so, by cracky."

Across the trail at the saloon a rifle barrel appeared above the batwing doors. A shot rang out and the hosteler slumped to the ground, blood gushing from a bullet hole in his chest.

"Sure enjoyed the show," he gasped. "Them tinhorns had it a cummin'. Reckon I'm gonna cash in my ch—!" A sigh came from his lips, the old one faded away into the painless aura of darkness. Bonner put the spurs to his bronc and headed out of town.

"Think Ill head to the east," he quickly decided, "I'll head for the Rocky Mountains."

At the saloon, droves of men were pouring into the street with their guns shooting. They were cursing and shouting, adding to the uproar that Bonner and the gamblers had started.

A barrage of red-hot lead put fear into the rider as he and the horse passed by. The young cowboy, Will Bonner, rode away fading into his awaiting destiny.

Will tried to shrug away the memories as he stirred from his hideaway on Squaw Mountain. Then he walked back to see how his old pard was doing. The horse was quietly resting and luckily appeared to be in fine health. His hair was spotted with residue from a recent roll in the ground litter. After giving Red another good rubdown and cleaning him up, Bonner cinched the saddle back on. They might have to leave in a hurry so he wanted to be ready to ride.

Returning to the hidden ledge, he prepared himself for the approaching riders. He removed his hat so that nothing showed above the slab of rock but his eyes and the rifle barrel.

The sun was hot and unforgiving at the summit. Bonner wiped the sweat from his brow and continued his silent vigil. He fidgeted to remain alert, as he knew the posse should be showing up soon.

Fuelled by a surge of adrenalin, excitement swept through the cowboy as he spotted the posse ride into view. They were on the long, steep climb that led nowhere but up. On both sides of the narrow trail, where they rode, cliffs dropped sharply off into empty space.

At first there was only one rider then six more mounted riders appeared on the trail riding single file, nose to tail. This is perfect Bonner reckoned, now is the time to teach this miserable lot a lesson from the good book.

He took careful aim on the lead rider, pulled the trigger on his Winchester and watched the mayhem that followed. His shot was a bit short, and smacked into the shale in front of the lead horse, then ricocheted as it whined a deadly tune. The animal squalled and reared in fright upsetting the rider. Both the rider and the horse tumbled off the trail, spilled over a cliff, and rolled down into the valley below.

The second rider fought to control his horse which bucked, and then they too tumbled off to the same fate as the leader. Will raised the sights of his gun a touch, and then pulled the trigger for the second time. This time the bullet hit the rider of the third horse who fell from the saddle, though he was sure that he had only winged him.

Panic spread through the remainder of the posse, as they managed to turn their wild-eyed broncs around and flee to the safety of the timberline. A horse with an empty saddle trailed behind.

Will Bonner was pleased with the results of his ambush. "A payback for the old timer at Wild Horse Creek," he spoke to the wind, "for gunnin' down the old hosteler who was an innocent, unarmed man."

Although he was sorry to know that two horses had tumbled over the cliff, he had no sympathy for the riders.

"An eye-for-an-eye my old pappy used to say. So says the good book!"

He left the barricade, picked up the reins of the sorrel horse, and together they walked on down Squaw Mountain Pass. The trail turned into a steep, sliding mass of shale. So he was forced to lead the sorrel. He sure couldn't chance a broken leg or a fall.

As the day wore on the severity of the trail eased up some. The cowboy and his horse had at last walked away from the Pass. He could sense the sorrel was finished for the day, totally spent. Old Red had performed surprisingly well considering what he had been through.

Behind the big mountain, the landscape remained barren; there was no sign of any vegetation. Will found a seep of water pooling in a small pocket of limestone, it was sufficient for the cowboy and his horse to quench their thirsts. "Reckon we'll make camp here, by this waterhole," he said, and pulled the saddle from the horse. "Sure hope a good night's rest, and this here water will give you enough energy to continue on in the mornin'. Reckon what's left of that posse is still a comin'. You and I need to get a little shut eye tonight."

The night passed without incident, and though gaunt and in need of food, the big horse looked much better. A few hours rest had made a big difference.

Bonner took one last look back toward the Pass; no one was on the trail as far as he could tell. Maybe the ruckus of the day before had convinced them to leave him alone and to head back across the Rockies where they belonged.

In the saddle he headed down the trail, Red was doing fine, walking cautiously and slowly. The old game trail was angling around the north face of the mountain. The cowboy relaxed, he was going to make it after all!

"Another fifty-yards Red, and then I'll walk some more…them green trees are gettin' close, mighty close!"

At that moment a powerful force struck him! The echo of a rifle shot bounced back and forth high in the crags on the mountain. Shock swept through his body. Drifting in and out of awareness, he gritted his teeth and prayed to the Saints above that he could stay in the saddle. If he fell to the ground he would be a goner for sure!

The bridle reins hung loose, the sorrel horse waited patiently for the comforting prompting of the old Spanish bit in his mouth. The horse sensed his friend was in trouble, smelling his blood and hearing his groans. The big cowboy was no longer talking to him.

Red's big head raised as his velvet nostrils searched the breeze for a scent of what lay ahead. His sense of smell caught a whiff of pine trees, wild berries, and green juicy plants. The horse continued on, ever mindful of Bonner slumped in the saddle. Will had both of his hands clasped to the rigging in a death grip.

A raven croaked nearby. High in the sky a golden eagle soared, on widespread wings, in the thermals. A canyon breeze sang a wilderness song to the horse as the pines sighed their pleasure.

* * * Chapter 31 * * *

The sorrel horse stepped off into the shale slide with caution as he started down to the forest. There was no trail to follow only gut instinct and smell guided the horse. The green of the pine forest below beckoned to the horse.

Trembling with fatigue, Red stopped often to make sure the gunshot cowboy was still in the saddle. It also allowed him a respite from the tedious descent. At one of these breaks, his wilderness honed ears sensed a hint of danger. It was a strange garble of sound, somewhat frightening to the horse, yet somehow familiar.

Red stared into the pine forest wondering why Bonner never touched him with his spurs. He heard the strange sound again, a sound that was so puzzling to the horse.

The scent of plants was overpowering and the sorrel was starving. He cautiously continued on. Entering the pine forest he immediately lowered his head and began to ravenously feed on the succulent forage. The horse grazed for a long time until it heard the strange noise again. This time it was much closer!

It was a foreign sound but the horse sensed that it would not harm him. He glanced back to make sure Bonner was still in the saddle and moved toward the sound. As he neared a huge chunk of rock that had fallen from the big mountain eons ago, the big horse could see a small animal in the gloom of the forest.

The little mule watched, with interest, the approach of the sorrel horse with the man swaying in the saddle. Without any warning the mule bounced to its feet and uttered an unearthly sound. The sudden flurry of sight and sound spooked the sorrel horse. He lunged violently to the side and unseated his gunshot friend. Will tumbled to the ground and landed amongst the greenery that grew there.

A deep rooted bond of loyalty would keep the big horse close to his fallen friend. His ears were laid back as a warning to the mule to stay away from the fever-wracked body of his friend. Staying close to the cowboy, the sorrel lowered his head to crop the lush plants that grew in this sheltered place.

As an irritation to the horse the mule insisted on lying on the far side of Bonner. She lay as close to him as she could get. With his ears laid back Red would attempt to shoo her away but she wouldn't budge. Her own ears were laid low, strange sounds came from her throat, yet Jenni would not move. She sensed the horse was only bluffing and would not harm her.

In disgust, Red would leave and continue his grazing. On occasion he would return to the cowboy and sweeping his velvet nose across Bonner's face he would check the cowboy's breathing. Will's breathing was so ragged that it ruffled the long hairs on the horse's nose.

One of Jenni's long ears remained pointing at the fallen cowboy the other was pointed out toward the Chief Mountain trail. She sensed someone was coming, and she knew who it would be. A voice sounded again, she still did not move from the cowboy's side. Several times though, one of her half-hearted brays, more of a snort erupted from deep inside her as if she answered the voice from the timber. The little mule knew that it was Lynn Duval calling her name. Everything would be fine now, the little Jenni mule knew!

With the arrival of the girl at the clearing, the two animals appeared pleased to have a human there. To listen to her feminine chatter, and to be a part of her warm friendly essence, was a comfort to the animals.

Lynn discovered that the cowboy was unconscious and burning up with fever. She helped him to drink a few swallows of water and opened his shirt to see the extent of his injuries. She found a bloody looking mess from the wounds of a bullet.

"He has been shot in the back!" she murmured.

After cleansing the wounds, she prepared a poultice with moss from a nearby bog and packed both the entrance and exit wounds of the bullet hole. The high fever was evidence that infection had already set in.

Lynn had grown up helping her old Nez Perce guardian, Sara Lame Deer; tend to the wounds of the frontier. She had learned about the healing properties of plants and carried many of the dried herbs, bark and roots, with her in her pack. She went to her supplies to get some dried willow bark to be used to make tea for the cowboy. The willow bark tea was a natural medicine that would reduce the fever. At the clearing she kindled a fire, placed fresh water in her coffee pot, placed the dried willow bark into the pot, and prepared the tea.

"I must keep him as warm as possible," she said, as the three animals looked up at the sound of her voice.

Lynn found a blanket roll tied behind the cowboy's saddle and she prepared a warm bed for him on the spot where Jenni had been nestled so close to him.

"How you know what to do Jenni…I'll never know! Reckon you've done your share of savin' this cowboy's life!" exclaimed the girl. "The rest is up to me."

The girl never strayed far from the cowboy, yet she accomplished the duties necessary to make the camp comfortable. She unsaddled the two horses and ground tied them close by.

She would glance now and then at Will Bonner but found that he was still unconscious. She hauled in dry wood for the fire, scoured the nearby woods for edible plants, and offered a prayer of thanks for the jerked meat that she found in the saddle bags.

She would be here for several days staying long enough to get the cowboy back on his feet. She could not leave him here to die. It was the cowboy way, that her Grandpa Brannon had taught her, to help others. Tears came to her eyes as she remembered the old patriarch of her family.

Forcing her thoughts back to the present, Lynn knew that she must not forget about the wild group of riders who had ridden down the trail, just a few hours ago. The trail was close, a mere fifty-yards above the big rock.

"What were they doing here, so close to her gold mine." she wondered. "Were they hunting this cowboy? Had they shot him, and left him to die?"

The mystery of the unknown bothered her. She was comforted by the presence of the three animals; her pinto mare, the cowboy's sorrel horse and her little Jenni mule. Jenni had discovered the cowboy and stayed by his side until she led Lynn to this place with her mule talk.

Lynn's camp was neat and secure, she checked on the cowboy once more, giving him another dose of willow tea medicine. Soon the willow tea would relieve his raging fever and ease the soreness of his wounds. She also checked the moss poultices, they would help the wounds to heal quickly she knew.

Lynn sat cross-legged next to the small smokeless fire, her Colt .44 strapped on her hip and the saddle carbine within easy reach. She had the cowboy's head resting in her lap, as she coaxed him to swallow small sips of willow tea. His eyes were tightly closed as they had been since she found him. He appeared as if he was asleep, though he would swallow Lynn's tea.

Lynn enjoyed the comfort of this human presence and the challenge of nursing him back to health. She wanted to find out his story, about how he had been shot and left to die. The animals were content; all three were busy eating the lush plants that grew in this sheltered place fed by a small freshet of water that flowed from beneath the big rock.

Under the shadows of the big Chief Mountain the night was closing in on the secluded glade in the pine forest. Lynn's blankets were spread not far from the cowboy, as he remained in a deep sleep. "Sleep is what he needs," Lynn reckoned, "sleep will help heal his poor mistreated body."

She lay on her blankets fully dressed, watching the faint glow from a fire fuelled with seasoned twigs from a willow tree. Jenni was bedded down on the far side of the cowboy watching something out in the forest. An irksome breeze moaned through the lodge poles swooping down to tease the small fire as it moved on carrying the smell of the campfire away with it.

The saddle stock were resting, their hungry bellies now sated with grass. Lynn noticed they were staring into the darkened woods. The animals sensed that something was moving close to the camp and communicated their warning to Lynn. Stirring from the blankets, Lynn sat up. "I know something is out there Jenni…sure hope it is not another bear!"

The location of her camp was only a half mile from where she had killed the grizzly, a half mile as a raven flies. The girl felt a bit uneasy, but kept her rifle near her so that she would be ready in the event that something did show up.

The pesky breeze was now at rest and the forest was quiet. Then she heard the sound of a twig cracking. The sound was ever so slight and the girl almost missed it. Then the unnerving silence was shattered by a frightening ruckus.

"Caw-w, Caw-ww!"

The raucous clamour echoed through the clearing causing Jenni to bounce to her feet, and readied both horses to leave this scary place. For an instant Lynn was shocked. She had her rifle ready to defend the camp. She didn't believe in ghosts or haunts, but this awful noise was terrible to hear. Then, much to the surprise of the three animals, Lynn Duval began to giggle, the giggle turned into a full-fledged burst of laughter.

"Well I'll be!" she said, her merry laughter still echoing across the clearing. "You sure had us fooled Crow…and frightened too. Come into the fire my friend—get in here right now, you hear?"

With a little movement in the forest, a shadow appeared, and as it approached it turned into a young Indian brave clad in buckskin. He wore an old felt hat that sported the wing feather of a crow. The brave packed a rifle and a long skinning knife hung on his belt.

239

"Oke-ei!" he greeted, the word oozed from his mouth, "Oke-ei, Miss Lynn...Little Crow has come to find you. Your mother is worried that something bad has happened to her only girl child. She has sent Little Crow to find you—and bring you back to Lariat Cross. She told this one," Crow said, pointing to his chest, "to tell you that she loves you...and misses you."

"I'm so happy you have found me Little Crow, it is good to have you with me!" she replied as she greeted him with a warm hug. "I cannot go home to Lariat Cross, not right now anyway. Come to the fire...I have some coffee for you...we will talk. I will tell you the many stories of my adventures here at the big mountain."

Though embarrassed by the girl's warm greeting, the boy known as Crow followed her to the fire. He was thrilled to listen to her stories. He had been listening to her stories since he was a small boy. The two were sitting cross-legged by the fire, as Lynn related her experiences.

Little Crow was puzzled over the strange silent figure that lay so still in the blankets next to them.

Lynn repeated her adventures, from her fight with the grizzly to the strange riders on the nearby trail. She told him how she had discovered Jenni and the cowboy here by the big rock.

"Ke-eei!" the Nez Perce replied, he was the youngest son of Sara Lame Deer, Lynn's Nez Perce guardian. They had grown up together at Lariat Cross. "Ke-eei, Lynn's stories are good to listen to!" Crow never let his eyes leave the mule or the sleeping stranger.

"Little Crow will never forget your stories; he will relate them to his children, and those that follow." Then abruptly the tone of his voice changed and he spoke again, "Miss Lynn's long ears—a wise animal—the sick cowboy is the long ear's friend now...he will be this way forever. This cowboy will get better, Miss Lynn's medicine is good—when next the sun comes to see us—his brown eyes will be open!"

With that said, Crow excused himself, said he must go and bring his spotted horse into camp. "Caw-w, Caw-ww." The sound echoed just beyond the clearing, much more subdued than before, with a slightly different tone.

Lynn appeared puzzled, "How does he know?" she asked herself, "How does Crow know the cowboy's eyes are brown, he has never opened them!"

Presently Crow returned to the fire, he had a broad smile on his face. Closely behind him trailed an appaloosa pony.

"I tell him to come with me," Crow said, gesturing toward the pony, "He wishes to be here...with people, and the other horses he knows as his friends."

The young Nez Perce would be a comfort to her and a help for the wounded cowboy. He insisted that he guard the camp so that she could get a much needed rest. He would wake her if trouble came, he promised. Perched on a ledge of the big rock, he watched, listened and protected the little camp.

The cowboy was peacefully resting and his fever was dropping. Lynn Duval was pleased with the results of her nursing.

Lynn awakened from her sleep to the sound of a chickadee, scolding the presence of the people and the animals. The tiny fluff of feathers was not used to so many strangers in its forest home. Knowing that she would be unable to go back to sleep, and that the sun would soon return to these high mountains, the girl arose and stirred up the fire. She placed a tin cup full of willow tea on a flat rock close to the embers.

Saddle bag in hand, the girl walked back to a small pool of water. The water had formed a pond as it seeped from under the big rock. The pool was large enough for Lynn to bathe in. From her satchel she brought out a hairbrush and gave her long hair a vigorous grooming. "My hair must look a mess," she fretted. "I have not been able to care for it as I should!" Her long auburn hair was a family legacy from her mother and grandma Brannon. She was proud of it and usually kept it well groomed and looking nice. Locating a small vial of perfume from the satchel, she applied a few drops of the pleasant scent to her hair, wrists and neck.

She felt refreshed and well rested this morning she realized as she walked back to the camp. At the campfire she added fuel and pushed the coffee pot next to the glowing embers. She picked up the cup of steaming tea and turned to feed the cowboy.

The light of morning flooded into the lodge pole forest. The small birds and animals were awake making their presence known with all manner of chirps, chatters and sounds.

Kneeling beside the cowboy Lynn noticed that he was awake. "Oh! Oh my!" she said, a smile spreading across her face. "You have finally come back to the living! I've been so worried about you—reckon you have been a real sick cowboy."

His eyes were open, and they were brown. They looked deep into her eyes; a weak smile replaced the sombre lines on his face.

"You've got pretty hair Ma'am, smells good too. Prettiest hair I've ever laid eyes on." He attempted to sit up; stopped by pain he groaned and settled back on the blanket.

"I don't know where I am...or how I got here—sure makes a hombre wonder." He continued to look into Lynn Duval's eyes as he spoke, "Reckon I must be in heaven—you nursing me and all." A feeble smile graced his lips.

"Don't talk any more," Lynn scolded. "I have some more medicine for you, and I must change the dressing on your bullet wounds...you have two of them you know."

"Reckon I should follow your advice, appears as if I'm in bad shape," answered the cowboy.

The girl was thrilled that he had finally awakened; now she could talk to him and help him to get better. Her cheeks reddened as she remembered his comment about her hair. She insisted that he drink some more tea, as she checked his wounds.

The bullet holes looked better, the redness and inflammation were subsiding. With a fresh batch of moss Lynn replaced the poultice.

"My name is Lynn," she volunteered as she worked. "What's your name?"

Shuddering from the tartness of the tea, he replied, "Right purty name...I reckoned you was an angel...must o' cashed in my chips and you was a breakin' trail for me to the pearly gates. Where am I anyhow? How did I get to this place? What in the deuce is this gol-darned critter a doin'...a layin' here beside me?" Will Bonner became restless, and though it pained him to move, he tossed and squirmed in his blanket.

"I remember now! I was shot in the back by a pack o' murderin' coyotes— bin on my trail forever it seems—on the far side of this big mountain. Have you seen anything of a bunch o' owl hoots who call themselves a posse?"

The girl prepared a broth from the remaining jerky for the cowboy. Then she spoke, "How can I talk to you if I don't know your name?"

"I didn't reckon it mattered much," he managed to say, "I'm just a wandering cowboy who has got himself in a heap of trouble! Will is my name, Will Bonner."

Lynn smiled. "Sure good to have you awake Will, and talking too. Sure been lonesome here, with you sleeping all the time. I like your name, Will Bonner, sure is a right strong name. I'll answer the rest of your questions later, but first you must drink this broth I've fixed for you. The broth will help you get your strength back"

All of a sudden Crow was standing beside her, his silent approach startled Lynn. This was out of character for the boy, who delighted in announcing his presence with the raucous crow call. She was ready to scold him for scaring her but the Indian quickly cautioned her into silence. He squatted down beside her and quietly spoke, "Bad men come now—on the trail that goes past big rock!"

Looking long at the cowboy in his blankets, he spoke again, "They look for a man, who they wish to hang from a tree!"

Lynn asked, "How do you know these things Little Crow?"

"I walk to their camp, hide in the trees, and listen to the words they speak. Crow did not stay at this camp very long—it is not far from here—one mile, maybe two."

"Reckon you're a mighty handy hombre to have around," Bonner spoke from his blanket. He had dozed off to sleep; the powerful treatment from the willow tea was working its magic, but he was wide awake now, alert and inwardly cursing his lot of being flat on his back at a time like this.

"What are we up against Will?" Lynn asked, struggling to remain calm. Will replied, "We can handle this bunch—but first we must hide the horses and this confounded mule so they don't give us away. Do you think you can keep the mule from wakin' the dead?"

"Don't you scold her, you hear?" Lynn retorted. "You would be dead now if it wasn't for my Jenni mule. She found you, you know, then led me to you with her mule talk!"

The cowboy could sense Lynn was upset and that he had spoken out of place. "I'm plumb sorry Lynn. Reckon I sure put my foot in my mouth."

The Indian had listened to the cowboy's talk and suggested, "Crow will take the animals away from here," he said gesturing into the forest. I know a place where they will not smell the strange horses. Crow will tell them to be silent, as silent as a shadow.

"Reckon that's the makin's of a mighty fine plan my friend," Will said. "We need you to come back and stand guard on top o' that big boulder over yonder."

"I will put out the fire," Lynn said, and immediately did so. "Are you able to handle a gun? With three guns we should be able to defend ourselves."

A mischievous grin spread across his face when he answered, "You can bet your poke on it—reckon we'll read'em from the good book."

Will Bonner was feeling much better this morning, his fever was gone, yet the pain from his wounds was still agonizing. Every time he moved a pang would surge through the gunshot wounds. He felt like he was being stabbed with a red hot poker. He was sure thankful that this pretty girl named Lynn had found him and was nursing him back to health. He knew that if the posse would have caught him, he'd be strung up and dead by now.

Lynn Duval was happy to help the cowboy. Though he was flat on his back from his wounds, his presence was very comforting to her. She knew that the three of them would be fine, she just knew it.

With the horses secure Crow returned to his roost on the big rock. From this vantage point, twenty feet up, he could easily alert those below of any danger.

"We must not allow the posse to know you are here Will, they will kill you sure!" Lynn insisted.

Looking long in the direction of the Chief Mountain trail, he answered, "Reckon our ambush will change their minds!"

Lynn's Colt was hanging at her side and her trusty rifle was in her hand ready for action. The cowboy's six-gun was on the blanket beside him, along with his rifle. "Let'em come," Bonner said as they waited for the posse. "We are as ready as we can get! Sure do appreciate you folks helping me out like this."

The minutes of waiting stretched so long that they made it seem as if hours had passed to Lynn and the cowboy. Only the sounds from the wild residents of the forest could be heard. Then a hush settled over the woods and no sound could be heard.

The muted talk of a crow disturbed the silence. Lynn looked up at the Nez Perce, he was looking down at her and signed that the posse was closing in.

Moving forward the leader passed by the big rock and continued on. Behind him, head to tail, the other three followed him.

The last rider of the string reined in his bronc and spoke, "Must be a fire close by! Thought I caught a whiff of smoke, and coffee...I swear I can smell coffee. Sure seems outta place here unless that killer we're chasin' has holed up close by. Hold up you jaspers! I'm gonna take a look behind that big chunk o' rock."

As word passed up through the riders, they all reined to a stop, heads turning back to watch. The rider who went behind the big rock was the one who had shot Will Bonner in the back. He had slid down off the pass in the dark, circled around the cowboy's scanty camp, and hid on the north face of the mountain. When it was light enough to see, he ambushed the cowboy and left him for dead.

A shot echoed through the forest, followed closely by another. "He's found'im!" the lead rider roared. "Move! Let's go give him a hand."

The mounted riders spun their broncs and thundered back down the trail. Two of them charged past one side of the rock, the other took the other side. Bursting into the clearing with six-guns blazing, a full-fledged war erupted; it was a scene of utter confusion.

Lynn was shooting her rifle and, from his blankets in the grass, the cowboy was also throwing lead with his Colt .44. From his perch high on the big rock, the Nez Perce was sniping with his battered old weapon.

The charging posse was voicing its arrival with the anticipation of an easy kill, only to scream and roar as they fell dying in the grass.

The war was over as suddenly as it had begun, an ominous silence engulfed Lynn Duval's camp in the lee of the big rock. In the distance the fading clatter of two mount-less horses was heard high up the Chief Mountain trail. The posse had been abolished.

The girl stood, smoking rifle in hand, her hair in disarray. "Are you all right Will," she called. She had begun to relax a bit from the adrenaline that had been flowing for those brief moments. She spoke again, her voice back to normal. "Reckon we sure enough read'em from the good book!"

"We sure did that," he replied. "I'm all right, a bit sore from all the moving around I was doin'—sure am relieved to see you never got hurt!"

Kneeling close to the cowboy, Lynn made sure his bandages were in place and fussed with his blankets to make him comfortable again after the big ruckus. Thankful that they were both still alive, she took his hand in her own, marvelling at the feeling that flowed between them. She knew that Will Bonner felt the same.

Their ambush of the posse had been a resounding success; the little war was now but a memory. It had been Crow's first shot that brought down the posse scout. The scout's convulsing finger had pulled the trigger on his six-gun, the bullet whining off through the pines. As the remainder of the posse came around the rock, Lynn and the cowboy had entered the battle. The girl's rifle, Will Bonner's six-gun, and Crow's sharp shooting had done in the intruders.

The young Indian brave scrambled down from his perch and scalped the posse scout that he shot to begin this melee. He then walked into the clearing beaming from ear to ear; the other bodies lay there with their hair still intact. The Nez Perce reckoned his coup this day would make him a mighty Chief.

Lynn's nerves were on edge when she saw the bloody scalp dangling from the barrel of Crow's rifle. He had his skinning knife out, all set to carve the scalps of the others, when she shrieked, "No! Don't take any more hair Little Crow. For heaven sakes, can't you be satisfied with the scalp you have already taken? It is a sin what you are doing—you are making me sick to my stomach!"

Disappointment spread across the brave's face. "Crow," the cowboy intervened. "I would like you to go round up the loose broncs that are here...the posse's horses!

"Could you to tie these dead hombres to their saddles, and then start them back up the trail. Them thar old ponies are mighty tired of the trail and will head for home."

"Ke-eei." The young Indian acknowledged his request and left the clearing.

Totally exhausted, Lynn settled to the ground by the cowboy's blankets. Looking at the cowboy she explained, "I am bothered by the fact that I had to kill someone today."

"Don't let it bother you Lynn, you handled everything just fine. We had it to do I reckon. It was shoot them or they would have done the same to us—worse yet to you!" replied the cowboy. "I'm mighty proud of you Lynn." With that said, his hand brushed across her hands that were folded in her lap.

Later that night Bonner insisted on sitting up to eat his supper. "Reckon it sure feels good a sittin' here," he said with a big grin. "Tryin' to eat and drink while flat on your back...ain't a fittin' or proper thing to do! Plumb mortifying in fact."

Lynn was pleased with his progress and told him so.

"Come mornin' I'm a goin' to stand on my feet...and start to walkin'." Will explained, "Don't seem right for me to be layin' here—and you a doin' all the chores."

"Oh, fiddlesticks!" she exclaimed in disgust. "You cowboys are all the same!" Old Grandpa Matt Brannon and Will Bonner were the only two she had really known. One of them was dead and in his grave, the other was sitting here in her camp, drinking her coffee. Will just sat and smiled at her, his smiles stirring her heartstrings.

"You would have done the same for me Will, and besides—!" She was blushing now, her thoughts were disordered, as she tried to piece together what to say next. "It pleases me immensely to have you in my camp. I don't mind helping you to recover from your wounds. I'll never forget the fight with the posse. The three of us fought them together Will Bonner; we shot and killed them. We were a team, and don't you ever forget it!"

* * *

The days passed swiftly, the cowboy was getting stronger and doing his share of the camp chores. They were together, never straying far from each other. The situation was soothing for both of them.

Little Crow ventured over to find the decaying carcass of the grizzly Lynn had shot, and to pay his respect to the remains of old Raven Wings. He prepared the old man's body for its journey to the happy hunting grounds. Little Crow was proud that he could do this for the old Flathead holy man.

He returned to camp beaming with happiness. Around his neck, strung on a rawhide string, were the claws of the grizzly who had tried to kill his friend, Lynn Duval.

Some time later as the cowboy and the girl were sitting around the fire, drinking coffee and enjoying each other's company, the cowboy spoke, "Reckon it's time for me to be a movin' on Lynn. This cowboy's got some ridin' to do."

* * * Chapter 32 * * *

Lulled by the chatter of swift-flowing water, Lynn Duval was standing beside the river that she loved so much. Her thoughts were like a double-edged sword, she was happy on one side, and melancholy on the other side.

She was thrilled as could be with her new cabin. It was situated on a well-grassed clearing in the cottonwoods; a mere stones throw from the St. Mary's River. To the girl it was a mansion, and even though it had only two rooms, it was still her mansion.

Lynn had decided to build her own place down on the old burnt out homestead of her Brannon grandparents on the St. Mary's river. After explaining her wishes to her mother and stepfather, old Paddy had hired a crew of Mormon woodsmen and set about building her a cabin.

"No gold will it cost ye for the labour of ol' Paddy n' his builders lassie, the materials and fixin's ye must pay for with th' gold from yer poke!" Paddy had explained a wide grin on his face as he spoke. Lynn had been as excited as could be with his offer, and a deal had been made on the spot.

She had been moved in for almost a month now, all her belongings were here. Her mother had given her only daughter a cook stove, a table and chairs. Along with her bed, which she had brought with her from Lariat Cross, her jovial stepfather had created built-in bunk beds. One set on a wall of each of the rooms, and a built-in cupboard for her dishes and food.

As an added feature, Paddy had piped in water from the spring. This was the same spring that had served her Grandpa and Grandma Brannon so many years ago. She was comfortable here and needed nothing more than some longhorns to graze the virgin grass that was so plentiful in the breaks of this river valley. She was a bit lonesome, and could really use someone to talk to.

Her thoughts drifted back to the cowboy and her stay with him at the big rock along the Chief Mountain trail. When she was nursing the cowboy back to health, she had sent Little Crow down the trail to Lariat Cross for provisions and with a message for her mother. She wanted her mother to know that she was doing fine and was in good spirits.

After a short recuperation, the cowboy had improved enough to saddle his horse and continue his quest. He had told her of his plans to purchase himself a ranch. It was what he had dreamt of since he was a small boy.

Will Bonner had thanked her for saving his life, and for nursing him back to health. In the final moment, before he stepped into the saddle, he brushed her cheek with a kiss.

"I'll return Lynn," he promised. "When I get settled...I'll be back! Reckon you and this cowboy have some talking to do!"

Lynn struggled to hold back her tears. The girl had grown close to the cowboy. In the short time that they had been together a fondness had evolved between them. She thought that she would never see him again so she had called after him, "Will! Will Bonner...wait up you hear? Don't you leave me here by myself!" Maybe she had been a bit forward, but it was her way to tell it like it is. "The least you can do, Will Bonner, is ride with me back to Lariat Cross! I want you to meet my folks and stay a few days."

With a sheepish smile, the cowboy reined his sorrel horse. "I'd love to Lynn...wasn't sure if I would be welcome or not."

"Oh fiddlesticks!" she told him. "You are my friend; my mother will treat you as one of the family." A blush spread across her cheeks when she realized what she had just said.

Lynn sighed as she remembered the events of that day and then settled in the grass under the shade of a cottonwood tree. "He was so kind and considerate to me," her thoughts were rambling again. "And he's a handsome hombre too, a real cowboy with brown eyes and dark hair." Would she ever see Will Bonner again? Did she want to? She was sure that he must have found his ranch by now. "Darn-tootin' I do," she reckoned. Yes! Yes I miss him so much, I surely do."

"I'm nineteen now," she sighed. Her birthday had happened while she was away at the Jenni Mine, and with all the events that followed, she had forgotten all about it. She hadn't remembered it until she arrived back at Lariat Cross. Her mother had insisted on making a birthday dinner with all the trimmings. Lynn O'Neil had even insisted on making a birthday cake as well. The girl's memories were strong upon her at this time, just wouldn't let her be.

Paddy had tucked the cowboy under his wing, and hustled him off to his quarters. "Come with me lad –'tis a good scrubbin' you'll be a needin' and a shave too. Ol' Paddy will take care o' Lynn's cowboy, he will." Lynn had giggled as she watched them leave, and then went to her own quarters for a much-needed bath and a change of clothes.

"Jumpin' Jehoshaphats!" Paddy gasped, when he saw Will's bloody shirt, and promptly gave him one of his own. "An' yer shoulder laddie, sure it must'ave bin a cannon...that shot ye."

With that said, he went for Lame Deer and her medicine. The old Nez Perce lady was pleased to inspect his wounds, and proud of Lynn for the fine job she had done. She insisted he take a small container of her secret medicine, it was a salve that would heal anything she assured him.

Everyone from Lariat Cross Ranch was seated when Paddy escorted the shy cowboy to the dinner table. Lynn was surprised and pleased when they arrived. Will looked so different now that he was clean and shaven. He had a moustache which Paddy insisted that he keep. "'Tis fine lookin' Will Bonner'twould be a cryin' shame to do away with that fine lip hair that ye'ave,"

The crafty old Irishman then seated him next to his stepdaughter. Lynn noticed that the bloody shirt with the bullet hole in the front and back had been replaced by one of Paddy's shirts. Lynn was pleased and would thank her stepfather later for his kindness to Will Bonner.

While at the Jenni Mine, with time to reason things out and all, she had forgiven her stepfather for their earlier differences of opinion. She put his constant nagging behind her.

Lynn looked just great, and she felt that way too. Her hair was washed and had been brushed till it shone like silk. She wore a long gingham dress. This was the first time the cowboy had seen her dressed in anything but jeans and a shirt, and he admired her. He enjoyed the roast beef and fixing's, but his straying eyes just could not leave Lynn alone.

Lynn knew he was watching her and enjoyed every minute of the attention. And her perfume! The scent was overpowering, nectar from the Gods as far as Will Bonner was concerned.

This was a happy time for the young couple. They were constantly together. Hand-in-hand, Lynn would lead him up to the aspen grove to visit her grandparent's graves. Then she would lead him down to the enchanting stream she knew as Lariat Cross. It was a peaceful, sacred place to Lynn, and had been since she was a small girl. The soothing music of this mountain stream was good medicine for their souls.

After a two-day stay at Lariat Cross the cowboy insisted that it was time for him to be riding on. He had enjoyed the long hours that he and Lynn had spent together. He had also equally enjoyed the time spent with Paddy O'Neil. Their gab sessions were good medicine for both of them. "Reminds me o' me old pard—Matt Brannon—he does," the Irishman had confided to Lynn's mother.

No persuasion on Lynn's part would convince him to stay longer. His only reason for coming to the Territories, he told her, was to find him a spread of his own. It was an awesome task, one that would give him no peace of mind until it was over and done with.

Will had leaned from the saddle to shake her hand, and looked deep into her lovely eyes. She stood on her tiptoes and brushed his cheek with a kiss, a kiss that the cowboy would never forget. Lynn could not hold back the tears when she watched him ride down the trail through the aspens. Will's eyes were damp too although he hadn't allowed Lynn to see that.

'He'll be back," Paddy had told her. "ol' Paddy knows! The cowboy is plumb smitten with ye Lynn—be a fool if he wasn't! Don't ye fret now lassie, ol' Paddy can tell...you like him too. All the banshees from the big for-rest will not be able to keep you two...apar-rt!"

Lynn shrugged away the memories as she arose and walked over to the corral to tend to her pinto mare. The Irishman and his woodsmen had built her a corral, and a small slab shed too. "To keep yer horses in Lynn," he had told her, with his usual Irish brogue. "And yer saddle and horse gear too. The rain and the snow'll not be a burden to ye anymore."

Lynn was almost angry with herself, because the memories were driving her crazy. "I must keep myself busy, find something useful to do." she said. After brushing Boots, and giving her a handful of oats, she wandered to the cabin and sat on the doorstep listening to the sound of the river.

She loved this river that flowed so close to her home. The sound of the moving water was soothing to her troubled soul. Even at night it would lull her to sleep.

But there was a feeling in her heart that would not go away. The feeling had grown since meeting the cowboy named Will Bonner. She sure missed him, dog-gone it all. She wondered if she had fallen in love with him.

The weeks passed by, turned into months, then finally a year. Still he did not return, "Where is he?" she fretted. Sure hope he hasn't been killed, or died of loneliness!

One day Lynn saddled her pinto mare and rode up to her Mom's ranch, it was only twenty-miles away, an easy ride for the girl. She just had to spend a few days at Lariat Cross, since she was homesick for her mother's companionship. She had also missed her daily sojourn in the aspens to visit her grandparents' graves.

While at Lariat Cross, Paddy O'Neil had approached her with a proposition. "We've all bin a talkin'...including ol' Lame Deer...that ye, me lassie, should take Little Crow back home with ye. He wanders like a banshee—gives ol' Paddy the creeps, he does. He would be a good worker...and guard yer river ranch night and day. He loves to hunt, the Nez Perce heathen does—would keep ye supplied with table meat too."

Lynn knew that her stepfather and Crow were not on the best of terms, and that Lame Deer would be delighted if she would allow Crow to come and live with her.

So out of respect for her Nez Perce grandmother, she decided to take him along. She knew Crow respected her and would help her do whatever she needed. She would have somebody to talk to and keep her company through the lonely times.

Crow's possessions were few. He had the clothes on his back, a smoke-tanned pouch, a rust-pocked rifle, a razor-sharp skinning knife and an appaloosa pony. He was a happy and proud Indian that day.

He would now be Miss Lynn's cowboy and her protector night and day. Crow's favourite time was when the sun went down. He would use secret charms and potions to harass and persecute the evil ones until the sun once again came to the land. The young Indian was superstitious, a trait he inherited from his mother, and dreamed someday of becoming a great medicine man. Yes, he was proud to be the girl's new hired hand and would give his life for her if need be.

With a pack horse in tow, Lynn and Little Crow headed down country towards her river ranch. She decided to ride into the Mormon town to pick up supplies. With Crow to feed, she would need an extra good supply of food on hand. Nearing a fork in the trail Lynn said, "I'm going to town to buy provisions, you coming with me?"

"Little Crow will go this way," the Nez Perce replied, gesturing towards the river, "I must be there to guard Miss Lynn's ranch...keep evil spirits away!"

A smile spread across her face, realizing that she would enjoy having him around. Crow would be an asset and a comfort to her in this lonely time of her life.

Much later in the day, as dusk was closing in, Lynn Duval rode away from the trading centre now known as Card's Town. She had a loaded pack horse in tow, and was riding south on the old Blackfoot trail that passed within a half-mile of her ranch. It was a fifteen-mile ride, and she was concerned that she had not been able to leave sooner.

It was the Allen's, Bob and his sister Sue, who were responsible for her late start. Their father was a prominent business man of the community, and owned the store where Lynn had purchased her supplies.

Bob had been hounding Lynn for months to be his wife, move into the town and settle down with him. Lynn had told him no many times. Today the Allen's had wanted her to stay and spend the night with them so she could get to know their folks.

Lynn was fuming mad all right, and vowed that the next time she needed supplies she would deal with the new trading post that would soon be open for business. "Hope we make it home before dark overtakes us," she said to her horse as she stopped to put on her coat that was tied behind the cantle of the saddle. The pinto's ears acknowledged that it had heard her.

As the sun went down, an eerie wind moaned through the prairie grass and a thunder storm was rumbling in the southern sky. "Reckon we better hurry Boots —'fore we get caught up in the storm that's a headin' our way." The horse recognized the gentle urging of the girl's spurs, and the tone of her voice, and changed her pace into an easy ground-covering lope. The pack horse found it hard to keep up.

She rode on into the gathering darkness. "Be home right quick Boots," she said, a torrent of rain blasted them in the face, "Just another mile or two."

Above all the hubbub of the storm, with its thunder and lightning, Lynn thought that she could hear the call of a crow. "Must be a hearin' things, them pesky critters should be holed-up in a tree…taking shelter from the storm." she thought.

Just as suddenly as it had arrived, the rain passed on, drenching the distant prairie far to the east. All was calm now except for a final clap of thunder, the intense sound booming along the breaks of the river valley, echoing far up into the nearby hills.

The wind and the thunder followed the rain on to another destination. Startling her, a voice spoke from out of the darkness. "Angry sky—now gone—bad noise and spirit lights have now left your river ranch." It was Crow, who had appeared, soaking wet, riding by her side.

"Oh!" the girl exclaimed. "Oh my, is that you Crow? You startled me so…sure didn't know anyone was around. I'm so happy you came to meet me, reckoned you would be up ahead, guarding the ranch."

"Little Crow ride this way—find Missy Lynn—bring her home to her cabin, safe from the evil ones, from spirit lights that fall from the sky!"

"I'm sure relieved my top hand is here, riding beside me. It was becoming spooky riding alone, the thunder and lightning and all."

A clap of thunder rumbled far out on the prairie, but it was too far away for the riders to hear the scary echo.

Though Crow never replied, an infectious smile spread across his face, the darkness of the night prevented the girl from seeing how pleased her words of appreciation had affected him.

The girl and the young Indian brave rode on into the night. Lynn's thoughts were of her warm cabin and getting out of her wet clothes. Crow was proud of himself for finding the girl. To have done so fuelled his desire to become a great medicine man.

After another stretch of silent riding, he broke the silence. "Crow find this," he said offering her a scrap of paper torn from a paper sack. "It is a talking paper, with magic words that tell us stories. Find on Lynn's cabin door, waiting for you to see."

The only light was from the stars, Lynn's gloved hand reached out in the darkness before coming in contact with the message, which she took and tucked in the pocket of her coat. "Thank you, Crow. I wonder who could have put it there. Too blasted dark to read it out here, we will have to wait till we get back to the cabin."

When they rode into the ranch, Crow insisted that Lynn go ahead into the cabin where it was warm and dry. He would bring in the supplies, he told her, and put the horses away.

Lynn was surprised to find the cabin warm; a fire was burning in the cook stove. There was even a pot of freshly brewed coffee on the stove ready to drink. She had made a good decision to bring Little Crow to live at the ranch.

Lifting the fire-lid from the stove, the girl added more wood, and noticed that there was sufficient light to read the note. Unfolding it she read:

> *Lynn*
> *Sure I'm a sorry hombre to find you not at home—bin*
> *lookin' forward to visit forever.*

Located a small spread along milk river must be a hundred miles east of your place three/four day ride small not much for grass a cabin to live in better than nothing, a start!

On trail of Herefords, at Judith Basin, Montana two-hundred head young stuff

Could you use some of herd? Too many for what savings I've got left.

Send word if you are interested.

Always a grateful amigo

Will Bonner

P.S. stayed two days waiting—had to move on, will explain later

Tears were flowing before Lynn finished reading the note. She was torn by emotion; elated that Will had finally made contact with her, yet saddened that she had missed him by a few short hours.

He had been here in her cabin. That's why the fire in the stove was already burning with the coffee pot, simmering on the back of the stove. It couldn't have been Crow. He would never enter the cabin without an invitation to do so.

Though her cabin was neat as a pin, she could tell the cowboy had been there. She knew he had slept in one of the bunks, and drank her coffee. How did she know this? His scent, a masculine, musky essence that was still evident to her sensitive nose. It was Will Bonner who warmed her cabin and left her a welcome drink simmering on the old cook stove.

Crow knocked on the door, entered with the provisions, then quietly left for the corrals. He wanted to sleep in the shed that sheltered the horse gear. From there he was free to wander in the night and continue his vendetta against the evil ones whom, he reasoned, must be lurking in every shadow.

Lynn never slept much that night, as she kept thinking about Will Bonner. She was heartbroken that he had left before her arrival. He must have seen the advancing storm and moved out in front of it.

Then she cursed the Allen's who had made her late in arriving home. Unable to sleep, she planned what she would do in the morning. Lynn Duval arose early and prepared herself for a journey. After spending most of the night considering the pros and cons, her decision was to saddle up and ride after Will Bonner. If luck was with her she could overtake him, and accompany him to the Judith Basin. She was in need of cattle for her ranch, so Will's offer to share the Herefords was a stroke of good fortune for her. It also gave her a good reason to follow him.

As certain as she knew her own name, she now knew that she could no longer be parted from the tall, handsome cowboy she knew as Will Bonner. In the short time they had been together, at the big rock and at Lariat Cross, Lynn Duval had fallen head-over-heels in love with Will.

She knew in her heart that she was in love with the big cowboy. It was Jenni's doing, her Grandpa Brannon's mule, who had lured her to the big rock along the Chief Mountain trail.

* * * Chapter 33 * * *

Crushed by disappointment, a forlorn cowboy rode away from the St. Mary's River country and Lynn Duval's ranch. He headed far to the east, deep into Milk River country towards the rough breaks of Writing on Stone.

Not far from the American border he had chanced upon an unclaimed piece of grass. An added bonus was a modest cabin situated near the river. The cabin was nothing more than a rundown shack, which had been used as a refuge by booze runners and undesirable transients. He had patched up the missing boards on the roof, cleaned it and made it as comfortable as a cowboy could. Will, like most cowboys, was unfamiliar with the intricacies of a saw and a square.

He waged a constant battle with mice, pack rats, and even the odd rattler. But it was a place he could hang his hat, and for all intents and purposes was his home.

Will Bonner was disappointed that he had not found Lynn at her ranch. He wondered where she had gone. Perhaps she found someone else and had forgotten about him. It irritated him to think this way, to agonize over the fact that he might have lost her. Yet it was his own fault, it had been a long year since he had last seen her.

He missed her auburn hair, her twinkling eyes and her cheerful disposition. He liked her infectious giggle, and she was a swell looking gal as well. He realized now, as the sorrel horse carried him on into the stormy night, that he had fallen in love with the girl from Lariat Cross. Love was an emotion that was new to him a powerful feeling that he had never known before! He vowed to the Gods in the sky that he would never rest until the girl became his wife, and eventually the mother of his children.

His thoughts were uncontrollable, coiled up inside him like an eight day clock. "I should have stayed until she came back. I really wanted to be there when she returned to her cabin on the river."

Cursing the fate that seemed to control him, his thoughts moved on to the deadline south of the border. The old cattle buyer had warned him, "If you're

257

serious about buying a herd, hustle on down to the Judith Basin country before some other rancher snatches up them thar Herefords. The herd is yours for six Yankee dollars a head...providing you have that much in your poke!"

Riding long into the night both Bonner and his sorrel horse were bushed. As it neared first light he rode into a sheltered draw and stepped down from the saddle. "Reckon we can sure use a rest, Red, and a bite to eat as well.

"I'm one hungry cowboy, hungry enough to eat the leather off my spurs, reckon you could use a good feed on this here prairie wool too," Will spoke as he referred to the abundance of short grass that grew here on the wind blown prairie.

First things first, Bonner pulled the sweat-dampened rig from his bronc. He stood the saddle on end near a clump of sage, and spread the blanket on the grass to dry. Then the cowboy gave the sorrel a vigorous rubdown with a fistful of grass. After performing a couple of rolls on the ground, Red lunged upright again and began to graze on the nutritious forage. The mainstay of all grazers in this wide-open country, the region became known as short-grass prairie, and with good reason.

He kindled a modest sagebrush fire and heated a pot of coffee. He grinned as he thought of his campfire coffee, which would sure take the bark off your tongue, as he compared it to the coffee he had back at Lynn's place. No comparison, the girl's coffee had his beat by a country mile.

Spreading his bedroll in the lee of a sagebrush clump, Will Bonner curled up for a few hours sleep. A tumble weed bounced down the draw and startled the horse. After it listened to the cry of a crow from far out on the prairie, the horse again lowered its head and continued to graze on the tasty prairie wool.

Bonner awoke with a start, the sun was well over the horizon, and he silently cursed. He had overslept and should have hit the trail hours ago. But dog-gone it all he had been bone weary and stewing over the girl from Lariat Cross had frazzled his nerves. The extra sleep had left him refreshed, ready to continue on to his claim along the South Fork of Milk River.

As he sat up, he noticed Red's ears pointed towards the west, the direction that they had come from the night before and there, sitting cross-legged by the fire with the morning sun at his back, was Little Crow, the Indian brave from Chief Mountain.

The brave was smiling, his hands flashing all kinds of signs, both to the sun above, and the earth below. "Oke-eei," he greeted.

"What are you doing here?" Bonner asked with a start. "You're the last hombre I would expect to see out here on this bald prairie."

The young Indian was in his glory and felt important. After a flurry of signs that left the cowboy in a quandary he spoke, "Big cowboy—must wait at this camp—for Miss Lynn. She is coming to ride with you…to find cows with white faces."

Still fidgety, and flashing signs that he knew Bonner could not recognize, he spoke again, "Miss Lynn happy you come to her cabin by the big river— she not happy you rode away—without making talk. She has many wise words to say to big cowboy."

Bonner could hardly contain himself; his heart was thumping like crazy. With a broad grin on his face he spoke, "How far back is she Crow? Reckon I'll ride back and meet her, escort her to camp."

Little Crow could sense the excitement building in the cowboy, and held up two fingers. "Two…maybe three hours…that way," he grunted, and gestured towards the western horizon.

"Thanks a bunch," Bonner told him. "You wait up for us, you hear? We'll be along before you know it."

"Ke-ei!" the Indian boy replied. "Ke-eei! Little Crow will guard your cowboy camp." He was eyeing the cowboy's simmering coffee pot as he spoke.

The cowboy rode out of the draw, put the spurs to the horse and headed west. Little Crow's keen ears picked up the sound of a fast moving horse and the fading echo of a cowboy, encouraging it to go faster.

Pouring himself a cup of coffee, Crow settled down by Bonner's fire and studied a vulture hovering in the eastern sky. He was content to be guardian of the cowboy's camp. He was also pleased that Will was riding back to meet Miss Lynn. Crow liked them both very much.

His attention stayed with the vulture. The vulture was a sign to him from the Great Spirit up in the sky. "Spirit say to Little Crow…bad spirits…not far away," the Indian muttered. A cold shiver rippled through the lean frame of Lynn Duval's native friend.

Opening his possible satchel he withdrew a pinch of dried sage leaves, crushed them in the palm of his hand, and sprinkled the sacred herb on Will Bonner's fire.

* * * Chapter 34 * * *

A pleasant breeze was sighing across the land, ruffling the grasses like waves on a mighty sea. Scattered at random across the open prairie, tumbleweeds were bouncing along. They were behaving to the whims of the mischievous breeze of the prairie.

Lynn Duval was excited to be riding into the eastern prairie to find Will Bonner. She was fretting over Crow, whom she had brought along to scout out the trails and of course to wrangle the Herefords they would purchase.

Crow had ridden ahead several hours ago, and she had seen no trace of him since. "I hope he hasn't run into any trouble," she worried. "He's my top hand now, in fact the only one I've got on my payroll."

This was new country to the girl from the St. Mary's river country, and she was enjoying every minute of the ride. She glanced back at the burdened pack horse; the sorrel gelding was doing just fine. Her eyes swept the horizon, looking for her Jenni mule. She hoped Jenni had stayed at the ranch as Lynn had asked her to.

It took Lynn some time to get used to the prairie, there were no trees, and the landscapes was flat and open to the sky above. Lynn was used to a more varied landscape since she was born in a high country of valleys, hills and mountains. Lynn liked trees. She missed the aspens, the lodge poles and the singing mountain streams that nourished them.

Turning in the saddle, her eyes scanned the prairie behind her; a tiny dark speck appeared on the bleak horizon.

It could be a mirage she reasoned, a strange phenomenon of the desert and prairie. The Mormon woodcutters had told Lynn and her mother of this unusual occurrence. Mirages were often seen, they told the two Lynn's, on their three month trek to the northern territories in wagon trains. They could not explain what caused the mirages though.

It could be her Jenni mule. The girl smiled and relaxed some; she knew the little rascal would follow even though she was a slow walker. "It doesn't seem to matter," she mused, "If I'm travelling five miles or fifty, my faithful Jenni insists on coming with me."

An hour passed, and then it was two more. The small speck on the horizon remained the same. "Jenni is coming," she told her horse. "She'll catch up to us when we stop for lunch." Shifting in the saddle, the girl smiled and relaxed some. A dark speck appeared on the eastern horizon now, and it was moving towards her. "I'm sure feeling better," she told her horse. "Little Crow is finally coming back to see us. He's sure a comin' fast…a puttin' the spurs to that appaloosa pony he's a ridin'."

The incoming rider was closing in fast, just three-hundred yards out before Lynn realized it wasn't Crow's appaloosa pony. It was a horse she had seen before, a big sorrel and the rider was wearing a cowboy hat.

"It's Will!" she shrieked, and put the spurs to her pinto mare. "I just know it is!" The mare lunged ahead, not used to the urgent demand of Lynn's spurs. The sorrel horse never wavered, continuing a rapid pace to meet up with Lynn Brannon's pinto mare.

"Lynn!" the cowboy shouted. "I'm sure a happy hombre," and reined the big horse to a sliding stop. The girl stopped Boots on a dime and jumping from the saddle ran to meet Will. In no time at all they were wrapped in each other's arms.

Lynn pulled his sun-bronzed face down to her own and gave him a long passionate kiss. "Oh Will, what have you done to me?" she moaned, still panting from the excitement. "This past year has been the worst year of my life…you riding away and all…not letting me know where you were, or how you were doing."

Lynn wasn't letting him out of her clutches, still hugging him as tight as she could when she said, "I thought that you didn't like me anymore—or had found someone else!"

"No! No, Lynn, it is not that way at all! I'm sure enough sorry for the way things worked out. I wanted to be with you in the worst way, I just wanted to get settled first. Find a small spread and the cattle to stock it with—a place to call my own. Only then could I ask you to be my wife!"

Lynn's heart leaped with joy at hearing the cowboy's words. She looked into Will Bonner's eyes and asked, "Are you asking me to marry you? Cause if you are, my answer is yes!"

Lynn continued to talk, "I love you, you know. Since the first time I saw you all shot up and sick, I have loved you!"

Will was shocked and at a loss for words. After another kiss, he managed to say, "I love you too Lynn, reckon it happened when you was nursing me back to health—you saved my life you know. It's just that I have nothing to offer you, I reckon you deserve more than a wanderin' cowboy can give you."

"Oh shoot!" she interrupted, and sparks were flashing from her eyes. "You and your cowboy pride! I need you so much Will Bonner; we can run my Grandpa Brannon's homestead on the St. Mary's together, build it into a ranch we can both be proud of. Raise our children there...and live out our lives."

With a dusty hat in hand, the cowboy's head was hanging low, staring at the ground as he listened to Lynn talk. Several long minutes of silence followed, he was deep in thought and Lynn waited patiently.

"Reckon you're right—let's do it—the sooner the better. You and this cowboy, Lynn Duval, will get hitched-up by the first preacher we run across!"

They agreed that they must continue on to the Judith Basin and buy themselves some cattle for their ranch back on the St. Mary' River. With a squeal of delight, Lynn flew into the cowboy's arms for another kiss, then one more, and another for good measure. Coming up for air Lynn gasped, "You have made me so happy, so very happy. I love you with all my heart, and always will. Don't you ever forget it Will Bonner—you hear?"

Will Bonner's smile was as wide as the distant horizons as he spoke, "Don't you worry none Lynn, from now on we ride through life together, side-by-side in all that we do. My feelings are the same as yours, just can't get enough of the wonderful kisses you're a givin' me though." Bonner continued, "Reckon we best be a headin' down the trail, pick up our Indian friend and ride on for Writing on Stone. I have a few things to pick up. I need to collect my savings I've got cached in an old nester's shack I've bin a callin' home."

The next day was long spent before the cowboy and his girl arrived at a spectacular break in the short grass prairie. Below them were the cliffs of Writing on Stone and the arid wind-swept valley of the Milk River. Little Crow had ridden ahead and was exploring the mysteries of the magic rocks. Writing on Stone the prairie tribes called the dramatic cliffs.

A fickle air current brought them the faint scent of wood smoke, yet the landscape below showed no sign of smoke. A look of concern spread across the face of Will Bonner. "Reckon there's bin a fire here, by the scent and all. Follow me Lynn; we'll cross the river and ride on to my place. It's over yonder, around the bend, hard to see it from here. We best ride with caution, could be an Indian camp, most likely meat hunters on the prowl for red meat to hang in their lodges, for the comin' winter."

Down an old Indian trail they rode, bottoming out on the valley floor. Then they rode on to the high bench on the far side of the stream. There to greet them was what remained of the cowboy's home. It was a heap of ashes. Nothing stirred only a wisp of smoke struggled to escape the rubble of the charred remains.

They ground tied their horses and walked over to the remains of the shack, the cowboy's head was hanging low. "Reckon I'm wiped out Lynn, what few belongin's I had and my money cache were in the small cabin. It sure seems like I'm just a hard luck son-of-a-gun!"

"Oh Will, I'm so sorry," she said, standing close beside him, her hand in his.

"Reckon this here fire makes a cowboy feel like a failure. I've not got much to show for a year of hard work—don't know what I'll do now!"

Wrapping her arm around his waist, she looked up into his eyes. "You look at me Will Bonner!" she scolded. "You and I are goin' to make out just fine. What is important now is that we have each other…you remember that Will Bonner!"

The cowboy was mindful of the girl's presence and thankful that he had her by his side. He looked into her eyes and the look that he saw there reminded him that he was very much in love. "Reckon you're right Lynn, can't help feelin' sorry for myself though, guess I'm only human."

Lynn said, "Let's find something that we can use as a shovel so we can dig in the ashes and maybe, just maybe, we might get lucky and find your gold."

The cowboy looked up smiling, "Thanks Lynn, that's a great idea. Don't know how I ever got along without you, you're always pulling me out of tough scrapes."

"Oh fiddlesticks Will. There's a piece of wood over yonder, let's get to work, she said, pointing to a tree branch. With the chunk of a weathered willow branch in hand, Will Bonner began poking around in the ashes. "I had my money stashed in an old coffee can," he said, stopping to glance at Lynn, "It should be right about here…was in the outer wall where an old chimney was standing. I had hollowed out a hole in a rotted log, cached the can inside."

Bonner paused a moment, staring into the ashes. Lynn stepped back and waited. She sensed her cowboy was deep in thought, and respected his silence.

Finally he spoke. "Reckon you must think I'm a losin' it Lynn. But that old coffee can we're huntin' has a certain sentimental value…old Red and I… have covered a bunch of country together with that old can in our saddlebags."

He was grinning when he looked at Lynn. She was smiling too and brushed away a tear that was trickling down her cheek. This young cowboy so reminded her of her grandpa.

She was so thankful to have been around the great cowboy, a strong man of the West capable of upholding what is true and right. Matt Brannon never backed down from adversity. He would meet it head on with blazing six-guns and blue flame flashing from his eyes.

* * * Chapter 35 * * *

After careful scrutiny of the ashes, Will Bonner uncovered the heat-charred can with its lid still in place. "Sure looks like we've hit the jackpot darlin'. Must be the coffee can, it's sure enough scorched black as sin!"

Lynn was helping him, and together they were able to manoeuvre the heavy can away from the smouldering ashes. The lid was warped from the intense heat, but they were able to open it. Out spilled the cowboy's stake in life, an impressive heap of Yankee double eagles none the worse for wear.

As they were counting Will's life savings, he told Lynn why the can held such sentimental value to him. Ever since he was a young boy, Will had dreamed of owning his own ranch. As he earned money, he would stash it in the coffee can. He figured that when the tin was full of double eagles, he would surely have enough saved to buy his ranch. All the money added together amounted to well over five hundred dollars.

Lynn turned to Will and gripped his hand. "Thank you for telling this to me, about your coffee can and all. What a wonderful story, one I will always remember and tell to our children some day. Why this coffee can story of yours will be part of our family heritage, history of the personal kind. Reckon you can tell me other stories any old time!"

The cowboy was beaming with a wide grin. A cowboy yell broke the silence of the lonely valley. Still smiling he turned to the girl, "I'm a happy cowboy sure. Now I will be able to pay for my share o' the herd o' Herefords…you and I are a goin' after."

Little Crow had returned to take care of his nightly chores which involved taking care of the three head of saddle stock and the sorrel pack mare.

The contrast in temperature from day to night on the arid prairie was much like that of a desert environment. Even though it was hot as Hades in the daytime, a distinct chill of approaching night crept into Milk River country.

Will kindled a cooking fire and they prepared a tasty supper of roast prairie hen, hot biscuits, coffee, and for dessert a can of peaches. Lynn had tucked away a few cans of peaches in her provisions.

That night after relaxing around the fire, Lynn and her cowboy took their bedrolls off into the shadows. They rolled out the blankets side by side. Their beds were next to each other until the Jenni mule walked into camp and laid herself down right in the middle of them.

Will Bonner fired up right quick and cursed at the mule. Lynn burst into contagious laughter, "Don't swear at her Will," she finally managed to say, "To get along with Jenni, you must realize that she has a mind of her own. She sleeps beside me whenever we are away from home. She is very protective and only tolerates you because I love you."

Will wore a big grin as he spoke, "Never once did I reckon I would have to share my best gal, with the likes of a mule!" The cowboy's eyes never closed until he was sure Lynn was asleep. "She's had a long, hard day," he said to the mule.

In the shadows on the far side of the fire, Little Crow sat with his back propped against his saddle. He was mumbling strange words, his eyes intent on the magical cliffs on the far side of the river.